Andrew Hammond began his working life in a cheap suit, sitting in the bowels of York Magistrates' Court, interviewing repeat offenders who always said they 'didn't do it'. After three years in the legal profession, Andrew re-trained as an English teacher. CRYPT is Andrew's first fictional series but he has written over forty English textbooks for schools and he can spot the difference between an adjectival and adverbial phrase at fifty paces (if only someone would ask him to). He now splits his time between writing and educational consultancy, and lives in Suffolk with his wife Andie and their four angels – Henry, Eleanor, Edward and Katherine – none of whom are old enough yet to read 'Daddy's scary books'. But one day . . .

By Andrew Hammond

CRYPT: *The Gallows Curse*
CRYPT: *Traitor's Revenge*

For Spud.

CRYPT
COVERT RESPONSE YOUTH PARANORMAL TEAM

TRAITOR'S
REVENGE

ANDREW HAMMOND

headline

First published in 2012 by
HEADLINE PUBLISHING GROUP

2

Cataloguing in Publication Data is available from the British Library

ISBN 0 978 7553 7822 7

Typeset in Goudy Old Style by Avon DataSet Ltd,
Bidford-on-Avon, Warwickshire

Printed and bound in Great Britain by
Clays Ltd, St Ives plc

Headline's policy is to use papers that are natural, renewable and
recyclable products and made from wood grown in sustainable forests.
The logging and manufacturing processes are expected to conform to the
environmental regulations of the country of origin.

HEADLINE PUBLISHING GROUP
An Hachette UK Company
338 Euston Road
London NW1 3BH

www.headline.co.uk
www.hachette.co.uk

GHOSTS ARE THE STUFF OF FICTION, RIGHT?

WRONG.

THE GOVERNMENT JUST DOESN'T WANT YOU TO KNOW ABOUT THEM...

THIS IS THE TOP SECRET CLASSIFIED HISTORY OF CRYPT.

In 2007, American billionaire and IT guru Jason Goode bought himself an English castle; it's what every rich man needs. He commissioned a new skyscraper too, to be built right in the heart of London. A futuristic cone-shaped building with thirty-eight floors and a revolving penthouse, it would be the new headquarters for his global enterprise, Goode Technology PLC.

He and his wife Tara were looking forward to their first Christmas at the castle with Jamie, their thirteen-year-old son, home from boarding school. It all seemed so perfect.

Six weeks later Goode returned home one night to find a horror scene: the castle lit up with blue flashing lights, police everywhere.

His wife was dead. His staff were out for the night; his son was the only suspect.

Jamie was taken into custody and eventually found guilty of killing his mother. They said he'd pushed her from the battlements during a heated argument. He was sent away to a young offenders' institution.

But throughout the trial, his claims about what really happened never changed:

'The ghosts did it, Dad.'

His father had to believe him. From that day on, Jason Goode vowed to prove the existence of ghosts and clear his son's name.

They said Goode was mad – driven to obsession by the grief of losing his family. Plans for the new London headquarters were put on hold. He lost interest in work. People said he'd given up on life.

But one man stood by him – lifelong friend and eminent scientist Professor Giles Bonati. Friends since their student days at Cambridge, Bonati knew Goode hadn't lost his mind. They began researching the science of disembodied spirits.

Not only did they prove scientifically how ghosts can access our world, they uncovered a startling truth too: that some teenagers have stronger connections to ghosts than any other age group. They have high extrasensory perception (ESP), which means they can see ghosts where others can't.

So was Jamie telling the truth after all?

Goode and Bonati set up the Paranormal Investigation Team (PIT), based in the cellars of Goode's private castle. It was a small experimental project at first, but it grew. Requests came in for its teenage agents to visit hauntings across the region.

But fear of the paranormal was building thanks to the PIT. Hoax calls were coming in whenever people heard a creak in the attic. Amateur ghost hunters began to follow the teenagers and interfere with their work. But it didn't stop there. Goode and Bonati quickly discovered a further truth – something which even they had not bargained for. As more and more people pitched up at hauntings to watch the agents in action, so the ghosts became stronger. It seemed as though the greater the panic and hysteria at a scene, the more powerful the paranormal activity became. There was no denying it: the ghosts fed off human fear.

So where would this lead?

To prevent the situation from escalating out of control, Goode was ordered to disband the PIT and stop frightening people. Reporters tried to expose the team as a fraud. People could rest easy in their beds – there was no such thing as ghosts. Goode had to face the awful truth that his son was a liar – and a murderer. The alternative was too frightening for the public to accept.

So that's what they were told.

But in private, things were quite different. Goode had been approached by MI5.

The British security services had been secretly investigating paranormal incidents for years. When crimes are reported without any rational human explanation, MI5 must explore all other possibilities, including the paranormal. But funding was tight and results were limited.

Maybe teenagers were the answer.

So they proposed a deal. Goode could continue his paranormal investigations, but to prevent more hoax calls and widespread panic, he had to do so under the cover and protection of MI5.

They suggested the perfect venue for this joint operation – Goode's London headquarters. The skyscraper was not yet finished. There was still time. A subterranean suite of hi-tech laboratories could be built in the foundations. A new, covert organisation could be established – bigger and better than before, a joint enterprise between Goode Technology and the British security services.

But before Jason Goode agreed to the plan, he made a special request of his own. He would finish the building, convert the underground car park into a suite of laboratories and living accommodation, allow MI5 to control operations, help them recruit the best teenage investigators they could find and finance any future plans they had for the organisation – all in return for one thing.

He wanted his son back.

After weeks of intense secret negotiations, the security services finally managed to broker the deal: provided he was monitored closely by the Covert Policing Command at Scotland Yard, and, for his own protection, was given a new identity, Jamie could be released. For now.

The deal was sealed. The Goode Tower was finished – a landmark piece of modern architecture, soaring above the Thames. And buried discreetly beneath its thirty-eight floors was the Covert Response Youth Paranormal Team.

The CRYPT. Its motto: *EXSPECTA INEXSPECTATA*. Expect the unexpected.

Jamie Goode was released from custody and is now the CRYPT's most respected agent.

And his new identity?

Meet Jud Lester, paranormal investigator.

CRYPT
COVERT RESPONSE YOUTH PARANORMAL TEAM

TRAITOR'S
REVENGE

CHAPTER 1

THURSDAY 9 JUNE: 11.57 P.M.

BOOTHAM, YORK

The man stared at the ceiling and allowed his eyes to trace the familiar route map of cracks that wove through the tobacco stains and patches of mould above him.

A clock on the far side of his apartment ticked its way through another monotonous minute, just as it did every time he lay down to wait for the spirit.

How many times had he done this? How much of his life had he spent lying waiting, watching the spiders crawl. Is that what they do? Crawl? he asked himself.

Or is crawling what four-legged creatures do?

Do they creep instead?

'Jesus, who cares!' he said aloud.

The stillness was disturbed before the tick-tocking resumed.

The man focused on his own breathing. He could always tell when he'd had a coffee too late in the day. He could feel the rapid rhythm bouncing in his ears and his breathing was unusually fast for someone lying down doing nothing.

Always *nothing*. Just waiting. He glanced over at the wardrobe, the rug and the floorboards beneath, where the old petrol can lay hidden. Was he about to use it again? Was carnage on its way? He prayed not.

At times like these he was no longer a conscious, thinking person. A receptacle, that's all. An empty vessel waiting to be topped up again with the regular dose of . . . of what?

What *was* it? And where did it come from?

The spirit had been reaching to him since he could first remember – since he was a boy – clouding his decisions, shaping his ambitions. Owning him.

He closed his eyes and relived the moment again – that first time he'd ever heard the voice. It was so clear. Even now, twenty-five years later – twenty-five years of sharing his life with this uninvited guest – the hairs on the back of his neck prickled at the thought of it. That first, terrifying moment when the voice had penetrated through his little skull and on into the private recesses of his head. He didn't know why or how or where it had come from; he only knew he wanted it to stop.

But it didn't. And it kept coming back, kept influencing him. Sometimes it seemed like he had no free will – like his life was already mapped out for him.

As a kid, his parents had told him he was 'dreaming again'. He'd thought at the time that perhaps they were right, because the voice only came at night, and had always been silenced by the morning.

But now, as a man, living in a bachelor flat, his parents dead and his girlfriend gone, there was no one to tell him it was a dream any more. No one to stroke his blond hair and place a cold flannel across his brow.

He shrugged away the self-pity and tried to empty his mind of thoughts, ready for his guest.

He waited silently, the clock ticking like footsteps.

And slowly the voice came.

'Tonight is our time, little one,' it whispered, still using the same name from way back. It had always done that. 'Tonight.

You'll silence him for ever and our quest will begin in earnest.'

'How, master?' said the man.

No reply.

'How shall I silence him? *Tell me!*'

'Ashes to ashes . . .' came the reply.

The man heaved a sigh. He knew what that meant. Just like before. Just like every time. The spirit's obsession had never abated.

Burn him to death.

The smell of petrol always lingered in the man's nostrils for days afterwards. And he could smell it on his fingertips, especially when eating.

He'd hoped it would be different tonight. He'd clung to the faint possibility that the victim could be dispatched differently this time. Not burning again.

At least it was only the smell of petrol that lingered. The man had usually disappeared well before the stench of burning flesh could ever reach him.

That pleasure was for the firemen. The poor souls whose job it was to go in and remove the blackened bodies.

No, the smell of charred skin would be too much for the man. Besides, if he'd hung around long enough to smell them burning, chances were he'd have been caught.

But he had often wondered. As a kid, he'd once thrown a frog on a barbecue and pressed it down with a fork until it gave its last croak. He remembered the smell vividly.

Was that what chargrilled people smelled like? Dead frog?

'Hurry, little one.' The spirit's voice shook the man from his pondering. 'The night is on us and the flames of hell are rising. We must dispatch him tonight.'

Whether it was the frog or the whisky or the fact that he hadn't slept properly for three days the man wasn't sure, but he just couldn't face it this time. The thought of slipping out into the dark, for another kill? Not tonight.

'Why, master?' he whispered into the empty room. 'Why *tonight*? I don't understand why I have to . . .'

He trailed off. The pain was coming. He should have known it would. Whenever he'd shown disobedience in the past, he'd felt the same sensation – a sharp, agonising jab, like a dagger piercing into his flesh. But he never knew where it would enter his weak body. The spirit liked to surprise.

A blood-red stain seeped slowly on to the cream duvet just beneath his right thigh. He was leaking again. Just like before. And as the blood ran from his veins, so his courage ran with it.

Why he'd been the one chosen all those years ago he didn't know. What he'd done in a past life to deserve it he could only imagine. All he knew now was that he belonged to the spirit, and he had the scars to prove it. His body was peppered with lesions from past moments of defiance. Would he never learn?

He grabbed his leg and pressed hard to stop the flow.

'I'm sorry, master!' he pleaded. 'Leave me! I'll do it. I will, I'll—'

'Rest, little one. Calm your head. I know you, better than you know yourself. I've watched you grow. And tonight is another step on our journey together – a journey that will end in triumph. You know it. And we shall reward you. Fear not. You are part of a much greater plan – so great it lies beyond your comprehension. But you will share in its glory.'

The man had heard the same speech many times before. But the crimson stains were spreading and his leg was paralysed with pain.

'I'll go now, master,' he said weakly. 'Please. Let me prepare.'

'Then our quest continues, little one. I shall return on the morrow, to hear the good news.'

He was alone again. The searing pain in his leg slowly eased.

He rose gently and limped to his chest of drawers. He fished around inside for the screwdriver.

Then he moved to the wardrobe. He put his shoulder to it,

pushed sideways, and the old beer-stained rug beneath it ruckled, revealing dark, dusty floorboards. He jabbed the screwdriver down between two boards and one came loose. He lifted it up.

There was the old can inside the felt bag. And the familiar smell. God knows he'd tried to wipe away the residue. He was fastidious in his cleaning every time, but there was always a trace, and it was enough to release the petrol vapours as soon as the floorboard was lifted.

He *had* to be more careful this time. Wipe the can clean.

Wipe it. Wipe it hard.

He shuffled to the kitchenette, precious can in hand, refusing to turn and face the bloodstained bed – evidence of another battle of wills lost. He'd deal with that when he returned. God knows he'd got used to washing away his own blood.

Reaching to the back of the cutlery drawer, he found the matches.

Moments later, hood up, the man left the building and entered the dimly lit street.

CHAPTER 2

FRIDAY 10 JUNE: 2.03 A.M.

HUNTINGTON, YORK

Flames licked up the banisters, engulfing the stairwell in pungent smoke from the petrol-soaked furniture below. With the smoke alarms disabled, the doors and windows locked shut and the whole place drenched in fuel, the man made for the door. Job done.

Sweating profusely, and choking from the fumes, he went to open the latch but had not seen the umbrella stand by the door. His leg caught it and he went down on the hard tile floor. As he landed, the petrol can slipped from his hand. The top had not been screwed securely and petrol spat over his chest from the open can.

Within seconds he was alight.

Frantically he staggered to his feet, threw off his hoodie and began pounding his chest furiously with the sleeves of his shirt. The pain was excruciating. But he *had* to get out of the house.

Still alight, head down, he grabbed the smoking hoodie, ran from the place and launched himself on to the wet grass outside.

The flames went out with a sizzle but the pain continued to rip through the man's chest. In agony, but acutely aware that without his hoodie he was now visible to the whole neighbourhood, he stood up, ran to the alleyway across the road and into the shadows of the park beyond.

Back in the house, doused in petrol, his victim never made it downstairs.

CHAPTER 3

FIVE YEARS LATER

TUESDAY 2 NOVEMBER: 7.01 P.M.

HOUSES OF PARLIAMENT, LONDON

'So what's the problem?'

'I saw someone down in the basement.'

'There's nothin' unusual in that, Kev,' said Mike. 'There's always someone down there. Probably working on the pipes. You know what the heating's like in this place.'

'I've checked the record,' said Kev. 'There was no one scheduled to do any work in that area today. Look, just wait, will you. Watch this. You'll see.'

'See *what?*' Mike was getting impatient. He'd just started his shift and was waiting for Kevin to sign off and leave him in peace. He'd got his coffee, his new magazine and his iPod. He was hoping for a quiet night.

The two men were squeezed into one of several security cabins flanking the rear gates to Westminster. Kevin looked tired and jaded from staring at the bank of screens all day. There were muffin crumbs and empty crisp packets scattered across the desk – the usual discarded clutter from one of his shifts. Kevin had a reputation for 'eating for England' to relieve the monotony of the job, and at seventeen stone his weight did little to counter the rumours. The chair creaked under him.

He was glad Mike had arrived to take over the shift, and was looking forward to getting home for a good dinner, but he just had to show someone what he'd just seen. He needed a second opinion. It had been so strange after all. Had the job finally got to him and he was now seeing things?

The work was monotonous but well paid. And he'd been there fifteen years this year, though the place was unrecognisable compared with back then. Since the global threat of terrorism had engulfed the country, the dark security buildings surrounding the Houses of Parliament had been constantly added to so that the complex now resembled a village in silhouette, surrounded by a maze of black concrete barriers. And at the centre of it all, still untouched, the gothic masterpiece – the vision of architect Charles Barry. The home of democracy.

Mike glanced disappointedly at the computer keyboard and the empty packet of Wotsits beside it. The keys were sprinkled with a cheesy dust.

'Come on, Kev, what're you tryin' to show me?'

'You'll see.'

'Where's the clock, by the way?'

'What d'you mean?' said Kevin.

'You know, the digital timer in the corner of the screen. It's not there.'

'Yeah, I know. It's weird. It hasn't worked all day. Anyway, it doesn't matter – you wait till you see this, Mike.'

Kev released his orange fingertip from the skip button and the action returned to normal pace. There was definitely someone there. Down in the basement, below Central Lobby.

'Big deal,' said Mike. 'So someone's down there. How long have you been working here, Kev? Honestly, sometimes it seems like I'm the experienced one and you're the new guy.'

Kevin smiled to himself. He knew what was coming.

'Just wait,' he said.

The images became pixelated at times and occasionally the screen flickered. There seemed to be some sort of electrical disturbance down there. But they could both see the shape of a man moving about. He had his back to the camera. It was hard to make him out, but it wasn't a particularly unusual sight. Both men had often watched engineers doing their thing in the basement. This seemed no different. And access was strictly limited, so it couldn't have been anyone else. The flickering seemed strange, but nothing alarming.

'Like I said, Kev, probably just inspecting the pipes or somethin'.'

'But—'

'Yeah, don't tell me,' said Mike. 'You said there's no record of it in the work book, but he probably just thought he'd inspect that area while he was down there. I can't see his face from this angle, but I bet it's one of the regular guys. And his equipment's probably interfering with the CCTV. So what? Look, Kev, if you don't mind, I really wanna get set up for tonight. You can clock off now. There's a programme on the radio about to start and I—'

Mike stopped. And stared at the screen.

'Holy shit,' he said. 'How did he do that?'

CHAPTER 4

TUESDAY 2 NOVEMBER: 8.01 P.M.

ALL SAINTS CHURCH, YORK

The icy wind was whipping up again, and Fiona pulled her coat tight into her chest. Her red hair was blowing across her aquiline face and a droplet of water was forming on the end of her nose. She watched her step carefully. The old pavements were uneven at the best of times, but with a light covering of snow on them, slowly freezing now in the night air, they were especially hazardous. Her work shoes didn't help, but her boots would have looked stupid with the skirt she'd chosen for work that morning. Vanity won over safety every time.

Coppergate was quiet tonight. Maybe it was the weather, she thought. It really was bitterly cold. Everyone would be safely tucked up at home by now, in front of their TV sets, mugs of cocoa in their hands (or a gin and tonic in Fiona's case). But it had been a chaotic day, with back-to-back clients all morning, and then a case in court in the afternoon, which meant she hadn't even started to catch up on her correspondence until teatime. No wonder she was running late.

She walked on against the wind, in the direction of the car park down on Stonebow.

Just time for one quick fag.

She stopped to fish for her cigarettes in the trendy but oversized tote bag that went everywhere with her.

Rooting through its random contents trying to find her lighter too, she dropped her phone on the floor. Thank goodness she'd just bought that fancy case – the one her kids had teased her about. She'd known it was worth having.

She stooped to pick it up.

Cigarettes located, she placed one to her lips and tried to light it on the move. The wind kept extinguishing the flame within seconds. She stopped, and cupped her hands around the lighter, cradling the bright flame.

She sucked on the cigarette, inhaled her first lungful of smoke of the day, and pocketed the lighter again.

Her green eyes were blinded momentarily by the brightness of the flame. But then, as they readjusted to the light, she saw something that made her stop.

And scream.

The handbag fell from her arm, spewing its contents across the ground as it dropped. A lipstick rolled into the road.

For a second Fiona stood there incredulous. Frozen to the spot. Then she regained her survival instinct and turned to run. But her foot slid out from under her on the slippery pavement and she dropped like a stone on to her back. Her head struck the edge of the kerb as she fell.

She was out cold.

A few steps ahead, outside All Saints Church, was a figure.

It wasn't walking purposefully. It was staggering aimlessly around the small garden, bumping into the solid oak door and crashing into the stone porch.

But it wasn't the reckless actions of the figure that had frightened Fiona.

It was the fact that it was headless.

CHAPTER 5

TUESDAY 2 NOVEMBER: 8.16 P.M.

WESTMINSTER, LONDON

The evening traffic was heavy down Victoria Embankment. Jud wove the Fireblade around the taxis and cars like a slalom. Strands of black hair tickled his eyes as they stared through the dark visor.

He felt impatient, as usual. Bonati rarely gave much information away when he sent agents on an investigation. He liked them to arrive with an open mind and let their ESP work its magic free of influence and speculation. Besides, it was dangerous if the agents arrived at a haunting already fearful. Of course, the CRYPT training programme tried to help them combat fear, but there was always a chance it would seep uninvited into their veins en route.

Bonati had always suspected that ghosts not only harnessed electromagnetism and static electricity in a room, they fed off something else too – human fear. And eventually he'd managed to prove it.

It had taken many months of field research at real-life hauntings to get the kind of solid, reliable data needed – and now he and Jason Goode were confident in their conclusion. The more fear expressed at a haunting, the more powerful the ghosts seemed to be. When human fear was rife, the radiation levels recorded by their field equipment were off the scale. And this meant more energy for the ghosts to harness. You could say the ghosts fed off human fear.

It was another reason why the work of the CRYPT had to remain undercover. They'd known for years that too many humans at a location interfered with their equipment – it rendered their data useless. But to discover that human fear itself – when expressed by too many people crowded into one place – actually strengthened the very ghosts they were investigating, well, Bonati knew it was a breakthrough.

So he was always keen to prevent fear from spreading, not only in the public at large, but among his agents too.

He'd said to Jud, 'Get down to the Houses of Parliament. I want you to go and watch some TV!'

Jud had replied facetiously that watching television was precisely what he and Luc had been doing at the time. And what was so special about the televisions at Westminster anyway? But the professor hadn't appreciated his humour. The film would have to wait.

The patchy details he'd gleaned from Bonati about this sighting in the basement amounted to no more than a security guard not doing his job properly – at least it seemed that way to Jud. Of course he knew there'd be more to it than that. Bonati was no fool.

But why did the calls always seem to come in when Jud was relaxing with friends? Why not in the middle of a boring meeting or an equipment demonstration or one of the countless training sessions that agents had to endure every week at the CRYPT?

The training programme for all recruits was rigorous and demanding. It was like a boot camp for the mind.

Each week an experienced agent – or skull, as they were affectionately known – was paired up with a new recruit, or zombie, and together they'd face a new challenge – a simulated haunting that would test their powers of extrasensory perception as well as their skills in taking readings, photographing and recording scenes, interpreting data and researching the past lives of the deceased.

Jason Goode, global entrepreneur and technology guru, spared no expense when it came to staging the simulated hauntings in the SPA rooms on the lowest floor of the underground CRYPT. Agents loved telling zombies to meet them in the 'spa' down in Sector 3. All thoughts of jacuzzis, facial treatments and massages quickly vanished when they realised what the Simulated Paranormal Activity rooms actually offered.

Knowing that whatever was coming at you in those rooms was not a real ghost but only a simulation did nothing to calm your nerves. It always seemed so real, so vivid and so frightening, it was hard trying to convince your senses they were being fooled.

Physical injuries were never sustained, of course – Bonati made sure of that – but assaults on the agents' senses were as powerful as they were unpredictable. It toughened them up.

Jud had endured many sessions in the SPA rooms, each one as unpredictable as the next. They always reminded him of the CRYPT motto, 'EXSPECTA INEXSPECTATA'; 'Expect the unexpected'.

And here he was again, en route to another real haunting, braced and ready for the unexpected. You never knew what you'd find. Each assignment was different.

The halogen headlights swung across the base of Big Ben and on towards Parliament Square. Sharp left into St Margaret Street, and soon Jud could see the long lines of concrete barriers leading to Victoria Tower, the tallest part of the Houses of Parliament. Strange how a building with towers over three hundred feet tall can be protected by a four-foot wall, thought Jud, as he slowly pulled the Fireblade up to the black security offices and dismounted.

A senior officer from Special Operations 17, Palace of

Westminster Division (the branch of the Met responsible for security at the Houses of Parliament) took Jud into the nearest security cabin, where Kevin and Mike were still staring at the screens.

'This is Mr Lester,' said the officer. 'He's here to ask you some questions.'

Looks about twelve, thought Kevin. 'Oh, right,' he said, trying to hide his surprise. 'And why is he—'

'We don't need questions from you. We need answers. Just show him the tape, please.'

Jud could sense there'd been an argument in the room already. He guessed this wasn't the first time voices had been raised tonight. An intruder in the basement at Westminster represented a serious breach of security, and someone would pay.

But he still failed to see why he'd been invited to join this little spat.

'You'll be touring the basement with us shortly,' said the officer, 'but first, I think you need to watch this.'

Kevin had already prepared the CCTV footage. He pressed play once again, and Jud watched the screen. It looked like any other industrial basement: pipes and electrical wiring; generators and boilers; air-conditioning units with giant metal pipes feeding from them and disappearing down the long corridor in the centre of the screen.

And then Jud saw the figure come into view.

It was obviously a man, his back to the camera, shuffling around.

'So this is it?' he said.

'Yeah. That's him.'

'OK,' said Jud, becoming impatient. 'So you've had an intruder. And you've already checked and there shouldn't have been an engineer in that area today. So you don't know who he is. It's a serious breach, I can see that, but I don't—'

'Sorry,' the officer interrupted, 'I think you should just wait a moment. Keep watching.'

Jud sighed and stared back at the screen. He slumped in the chair and wished he was back at the CRYPT with Luc, finishing the action film they'd started watching.

And then he sat upright. He'd seen it: the reason why the CRYPT had been called; the reason why this was no ordinary breach of security.

The dark figure shuffling around in the basement had stopped momentarily, turned and then passed straight through the wall.

CHAPTER 6

TUESDAY 2 NOVEMBER: 8.41 P.M.

BRIDGE STREET, YORK

Blue flashing lights swept across the Piccolino Ristorante window as an ambulance raced past in the direction of Coppergate. Simon Thacker, MP, helped himself to another glass of Chianti.

'So, how's the new job, Simon?' asked Barry, the local party chairman.

Barry had been a stalwart of the York Conservatives for thirty years. In that time, there hadn't been one event he'd missed, from leaflet dropping and canvassing across the city to fund-raising events and party meetings. Barry had seen it all.

And he'd seen his fair share of MPs and candidates in that time too. There was Sarah Barstow, a local businesswoman who'd risen to prominence in the 1980s and then suffered a heavy defeat to Labour; David Miller, who had a brief spell as local candidate but had never won the seat; Raj Chander, who fought well and won a majority before famously defecting to the Lib Dems, and then the most prominent of them all, Brian Maxwell, MP for York and Justice Minister – until his untimely death in 2005. Barry could remember receiving news of his death as if it were only yesterday. The phone call from Brian's sister had woken him early that morning, and through her tears she'd told him Brian was dead.

And then the by-election, and the rise of the young man seated before him, Simon Thacker. Thacker had been a member of the Young Conservatives ever since he'd been old enough to join. Barry knew his parents well, and young Simon had viewed Barry as his mentor through those early years. Like Barry, Simon had not missed an opportunity to evangalise about the party and the Tory vision (which changed with the times, of course).

But now Simon had grown from young Tory mascot to serious politician. And here he was, a few weeks into his first junior ministerial post – Police Minister.

'So come on then, Simon,' said Barry cheerfully. 'Tell us how the plans are going.'

The others listened eagerly. Mary Foxton, local party treasurer, and Nigel McGrath, party secretary, both shared Barry's pride in their new boss and marvelled at Simon's meteoric rise from newly elected MP to junior minister.

Having known Simon since he was a boy, Barry knew that he harboured a fascination not only for Westminster politics, but for the buildings too. He talked of little else. Barry had arranged for him to have tours of the Houses of Parliament more times than he cared to remember, and on each occasion Simon had been transfixed by the architecture.

Of course, Simon knew exactly what Barry meant by 'plans'. The State Opening of Parliament was just days away, and as Police Minister, Simon's diary had been filled with meetings and conference calls with the various security forces who guarded the House and the legions of civil servants who were responsible for the administration of the place, under the watchful eye of the Black Rod. The House Authorities, as they were known by MPs, could be officious at the best of times, but when a royal event loomed, some were downright obstructive.

'Going well, thanks,' Simon said. 'Busy, but we're nearly

there. The security forces are happy. Rehearsals are under way, and I think even Black Rod's satisfied. He's a fussy customer.'

'And so he should be!' said Barry. 'It's an important office he holds. His head's on the block if anything goes wrong . . . Do you remember when I took you to the State Opening back in '87?'

'How could I forget!' said Simon.

It had been the most amazing event he'd ever witnessed. The pomp and ceremony, the pageantry, the robes, and of course the strange customs adhered to: that moment when Black Rod, representing the House of Lords, approached the House of Commons only to have the door flung in his face as a sign of the MPs' independence. The young Simon had loved it all, and had vowed to be part of this weird world one day.

'The Sergeant at Arms in the Commons keeps winding up Black Rod. It's like a scene from a historic comedy sometimes. Honestly, Barry, how those people ever make a decision I don't know. My police guys just sit and watch and chuckle.'

'Yeah, but you love it, Simon, don't you!' said Mary Foxton.

'Certainly do,' he replied, smiling. 'I tell you, meetings at the House are more enjoyable than most meetings at Scotland Yard!'

'I'm sure,' said Nigel. 'Police Minister's a good job, though. You've done well, Simon.'

'It's only a junior ministerial post,' said Simon. 'But it's a rung on the ladder. You watch. Onwards and upwards from here.'

They raised their glasses to that. Thacker was certainly the most energetic and ambitious of all the York MPs they'd served. It seemed like he'd been born to be a politician. He'd thought and talked of nothing else since that trip in 1987.

Their starters arrived and they tucked in. Simon regaled them with more tales from Whitehall. They always enjoyed his regular updates. The fierce debates at Westminster, the back-stabbing and the whispering in the corridors outside, and the revelry in the clubs and inns that fed off the MPs' less respectable habits.

Outside, the blue lights returned as the ambulance flashed past again in the opposite direction, carrying a shocked and terrified woman from All Saints.

CHAPTER 7

TUESDAY 2 NOVEMBER: 9.03 P.M.

HOUSES OF PARLIAMENT, LONDON

The old metal lift juddered to a halt and the doors clattered open. Jud stared out at the mass of pipes and joists and metal fencing that lined the walls of the basement below Central Lobby.

'Come on,' said Kevin. 'The CCTV captured the figure in the sewage ejector room. It's this way.'

'The what?' said Jud quizzically. This didn't sound like it was going to be fun. 'Did you say *sewage ejector*?' It wasn't what he'd had in mind when Bonati had told him he was going to the Palace of Westminster.

'Yeah, 'fraid so.'

An engineer appeared from a corridor to Jud's right.

'It's OK, I'll take him from here. I was told you were coming down.'

'It's all right, I don't mind,' said Kevin, stopping. 'I know where it is.'

'No, you might as well get back. I'm down here anyway,' said the engineer.

Kevin shrugged his shoulders and returned to the lift. 'See you later then.'

'I'm Jones. Neil Jones,' said the engineer, turning to Jud and extending a hand. He wore heavy-rimmed glasses with lenses that made his eyes look tiny. Jud wondered if he'd never heard of contact lenses. 'I'm one of the senior engineers on site. They said you wanted to take some readings?'

'Er, yeah, please,' Jud replied, omitting to give his name.

'What's this all about then? You an engineer as well, are you?'

'No, I work for the police,' said Jud. 'Ballistics. Fingerprints, you know.'

'Oh, I see. So this imposter then, huh? How did he get in? Or out? It's weird. I mean, the place is locked up. Access is always limited to just a few of us.'

Jud was relieved – the man's questions proved he'd not been told about the strange way the figure had vanished through the wall. At least that had remained a secret. For now, he thought.

'Look, do you mind?' said Jud politely. 'It's just that I tend to work alone, you see. Fewer distractions. I'd prefer just to get on with it. The security guard said something about the sewage ejector room?'

'Oh yeah, of course,' said Jones. 'I'll show you where it is and then leave you to it. I'm due to clock off soon anyway. Just remember your way back, yeah? You don't wanna get lost down here!'

Jud nodded and followed him into a long, narrow corridor running from the Central Lobby's basement.

'This is the main pipe shaft,' said Jones. 'It was built years ago to help with ventilation for the rooms above. It connects via some vents to a vertical shaft that runs the full height of Victoria Tower. It takes in clean air from the top of the tower and sends it down these pipes, then the air is funnelled up into the Central Lobby and offices above us.'

Jud stared at the rows of pipes along both sides of the narrow corridor. Above him were miles of trunking carrying electrical wiring. The place was like some hi-tech rabbit warren.

'It's amazing,' he said. 'I mean, to think, all those statues and fancy chambers above us, and then you've got this ugly maze of metal pipes and wiring below. It's like being on a submarine. You'd never think it when you're up there.'

'Yeah, it might look like a museum in the House – especially with some of the old fossils that work there – but down here you might as well be inside a factory. There's fifteen miles of pipes, you know. Different ones for heating and air-conditioning and water. It's quite a feat of engineering.'

They walked on, and Jones led Jud into a large square room lined with stained white tiles. In the middle was a giant metal sphere.

'That's the sewage ejector. Gets rid of the foul smells in this place.'

'Yeah,' said Jud, smiling. 'Full of shit, these politicians, aren't they?'

Jones laughed. 'It's over a hundred years old, that thing. Lasted well, though.'

Jud continued to glance around the room and recognised the stretch of wall and mass of pipes that he'd seen on the CCTV footage in Kevin's office.

'So this is where the man was spotted?'

'Apparently so,' said Jones. 'I've been working at the other end of the basement all day, haven't been down here, but that's what they say. I don't know how he got in here, I really don't.'

'Thanks,' said Jud. 'You don't need to stay. I'll find my own way back.'

'Sure?'

'Yeah, no worries,' said Jud. 'You can get back to what you were doing at the other end. I'm fine here, honest.'

Jones wandered back down the main pipe shaft, his whistles echoing around the metallic pipes and blending with the pounding of his footsteps on the stone floor. He was glad to be able to knock off shortly. It had been a long day.

As the sound of the man's whistling faded to nothing, Jud felt relieved to be alone at last. The only sound was the steady hum of the metal machinery that surrounded him, and the irregular trickle of water down distant pipes.

He took off his backpack and began emptying its contents on to the floor: the Tri-Axis 333 EMF meter, the Geiger counter, the electrostatic locator and his motion detector. His precious EM neutraliser would remain in the bag. He didn't want to run the risk of losing it – there were times in the past when he'd misplaced it but not realised until the moment he'd needed it most. He wasn't about to lose it again.

After setting the instruments down on the tiled floor, he stood up to look around. His dark eyes scanned the room with robotic efficiency. Even with all his equipment, he knew that his first line of defence was his extrasensory perception. With Jones gone, he was now free to clear his mind and take in the atmosphere alone. Just the way he liked it.

There was energy in this room – and emotion too. Jud could feel it. He closed his eyes and breathed deeply.

There was a palpable anger, a bitterness of some kind.

It was rare for Jud's ESP to scare him, but he had to admit that down here in this room, there was a ferociousness to the atmosphere that he'd never experienced before. As though the air itself was angry.

He breathed in again and ran his hand along a metal pipe. His thin, artistic fingers jolted as a surge of static electricity jabbed into them. There was a clear residue of something here. He grabbed the hand-held electrostatic locator and switched it on. The readings were high. He pressed the 'quick zero' function to repeat the test, and again the needle soared. He'd expected above-average readings, given all the equipment down here, but this was way higher than he'd anticipated.

He knew he'd not been imagining it. Bonati had told him enough times that just as ghosts could leave a residue of electrostatic energy on the objects surrounding them, so too could they leave a residue of emotion in the air. It didn't disappear instantly; it hung like a fog.

Jud had often pondered the origins of emotion. Where did it begin? It was often said that it started in the heart, but you could feel it in the pit of your stomach. And when it passed into the air, as it always did (he'd walked in on enough fights between his parents to know that emotion could linger in the air), how did it leave the body? Did it pass through the skin like sweat? Did humans radiate emotion like they radiated heat?

Whichever entity had given off this emotion down here in the depths of Westminster, it was certainly lingering. There was no doubting Jud's powers of perception. He could feel the resentment, the bitterness.

Or was it some kind of desire for revenge? Was that what it was?

He steadied himself and listened. At moments like these he was doing more than listening – or watching or smelling, or any other of the usual senses. It was tuning in – going beyond listening, to engage with the world on a deeper level.

And as he continued sensing, the initial anger he'd perceived altered. Was it revenge? Or was it suffering? He could feel both – they were not, after all mutually exclusive. Suffering often led to feelings of revenge.

But why here? Why now? If the figure in the picture had indeed been a spirit, why was it here, and emitting such strong feelings? He thought of the eccentric, power-crazy politicians this place had seen over the years – and the amount of fighting and back-stabbing that must have gone on. There was no doubting there would be deceased politicians who might not be resting so peacefully – but *revenge*? And at such high levels?

He picked up his Geiger counter and moved to the stretch of wall he'd seen the figure pass through. It was a part of the room clear of pipes – just a wall of faded white tiles. He pointed the

Geiger probe at the tiles and slowly moved it up and down. A series of clicks began emitting from the main unit – proving that there were levels of ionising radiation here. The clicks increased and decreased in volume as Jud moved the probe around. The levels were certainly highest in the stretch of wall where the figure had appeared to pass through. Jud knew it was entirely possible for a spirit to pass through a wall and leave traces of ionised plasma behind.

But it must have entered peacefully and then been angered by something once inside. As Jud was aware, ghosts could pass through walls as non-conflict plasma provided the electrical current was low. Professor Bonati had shown in experiments that spirits were made up of ionised plasma and that the electrical current passing through the plasma could be raised by the spirit's own emotions. If a spirit was at peace, the plasma could pass through solid barriers, but if it was angered, the levels were raised and the ionised plasma would become opaque and eventually harden.

So if a ghost was in here earlier, something must have angered it once it had entered. Then, just as it had arrived peacefully, it must have left once this emotion had abated. But what or *who* was here?

And why?

Jud stopped.

What was that?

He spun around. There was a whisper. He was sure he'd heard it. Was someone or something communicating with him?

He set his instruments down again and closed his eyes.

Come on, listen. He told himself.

Slowly the whisper returned. A low, guttural kind of croak, its words indistinguishable but recognisable as speech of some kind. Jud concentrated and felt another surge of anger seeping in through his invisible antennae. The strange noise settled into a regular rhythm – a mantra of the same words repeated.

'Martyrs . . . for the martyrs caritatis . . .'

Jud opened his eyes and glanced quickly back at the wall.

There was a face coming through the tiles.

He fell backwards with shock, crashing into the great metal sphere that housed the sewage ejector. His spine struck solid metal and he winced in pain as he dropped to the floor.

It was a pale, lifeless face, translucent at times passing through the solid wall, but now becoming visible. Jud looked down and saw the rest of the ghost's body passing through. It was almost like a projection – a cloudy image but getting more opaque by the second. He could see the outline of a long dark coat and heavy boots.

Should he reach for the EM neutraliser?

He decided not yet. CRYPT protocol stated clearly that you shouldn't use your neutraliser the moment you saw a ghost. You had to see what was entering first. And try to understand why it was there.

He stepped back and watched the whole image emerge.

It was the same figure as the one he'd spotted on the CCTV. It had to be. As the plasma hardened and the shape came into view, he could see it was the body of a man. The ionised atoms were trying to assemble themselves into a solid shape.

But it just wasn't setting.

Though Jud had witnessed countless paranormal visions, he couldn't stop his heart from racing now. This was surely the most chilling sight he'd seen. It wasn't just the intensity of the ghost's piercing eyes that shocked him – he'd seen this before and knew that the eyes offered a window straight into a spirit's emotions; it was the way the face was shifting and contorting, shrunken one moment and then hideously swollen the next. The eyes widened, then tightened; the jaws sank, then rose up, and the head, buried beneath a shock of brown hair and covered in dark bristles, was stretching and constricting like an image in a hall of mirrors.

The speed with which a spirit assumes the ghostly shape of the body it once occupied in life is usually quite fast. The electromagnetism it emits attracts the ionised plasma in a uniform way, following the original outline of its body. Like a blueprint. But this was different. It was more fluid. And it shifted and pulverised to produce hideous images of a misshapen human.

As the ghost formed in front of him, reality struck: his bag containing the EM neutraliser – the only hope of reducing the ghost's power – was slumped against the wall near the entrance to the room. There wasn't time to get it now. His decision to wait and see what happened before using it had been the wrong call. He knew that now.

Jud stepped further backwards and felt the metal machinery behind him again. Keeping his eye on the ghost, he moved round until he was at the other side of the great sewage ejector.

But the ghost had already seen him, and once it was clear of the wall, it sloped towards him, its shape now fixed.

A bulbous, ugly face, with prominent cheekbones and a sturdy jaw. His hands were blackened and worn. And his eyes seemed almost buried beneath a great bulging forehead.

His mouth opened and that familiar croak was emitted again, 'For the martyrs caritatis . . .'

Jud shifted so that the great metal sphere remained between them. If he could keep the ghost approaching, he could move further round until he was opposite the entrance to the room, and then flee down the main pipe shaft.

But then, without warning, the ghost went for him. It flew up and over the giant machinery. Its hands went for his neck. Jud was held tight. The strength of the ghost was incredible. Jud tried to push it away, but the hands gripped him tightly.

Don't be *afraid*, he kept telling himself. Don't let your fear give the spirit strength. *Stay calm*. But he couldn't resist pushing and kicking at it.

The ghost's hands were constricting further. Jud could feel

the sinews in his neck being pressed, the ghost's iron fingers jabbing into his flesh. He knew his skin had been punctured – he could feel the blood trickling down and seeping into his shirt. It was just a flesh wound, but he knew that any second the spirit's fingers would find a main artery. Or strangle him instead.

He was still lashing out at the ghost, punching and kicking its frame, but it was having little effect. This was one of the strongest ghosts he'd encountered.

Suddenly there was a strange and deafening grinding noise.

The workings inside the great sewage ejector were pounding into action. Jud had no idea what was happening but neither did the ghost, and the sudden noise had startled and weakened it. Jud saw his chance and rammed the ghost into the metal sphere behind it. It released its grip and staggered around for a moment.

But then it flew at Jud again and this time caught his jacket. He could feel the ghost's razor-sharp fingernails digging into his arm. He tried to wriggle free, but the ghost clung on. He knew it had pierced his flesh. He could feel it.

The ghost pulled hard and ripped part of Jud's jacket sleeve, revealing a jagged wound beneath.

The great machine began grinding again, as pipes and valves shifted deep within it. The noise was deafening.

Jud watched as the ghost moved away from him, almost retreating.

But it didn't disappear. Though obviously weakened – either by the tussle with Jud or by the shock of the grinding noises from the machine – it didn't fade away altogether. Jud watched as it steadied itself against the wall. He could even see his own blood on the ghost's hand, where it had punctured his arm.

He seized his chance. His equipment was strewn across the floor. He knew he couldn't leave it behind – he'd made that mistake before. With the ghost still recovering, Jud went for his instruments, threw them into the rucksack and made a dash for the door that led out to the main pipe shaft. Without stopping to look back, he ran down the long corridor and out into the main basement below Central Lobby.

He hurriedly pressed one of the lift buttons and waited, glancing over his shoulder down the long shaft towards the ejector room.

A dark silhouette was approaching him down the shaft.

With seconds to spare, the lift doors finally slid open and Jud was inside.

Behind him, the ghost swept straight past the lift and on, deeper into the basement, a piece of Jud's torn jacket clutched in its skeletal fingers.

CHAPTER 8

TUESDAY 2 NOVEMBER: 9.32 P.M.

YORK GENERAL HOSPITAL

Fiona touched the back of her head and felt the bandage.

'Honestly, I just don't know what happened. I mean, one minute I was standing there, and the next I was waking up in an ambulance on my way here.'

Her husband looked concerned.

'You must have been terrified, darling. It's incredible – what you saw, I mean. Are you sure about it? It was a dark night. Misty too, wasn't it?'

'It's *true*. I'm not making it up, David.'

He could see she was getting tense again. She only ever used his full name when she was angry. Her head was obviously pounding and her colour still hadn't properly returned.

'I know. I'm sorry, Fi,' he said. 'I'm just saying it might have been your eyes playing tricks on you, that's all. The moon casts funny shadows, especially in the snow. And it was definitely foggy, wasn't it? Hard to see anything properly, I'd say. Look, I shouldn't have brought it up again. I'm sorry, love.'

'It wasn't a trick of the light! Why do you think I fell over with shock?' said Fiona. 'I might have passed out briefly, but I can still remember it as clear as anything. It *was* a figure, David.

In the shadows, stumbling around in the graveyard. I saw it! At All Saints.'

'And it was . . . *headless*, you said?' David whispered.

'Yes!' She looked like she was going to cry again.

'I'm sorry,' he said, staring at her. She was such a level-headed woman. The source of common sense in the family. David was the one with the big ideas, the dreamer. If he'd said he'd seen a ghost, people would have just thought he was off again on one of his usual stories. But Fiona? She wasn't the sort to make stuff up. It wasn't like her.

'I just wish I'd been there, that's all. I wish I'd seen it.'

'So do I, Dave,' said Fiona. 'At least then you'd have believed me!'

David stroked her pale, freckled hand again. It seemed strange seeing her in a hospital bed. The last time they'd done this was six years ago, with the birth of their youngest. It had been much happier circumstances then.

'So, you're sure you're all right?'

'Yes! Stop fussing, will you.'

'OK, OK, I just think you've been overdoing it lately,' said David, looking concerned again. 'You know you have, Fi. I realise better than anyone how hard you've been working. I just wondered if . . . well, if . . .'

'If I've been seeing things, huh? Losing my marbles, you mean? In need of a rest and holiday? All that kind of crap.' Fiona sat up in bed. She looked furious. Patients in nearby beds looked over.

'OK. Let's drop it,' said David. 'No need to raise your voice. You need some rest, whether you like it or not. I've called Tony Woodhead and we've agreed you're not going in for the rest of the week.'

'What? You've called my boss? You've only met him once! How the hell did you get his number?'

'It's in the address book in the kitchen.'

Fiona shook her head. 'Brilliant. So now Tony thinks I'm going crazy too.'

'No, I just said that you'd tripped in the street and had a bad fall. I didn't say anything about seeing ghosts, Fi.'

'Ssh – keep your voice down!' whispered Fiona.

A nurse with a warm smile approached the bed.

'Mrs Peters, the police are here to see you. They'd like a word, if you don't mind. Do you think you're up to it?'

'No, she's not,' David snapped at the nurse before his wife had had a chance to speak. 'Tell them to come back tomorrow. She needs—'

'It's OK, Nurse,' Fiona interrupted him. 'I'm not sure why they're here – I mean, there was no one else involved or anything – but I'm happy to speak to them.' She turned to her husband. 'Darling, you go and get a coffee. Are the kids all right, by the way?'

'Yes, your mother's with them now.' He rose reluctantly and made for the coffee machine outside. He glared disapprovingly at the two men in suits waiting by the door.

David had a horrible suspicion it wasn't a police officer his wife needed right now – it was a therapist.

CHAPTER 9

TUESDAY 2 NOVEMBER: 9.51 P.M.

HOUSES OF PARLIAMENT, LONDON

'So the camera's not working at all now, you say? You didn't see what happened?'

Mike shook his head slowly. 'I can't understand it,' he said. 'The last footage we have is at 9.16 p.m. We saw you enter the sewage ejector room. I watched you moving around – I mean, to be honest, the boys and I wondered what you were doing down there. I thought you were here to take fingerprints an' all that. That's what they said. Anyway, then the picture just went hazy.'

Jud had guessed what must have happened. Given the amount of electrical energy in that room, no wonder the CCTV camera had fried. It must have been pretty close to breaking point when the spirit appeared earlier – and it explained the pixelated images and the flickering the guards had seen. But when the ghost returned again, the surge of energy would have been too much and the tiny camera would have fizzled out.

Along with any concrete evidence to prove that Jud had not been making it all up.

'So, tell me – what *did* happen down there then? What

is it we've missed? You look like you've been in a scrap or somethin',' said Kevin. It was way past his clock-off time, but this was becoming too intriguing to leave now. Dinner could wait.

Jud paused before answering. Information about any CRYPT investigation was strictly on a need-to-know basis, and these security guys didn't need to know.

But how was he going to explain the ripped jacket? And the blood on his shirt? If they'd not seen his encounter with the ghost, how was he supposed to explain that? His arm still stung from the puncture wound.

'Oh, this,' he said nonchalantly. 'Well, I tripped over some wiring down there. I went to break my fall and caught my jacket on one of the metal fences. It looks worse than it is. Don't worry about it.'

Kevin looked at him intently. *Was that the truth?*

'OK. So what *did* you find down there?'

Jud felt trapped. He couldn't tell them what had *really* happened. Not yet, at least. It was against all CRYPT rules. Fear could spread like wildfire.

He thought for a second. The guards were watching him.

'Not much,' he said. 'I could see a few handprints on the rails, which was useful, but not much else. And as for this disappearance, I'm not completely sure it wasn't a trick of the camera, to be honest. You see, if there *is* some sort of electrical disturbance, caused by static electricity or a faulty appliance in the vicinity, then the camera could well have skipped and jumped ahead. It might have looked as though the imposter disappeared through a wall when in actual fact it's almost certain he didn't – it just seemed that way.'

Jud watched the two men as they looked at one another. Were they buying this crap? At least Bonati would be pleased he was trying to cover up the ghost incident until they'd had time to get an action plan together. They certainly needed to – there was some serious paranormal activity down there, and Jud had a feeling it had only just begun.

Mike gazed back at Jud for a moment before he spoke. There was something about this young man. He looked younger than they'd expected, and now, since returning from the basement, he seemed on edge. It was hard to put your finger on it, but this kid seemed rattled.

'So nothing happened down there then, huh?' he said.

Jud ignored him and instead replied with a question of his own.

'Are the other cameras defunct too? I mean, has the whole circuit blown?'

'No. Just the one in the sewage room.'

'So the one in the main pipe shaft is working?' asked Jud quickly.

'There is no camera in the main pipe shaft. Don't need one. The camera in the sewage ejector room can be manoeuvred around. You can see right down the shaft from there.'

'But not if the camera's broken,' said Jud.

'Exactly,' said Kevin.

'So no footage at all?'

'None.'

'OK,' said Jud, trying to hide his relief. He knew that the last thing the CRYPT needed was for one of their agents to be filmed battling with a ghost. But the guards had seen his expression change.

'You seem pleased about that,' said Kevin.

'What?'

'It's just that you look relieved now – that there's no footage, I mean.'

Jud felt a surge of panic.

'Relieved? What're you talking about?' he said. 'I'm not *relieved*. I'm not bothered either way.' What were these guys suggesting? That he had committed some crime he now wanted to cover up?

'Look, I really need to report my findings to the police,' he said, changing the subject. 'But we may have to return later. You'll give us access again, yeah?'

'Whatever our orders are,' said Mike. 'The police already did a sweep of the place before you came, and no doubt they'll do another one now. If they feel a further inspection is needed, then we'll let you in. It's up to them.'

Gee, thanks, thought Jud. He told the two men he was going outside to make a call and would keep them informed of the next course of action. After all, CRYPT was in charge of this investigation now, not them.

He was thankful to be outside in the cool night air. He heard the phone ring inside the security cabin as he left. He watched through the window as Mike picked it up. He waited a few seconds, realised the call wasn't for him and then walked away to find a quiet corner where he could call Bonati.

The professor had to be briefed, and quickly. Jud knew MI5 would be expecting answers from him. He might have escaped on this occasion, but he knew full well that he needed to get back into that basement as soon as possible. This time with more agents – and more neutralisers.

He sat down on one of the concrete barriers that surrounded the complex. The late-evening traffic beyond the perimeter offered a comforting sense of normality. It was cold, though. His breath was illuminated in the orange glow from the street lamps and floodlights.

Before he did anything else, he knew he had to make notes on the incident, collect his thoughts. He'd not had a chance to record his observations as he often did, so a quick written report on the iPad was all he'd be able to do for now. At least he could refer to it when he rang Bonati.

Experience told him that incidents like these could play tricks on the mind. You remembered things differently sometimes, the order of events or the places in which they happened. It was vital to get the details down either at the site or straight after an incident.

Once he'd made a few notes on his iPad, he decided it was time to call Bonati and brief him. A myriad of thoughts ran through his mind as he fished around in the rucksack for his phone. They would have to seal off the basement, make up some reason. Tell the security guards to back off, that it was all under control. The two guys in the cabin seemed to have bought his story about the fingerprinting. But they wouldn't buy it a second time, that was for sure.

He needed to work out a plan with Bonati – and fast.

He'd just started keying in the special CRYPT number when he heard the cabin door swing open and saw the two security guards walking quickly towards him. Kevin was signalling to someone over Jud's shoulder. He spun around. Two armed police officers were approaching him from the opposite direction.

He pocketed his phone quickly.

'Wait a minute, what's going on?' he said, as Kevin took his arm. 'What're you doing?'

'I think you'd better come back inside,' said Kevin coldly.

'No,' said Jud, pulling his arm away. 'Get off me. Tell me what's going on first.'

The police officers intervened, marching Jud back inside the cabin and shutting the door.

Mike turned the key and pocketed it.

'You're going nowhere, son,' he said.

'What're you talking about?' protested Jud. He could feel the tension rising in his veins. His heart resumed the same pounding as before. This was turning into a testing assignment. Where would it lead next?

One of the police officers said, 'You look like you've been in a fight, young man.'

Jud looked down at his ripped sleeve and the bloodstained shirt beneath.

'What? Oh no, it's nothing. I was telling these guys earlier, I tripped over down in the basement. Fell against one of the metal fences. Ripped my damn shirt. Don't worry about it. Now will someone tell me what's going on?'

Kevin spoke. His face was deadly serious.

'You'll remember the engineer we met when we were down in the basement, yes?'

'Er, yeah,' said Jud.

'So you *did* meet him then?' Kevin said, glancing across at the police officers. 'You can confirm that?'

Jud was confused. 'What? Of course I met him. You were there at the time, don't you remember! Look, what *is* this?'

'Yes, I was there,' said Kevin, ignoring his question, 'And then I left you alone with him. I went back into the lift, correct?'

'Yes. Why are you asking these questions?' said Jud. He was beginning to feel nervous now. What was happening here? Why was everyone staring at him, watching his reactions to these pointless questions?

Kevin spoke again. 'So, just to clarify, you were left alone with the engineer in the basement?'

'I just said that!' said Jud, trying hard to hide his nerves. 'Look, has something happened that you're not telling me?'

Mike spoke up. 'The engineer, Neil Jones, was due to clock off around the time that you met him.'

'So?'

'Well, that's just it, you see. He hasn't showed.'

'What do you mean, he hasn't showed?' said Jud.

'I mean, according to our records, he still hasn't clocked off. We have a strict system which helps us keep tabs on who's down there and when. And according to the log, Neil Jones hasn't clocked off yet.'

Jud was getting frustrated now. What the hell did this have to do with him?

'Look,' he said, 'why are you telling me this? So the engineer's working late. He's obviously still down there. So what?'

'Our officers were patrolling the basement moments after you came back up here, young man,' said one of the policemen.

'Yeah, *and?*' said Jud impatiently. If he heard the phrase 'young man' once more, he'd swing for somebody.

'There's no one down there. No one at all.'

'What?' said Jud. His breathing was speeding up. They'd all noticed it.

'I *said*,' the officer replied laboriously, 'there is no one down there now. Which leads us to one question: *Where is the engineer?*'

There was a knock on the cabin door. Kevin opened it quickly. A third officer walked in.

'Ah, here he is,' said the first policeman. 'You've been patrolling the basement with the others, haven't you, Paddy?'

Paddy nodded. And passed something over to him.

Jud's impatience was getting the better of him. He stood up. 'Look, what is this? What's going on?'

The first officer got up from where he was perched on the desk and walked straight towards him. Whatever Paddy had passed to him, he now had it behind his back.

'Sit down. I'll tell you why we've asked you back in here. Because you were the last one to see Neil Jones, that's why.'

Jud fell silent.

'And Neil Jones has gone missing. But my colleague here found something while he was doing a sweep of the basement just now, didn't you, Paddy?'

The officer revealed what was in his hand.

Jud could see instantly what it was. He needed no explanation. Jones's specs. One of the thick lenses was shattered and the frame was bent.

'Right,' said Kevin, stepping closer to Jud, who stood pondering which was worse, his oversized gut or his cheesy breath, both of which were invading his personal space. 'I'll ask you again, and this time I want the truth, son, because I don't think you gave it to us last time.

'So what exactly happened down there?' A police officer added. 'I suggest you begin at the beginning. We've got all night, young man.'

CHAPTER 10

TUESDAY 2 NOVEMBER: 10.18 P.M.

MICKLEGATE BAR, YORK

Snow had been falling for several hours and the pavements and buildings that lined the street looked like a picture postcard. Up ahead, the Roman walls that flanked Micklegate Bar, the grandest of four ancient gateways into York city, were sprinkled with a layer of white icing.

It looked like a stage set. Or a scene from A *Christmas Carol*.

But Ted chose not to stop and admire the Dickensian picture. After all, he'd trudged home this way every quiz night for fifteen years now – in all seasons. And it made no difference when you were pissed anyway. Ted liked his beer, and his team had scooped second prize tonight – two free pints apiece, on top of the ones they'd already had. It had been a good night.

He trudged onwards over the snowy ground, his flat cap pulled low over his faded hazel eyes and wrinkled face. He knew the journey home from the Bay Horse so well he could have done it with his eyes closed.

He crossed Queen Street at the lights and entered Micklegate, the ancient bar towering ahead of him. The streets were quiet now – probably the snow. Amazing, he thought, how a bit of snow sent everyone running indoors to crank up the central heating and plan their excuses for missing work the next day. It never used to be like that sixty years ago when he was a lad. If it snowed, no one said anything about missing school or work. Life went on.

Why does everyone go weak at the sight of snow these days? he thought to himself.

As Ted saw the bar ahead, he wondered what the stonemasons who built it in the Middle Ages would have thought of modern living. Nearly a thousand years of progress, and for what?

'We've all gone soft,' he mumbled into his coat, and plodded on towards the archway that ran through the bar – once home to the portcullis that barred undesirables from entering the city, or stopped certain residents from leaving.

The snow was falling heavily now, and any trace of footsteps from earlier shoppers had gone. The ground was crisp and white, or would have been but for the orange glow of the street lights behind him.

Just before he entered the archway, Ted's eye caught something on the ground beneath him. It was a darkened patch of snow.

What was that?

He stooped to peer at it. It looked dark reddish. It wasn't blood, was it? It couldn't be! It was too early for the late-night scraps. And he could see no one else further up Micklegate, through the arches. He was alone.

He prodded the stained patch with his shoe. Maybe someone had dropped something?

As he touched it, he was struck by the horrid suspicion that it was dog shit.

But it looked different. It was definitely a liquid of some sort. A stain rather than something on top of the snow. He was almost sure it was blood.

And then he felt something splatter on to his shoulder.

He strained his neck and tried to refocus his tired eyes on his coat, just inches from his face.

What the hell was that?

He touched his shoulder and scraped something off.

It felt and looked like a piece of raw liver – bloodied and slippery.

He quickly threw it to the ground, disgusted. As it landed, the red, pulpy mess caused the same staining in the snow that he'd seen before.

My God, it *was* blood.

He dared to glance up at the bar. Holding on to his cap, he allowed his eyes to scan the old stones that made up the impregnable walls of the gatehouse. Higher they went.

Suddenly he staggered backwards and held on to the wall. It was like someone had struck him in the gut, leaving him light-headed and shaking. The shock quickly drained his face of colour and shook him into a cold, sober state.

There was a severed head.

Rotting on a spike. Jutting out from the stone defences that towered above him.

Ted stood there, transfixed. From where he was standing, he could see it was the head of a man. Its petrified gaze and its grey, rotting skin were chilling to look upon. He felt sick.

The severed neck, which had been so brutally forced on to the spike, was still leaking blood, and it was from here that remnants of the man's flesh were falling.

Ted dropped to his knees trembling as another syrupy blob plopped onto his coat.

And then the pain struck.

At first it was like a hollow thump inside his chest. Then a tightening across the top of his body, and a paralysing tingle down his left arm. He fell backwards. The archway above him blurred.

His heart was failing him. And he knew it. All those false alarms he'd ignored. Those pains he'd blamed on indigestion. Was it too late now? Was this it?

As he went down, his last glimpse was of the severed head, its eyes mirroring the fear now written across Ted's own face.

He spat his last words up at the stone tower:

'Why me?'

CHAPTER 11

TUESDAY 2 NOVEMBER: 10.37 P.M.

HOUSES OF PARLIAMENT, LONDON

Jud sat in the chair, speechless.

Bonati had only been at Westminster five minutes and he'd already blagged himself half an hour with the 'suspect'. He'd negotiated a room within the building and a little time to do some straight talking with Jud. The police had reluctantly given him until eleven p.m., after which time they would take over. Bonati had wondered just how they proposed to do that, given that he was already in direct communication with MI5 and senior officers at SO17, but he didn't think it was wise to argue right now. Better to let these people believe they held the power, at least for now.

But he'd been angered by their refusal to let either him or Jud revisit the basement. All they had to go on was the pair of bent specs belonging to Jones. Was that really enough to suggest the engineer had been cruelly dispatched. And by Jud? The case was flimsy to say the least, and Bonati wanted to kick ass.

But they had twenty-three minutes left on the clock and he needed better answers from Jud than he was getting so far.

'Come on, J!' he said. 'Tell me what the hell happened down

there. You know I'll protect you, but I can only do that if you give me the whole story.'

Jud was getting exasperated. 'Look, sir, I've told you everything that happened. *Everything*.'

'But nothing you've said explains the fact that moments after you left the basement, the police made a search of all sectors and found the engineer had gone missing.'

'But no one's found a body, sir. I mean, there's no evidence of foul play, is there?'

'Well they found his mangled specs, Jud. It doesn't look good, does it? After all, you were the last one to see this Jones guy, and no one else was in there, no one except this *ghost*, of course.'

Jud thought he heard something in Bonati's tone that suggested he didn't even believe his story about the ghost.

'Oh, so you think I'm making up the ghost now, is that it?' he snapped at the professor.

Bonati stopped his pacing and threw a steely glance at Jud.

'That's enough,' he said. 'I never said that at all. I've never doubted you, J. But you lose your temper with me, and I can't help you any further.'

'I'm sorry, sir. I just don't know what's going on. I mean, you never really told me why I was here in the first place.'

'OK. DCS John Braithwaite – whom I've known for years – contacted me to say they'd had reports of an intruder in the basement. And as you know, because you've seen the CCTV footage, there was talk that the figure disappeared through a wall. Braithwaite wanted it dealt with quickly and discreetly. So he called us in. That's all I know.'

'But that tells us nothing!' said Jud.

'I know, J. But let's just think this through, shall we. Is there any way we can prove to those men outside that the engineer was alive and kicking when you left the basement?'

'Well, surely the camera caught him leaving?' Jud said. 'I

mean, it hadn't packed up at that stage, had it? The ghost hadn't arrived at that time. It was working, surely.'

Bonati nodded. 'That's true. But the camera didn't capture the engineer leaving, did it? You already asked the security guards if it showed anything in the main pipe shaft, and they told you it remained on you, in the sewage ejector room, remember? It's worked by remote, and it never followed the engineer down the pipe shaft.'

Jud looked despondent again. 'So it seemed like he never left my side.'

'Exactly.'

'But the lift,' said Jud. 'I mean, at the other end – at the top. Someone must have seen him leaving the lift. Maybe he didn't clock off as he should have done. He *must* have come back up.'

'Jud!' said Bonati. 'Slow down and think. They're saying he never even made it inside the lift! They found his broken specs in the basement. Why would he have left without them?'

Jud fell silent. He was trapped. Cornered. There was evidence that he had met the engineer – the security guard, Kevin, had taken him down and introduced him to the man. Then Kevin had returned to the lift and left the two of them alone down there.

Later, Jud returns to the ground floor, sweating and looking nervous. His coat is ripped and there's blood on his arm. And while he's in the cabin giving Mike and Kevin some cock-and-bull story about fingerprinting, police officers do a sweep of the basement and find nothing but Jones's mangled specs.

And the last person to see Jones alive was Jud.

OK, this was getting serious now.

CHAPTER 12

WEDNESDAY 3 NOVEMBER: 8.02 A.M.

THE CRYPT

The briefing room was alive with gossip.

'*Arrested?*' someone whispered.

'What're you talking about?'

'Jud's been arrested.'

'What?'

'Who's been arrested?'

'Jud.'

'Why?'

'What's going on?' said Dr Vorzek as she entered the room and heard the excited chatter.

Silence eventually fell on the group.

'Go on,' whispered Grace to Bex. 'Tell her about your text!'

'No!' said Bex. Telling everyone in the room that she was receiving texts from Jud would only cause the usual jeering.

'Go on,' said Grace again. 'It's important, Bex.'

Eventually Bex nodded and began.

'I had a message from Jud last night, Dr Vorzek. Can I ask you what's going on? He's in trouble, isn't he?'

Vorzek frowned. She knew exactly what was going on. She and Bonati had been telephoning each other to discuss Jud's case for most of the night. Events had taken a turn for the worse and Jud had been removed to Scotland Yard for some serious questioning. But she wasn't about to say that here, in front of the other agents.

'I appreciate your concern, Rebecca, but everything's in hand. We needn't worry about that now.'

'So why's Bonati not here?' Bex whispered to Grace, who shrugged her shoulders in reply. The professor almost always gave the morning briefings, and his absence spoke volumes.

And where was Jud anyway?

Now it was the turn of the agents to frown. Was that all Vorzek was going to say? The word on the grapevine was that Jud had been arrested at Westminster – but no one, not even Bex, knew why. His text had been cryptic, to say the least. *Don't believe what you hear. I didn't do it*, was all it had said.

Vorzek was certainly not going to be let off that lightly. Bex pressed on.

'I'm sorry, Doctor, but Jud gave me no details other than to say that he didn't do whatever he's being accused of. I'm really worried. Can't you give us any more information? I've tried calling him today but—'

'That's enough!' snapped Vorzek. 'It's not appropriate to discuss the matter here. It's in hand. Bonati's doing all he can. And I've got a lot to get through.'

Luc spoke up next. He too had been worried, as he'd not heard anything from Jud since he'd left him watching the movie the night before.

'But this is weird, Doctor. I mean, I was there when the call came in for Jud to go to Westminster. He didn't know anything about why he was going there. He didn't know what to expect. If something's happened, Jud certainly didn't plan it.'

There was another rumbling of speculation. Vorzek knew she

couldn't stop the agents from caring about one another. If one of them was in trouble, everyone wanted to know about it. They were a tightly knit group. Bonati liked it that way. Camaraderie and teamwork were encouraged at all times. Just ten agents were recruited each year, so everyone knew each other well.

'I'm sorry. That's all I can say. We're doing what we can. As soon as I have something to report, I'll tell you.'

'So something's definitely happened, then?' said Luc.

Vorzek shot him a stern look and ignored the question. 'Right, listen, everyone. We've received reports from our contacts in the north that there have been some incidents in York.'

She turned to the vast screen built into the wall behind her and switched it on.

The briefing room was unlike any other at the CRYPT, not just because it was large enough to seat everyone in the organisation, but because of the lavish equipment it housed.

Having the owner of Goode Technology PLC as its co-founder helped when it came to resourcing the CRYPT. Every month there was some new form of communications technology installed somewhere in the place.

The 72-inch rear projection screen with a 1,300-lumen LCD projector was one of Jason's latest gifts to the agents. And there were multi-system links installed so that live video casts from Goode's penthouse could be pumped into any one of the meeting rooms underground.

The main briefing room was fitted with a ten-speaker surround-sound system and new lighting rigs that enabled whoever was giving the briefing to program lighting and sound patterns to match their presentation (and keep the agents awake at all times).

It was the same state-of-the-art speaker system that had pumped out the customary thirty-minute warning prior to the morning briefing. The timing was always the same, but you never knew what would be playing. The choice this morning had been 'Hotel California' by the Eagles. Goode always enjoyed programming the daily alarm sounds to give his agents the best musical education he could. Monday had seen the zombies and skulls rising to Stevie Wonder's 'Higher Ground' and Tuesday had brought an unexpected blast of P. Diddy's 'Ass on the Floor'. Goode was nothing if not eclectic in his tastes.

He had even been known, on occasion, to use the giant screens in certain rooms to surprise the agents with excerpts from the latest horror movies. The screens would come on when they least expected it. Goode said it kept them on their toes. Bonati just thought it distracted them, but who was he to argue with the man who owned the building?

No such horror scenes that morning, though.

Instead it was an ancient-looking stone church that filled the giant screen in front of them.

'Worrying reports,' said Vorzek. 'Inexplicable sightings. Police have spoken to a woman in the area who claims to have seen a headless figure outside this church in the centre of the city.'

Now the zombies and skulls were hooked.

'When?' said Grace.

'Last night.'

'Any other witnesses?' said Luc.

'The police are on it now. They're interviewing, but it's hard. You can't walk up to someone and ask "Have you seen a headless ghost recently?"' Vorzek didn't mean to sound facetious, but lack of sleep was playing havoc with her nerves.

She continued, 'The woman was adamant about what she saw. She tried to run but apparently slipped over and knocked her head. She was out cold for a while.'

Some of the agents were thinking the same thing. Bex articulated the mood. 'Are they sure it was in that order? I mean, she didn't slip, bang her head and *then* see something weird?'

'Bex, please,' said Vorzek. 'You know as well as I do that evidence comes to us from the security forces only when they're satisfied it's genuine and worth investigating. That's not all, anyway.'

'What else?' said Grace.

'Well, it seems that an elderly man was found later, at a place called Micklegate, collapsed in the street – a mild heart attack. He survived, but only because of the quick thinking of a motorist.'

'Don't tell me. The shock of seeing another ghost?' asked Grace.

'Well, could be.' A picture of the medieval arch appeared on the screen. 'This is Micklegate Bar,' said Vorzek. 'Built in about 1200. It's one of four gateways into the city. But it wasn't just used as an entrance. It had a more sinister function. It's where they used to display traitors' heads on spikes. A kind of deterrent to would-be criminals. And that's exactly what the man claims he saw.'

'What?' said Bex. 'He saw a *severed head*? On a spike?'

'Yes. Exactly. And the shock very nearly killed him, apparently.'

Some of the older zombies were not convinced. Some wanted to know what he'd been doing prior to the sighting. Drinking, perhaps? But no one was prepared to question it, given the doctor's mood. It would all be covered in the full report when they got a chance to read it anyway.

Vorzek could sense the scepticism in the room. She continued, 'The point is, he wasn't the only one who saw it. The motorist saw it too.'

'So was it a real head or was it a ghost?' someone said.

'And was it recognisable?' said another.

'One at a time,' said Vorzek. By the time the police were at the scene, the head had been removed. Now, that could mean it was a ghost that dematerialised, but it could just as easily have been a real head. If someone put it there, they could also have removed it. And no, the face wasn't instantly recognisable, as it's features had been badly beaten or burned.'

54

'So no evidence?' said Grace.

'Well, there is something.'

Suddenly the group gasped as they caught sight of the gruesome image on the giant screen. It was impossible to see the face from the angle at which the shot had been hurriedly taken, but it was obviously a disembodied head.

'The motorist who saved the man in question captured it on his phone.'

'It's horrid,' said Grace. 'No wonder the shock nearly killed the old man.'

'I know. It's a disturbing image . . . which is why he sold it.'

'He *what*?' said Luc.

The room fell silent. They feared what was coming.

'*Sold* it,' said Vorzek again.

The front page of the *York Press* now filled the screen, with the same gruesome shot of the head emblazoned across it, accompanied by the headline THE MICKLEGATE GHOST.

'Great,' said Luc sarcastically. 'Helpful headline. Anything to sell papers.'

'How are we going to take readings if everyone's swarming over the site?' said Grace. 'And now that we know what human fear does to ghosts, this will only get worse. How're we going to investigate it, Doctor?'

'That's up to you, Bex,' said Vorzek. 'I've booked you a ticket on the nine twenty-five from King's Cross. You've got an hour.'

Bex stood up quickly. 'But what about Jud? I mean, we still don't know if—'

'Thank you, Rebecca. Go and pack, please.' Vorzek was relieved that she and Bonati had found a job for Bex, and one which took her away from the CRYPT for a while. They knew that she'd be concerned about Jud, but they couldn't allow her worry to spread. Vorzek turned to the other agents, most of whom were staring enviously at Bex.

Grace stood up. 'I'm going with her,' she said.

'I'm sorry,' said Vorzek sternly. 'Agents don't appoint themselves to cases.'

'Yes, but she needs—'

'Sit *down!*' said Vorzek. She was in no mood for another argument.

'But—'

'No! Bex is perfectly capable of investigating this one alone. Ordinarily we'd send two agents, it's true, but we've already got enough cases to fill every agent's diary twice over. We're stretched, Grace. We need you here. If you'll let me get on to the rest of the agenda, you'll see how many more incidents we've got to investigate.

'Right, next report. The rector at St Peter's in Clerkenwell has been in touch again. It seems the ghost's back.'

Bex exited the room.

But she resolved to call Jud from the train – and keep calling him until she got some answers. York or not, she wasn't going to give up on him that easily.

CHAPTER 13

WEDNESDAY 3 NOVEMBER: 9.11 A.M.

SO17 PALACE OF WESTMINSTER DIVISION, NEW SCOTLAND YARD

It had been a long night.

Bonati and Jud had talked and then talked some more, but Jud just couldn't come up with any more answers. Nothing. Surely the police had no evidence to prove he had anything to do with the engineer's disappearance? But then Jud had no way of proving the contrary either. The camera in the sewage ejector room had packed up, robbing him of an alibi. He could've been anywhere in that basement – including the area where the engineer was last seen.

The security guards and police officers had been true to their word. They'd arrived to collect their suspect at eleven p.m. When Bonati was unable to give them any more answers, they'd carted Jud off to New Scotland Yard for questioning.

Frantic phone calls from Bonati to SO17 and MI5 had not prevented them from taking him. The professor had insisted that he should at least come too, but was denied at first, until he'd pulled some strings even higher up and was finally given clearance. Bonati would take the place of a lawyer, the only person usually authorised to accompany a suspect during interview.

There was no way he'd abandon Jud now. He believed his story. He *had* to. After all, the alternative was unthinkable. There were too many painful reminders here of the case involving the death of Jud's mother. The accusations, the denials, the insistence from Jud that 'the ghost did it'. Bonati vowed he would be there every step of the way.

On arriving at the station, Jud had been thrown into one of the cells. And left to stew.

Bonati had been furious. Why make him wait? They were playing with Jud and the professor knew it. But just as Jud sat miserably on the other side of the bolted metal door, Bonati too had had to wait, and wait, until the officers decided it was time to begin the interview. That was at 6.15 a.m.

And now here they were, still sitting in the interview room three hours later and still going round in circles. The morning sun was streaming through the small window at the far side of the room, but it brought little comfort. Rather it struck Jud's face like an interrogation spotlight.

Neither Jud nor Bonati had been allowed to revisit the basement at Westminster. All they had was the word of the police.

Bonati had questioned them constantly since arriving at the station, wanting to know the exact circumstances of the engineer's alleged disappearance and just why Jud was implicated. But the officers had been cagey. It wasn't unusual to conceal evidence from the suspect, they said – the more Jud knew, the easier it would be for him to deny it all – but the professor had been especially furious that he too had been denied access to the basement. It didn't make sense.

The officers had just kept using the same reply: 'All in good time, sir.'

But it was now after nine in the morning and they seemed no closer to charging Jud with anything. How much time did they need?

If the case against Jud was so strong, why hadn't they charged him? Why hadn't they finished the interview by now and slung him back in the cells?

Bonati knew they were in a race against time, not just because of the legal limit of holding a suspect without charge, but because Jud's temper – something they'd been working so hard to improve recently – was bound to blow soon. And that would mean disaster. You exploded in a police interview and you might as well confess to doing the crime.

'Look,' said DS Barton, one of the two detective sergeants who'd been staring silently at Jud from across the small table for several minutes now, 'I know you've told us over and over again that you were nowhere near the place where the engineer had been working – you said it was at the other end of the basement, yeah?'

'Yes!' said Jud, again.

'So how do you know where he was?'

'What?' Jud shifted awkwardly in his chair. Was this yet another trap they were setting? 'Because he told me!' he thundered, thumping his fist on the table so that it rattled on its wobbly legs.

Bonati turned and flashed a look at him. 'OK, J,' he whispered. 'Take it easy.'

For Jud to erupt now in a violent temper would mean game over for sure.

'OK,' said Barton's colleague DS Colville, realising that they'd reached a dead end with that line of enquiry. 'So what exactly were you doing in *your* end of the basement?'

Jud put his head in his hands. 'Oh come on,' he moaned. 'We've been through this already. How many times? Look, I've told you. *Investigating.*'

'But unless you can account for your time in this sewage ejector room with something more than just "investigating", what are we supposed to think, huh? No one else was reported down there. The security checks on that basement are as strict as hell. We can see exactly who's down there at any given time – when they go down and when they come back up.'

'Well that's clearly not true!' interrupted Jud. 'I mean, why was I there in the first place, huh? To investigate an intruder, I thought.'

The officers chose to ignore that. 'You went down with the security guard at 9.03 p.m.,' said Barton. 'The camera in the lift sees you exiting. Then the camera in the sewage ejector room sees you enter it at 9.05 *with* the engineer. And we can see you moving around for a few minutes, lookin' at the walls.'

'Yeah,' agreed Jud. 'I was checking for fingerprints.'

DS Barton looked unimpressed. 'For God's sake, son, who do you think we are? Do you think we don't know what's going on here? Do you think we don't know who *you* are? Is that it? Are you trying to cover up what you're doing? Why do you think we let Bonati in? We know about the CRYPT, so let's stop this silly pretence.'

Bonati could see Jud's fists were clenched beneath the table.

'OK!' Jud shouted. 'I was trying to find some evidence of paranormal activity. OK? You *know* that. I was seeing if the intruder that had been reported really was a ghost. That was my brief.'

Bonati was nodding in agreement.

Jud looked at the officers across the table. All these questions and they'd got nowhere, it seemed to him. Achieved nothing. What kind of investigation was this?

Of course Bonati knew exactly what the detective sergeants were doing. Going over the same ground time and time again so that Jud would answer differently just once and then they'd jump on his inconsistent story-telling. Guilty as charged.

Or, even better, they'd keep asking the same questions, keep rattling the suspect in the hope that he'd crack in the process and offer a confession just to shut them up.

And Jud was taking the bait. He could feel his heart racing, and in his lap his knuckles were going white with tension. His legs were fidgeting under the table.

'Look!' he shouted. 'Either you accept my version of events or you just bloody charge me and—'

'Jud!' Bonati said quickly. 'Cool it!'

The officers glanced at one another, smirking

'Don't worry, Professor,' said Colville, turning to Bonati with a grin across his face. 'We know all about this young man's temper. Oh yeah. Vicious. There's a lot of us who know about your temper, *Jamie.*'

Jamie? thought Jud. Now things were slipping out of control. If they knew who he was – or who he used to be – and the previous conviction that had robbed him of his identity, then things had just got a whole lot worse.

'Gentlemen,' said Bonati sternly, rising from the table. 'Can I have a word outside, please? Now.'

There was something in his authoritative tone that left the men unwilling to defy him. It wasn't his words so much as the aura that surrounded him. It was so rare for him to show anger that when he did, people sat up and listened – even those who didn't know him could sense he meant business.

They slowly rose to their feet and followed him out.

'What the *hell* do you think you're playing at?' he bellowed. 'What's going on here?'

The two officers looked incredulously at him but said nothing, like naughty school kids.

Bonati wasn't deterred. 'You know perfectly well that you can't refer to previous convictions when interviewing suspects – and Jud is no different. You mention the name Jamie again and I'll have you sacked. I know what you're trying to do. You're trying to provoke a reaction. A bit of bear-baiting, is that it? Wind him up and get a quick confession? Nice and easy for you.'

The officers remained silent. One of them dared a smirk.

'And where the hell is John, anyway?' Bonati continued.

'John?' said Colville, looking bored.

'Yes! Detective Chief Superintendent John Braithwaite. Look, I spoke to him last night, but since then I haven't heard anything.'

'I think the DCS is a busy man, sir.'

'Don't patronise me,' snapped Bonati.

The whole thing had been odd from the start. First the phone call from his usual contact at MI5 yesterday evening to brief him on what would follow. Then the call from Braithwaite. An intruder seen in the basement at Westminster. Nothing unusual in that, but according to the security guards, the figure had passed right through a wall. Could it have been a ghost? They'd sounded genuinely concerned.

He'd had dealings with Braithwaite in the past and he knew he could be trusted. Braithwaite was a decent guy. He knew the story and was one of the few guys at the Met who was sympathetic to the CRYPT. Most coppers, when dealing with agents, retained a distant coolness – a cynicism about Bonati's 'kids' army'. They scornfully called it the CRIB, on account of its young investigators. But Braithwaite was different. He'd seemed sure that Bonati's agents would tell them if there was something paranormal going on. So Jud had been dispatched. Braithwaite had shared MI5's concern about a possible haunting in such a high-profile location, but had said he was confident that the CRYPT would set their minds at ease.

But events since then had not been so straightforward.

No sooner had Bonati dispatched Jud to Westminster – it was his turn, and he was always hell to be around when he had no case to work on – than he received another phone call from Special Ops. But it wasn't Braithwaite this time.

And the allegations involving Jud were beyond comprehension.

Bonati still believed that Jud was innocent – no question – but convincing these coppers, and proving what really did happen down there in the basement was going to be difficult.

And something didn't add up. Why was Braithwaite no longer on the case? Bonati had not yet had a chance to call his contact at MI5 again and ask some serious questions, like why had Braithwaite sent these two detective sergeants instead? And who the hell had briefed them about Jamie Goode? A story like that would have been like gold dust to them. But this was classified information, only for a select few at MI5 and just a handful of senior officers at the Met. Who was spreading it around the lower ranks now?

'If you're not going to tell me where Braithwaite is,' continued Bonati, 'then perhaps you'll tell me why we've had no access to the basement since the engineer went missing.'

Barton spoke first. 'You know very well, sir, that we don't have to do that. We put a case together, we find evidence, we charge, and then we move to a conviction – we're not obliged to show you that evidence until the trial, and that includes the crime scene.'

'Crime scene?' said Bonati. 'What bloody crime are you talking about? You've no evidence to suggest Jud has done anything.'

'You're forgetting the glasses, sir.'

'Oh, I see. So you find this engineer's broken glasses and that immediately leads you to the conclusion that Jud has killed him and hidden him somewhere, is that it? I take it you've checked the specs for Jud's fingerprints?'

'We're on it now,' said Colville. 'And we're continuing our enquiries. We've got twenty-four hours to hold him without charge and we—'

'Oh shut up!' Bonati said. 'I don't need a lesson in procedure. I know you've got a few more hours before you have to charge him or let him go, but I'm not stupid. I know you'll apply for an extension, and that you'll get it.

'Look, there's a kid in there who's terrified. Understand? Terrified because you just called him Jamie. Now I don't expect you guys to understand the full significance of what that means to him, because you've probably only been told half the story. But you obviously know enough to use it to provoke a reaction. Yeah? Well you've got it, OK?

'Now, either you show your hand and decide what you're going to do with Jud, or I'll take this further. Right here, right now. I'll call Braithwaite, then the Commissioner, then MI5, then the Home Office. And I'll get clearance to handle this case myself. Now, what's it to be?' He took out his mobile and looked ready to dial.

'Handle this yourself?' scoffed Barton. 'If you could do that, you'd have done it already! Don't threaten us, sir.'

'You really don't get it, do you?' said Bonati. 'We try to work with you every step of the way. It's how it's always been. We do things properly. We follow protocol because we trust you – and you trust us. There's a system and it usually works. But I'd say you abused that system when you dragged up Jud's past, and I could have you disciplined for that. When you brought that up, you broke the rules of the game. So what's it to be?'

Colville and Barton thought for a moment, exchanged glances and then nodded surreptitiously. They too had wondered why Braithwaite wasn't on the case any more, but they had their orders to follow – orders that had come from 'the very top', as their senior officer had said.

But maybe this guy Bonati really did have friends in high places.

It had been a long night for them too, and all they wanted was a coffee, a bacon sandwich and a comfortable seat instead of those horrid plastic chairs in the interview room.

'OK,' said Barton. 'I tell you what we'll do. We'll bail the kid into your care. That's not to say we won't call him back and charge him later, though. We might. But he stays at the CRYPT, he goes nowhere and he sees no one until you've heard from us again. He *is* still a suspect, after all.'

Getting Jud bailed into his care – just like he and Jason Goode had done the first time round – was the best option for now. But Bonati sensed something strange in the offer.

'That's what you were intending to do all along, wasn't it?'

The officers shook their heads and shrugged.

'Yes it was! I don't imagine you were ever going to charge him. At least not yet. But you wanted him out of the way . . . those were your orders, weren't they? Keep him locked up for a while and then play games with him in the interview room? Something's going on here, and I will find out what it is.'

CHAPTER 14

WEDNESDAY 3 NOVEMBER: 9.36 A.M.

WINCHESTER STREET, PIMLICO, LONDON

Daylight was struggling to break through the faded brown curtains, which remained closed. It wasn't the first time the man had slept in, even on a weekday.

He lay cocooned inside the duvet, in a room barely bigger than his double bed. The radio had blasted out and been silenced by a slap on the snooze button several times already.

The man was not getting up. He couldn't. Not yet.

He glanced across the cluttered room to the hallway through the open door. He could see the kitchen beyond. Foil wrappers from last night's takeaway were still sitting on the worktop, blobs of congealed sweet and sour sauce clinging to their sides. Discarded cans of Strongbow were stacked in the corner.

Would he ever grow out of student mode? Would his flat ever be clean? Not unless he had a visitor, and that was rare these days. Until then, there was no point in washing up. A waste of time and water.

Washing up was on a needs-must basis only. When he'd used the final coffee cup and all the others resembled giant Petri dishes harvesting their own elaborate forms of mould, then he would run one under the hot tap. Only the treasured whisky tumbler was treated to a more frequent wash. But a faint malty whiff lingered from it this morning, from where it had been abandoned last night on the bedside table.

He turned on to his back and contemplated the events of the night before. It had certainly been a busy one.

He'd followed the master's instructions to the letter.

His target hadn't returned to his house in Lambeth until gone eleven. The man had been waiting in his car a few yards down Pearman Street, listening to Classic FM. He'd always preferred something classical, especially on the night of a killing. It settled his nerves.

He gave the victim a good hour to unwind – he was probably grabbing a snack and enjoying a nightcap. Why deny a man his last drink? He wasn't completely heartless, he thought.

He watched the lights go out on the ground floor and the bedroom light go on upstairs. Twenty minutes later that too was turned off and the house was finally in darkness.

Hidden from view by the usual black hoodie, he crept up to the door and picked the lock with ease. There wasn't even a deadlock or a chain and bolt system.

Shoddy security for a senior copper, he thought. The lock picked, he welcomed himself into the hallway and tiptoed down the chequered tiled floor.

Luckily his target lived alone. He always preferred it that way. Family members were a nuisance. It wasn't the killing. He'd lost all trace of a conscience years ago – the spirit had put paid to that. It was the hassle of having to visit their rooms and make sure they too were silenced. It just took extra time.

No petrol can tonight. Too risky. Pearman Street was lined with Victorian houses, some divided into flats, some family homes, but all filled with too many good Samaritan neighbours who'd try to save his victim as soon as they smelled the smoke and saw the flames licking at the windows. It wasn't a clean enough killing and he knew he couldn't run the risk of failing tonight. The master would never accept that.

The man's left hand was still clutching the Glock 17 9mm, hidden inside his hoodie pocket. The Evolution-9 silencer was its perfect companion, affording a killing that was as discreet as it was fast.

His target was snoring. Ugly bastard, too.

One quick thud to the temple, and his snoring stopped.

Then it was back to his snug flat in Pimlico and a well-earned whisky. The rich, pungent liquid always soothed his throat and warmed his cold frame. It was a ritual. He even called it his killing bottle. His cabinet was lined with other drinks, but the oak-aged single malt was king on nights like these.

And now, as the morning sunshine poured in through the curtains, he felt pleased with himself. Everything was going to plan. The master would be happy.

Wouldn't he?

He stared at the ceiling. And waited. Just like before. Like every time.

It didn't matter where he was – he could be in a fancy hotel suite, a room at the club or here in his Pimlico flat – he always felt the same. Like a kid. Lying in his little bedroom at home in York, just waiting for the spirit to come.

He knew he shouldn't still be in bed when there was so much to do. But there was something appealing about hiding under the duvet while the frantic sounds of commuters and shoppers drifted in through the window.

Smug. That was it. He felt smug at the thought of all the losers on the streets below, stuck on the hamster wheel of life, the rat race – no control, no life and no time for themselves.

But not him. He was different. He was the chosen one. Always had been.

He knew that the spirit was coming, because he'd dreamed it. That was the way it often worked. If he received a visitation in his dreams, he knew he would be communicating in the morning. He'd never seen the spirit face to face, only heard him. His voice often penetrated his dreams. And when it did, he only saw a shadow. Always a black, featureless silhouette. And when he awoke at dawn, he knew the master was coming.

Of course he never minded lying and waiting in the mornings. It was easier than when the spirit came at night. Trying to stay awake, especially after an exhausting day, ready to hear the master's voice, was a trial sometimes. But the mornings were different. It gave him a welcome excuse to stay under the covers. (Though colleagues at work had become suspicious about the amount of dental work he'd been having, each appointment causing him to be late for work *again*.)

Eventually, after he'd slammed the snooze button to stop the radio interrupting for the sixth time, the man heard it. As always it was soft, probably imperceptible to most people, but to the trained ear it was unmistakable.

'Hello, little one,' it whispered. 'Well, it has begun.'

'I know.'

'Last night our friends in the northern shires did not let us down. They are gathering.'

'And here in London too, it seems.'

The spirit emitted an ominous chuckle. 'Indeed, my friend. Just as we'd planned. We in the spirit world do not falter. We are not cursed with the doubts and weaknesses of living men. We have friends in London too, and they are rising. They have delivered once again, ensuring that our plot may flourish unabated.'

The man felt a twinge of jealousy.

'I too have delivered, master,' he said quickly. 'It was a long and difficult night, but it was worth it. I have fulfilled your wishes.'

The spirit spoke kindly. 'You have never disappointed me, little one.'

The man was gratified, but he was not about to relax. He

knew that beneath the master's thin veneer of kindliness lay a ruthless, volatile temper. God knows, the man knew about that.

But the sun was shining outside, the day was unfolding cheerfully and he had no desire to spoil the rhythm of things by pricking the spirit's temper. He couldn't afford another injury to his already battered body by upsetting the master today.

'Thank you,' he replied. 'And your friends in the north? They are revived by news of the uprising?'

'Indeed,' said the spirit. 'The martyrs caritatis are stirring. This will be their time.'

The man was nervous.

'More bloodshed?'

'They are martyrs caritatis, little one. They died for love. Love of their God. They are not killers. They were the ones who suffered death, remember.'

'Yes, I know,' said the man, only too aware that this was a dangerous subject. The spirit's love and admiration for the martyrs had always been present. It defined him, just as it had shaped him in life. But news of the ghostly apparitions in York had unsettled the man. 'They are religious martyrs, I understand that, master, but there have been two injuries already. Will there be more?'

'No!' the spirit shouted. 'Do not anger me. The injuries of which you speak were not caused by my friends in the north. They are stirring, yes, and some have been seen – many more will appear in the days ahead, you can be sure of that – but they are not violent. I will not have them dishonoured. They were witnessed by weak people, shallow victims of their own short-sightedness, who failed to see beyond the shocking images of the martyrs' broken bodies to find pity and compassion. All they felt was fear, and it was their own cowardice that caused them injury.'

'I'm sorry, master,' said the man, now fearing for his own safety. He tensed his body beneath the sheets, bracing himself for a punishing blow.

'You will see I am not the only one stirring,' the spirit continued. 'The plotters may have chosen to act, as we did back then, but you cannot stop other souls from rising. The sacrificed ones. In the hours that follow, there will be more. Not just in the north, but in the capital too. Anger is rife throughout the land, my friend, just as it was back then. The plan – our plan – reaches far beyond you and me and the group I hold dear. My friends are rising, but there will be others. If only you knew, little one. If only you knew what they did to us. To our brethren. But our pain and suffering will soon be over. Justice *will* be done. The country will be changed for ever. We are but days away.'

The man was relieved that the moment was now so close. But what might happen in the time remaining? He was doing everything the spirit asked of him. Risking everything. But would it end as the spirit wished? Would he and his friends ever rest in peace?

Would the man *really* get his life back?

Doubts had been creeping into his mind of late. He knew it was wrong. Negative thoughts seeped into him and festered like an infection. He pushed them away for another time.

'I sense you have doubts and fears too, little one.'

The man could never hide anything from the master. He knew him too well.

'I worry, it's true, master. I shall not fail you, but there will be those who try to resist us.'

'Just as there were back then,' said the spirit. 'History repeats itself.'

'You know who I am talking about, master. I have told you of them before.'

The spirit's voice emitted an eerie chuckle.

'Rest, little one. You refer to the babies once again, I assume?'

The spirit had never taken the man's concerns seriously. He'd told the master about the CRYPT and its arrogant agents who thought they knew all about paranormal things, but the spirit had mocked him. He did not share the man's fears that the agents might destroy their plans. He had simply called them 'babies'.

But the man was less charitable. He hated the way the CRYPT considered themselves so superior. The 'chosen ones'. Self-centred, meddlesome children who claimed to communicate with the afterlife, as though they were the only ones who had the gift. The conceit of them! To presume to know why spirits were returning and to try to send them back – before justice was even done! They would *not* succeed this time.

Last night's victim had been too close to the CRYPT. Too supportive. The man had been pleased when the master had named his latest target. He welcomed the chance to take out another friend of the CRYPT, and so isolate them further.

'Do not fear them!' said the spirit, reading his mind again. 'They are but children. They are nothing! And soon they shall be disgraced by their own kind.'

'You are right, master,' said the man. 'Forgive me. They are babies in a crib. And we shall soon be rid of them. The path is now clear. They will implode around their disgraced agent. He has killed before, so it will be easy to prove that he's killed again. The organisation won't survive the scandal. They'll—'

'Rest,' the spirit interrupted. 'Breathe easy. There are more important things to discuss.'

He felt his anger subsiding again. He could feel the warmth of the spirit's love running through him.

But of course he knew that visitations like these were never just for polite, self-congratulatory words. The spirit always wanted something more. Even after the events of last night, the man knew another mission was only moments away. The master hadn't just come to say thank you. It never worked that way.

'What will you have of me now?' he asked directly.

There was silence.

'Master?'

Was he being too impatient? Had he said too much already? He knew he'd done a lot of talking this time – far more than usual. Would he be put in his place now? Silence was never a good sign. He braced himself again, tensing his muscles as a boxer tenses his torso ready for the next punch.

The spirit whispered, 'I have no task for you today, little one.'

The man felt confused and cautious. 'Then why the visit?' he said tentatively. This was the first time, for as long as he could remember at least, that the spirit had come to him twice in as many days. Was he just returning to say thank you for last night? Unlikely. He'd never done that before. There was something else. He could tell. The hairs on the back of his neck stood up, as they always did when the master came.

'You are tense,' the spirit said softly. 'Worry not. You have fulfilled your latest task. You have nothing to fear this day.'

Now the man really was frightened. He'd known the spirit practically all of his life. He'd known the pain he could dish out at a stroke. But this was unlike other encounters. The softly spoken words unsettled him more than the anger he'd so often experienced in the past.

'The gang is assembling, my friend. My closest allies are back. But there is something further. Something I have not yet shared with you, little one.'

The man was transfixed. The master's words were soft and calm and intimate. But there was a sense of foreboding seeping into the room. The sun had passed behind a dark cloud, casting the room into shade. There was a lull in the traffic and the passing footsteps on the pavement had abated.

He felt acutely alone.

'You know how weak I have been,' said the spirit. 'How I have always yearned for physical form, but have lacked the energy to materialise.'

The man's eyes widened with fear. His stomach began to turn somersaults. Where was this leading?

'Well, it seems my martyred friends have strengthened me. News of the uprising has rekindled energy in us all. Their strength has renewed something in me. Something that has lain dormant all these years.'

'What . . . you mean . . . ?' The man couldn't form the words.

'Oh come, little one. We know each other better than we know ourselves. You know my pain. How I've been weak for so many centuries. Locked in a realm of darkness, longing to return to the world in form as well as spirit. To connect with you beyond these whispered words.'

'Master?' He felt sick with nerves. Was the shadow figure he'd known in his dreams really going to reveal himself? Was the voice about to gain a face after all these years?

'Patience, little one. I know you are as keen as I am for us to meet. Well, it seems the martyred souls are grateful to be rising again and joining us. They have repaid me. They have poured their energy into me. I have trapped it, harnessed it . . .'

Nerves had merged into cold, hard fear, which pulled at the man's stomach and brought a dryness to his throat. He'd not been expecting this. Perhaps not ever. He was still lying on his back, staring at the ceiling. He pulled the duvet up to his chin, over the scarred skin on his chest and at the base of his neck – the wounds that had lingered some five years now, since the York killing. Would they never go?

The room was filling with electrical energy. He could feel it surging through him. Tiny sparks danced up the metal struts of the bed frame. A strange tingling sensation came over his face, like pins and needles. He quickly rubbed his forehead, and then pulled the duvet even higher, up to his eyes.

'I have found my fellow men,' the spirit continued. 'Those whom I held dearest. I shall be with them at last, to stand beside them as we make history once more.'

The man peered over the top of the duvet at the faded white ceiling above him.

74

And then he saw something.

Was it a stain he'd not noticed before? A patch of mould seeping into the ceiling from the roof above? There had been heavy rain in the night; he remembered hearing it in the small hours. The clouds had cleared and the sun had burst through gaps in the curtains once more, but he knew it had been a rough night. Had the roof begun leaking?

He scanned the rest of the ceiling, looking for similar patches. Nothing. He glanced back directly above him. The patch, whatever it was, had darkened still.

And it kept darkening.

The man looked on incredulously as the mottled shapes spread across the ceiling like a miniature oil spill.

'Hello?' he said quickly. 'Master?'

Silence.

But the shapes were still shifting and intensifying above him. Energy in the room was growing. He could feel his heart racing and a prickly sensation running down his arms, bringing heat beneath the sheets.

What the hell was happening?

With trembling hands the man gripped the duvet tightly and covered his whole face. Was he dreaming? Had he slipped unknowingly into unconsciousness?

Under the covers he gripped his own leg and squeezed hard. A pinching pain ran through his thigh. He *was* awake, or so it seemed.

Still hiding beneath the sheet, the man heard the spirit's whispered voice once again.

'Hello, little one. Show yourself to me. I shall not harm you! But please forgive me if I am not what you had hoped for. I am a shadow of my former self. Centuries of cruel treatment have taken their toll. But my soul is intact, and at last I can appear to you.'

The man refused to pull the covers back. Instead he screwed his eyes tightly shut and willed the nightmare away.

'Show yourself!' the spirit boomed, sending a wave of terror through his body like a tsunami. 'Little one! Don't anger me! I have waited long enough to summon the strength to reveal myself to you. I have longed for this moment. Now *look at me!*'

A stabbing pain struck the man's right leg. It was the same leg he'd just pinched, but his hands were now tightly clasped beneath his chin. He knew exactly what was unfolding. He'd angered the spirit, and now his punishment was due. Soon he would feel the familiar damp patch on the sheet below him. His own blood would seep from the flesh wound inflicted.

Left with little choice but to appease the spirit before his body was punctured, the man slowly opened his eyes and began sliding the duvet from his face.

There was a head.

It wasn't fully opaque. But it was more solid than a hologram. It looked like it had pushed its way through the plaster above him, though nothing had fallen from the ceiling.

Black, bedraggled hair hung down from a pallid alabaster face, its features thin and aquiline. The face was not skeletal – a layer of white skin stretched across the skull, but it was so thin it revealed veins like marble grain.

But it wasn't the jet-black hair or the sickly pallor of the face that terrified the man as he stared transfixed at the ceiling; it was the milky white eyes.

They had no pupils.

Just white eyeballs, like a statue's. The solid, stone-like visage of the master, disembodied.

But then it moved.

And as the master's lips cracked and shifted apart, black, congealed mucus seeped from the corner of his mouth.

'It's been a long time, hasn't it?' the spirit said, breaking into a smile.

CHAPTER 15

WEDNESDAY 3 NOVEMBER: 10.12 A.M.

TRAIN BOUND FOR YORK

'Where the hell have you been? What's happened?' Bex couldn't hide her concern, even down the phone.

'It's OK,' said Jud. 'I'm back at the CRYPT now.'

'So?'

'What d'you mean, *so*?'

Bex had been trying to raise Jud on his phone since his text the night before. And now here he was, evasive as usual. Shutting her out, just like he always did.

'Why won't you talk to me?' she implored.

Passengers in the seats opposite her looked across disapprovingly.

But Jud was in no mood for an inquisition. He'd had enough of that from the police.

'Look, I'm tired, Bex.'

'*You're* tired! You send me a text in the middle of the night to say you've been arrested – no other details – so I spend all night wondering what's going on, and then you tell me you're tired.'

Others on the train were listening now. This was a strange

77

conversation for a kid to be having. Even the passengers who hated mobile phones were now hooked.

Jud could picture Bex's face at the other end of the line. The way she frowned when she was angry, the wrinkles running like contours across her unblemished skin. He felt for her. Last night couldn't have been easy for her either. He shouldn't have sent the text. It had only made her worry.

On arriving back at the CRYPT, his fellow skulls had filled him in on the latest news and briefing information.

'So you're on your way to York then, Bex?' he said more kindly, lying back on his bed. He still had his jacket and boots on. Hadn't even changed yet.

'Yeah. Vorzek has sent me up here. I think she wanted me out of the way, to be honest.'

'Really? Why?'

Bex thought for a moment. She didn't want to tell Jud the real reason, that she'd been bothering everyone with too many questions about his whereabouts. She suddenly felt embarrassed that she cared so much.

'I dunno,' she lied. 'Probably my turn for a new case, I suppose.'

'Where are you staying?' asked Jud.

'Dean Court Hotel, I think. Why?'

'Nice. By the Minster. I know it well. I had a school friend whose parents lived in York. I used to go and stay with them when my own folks were in America. Spent many a summer up there. Great city.'

'Yeah, well this isn't a holiday trip, Jud.' There was an awkward silence. 'You know, that's the first time you've ever mentioned your parents to me,' said Bex. 'You *never* talk about them!'

Lack of sleep must have been catching up with him. What the hell was he doing? This was a dangerous topic. But there was something in Bex's soothing voice – even on a mobile – that put him at ease and made him want to tell her everything.

Be careful, he thought to himself.

Images of his parents, together and happy, flickered through Jud's mind like a slide projector. He was tired and worried and hungry and confused – just the wrong time to be allowing himself such self-pitying thoughts of home. He knew they always led to grief – for his late mother. *Move on*, he told himself.

'Jud?' Bex had detected the silence. 'You still there?'

'Yes, I'm here,' he said miserably, lying back on the pillow. His eyelids felt heavy.

'Sorry.' She'd detected melancholy in his voice. 'I shouldn't have mentioned it. Forget I ever said it, Jud.'

'Whatever.'

'So you're not going to tell me what's been going on, then?' Bex was feeling frustrated again. Why was Jud always so non-committal on the phone? So monosyllabic. Or was that just a boy thing? Phone calls to her girlfriends were always three times as long.

'I'm sorry, Bex,' said Jud. 'I mean I'm sorry for texting you last night. I wasn't thinking straight. I shouldn't have told you.'

'No,' said Bex. 'You *should* have told me. Just like you *should* tell me now! I thought we were friends. I'm allowed to worry about my mates . . . Jud!'

He shouldn't have laid his head back on the pillow. Big mistake. It had only taken a few seconds.

'*Jud?*'

She heard the snoring. She listened to his breathing for a while. She felt close to him for a brief moment and could imagine him sleeping peacefully, his dark hair falling across his olive skin, his eyes gently closing and his body finally relaxing for once.

Then suddenly she knew she was intruding. Even at this distance she felt an intimacy creeping up on her which she wasn't ready for. A kind of closeness that felt uneasy.

She ended the call quickly. She felt suddenly self-conscious.

But Jud's sleeping face remained in her mind for the rest of the journey. She tried to read, of course, and listen to her iPod, but try as she might, she couldn't stop thinking about him.

Eventually the train pulled into York station. The great vaulted roof – a masterpiece of mathematical engineering – towered over her as she disembarked, climbed the steps of the footbridge and walked out into the cold Yorkshire air.

Across the road she was thrilled to see that the great stretch of wall, which famously spanned the full perimeter of the city, was white with snow. It was a picture.

But her excitement was short-lived. As she turned left to begin the short walk across the river to her hotel, she passed a newspaper billboard.

THE MICKLEGATE GHOST, ran the headline. It was true.

She bought a newspaper. There, spread across the front page, was the same gruesome image of the disembodied head, exactly as she'd seen it on the screen in the briefing room earlier that morning.

Vorzek was right. The good Samaritan who'd helped the old man at Micklegate had seized his chance to make a fast buck and sold the photo to the local press. The ancient city that stretched out before her, with its historic spires and medieval walls, was now awash with fear and speculation.

This was not going to be easy.

CHAPTER 16

WEDNESDAY 3 NOVEMBER:
12.15 P.M.

THE CRYPT

The ghost's head was shifting and stretching as though it was gelatinous. Eyes wide one moment, then deep-set and pig-like the next. The great bulbous nose shifted and contorted across its face, which itself was expanding and constricting like an image in a hall of mirrors.

Jud felt sick. The human form was not meant to be so fluid. The usual orientation of two eyes, two cheekbones, a nose and a mouth meant nothing any more. Instead, the image in front of him kept shifting shape in a disturbing way.

And the head was now inches from Jud's face.

Its giant jaws began expanding, revealing a large black hole. The stench was unbearable. But still the ghost was coming closer. Jud could feel its foul breath wafting over him. It was like pricking a stagnant pond with a stick and waiting for the gust of hydrogen sulphide to hit you. He almost retched.

The great jaws widened still and Jud braced himself for the end. Eaten alive by a sulphurous spirit.

And then the phone rang.

He sat bolt upright on the bed and wiped the dribble from his chin. It had been a deep sleep. Stupid decision to lie down – what was he thinking?

'Yes?' he said sleepily.

'Yes, *sir*. It's Bonati here.'

'Oh, I'm sorry, Professor.'

'Well?'

Jud still felt dazed. Images of the great ghost's head continued to flash across his mind.

'Er, I'm sorry, sir. I don't know what you mean. Well *what?*'

'Jud. Look at the time! I thought you were coming straight to my office after freshening up. What have you been doing? Sleeping or something? Get a move on, lad!'

Bonati rang off.

Jud stood up quickly. It was all coming back to him. How long had he been asleep? He glanced quickly at the alarm clock. Twelve fifteen. He'd been back from Scotland Yard for two hours and he still hadn't even taken his jacket off.

He scratched his head and looked at the mess around him. It was like being at school all over again, only this time there was no housemaster to nag at him for being untidy. No prefects to grass him up to Matron. The floor was strewn with discarded clothes and detritus from previous days: trousers and boxers bound together as sculptures on the carpet, still in the position they were in when he'd discarded them; odd shoes placed in precisely the right spot to trip him up every time he walked in; empty crisp packets and mugs – so many mugs, each one nurturing its own specialist form of bacteria.

He knew that one day he would tidy up. Or at least someone would. He'd pay some newly recruited zombie to do it for him in return for the loan of an Xbox game, or a DVD. You could always find newbies to do your dirty work.

He saw his mobile on the bedside table and thought of Bex. Hadn't he just been speaking to her? He vaguely recalled her voice but couldn't for the life of him remember what they'd talked about.

He thought of her up in York, alone. The distance troubled him. She should be here, in the safety of the CRYPT.

He gazed out of the basement window, up at the street above him. Maybe he hadn't realised just how much he valued his security down here. He was safely cocooned in the CRYPT. It cradled him. Kept him safe.

He felt tempted to phone Bex again. Just a quick call before he met Bonati. He picked up the phone. *Missed call.* She'd already phoned. He must have slept right through the ringing!

The phone sounded its shrill scream again.

He knew who it was, and he wasn't going to incriminate himself by picking it up just so Bonati could blast him for still being in his room when he should have been in his office in Sector 2.

He made for the door. Bex would have to wait.

CHAPTER 17

WEDNESDAY 3 NOVEMBER: 12.19 P.M.

THE CRYPT

Bonati and Vorzek were seated at the cherrywood table, each behind a steaming bowl of soup. A salty fish smell wafted into Jud's nostrils as he entered the room.

'Hungry?' asked the professor.

'Yes, sir. I suppose I haven't eaten since yesterday lunchtime.'

'Agents need sustenance,' said Bonati. 'Helps the brain function. That's why we're eating this.'

'Fish soup?' asked Jud.

'Exactly,' said Dr Vorzek. 'Omega-3. Good brain food. Fights depression too. You should try some.'

Jud didn't take the bait – Vorzek's not-so-subtle crack at his propensity for dark moods washed over him. He was too tired to respond.

He sat at the table and ladled the steaming, creamy liquid into a bowl. There was a giant crusty loaf on a chopping board beside the soup tureen. He dispensed with the knife, ripped himself a large hunk and dipped it into the soup. It was delicious and it reawakened his appetite. He tucked into it like a starving dog.

'Now, Jud, I know you don't want any more questions. Those jokers at the Met asked enough last night.'

Jud rolled his eyes and wiped soup from his chin.

'But we've got to establish what happened. You've been bailed here. It's not over. They're building a case against you. This is serious.'

Jud put his spoon down and looked directly at the professor. There were dark shadows beneath his brown eyes, which felt so tired they stung whenever he closed them.

'I *know* this is serious, sir. I'm aware of the circumstances. But you do know I didn't do anything, don't you? I mean, you do believe me?'

'Of course,' they both said in unison.

Vorzek smiled sympathetically as she spoke. 'Look, Jud, if we're going to strike you off their list of suspects, we need something more from you. Obviously we'll need to get back to that basement and take more readings. We might even find some clues as to what happened to this missing engineer.'

'I can tell you what happened to him!'

'Go on,' said Bonati.

'I've already told you I had to escape the ghost. When I ran into the lift, I could see it was following me. My guess is it swept past me in the direction of where this engineer was.'

'And attacked him?' said Vorzek.

'Exactly. But they won't believe my account of the ghost, will they? They won't believe a ghost has done it.' Jud exchanged a glance with Bonati. They both knew the true significance of what he'd just said. It was a haunting reminder of his previous life.

'Surely they've got some proof that I wasn't the only one down there!' Jud continued quickly. 'I mean, the ghost in the basement was the reason I was sent in the first place. The reason we were called, sir!'

Vorzek and Bonati looked at one another.

'Well that's just it,' the professor began. 'I've had another call from Scotland Yard.' He looked stony-faced.

Something was up. Jud knew it.

'Well?'

'They've been in touch again, J. The guys at SO17. It seems the security guards rang them just after we left there this morning.'

'Yeah? And?' said Jud. 'Have they found the engineer, this Jones guy?'

'No. Security at the House have said they've now identified who the intruder was. The man they first saw on the CCTV.'

'*What?*' Jud was incredulous. He dropped the spoon into the soup and pushed the bowl away. He'd lost his appetite. 'What do you mean, *the man?* It was a bloody ghost! And it nearly killed me!'

'The man they saw – you saw – on the screen last night was *not* a ghost, they now say; it was one of the engineers after all, a guy called Pete Walters. He'd been working at the other end of the basement but needed to shut off the sewage ejector machine in order to access a section of the drains further along the building. He can account for his movements and he says it was definitely him in the room.'

Jud stood up sharply and began pacing the floor. He ran his hands through his dark, greasy hair – he always did that when he was thinking hard. But he was shaking his head as he did so. His frown showed the others he was having none of this. It just made no sense to him.

'But sir, this "man" disappeared through a wall! That's why we were called there in the first place! Why else would they have called CRYPT!' He thumped his hand down hard on the table, close to Vorzek.

'Hey, that's my table!' said Bonati, trying to humour him.

Vorzek looked up and gave Jud a warm smile. 'Look, we know this is worrying for you,' she said. 'But we're on your side. We want to help you.'

Though Vorzek was trying to reassure him, her words had the reverse effect on Jud. When someone told you they wanted to help you, it just emphasised the fact that you needed help.

'Oh, come on! This is ridiculous,' he snapped, as he backed away from the table and began pacing the floor again. 'I mean, how did this engineer disappear through a wall then, huh? Tell me, *how*?'

Bonati couldn't hide his own growing concern. He was worried too, Jud could tell. The case was slipping out of their hands and they knew it. The professor's kindly face looked tired and worn.

'Well that's just it. They're saying that it was a trick of the camera, Jud. A blip.'

'A *blip*?' said Jud disbelievingly. 'Oh come on!'

Bonati went silent for a moment, deep in thought. The sound of traffic entered the room and there was an alarm blaring somewhere in the distance – an omen for what might follow. The professor shook his head. 'Jud . . . they said that's what *you* told them.'

'*What*?' Jud stood still, open-mouthed.

'Apparently you said that if there was some sort of electrical disturbance, caused by static electricity or a faulty appliance, then the camera could have skipped and jumped ahead. It might have looked like this figure disappeared through the wall when he didn't at all. It was just a blip.'

Jud slumped back into his chair. He had a sinking feeling inside and he knew it wasn't the soup. He was trapped by his own words. He couldn't deny it. The professor was right. He had said exactly that.

'But sir,' he protested, 'I said *that* to try and stop the panic. I gave the guards that explanation so they wouldn't worry and tell everyone there were ghosts down there. You always say we should try to cover our tracks, stop the fear from spreading and all that.' He turned to Vorzek; his face looked like he was pleading.

'Doctor, please, you've said that too. You always say how we should keep it quiet and—'

'So you wanted to stop people going down there, did you?' interrupted Bonati.

'What? Er, yes, sir.'

'You wanted to prevent them going back down to the basement, where you'd just been?' His voice sounded harsher now, almost accusatory.

'Yeah, well, I mean *no*.' Jud could hear how this was sounding. 'I mean I wasn't *hiding* anything . . .'

An awkward silence fell as they all stared at the table, trying to avoid one another's gaze.

'Oh God,' Jud said. 'This looks bad, doesn't it?'

'Well, it's not the best situation,' said Bonati.

'But hang on,' said Jud, looking up. 'There's usually a time counter on these cameras. I'm sure there is. In the corner of the screen. They can surely see from that that the camera hadn't skipped a few seconds. That it must've been a ghost passing through the wall.'

'Already asked them that,' said Bonati, shaking his head. 'Apparently there was no timer on there. It had been switched off.'

'*Switched off?*' said Jud disbelievingly. 'Well surely that's enough to arouse suspicion, sir?'

'Yes. And I've asked them to look into it, believe me,' said the professor. 'But it doesn't change the fact that this Walters guy is claiming it was him and not a ghost in the sewage ejector room. And so you can't say it was a ghost who might have attacked Neil Jones. They'd say it had to be someone else.'

'You mean me,' said Jud despondently.

'Well at the moment that's what it looks like,' said Bonati.

'So it was a trap.'

'We don't know that for sure,' said Vorzek. 'But we're working on it.'

'Hold on,' said Jud. 'If Walters was down there before me, then why aren't they accusing *him* of taking this other engineer, the Jones guy? He could've been hiding down there until I'd left, and then pounced on him. I mean, why am I the only suspect?'

They stopped and stared at him.

'There's something else we haven't told you yet, J. And . . . frankly, well . . . I don't know how to say this.'

Jud felt sick. What else was coming? How could this possibly get any worse?

'Go on. Tell me, sir!' he said impatiently.

'Well, when Special Ops called just now, they said they'd found something else down in the cellar. Quite close to where they found the broken glasses.'

'Yes? *What?*' said Jud, desperately. He didn't appreciate Bonati's cautious way of broaching the subject.

'They found a ripped piece of clothing. It was blue.' The tone of his voice was sombre. 'They said it matches the colour and material of your jacket, Jud. The one you were wearing last night.'

Jud stared at them incredulously. And said nothing.

'But that's not all,' said Bonati softly. 'They said there was blood on it too.'

Jud stood up again and pushed the chair towards the table. He was shaking his head and looking imploringly at Bonati, 'Look, this is getting out of hand, sir. I mean, I can't keep up with it.'

'Whoa! Take it easy, J,' said Bonati. 'Sit down. Let's take this one step at a time. Walters has said he was back up from the basement and on his way home before you'd even arrived at Westminster. So whatever happened to this Neil Jones, Walters *couldn't* have been involved.'

'That doesn't help me, sir.'

'No, let me finish. We've got to think how the police will be thinking.'

'Besides,' said Vorzek, 'the engineer who's gone missing – Neil Jones – was certainly alive when you went down to the basement – and this was after Walters had left.'

'Gee, thanks. This isn't helping,' said Jud. 'But you're right. I met Jones when I got down there. He showed me to the sewage ejector room.'

There was silence again while everyone tried frantically to make sense of this.

'And you said, didn't you, that the ghost went for you and ripped your coat?' said the professor.

'Yes, sir.'

'And now this same piece of clothing is found near the missing engineer's broken specs.'

'That's what you said, sir.'

'But it's all just too convenient, J. Either the ghost dropped it when he went for the engineer – if that's what he did – or . . . or?'

'Or he took a piece of Jud's jacket deliberately,' said Vorzek.

'Are you saying what I think you're saying?' said Bonati.

'That the ghost in some way helped to frame Jud? Yes, that's exactly what I'm saying, Giles.'

The three of them fell silent once again. This was new territory. Never in the history of the CRYPT had they encountered a haunting where a ghost was so calculating, so strategic. Could it really be working *with* a human?

'So the ghost took the fragment of coat and planted it near the engineer's specs deliberately, you mean?' said Jud. 'Is it *really* possible, sir?'

Bonati was still deep in thought.

'Well, all I'll say is it's improbable – but not *impossible*.'

CHAPTER 18

WEDNESDAY 3 NOVEMBER:
1.40 P.M.

MICKLEGATE BAR, YORK

Bex peered through the narrow window down at the traffic below.

It was quiet in the tower. Micklegate Bar Museum had been closed. Police tape surrounded the building. Even the daily traffic, which usually thundered over the cobbles through the archway below, had been diverted elsewhere.

Bex had the place to herself.

The colourful display boards and the books and gifts that lined the room at the top of the tower did nothing to ease the tension in the place. Bex could feel it. The austere stone walls and the dark wooden floorboards beneath her feet gave the room a cell-like feeling.

She leaned against the wall behind her and closed her eyes. She'd been there for several minutes and the feeling remained the same.

Anger.

Like all agents at the CRYPT, Bex had been trained to use her ESP not only to identify the types of emotions that hung in a location, but to measure their intensity too.

And this place was wild. She was in no doubt that anger of this magnitude could not be emanating from one spirit alone. There had to be hundreds of spirits connecting with this place to produce the levels of emotion she now felt.

It was always so hard to articulate what you were feeling to those who didn't have ESP. Only Bonati and the other agents understood. It began deep inside the stomach, like an acute case of butterflies, but it didn't stop. It spread through the body like water seeping into a room. Some of the agents called it an invisible glow. Others likened it to feeling hot or cold.

Bex had discussed it with Grace often. They'd said it was like the shivery, prickly sensation that ran across your skull when you got a sudden fright. Only most people couldn't control this feeling – and they only experienced it rarely.

Bonati had often said that what made CRYPT agents so special was their ability to feel shivers or prickles on demand. They could tune into a place and within a few moments their mind and body were awash with an array of emotions, from fearful shivers to adrenalin-fuelled anger. Even when there was nothing present to provoke such feelings in ordinary people, agents could feel something. And what was more, they could ascertain from the intensity of the feeling how many spirits were connecting with the place.

And here, in the small stone cell at the top of Micklegate Bar, Bex felt the most intense feelings she'd ever known.

Still with her eyes shut, she steadied her breathing and focused on turning the physical sensations into something meaningful – something she could articulate.

It wasn't just anger. No. It was more complicated than that. It had something to do with justice – for some suffering endured.

Yes! That was it. *Suffering*.

She kept her eyes closed and listened in further, making a deeper connection with the site.

Then she heard something. At first it sounded like a series of strange clicking noises, like a rattling flagpole or a tarpaulin flapping in the wind. She felt a growing panic inside. These clicks were often the early signs of some spirit trying to communicate. She remembered the frenzy of sounds they'd heard at the cursed site at Tyburn. Was something or someone coming?

But then the clicks slowly formed into words. Or was it the same word being repeated? It was hard to tell. Eyes tightly closed, breathing reducing to a steady, almost imperceptible rhythm, she concentrated hard. And there it was. A repeated phrase was coming through to her.

'Martyrs . . . martyrs caritatis.'

She opened her eyes.

The room looked different.

The display boards had gone.

In fact there was no evidence that this place was a museum at all.

What the hell was happening?

She blinked and looked again.

This was weird.

Quickly she ran to the window. The glass had gone. Just a long, narrow hole, like an arrow slot.

She looked down at the street below and her mouth opened in surprise.

The shops and the cars and the traffic lights had gone. Instead she was looking down on a scene from a history book. A cobbled street was flanked by half-timbered buildings. A horse-drawn cart was moving gently down the road, away from the bar. A couple of men dressed in dowdy tunics, dirty brown breeches and stockings were shuffling along the far side of the road.

Bex could feel her heart pounding inside her chest.

She ran to another window and peered out.

The sight was even more disturbing than before. Between Bex and the street below was a severed head.

Though she was viewing it from behind, her overactive brain

painted chilling pictures of its lifeless face. She could just make out the wooden stake below it, thrust up into its neck.

Was she dreaming?

The rancid smell of rotting human flesh wafted through the open window, making her gag.

She turned and glanced again at the tower's interior. Just bare stone walls and an old wooden bench.

She heard distant shouts from outside. They were coming from the other side of the tower, in the direction of the city. She ran to the opposite window and looked out.

There, slowly approaching the bar, was a crowd of people. At the centre was some kind of priest. His hands were bound and he was being pushed and pulled by guards.

There was a party of people following them. All dressed like they were out of some historical painting. But they were *real*. Men and women. Some were screaming, 'Mercy!' and 'Release him!' while others yelled, 'Hang 'im! Hang 'im!'

She watched as the priest was beaten and dragged towards the tower.

My God, are they coming inside? she thought.

She watched the angry mob approach the bar and then pass right underneath it.

Their shouts rang upwards.

Back at the other window, she could see the party continuing down the cobbled street.

Bex sank down on to the floor. Her hands were trembling. She closed her eyes tight and tried to work out what was happening. How could this be? Was she hallucinating? Was it possible that her extrasensory powers had switched into overdrive? Was this what they called *hypersensing*?

She had heard the word before. Rumours abounded at the CRYPT that some agents had been known to experience extreme phenomena when using their ESP at a location. She'd dismissed it all as scaremongering by the skulls, just trying to wind up the fresh-faced zombies. But the brain could do strange things. No one, not even Bonati, knew the limits of an agent's ESP. Was it possible that her powers of perception had been heightened to such an extent that they were defining a new realm, and the rumours of hypersensing were true? What little she knew of philosophy was enough to tell her that humans only had their senses to tell them if the world was real or not. What we know as *reality* can only ever be defined by our perceptions, she reminded herself. *So was this real now?*

Where was the old world?

Had her extrasensory perception connected so strongly with a moment in history that it was now becoming a reality for her? Like it was projecting it into her eyes? If emotions were left as residue in a place, like static electricity, was it possible that images could be too? Hypersensing must mean seeing them as if you were there at the time, she thought.

Whatever this was, it *felt* real – whatever that meant. But it couldn't be! Time travel was the stuff of fiction. Right? Bex wasn't going to fall for it.

With her head buried in her hands, she tried to breathe deeply and slowly. She could feel that her eyes were moist with tears, but she resolved to think her way out of this. After all, if she could turn her ESP on, then surely she could switch it off.

Relax, she told herself. You can remove the images and disconnect with this. You're in control – if you can start hypersensing, then you can stop it. This is an illusion created by a heightened extrasensory experience, causing your imagination to play tricks. It's an hallucination. That's all.

Breathe slowly.

She tried to think of something else. If she could refocus her mind on something in the real world, she could close the pathways through which her senses were deluding her.

Jud. Sleeping on the bed, back at the CRYPT. The sound of

his gentle snoring. She pictured his smooth face, lying peacefully on the pillow.

She waited a few more moments before daring to open her eyes. In her head she was at the CRYPT, in the games room, chatting with Grace and watching Jud and Luc battle it out on some video game.

Tentatively she opened her eyes.

The room was changing.

It looked as though a myriad of 3D projections were mingling in the centre of the room, creating holograms – images of the modern room she'd once been in. The walls were sturdy. The floor had not changed, thank God. She wasn't floating or swimming or travelling. She was still there. But the images were shifting, one moment solid and opaque, the next translucent. Moving in and out of the physical world, from plasma to solid.

She could feel her heart speeding up again. There was a nervousness in the pit of her stomach that wouldn't go away. Anger and resentment were seeping into her body – it was her ESP kicking in again.

She could see the display boards, the modern signs and the books for sale, but they were cloudy. *Focus!* she said to herself. She knew she needed to concentrate and control her thoughts, or she'd be in hyper mode again.

She closed her eyes once more and steadied her nerves. She could *do* this. She could relax and disconnect. There would be time for an investigation of what had gone on here, when she was back safely at the CRYPT. Bonati would tell her what had happened. He'd explain everything, like he always did. But for now she needed to breathe. Just breathe.

A few seconds later she opened her eyes again.

The room looked as it had when she'd first entered. The display boards depicting impressions of how the place had once looked in medieval times. Seemed ironic now.

The windows behind and in front of her were sealed with a

thick smoky glass and leaded mullions. She stood up and peered through the panes on to the street below. The police tape was still there, marking off the location. And in the distance, the diverted traffic stacked up at the junction. Never had she felt so comforted to see cars and vans moving bullishly over the ancient cobbles.

CHAPTER 19

WEDNESDAY 3 NOVEMBER: 1.51 P.M.

HOUSES OF PARLIAMENT, LONDON

Simon Thacker sat at the end of the long mahogany table, drumming his fingers over the thickly polished top. This was taking so much longer than he'd thought. What else was there to discuss? He should have been at the gym by now, hammering a ball around the squash court. But the House authorities would not be rushed. Not when it came to the State Opening of Parliament. Everything had to be checked, cross-checked and then double-checked. With so many high-profile figures on the premises, and so many strict procedures and protocol to follow, nothing could be left to chance.

Seated at the opposite end of the table was Brigadier Geoffrey Farlington, Gentleman Usher of the Black Rod, the man with ultimate responsibility for security in the House of Lords. If anyone entered the House, he had to know about it.

'We are grateful to our esteemed Police Minister, Mr Thacker,' Farlington said. 'Not only for his close personal attention today, but also for his assistance in dealing with the difficult events of last night.'

Everyone knew that Black Rod was referring to the strange occurrences below ground, though few people had been told the exact truth. It had been a trying time for them all, especially the security forces. But the matter had been dealt with swiftly and decisively as far as he was concerned. So far in the meeting they'd been able to avoid the issue – he'd preferred to slip it in at the end.

'May I thank you, Minister, and everyone at Scotland Yard, for handling such a sensitive breach of security so discreetly. Can we say the matter is closed, subject to the obvious court proceedings that will follow?'

'Most certainly,' said Simon. He turned to the representatives of Special Operations, seated to his left. 'I am pleased with the way the incident was handled. Our boys at the Yard have done us proud.'

A junior member of Black Rod's department, seated to Simon's left, shifted in her chair, and cleared her throat.

'Forgive me, Minister, may I speak candidly for a moment?'

There was silence in the room. All eyes turned to her.

'Is there a problem, Janice?' Black Rod fixed a steely gaze on her from the other end of the long table.

'Well, er, no, sir,' she said nervously. 'I just wondered if we ever got to the bottom of why the camera in the basement was faulty in the first place? I mean, it's fixed now, isn't it?'

'Of course,' said Black Rod. 'We've had our engineers on the CCTV system all morning. And our friends from security have checked it too. We're fully functioning again.'

'So what *exactly* happened, sir?'

Black Rod gave her a disapproving look. 'I'm sorry, Minister,' he said, turning to Simon. 'Janice here was recruited earlier this month. She is inquisitive and keen, which is quite charming. But it's been a long meeting and I think we all need to–'

'No, it's okay,' said Simon, raising his hand. 'It's a good question, Brigadier. We all need reassurance that the building is secure once again. It was a frightening situation.' He turned to Janice, who by now was flushed with embarrassment.

'May I assure you we've had the very best surveillance teams in the basement all morning. I am satisfied that what the security guards saw on their screens was the result of a malfunction in the camera located in Sector 4. I don't know what you have heard this morning – the place is awash with rumour and speculation, no doubt – but the matter has been resolved.

'The strange "intruder" caught on camera was in actual fact just an engineer after all. A man by the name of Pete Walters. The faulty camera made it especially hard for the guards to recognise him, but the matter is safely resolved now. It was a misunderstanding.'

People around the table looked confused, but no one wanted to press the minister further. Except Janice.

'So why is there talk of a missing engineer, Minister?' she said boldly.

Black Rod glared at her once more.

'I'm sorry, Minister,' he said.

Thacker waved a hand once again and said, 'No. It's fine, Brigadier.

'Look, the guards called for expert help when they couldn't recognise the imposter. However, it turns out that the outside agent who then came to visit the basement may not have been who he said he was. And it may have been he who was responsible for what happened next.'

'Which was?' said another member of the group. Everyone was listening intently now. Perhaps the truth would finally be revealed.

All eyes were on Thacker.

'Well, the police then found the broken spectacles of a different engineer who'd been working down there during the day. A man called Neil Jones, I'm told. It was Jones who initially showed the "security expert" where to go in the basement, when he first arrived on the scene. The same engineer who has now, it seems, gone missing.'

The young woman, together with several others in the room, had resumed a solemn expression. No one except the police had been allowed access to the basement since last night. But speculation had spun its way through the echoing corridors, and now everyone was talking about the alleged murder of an engineer in the cellars.

Simon detected the mood change in the room and was quick to alleviate fears.

'*However*, ladies and gentlemen, let me reiterate that we are investigating this strange sequence of events fully. Rest assured that the very best people are on the case. It need not concern us now. The matter has been dealt with, and can I echo Black Rod's sentiments in thanking my colleagues at Scotland Yard and members of the House staff here for their diligence and professionalism. I consider the matter closed.'

'So . . .' Janice hesitated. Should she push her luck and ask another question? She took a deep breath and continued. 'So, this talk of *ghosts*? Was there any truth in it, Mr Thacker?'

The group looked up from their papers again. The issue had been on everyone's minds, though no one else had been brave or foolish enough to bring it up at the meeting. But the rumours were still flying around.

Simon knew it needed addressing if he was to stop an outbreak of fear running through the place.

He smiled gently. 'Janice, is it?'

'Yes.'

'Well, Janice, there were those last night who did indeed suggest that there may have been some paranormal activity. It was discussed earlier in the evening. Let me explain the origins of it.

'You see, I'm reliably informed that the CCTV, which was faulty yesterday, gave the security guards the impression that the figure they'd seen in the basement actually disappeared through a wall!'

The assembled group looked suitably surprised. Some even chuckled.

'Yes, I know. It's ridiculous when you think about it. As I've said, it was a faulty camera that prevented the guards from recognising the true identity of the engineer. But it's all been sorted out now, and I can assure you, there are no ghosts in this place. Though I can't promise there aren't any former prime ministers looking down on us! Don't you agree, Brigadier, what?'

Black Rod wasn't chuckling. The events of last night had struck him as bizarre, and yet he'd not been here to help. He'd been across town at King's College, giving a lecture to some second-year politics students. And since then the security forces had been particularly tight-lipped about the whole affair.

'Well, no indeed,' he said reservedly.

Simon's face was appropriately sombre. 'But let's not jump to conclusions too soon. The engineer has been reported missing, it's true. And yes, it is also true we have found his broken spectacles. But there's a reasonable explanation, I'm sure. And talk of ghosts is ridiculous. Anyone can see that. Right, let's move on.'

There was a palpable sense of relief in the room. A dead body on the premises was the last thing they needed, especially with the State Opening so close. And there was no one in the room who didn't share the view that the whole incident was best kept under wraps. The press would have a field day if they knew about it. The story would run and run.

As it was, there had been no press releases, no conferences and no leaks from any loose-tongued staff. Anyone even vaguely near the scene the night before, and all those involved that morning, had been briefed by members of the Palace of Westminster Division to remain discreet and go about their business as usual.

It had been described by some senior figures in the House as a 'non-event', which they all knew meant 'cover-up'.

But there was one thing you could always rely on when it came to anyone working at the House – their loyalty. The House Authorities, not to mention the security forces, would settle for nothing less – for the sake of Parliament, democracy and ultimately the nation's peace of mind, it was best to keep the story well and truly buried. Besides, there were enough people who'd lose their jobs if word got out.

The Palace of Westminster was the very heart of the country. If it became known that that heart had been punctured and a serious crime committed within its walls, then fear and speculation would sweep the nation. The public inquiry would last for ever.

'Thank you, Minister,' said Black Rod quickly. 'Well said, sir, if I may be so bold! We do indeed need to move on! I must say this is the first time since I can remember that a minister has been so heavily involved in security at the House. And we are most grateful to you.'

Black Rod had an uncanny way of saying one thing and meaning precisely the opposite. His tone sounded disingenuous and Simon heard it. He knew that his own presence at the meeting challenged Black Rod's authority; the brigadier was instrumental to the plans for the State Opening. This was his gig, his time in the spotlight. As the personal attendant to the Queen whenever she was at Westminster, and as secretary to the Lord Chamberlain too, Black Rod had power. And his head was on the block if the State Opening didn't run like clockwork. The events of last night had been beyond Black Rod's control. Indeed he hadn't even been in the building at the time. And now, listening to Simon lecture everybody on the details of the events, he was in territorial mood. This was his precinct. Besides, a stranger in the basement below Central Lobby? A breach of security of such magnitude might have meant an inquiry, and that might have raised question marks over his own competence, given that he was ultimately responsible for security in the building, whether above or below ground.

Black Rod held so many offices it seemed like he owned the place. He was Sergeant-at-Arms, responsible for arresting any lord guilty of contempt or disorder in the House. As Keeper of the Doors of the House, he oversaw the admission of strangers into the House of Lords. So when it came to planning the annual State Opening of Parliament, the brigadier was key.

But meetings like these were never easy. There were so many interested parties. It wasn't just the House Authorities, the civil servants who herded the MPs and peers around the building like sheep; it was also the security forces: the civilian security guards and also the police officers who, as members of the Palace of Westminster Division, patrolled the building daily – and had been especially active since the incident last night.

And then there was the RDPD – the Royal and Diplomatic Protection Department – SO14, the guys responsible for shadowing the royal family wherever they went.

And now this new Police Minister, Simon Thacker, who seemed very hands-on, to say the least. Brigadier Farlington could see he wasn't going to be pushed around or pigeonholed by 'experts'. He admired that, but it was making meetings like these even more complicated.

'So, ladies and gentlemen,' Black Rod continued. 'I think that just about wraps up the meeting. I'd say we're on course for another successful day. I can report back to Her Majesty that everything is proceeding as it should.'

He said it as though he and the Queen were old mates. The lower-ranked civil servants in the room rolled their eyes. It was true that the brigadier had held the post for some years now – fiercely clung to it, in fact – but no one believed he was as well connected as he made out. His authority went with the post; it wasn't about personalities. But from his bushy eyebrows and bulbous, weather-beaten face, to his clipped military manner, the brigadier played the part well.

Simon collected his papers together.

'On behalf of the PM,' he said, keen to trump Black Rod's boastful name-dropping, 'can I thank the brigadier for his fastidious attention to detail. I am satisfied that this year's State Opening will pass as smoothly as ever. Congratulations to everyone. I look forward to the day immensely.'

With that he rose and the others stood up too, gathering the coffee cups and plates together and exchanging polite comments about the quality of the sandwiches they'd enjoyed earlier.

There was a sudden knock on the great oak door at the end of the room, followed by three more rapid knocks, of the kind that left the knuckles bruised.

Black Rod walked quickly to the door and opened it.

A security guard burst in. It was Mike, still looking jaded from the night before.

Everyone stopped. Silence fell on the group. It was obvious something was up. Mike's hands were trembling and his tired eyes darted across the room as if haunted by something no one else could see. Something inside his head.

'I'm sorry to disturb you, sir, but . . . well . . . er . . . there's been . . . another *incident*.'

'What?' said Black Rod.

'Down in the basement, sir. We saw it. Just now. I mean we watched it on the screen. Just like before. It's back!'

'*What* is back?'

The guard looked like he was going to keel over. Simon quickly offered him a chair and spoke calmly. 'Now slow down, and tell us what has happened. I'm sure there's a reasonable explanation for what you've seen.'

'It was a ghost! I'm certain of it.'

'Wait a minute,' continued Simon, determined to calm the atmosphere in the room. 'What's your name?'

'It's Mike. I'm telling you it was—'

'Listen, Mike, you need to slow down. You need to take a breath and tell us calmly what you think has happened. There was some silly talk of a ghost yesterday and I think we've proved there wasn't one, haven't we?'

The assembled group looked at one another nervously. No one spoke. But fear had blown into the room like a cold wind. Some returned to their seats and stared in confusion and disbelief at Mike.

'No, it must've been, sir,' he said. 'I saw it. We all did. It appeared on the screen just like before. But this time we saw what it *did*. Oh God, it was awful.'

'*What* was?' said Black Rod quickly.

'The attack,' said Mike. 'It *was* a ghost after all.'

CHAPTER 20

WEDNESDAY 3 NOVEMBER: 2.17 P.M.

VICTORIA EMBANKMENT, LONDON

'So let me get this straight,' said Luc. 'It's happened again, sir?'

Grace watched Bonati's eyes in the rear-view mirror; she too was keen to hear the latest.

'It seems so. That's what they said.' Bonati didn't take his eyes off the road ahead, but Grace saw a slight twitch.

He manoeuvred the black Mercedes SLS AMG through the busy street. It had always surprised the newly recruited zombies at the CRYPT to learn that Bonati was a car freak. It somehow conflicted with his image as a serious academic. Only Jud knew how the professor had always held a secret passion for high-performance cars and used to think nothing of driving hundreds of miles to indulge his love at amateur track days across the UK. He recalled many fiery debates his father and Bonati had enjoyed in those early days, whilst Jud listened from the top of the stairs at night. Jason Goode was strictly a Maserati man, and nothing Bonati said would convert him to Mercedes.

Bonati saw being a car fanatic as entirely complementary to being a scientist. Unlike so many lovers of the SLS AMG, he wasn't interested in the sleek lines or the romantic retro chrome or the astonishing gull-wing doors. For him, the car's real asset was hiding under the bonnet. The 6.2-litre V8 engine may not have been easy on the wallet at the petrol station, but the thrill of 197 mph on track days meant it was worth it. And achieving 0–60 in 3.8 seconds always pleased him on quiet roads. It was an astonishing piece of engineering, as he so often reminded the agents whenever any of them strayed on to the subject of cars, which was often.

'MI5 have said it's pandemonium now. They were as astonished as we were by what happened last night. They didn't believe the stories of the mystery engineer or the faulty camera any more than we did. And believe me, Luc, we were looking into it. MI5 were already making discreet enquiries to find out who was at the root of the cover-up. And I was just about to come here to Westminster myself when the call came in.'

'So it's only just happened, then?' said Grace.

'Yes. About an hour ago, apparently. A security guard – probably the same one Jud saw last night – was watching his screens as usual and saw something in the basement, just like before. Only this time the ghost didn't disappear through a wall. The guard saw everything. And by all accounts it was a brutal killing – one of the police officers patrolling down there.'

'Same place as before?' said Luc.

'No, not quite. Still in the basement, but a different sector. Below the House of Lords, apparently.'

'Blimey. I bet that rattled the members of the House!'

'They don't know about it,' said Bonati. 'Just like nobody knows about last night, or very few do. I tell you, there's something going on here.'

'Well, there's ghosts for a start. I knew Jud could never have done anything wrong,' said Luc.

'I know. We all knew that. But there's something else. It doesn't add up. The first incident still doesn't make any sense.

Why would they call us all in a panic because of some alleged haunting, and then hours later deny it ever happened and blame Jud?'

'He was set up, sir, we know that,' said Grace.

'Not for certain, but it's beginning to look that way,' said Bonati thoughtfully. 'But whatever plan they had in mind, it's backfired now.'

'I guess whoever set this up wasn't banking on the ghost returning,' said Luc.

'Exactly. But that's what's so strange. It's almost like someone knew the ghost was going to be there the first time. Last night, I mean. If you think about it. It's like this was all planned from the start. The way we were called in. The way Jud was sent down to the basement.'

'Are you saying that someone is working *with* the ghost?'

Bonati was deep in thought. 'It can't be possible, Luc, can it? I've never heard of an adult retaining their powers of ESP to be able to continue communicating with the spirit world. It can't happen. We're not built like that. The gift of ESP is highly rare anyway, and it's only ever been recorded in teenagers. It fades as you reach adulthood. That's why the only people I know who have it are back at the CRYPT. And, like you, they're teenagers. I can't believe that there's someone at Westminster who is in cahoots with a ghost!'

'It's the stuff of fiction, isn't it?' said Luc.

'But someone used the ghost story as a way of getting Jud involved, I'm sure of it,' said the professor. 'Then when it suited them they denied there was ever a ghost there.'

'But there *was* a ghost,' said Luc. 'And now it's killed again. Doesn't that mean Jud is off the hook?'

'Exactly,' said Grace. 'So why isn't he here, sir?'

'Too risky,' said Bonati. 'Whether someone is targeting Jud personally or the CRYPT in general I don't yet know, and I'm not prepared to take the risk until we find out more.'

'So is he stuck inside? He won't like that,' said Grace.

The professor laughed. 'No, we thought of that. But the further he is from Westminster the better right now – so he's off to York to meet Bex.'

'Oh,' said Grace, disappointed. She had been keen to accompany Bex but was told they couldn't spare any agents. However, she felt now was the wrong time to be arguing about it.

'So how's Bex getting on?' said Luc. 'Have you heard anything?'

'No, and that's why I've sent Jud up there. He knows York well, apparently, and will be able to give Bex the support she needs.'

'*Support?*' said Grace quickly. She'd not heard anything from Bex and was already beginning to worry. 'What do you mean, *support?* What's happened, sir?'

Bonati tried to hide his concern. 'Oh, nothing. I meant *company*. Jud's gone to provide some company. Look, we're here now.'

He swung the car out of Victoria Embankment on to Bridge Street and the Houses of Parliament towered ahead of them. They were both relieved to see the place was clear of TV vans and reporters.

'At least we won't be doing any press conferences down here,' said Bonati, changing the subject.

'Not yet,' said Luc. 'Will we get access to the basement again?'

'You bet. That's why I've brought you both. I want you to find out all you can down there. Just stay alert, mind you!'

'Is the body still there?' asked Grace.

'Which one?' said Bonati sarcastically.

'Well, the second one. I mean, no one ever found the first, did they? I thought he was still missing.'

'He is. Very suspicious.'

'I'd say this Neil Jones is alive and kicking at home. Probably left through some back door last night,' said Grace.

'We could find out,' said Luc.

'Oh, believe me,' said the professor, that's exactly what I was going to arrange before this call came in. Some simple policing is all we need, like you see on the TV. Get a copper to park up outside this guy's house, drinking coffee and eating a sausage roll. You get the picture. I've put Vorzek on to it. I want to know where this Jones character is, what happened and why they tried to pin it on Jud.'

'But the victim of today's attack is still there? I mean, his body hasn't been moved, has it, sir?'

'No, definitely not. I got a message to forensics to leave the corpse where it is.'

'And the ghost? The one Jud saw?' said Luc.

'Well, you can't ask our supernatural brethren to hang around until we get there, Luc. I think the ghost may have moved on.'

'No, I didn't mean that, sir. I meant do the House Authorities believe it now? That a ghost has done this?'

'Believe it? Finally they do, yes. There's a change of tone coming from Westminster now, I tell you. They got quite a fright by all accounts. I'm still going to ask some serious questions about how and why Jud was framed the first time – there're plenty of conspiracies flying around, and I won't let it drop – but for now, they're concentrating on finding out where this apparition has come from and why it's still haunting the place. All they want to talk about now is ghosts.'

'But not to the press, sir? I was expecting to see TV vans here,' said Grace.

'Oh, they can keep stories out of the papers if they wish,' said Bonati. 'The ones we read about are the ones they *want* us to see.'

'Great,' said Luc, smiling. 'So we can investigate in peace.'

'Let's hope so,' said Bonati sombrely. 'But somehow I don't think we'll say "great" when we see what the ghost did down there. Brace yourselves. It's not going to be pretty.'

CHAPTER 21

WEDNESDAY 3 NOVEMBER: 2.34 P.M.

HOUSES OF PARLIAMENT, LONDON

The basement was far from peaceful. The lift reached the bottom with a thud and the metal doors swung open to reveal a crowd of police officers, security guards and members of the House Authorities. Up ahead were figures in full white body suits and masks – the forensic team whose job it was to get up close and personal with the corpse.

A middle-aged man in a suit pushed his way through the crowd and greeted them.

'Thank you for coming,' he said. 'I'm Geoffrey Farlington.'

'Ah, the Black Rod,' said Bonati, half bemused by the ridiculous titles that were handed out at Westminster. 'Good to meet you, Mr Farlington.'

Their host resisted the temptation to correct Bonati by asking to be addressed as Brigadier. This was not the time to talk protocol.

'Giles Bonati, and these are two of my top agents, Grace Calder and Luc Dubois,' said the professor. 'We're here at the request of Special Ops.'

'Yes, I've been briefed,' said Black Rod. 'I understand you're crime-scene investigators. I must say I thought we had enough of those, but clearly not.'

Bonati ignored the poorly veiled insult and asked to be taken straight to the scene. He assumed there would be someone in the basement who knew the real reason why he and his agents were there and would be able to clear the place temporarily while they set up their field equipment.

Black Rod led them towards the section surrounded by police tape – a large storage area, gated with metal fencing and lined with containers and piping. There were too many people there for Bonati and the others to see the corpse, but as they approached, the brigadier ushered police officers to one side.

As the crowd parted, they saw the body.

Luc felt sick. Grace gasped loudly.

Still dressed in police uniform, the victim was stretched between two giant pipes. His hands and feet were fastened at each end and his body lay suspended and bent like a human hammock.

He was on his back, facing upwards, though his head had slumped to one side, an appalling expression of pain fixed across his pallid face. His eyes were open but lifeless.

'My God,' Bonati said. 'He's been . . .'

'Drawn and quartered,' said Grace, soberly.

The man's middle section was a macabre mess of ripped clothing and open flesh.

A vast pool of blood was congealed on the stone tiles. The man's intestines had spilled out of his body: a grey, pulpy mass of vascular tubes and veins. There was a gaping wound running from the pit of his stomach to halfway up his broken, mangled ribcage.

Never had they seen a victim so cruelly dispatched.

No one said anything for a moment. All eyes were on Grace.

It was obvious she was the youngest member of the assembled audience forced to view this medieval ritual, and there were those who thought she might not handle it.

'You OK?' An officer turned to her and placed a hand on her shoulder.

'Yeah,' she said defensively. 'I'm all right. Are you?'

A young man in a pinstripe suit approached Bonati. The professor knew instantly who he was.

'Mr Thacker, I'm so sorry to meet you in these circumstances.'

The MP seemed equally shocked. He looked awful. His eyes were ringed with dark shadows and he trembled as he spoke.

'Good to see you, Bonati.'

'Are you all right?' asked the professor.

'Yes, yes,' said Simon. 'Just lack of sleep. It's been a trying time.'

'Luc Dubois and Grace Calder,' the professor replied, turning to his agents. 'This is Simon Thacker, the new Police Minister.'

'Good to have you guys here,' said Thacker, smiling. 'Thanks for coming.'

They stared at the body for a few silent seconds. It was hard to take in. It was like a waxwork scene from a museum of horrors, only this was a real man who'd got up that morning, probably had some breakfast, kissed his family goodbye and set off for work.

Now he lay stretched out like a rag doll whose insides had split open.

Bonati shook himself out of the trance that had engulfed them all and cut to the chase. 'Did you summon us, Minister?'

Thacker motioned for Bonati and the agents to move away from the crowd before answering. They found a quieter corner of the storage room. Thacker was whispering now.

'No, I'll be honest with you, it wasn't me who called you, Professor. Naturally I know who you are and why you're here. But I'm somewhat sceptical myself. It was the brigadier who put in the call to the Met initially. He must've mentioned the word "ghost" for it to have got as far as you. But he doesn't know who you are.'

'Yes,' said Bonati. 'MI5 called to say they'd received reports of a haunting here. Again.'

'*Again?*' said Simon.

'Well, last night, you know.'

Simon shook his head and smiled. 'Look, don't believe everything you hear, Professor. Some of us take more convincing than others. And we don't indulge in scaremongering.'

'No, quite.' Bonati considered it best to avoid an argument about what really happened last night. There was enough to cope with here. But he was interested to know what Thacker thought of today's incident.

'You think this is the work of a human, do you?'

'Well, let's face it, Professor, which is more likely? I didn't hold with this theory about ghosts last night and I don't now. But I'm not going to stop you investigating. Of course not! I admire your work enormously – what little I know of it, at least. Since taking up office, I've heard the name CRYPT mentioned, though MI5 have been somewhat reluctant to shed much light on what you actually do.'

'Well, that's a deliberate policy,' said Bonati. 'Experience has taught us that the fewer people who know about us the better.'

'I see,' said Simon. 'Well, I'm very grateful you were able to respond so quickly.' He lowered his voice even further. 'Look, between you and me, I have my doubts about the brigadier. His judgement, I mean. He is a little prone to melodrama.'

'Well, it's a gruesome crime,' interrupted Luc. 'It's hard to see how you could overdramatise something like this.'

Thacker smiled. 'You're right, of course – Luc, isn't it? Well, Luc, I agree with you entirely about the appalling nature of the crime here. It's an atrocity. I suppose what I meant was I don't share Black Rod's views about the perpetrator.'

'You don't believe it was a ghost,' said Grace.

'Absolutely not,' said Thacker. 'Just like last night. I was away at the time, but I've heard what happened down here. I'm sure it's the work of a human. Ghosts don't have the monopoly on being evil, you know.'

Luc and Grace stared at him. This was surreal. Did he not know what had occurred? How Jud had been arrested?

Bonati was obviously thinking the same thing. 'Mr Thacker, you know what happened to my agent last night, don't you?'

'No? What're you talking about?'

Bonati couldn't hide his surprise. 'This is not the first time a member of my organisation has visited this basement, Minister.'

'Only last time,' interrupted Luc, 'our agent was accused of being the perpetrator, not the investigator.'

Thacker looked puzzled. 'I knew there was an incident last night. But I didn't know it was a member of your agency who was arrested.'

Both Grace and Luc found it hard to believe that he was unaware of the details of what had gone on.

'Were you not briefed, then?' asked Grace.

'Forgive me,' said Thacker. 'I was out of town last night. And in any case, I'm not briefed every time there's a crime committed, even somewhere as important as here. I was informed that something had happened – an engineer went missing, apparently. But I can't attend a crime scene every time something happens.'

'You're here now, though,' said Luc.

'Yes, indeed. But that's because we were all upstairs anyway. I was here for a scheduled meeting with Black Rod's department. We were finalising plans for the State Opening.

'Had I known that a member of the CRYPT team had become embroiled in accusations of this kind, I would have intervened on your behalf, let me tell you. All I was told was that an intruder was apprehended and is being dealt with. Are you saying that was your agent, Professor?'

'Yes,' said Bonati. 'Though he could hardly be described as an intruder. But let's not trouble ourselves with that now. The fact that another crime has been committed – while the agent in question has been bailed into our own custody – proves that he cannot have been involved in this one at least. He cannot be in two places at once, can he!'

'No indeed,' said Thacker.

Luc and Grace thought he seemed genuine enough. They supposed it was impossible for any Police Minister to be on top of every crime committed. That was not his role, after all. But at Westminster? It seemed pretty high-profile stuff. Nevertheless, Thacker seemed perfectly happy to welcome them now.

'So will it be possible to have some space here?' said Bonati. 'Your forensics people need to work on the body, of course, but we have our own investigations to carry out too, for which ideally we'll need an hour alone.'

'I don't have any objection to that,' said Thacker. 'Let's face it, the body's not going anywhere, is it?'

'Who is he?' said Grace.

'Chap called Freddie Jenkins. Works for SO17. Nice bloke, by all accounts. Family man. Two kids and a wife. Labrador. The whole package.'

Bonati shook his head. 'I just hope his wife's not at the coroner's inquest,' he said. 'I hope she never sees the photos.'

'No, quite,' said Thacker. 'I tell you what, I'll go and speak to Special Ops and see if I can get you some time alone with the body. You can come if you wish, Professor. I'm sure you'll help me persuade them.'

'Thanks. My agents will need this place cleared, ideally. Our field equipment is sensitive and too many bodies can interfere with the readings,' said Bonati.

Thacker couldn't hide his cynicism, but he agreed to see what he could do.

'Wait here,' Bonati said to Grace and Luc. 'Get a feel for the place. Tell me what you sense.' He followed Thacker while the agents set their backpacks down and looked around.

'Oh, another question if I may,' said Bonati as he followed the minister towards the crowd of officers.

'Yes, Professor?'

'Well, I wondered what had happened to Braithwaite?'

'Who?' Thacker had stopped.

'Detective Superintendent Braithwaite. From Special Ops.'

'Oh, right. Nothing's happened to him. Why do you ask?'

'Well, he seemed to be in charge of the case last night, but I haven't heard from him since,' said Bonati. 'It just seems odd, that's all.'

'I understand Braithwaite started his annual leave yesterday. He shouldn't have been in at all. He'll be on a plane by now. All right for some, eh?'

'I see,' said Bonati.

They disappeared into the crowd. Within a few minutes, officers and forensics started to file past Luc and Grace in the direction of the corridor that led out to the lifts. Some were glaring at them quizzically, but Grace's expression was sufficiently defensive to prevent any of them from making a wisecrack. Only Black Rod had something to say as he breezed past them.

'I hope you manage to find whatever it is you're looking for,' he said. 'I can't tell you what will happen if we don't clear this up fast. People up there are asking questions.' He was pointing to the ceiling. 'The Lords will not put up with such secrecy in this place . . . and neither will Her Majesty. This is a place of openness and democracy. There should be no secrets here.'

Yeah, right, thought Grace. No secrets in Westminster? How old did he think she was?

They stood for a few seconds staring at the appalling sight across the room. It was no less shocking this time.

'Well?' said Grace. 'What do you feel, Luc?'

'Apart from disgust, you mean?' he said.

'Yes. I mean the atmosphere. Do you detect any residue of emotion here, before we start taking readings? I can definitely feel something.'

Luc closed his eyes and breathed deeply, letting his perceptive powers reach like feelers into the metallic shell of the basement.

There was something. Something almost tangible. Was it revenge? A palpable feeling that someone had been wronged. Some great injustice that needed to be righted.

'I feel something. Some bitterness or resentment.'

'Revenge?' said Grace quickly.

'Yeah, maybe,' said Luc. 'Like a terrible crime's been committed here. And I don't mean the body we're looking at. I mean something else. Something even greater.' There was a crackle in his voice.

Bonati approached them. He was staring at Luc. 'Are you all right?' he said.

'I . . . I don't know, sir. I just feel . . . *heavy*.'

'Talk to me,' said the professor.

It was hard. Like so often before, it was difficult to articulate the feelings that swept through him. He could feel the tears creeping down his dark, smooth cheeks. This was embarrassing. And with Grace here too.

'I'm so sorry, sir. This is pathetic,' he said.

'No, on the contrary,' said Bonati. 'This is important. It's why you're valuable to us, Luc. And you, Grace. Are you feeling something too?'

Grace was looking equally pensive. She was frowning, as if preoccupied by some disturbing thought now triggered in her mind. 'I don't know. It's a sense of . . . bitterness, sir. A kind of revenge, but it's more complex than that. It's like someone has suffered – I mean *really* suffered. And they're still suffering now. It's like an overwhelming self-pity. There is revenge here, yes, but it's tempered with sorrow. I don't believe there is *evil* at work, do you, Luc?'

He was shaking his head. 'No, I don't. It's not as easy as that. There's real emotion here – I can feel it – but it's not evil like we've sensed in other places. This is *different*.'

'OK, agents,' said Bonati. 'You've got an hour. I've managed to persuade the people here to hold off for that long. I'll leave you to it. There're plenty of people I need to see upstairs. Thacker says they're asking all sorts of questions, and I need to try and smooth things over – keep as much of this under wraps as I can. You'll be OK down here, yes?'

'Of course we will!' said Grace. 'It's what we do.'

Bonati nodded, but he was looking worriedly at Luc, who was clearly sensing something. 'Look, just stay safe, will you,' he said.

They watched him go and then decided to move closer to the mutilated body.

'Hard to think evil is not at work here when you look at that, Luc,' said Grace.

'But it's not, is it,' he said forcefully. 'I mean, it looks like an act of evil, yes, but it represents something – the suffering I'm talking about. This is how the spirits are *feeling*.'

'Explain?'

Luc stared at the viscous wounds inflicted on the corpse. The blood that lay on the stone floor.

'It's a metaphor,' he said.

'What do you mean?' said Grace. 'A metaphor for what?'

'Someone in the past – or judging by the strength of the feelings in the atmosphere, a great number of people in the past – has suffered death and persecution, and this is a way of articulating their pain. This body represents what the spirits feel. This is a message for us.'

'A plea for help, you mean?' said Grace.

'Yes, exactly.'

'So we have to understand their pain?'

'That's right,' said Luc. 'It's a plea for justice. This man was a sacrifice, Grace. Just as the engineer was last night. It's a cry for help.' His voice was faltering again. Grace could see globules appearing in the corners of his large brown eyes.

'Hey, come on, Luc. I can feel the emotion too, but you're gotta let it pass. You can't absorb it all.'

'No!' he shouted. 'You're not listening.'

'What? I am listening to you, Luc, I'm here. What's wrong? Tell me!'

Luc was shaking his head. 'Don't listen to *me*. Just *listen*,' he said, his voice still breaking with emotion.

They stood there silently for a few moments, their extra-sensory perception extending like antennae into the metallic void around them.

Slowly, Grace heard it. Luc could tell she was detecting something from the expression on her face.

'See? You hear it?' he said.

'I hear something. It's hard to make it out. It's a repeated phrase of some kind.'

'Martyrs?'

She listened in further. 'Yes! For the martyrs – the martyrs caritatis,' she said.

'Exactly,' said Luc. 'It's why I feel so—'

'Whoa,' said Grace, seeing his eyes suddenly roll up towards his eyebrows. 'What's happened?'

'I feel dizzy,' he said weakly. 'I don't feel—'

And then he dropped to the floor like a stone.

Grace quickly bent down to him, feeling a sense of abandonment – a twinge of loneliness with the sudden realisation that she was alone with nothing but a brutally violated corpse and an unconscious friend for company.

'Luc! Luc, can you hear me?' She was smoothing one hand

across his closely cropped black hair and supporting his neck with the other. 'Luc?'

Slowly he opened a tear-stained eye. The whites around his brown pupils shone against his dark skin.

'Can you see me? Talk to me,' Grace said. 'Luc!'

CHAPTER 22

WEDNESDAY 3 NOVEMBER: 3.01 P.M.

DEAN COURT HOTEL, YORK

'So how do you feel now?'

'Well at least I'm not trembling any more!'

'No. You sound more relaxed and that's good.' Vorzek continued to be sympathetic. It was clear that Bex was still shaken, even though more than an hour had passed since her ordeal at Micklegate. Her first phone call to the CRYPT had been fraught to say the least. Whatever had happened in that tower, it had left her trembling and almost incoherent.

Vorzek had told her to return straight to her hotel room and try to relax, and she'd call her again in an hour.

And now it seemed that Bex was at least able to give a clearer account of what she'd experienced.

'It certainly sounds like what we might call hypersensing, Bex,' said Vorzek.

'So it's happened before then, Doctor? I mean, I'm not the only one?'

'Well, there's little evidence for it – it's early days in our research – but it's a phenomenon that has occurred before, though I've never met anyone else who's experienced it first hand.'

'So no one at the CRYPT has gone through it before?'

'No. At least they haven't told us if they have. Agents know about hypersensing, for sure. They've probably heard the expression, just as you had before today, but I can't say it's happened to any of them. You're the first, Bex.'

Knowing that she was the first to experience something so frightening did nothing to calm her nerves. She felt no pride, only loneliness. She'd hoped that there were other agents at the CRYPT who might have been able to understand what she'd just been through. At least then she might have felt less like she was losing her mind. As it was, despite the assurances Vorzek had been trying to offer her over the phone, Bex felt scared – scared she was becoming delusional.

Was she really sick?

Loneliness was creeping up on her. Just like when she first discovered she had powers of extrasensory perception. It might have been three years ago now, but she could remember it as if it were only yesterday.

She'd been away on a school trip at the time. They were staying in a large Victorian house on the crumbling Dorset coast.

They'd been out walking all day. She and her mates were tired and the boys were showing off back at the house before tea. Her teachers had suggested – why did teachers always 'suggest' stuff that you knew you had to do? – that they retire to their dormitories for a rest until dinner was served.

But Bex was in no mood for resting. She always had too much energy for that. So she and her best friend had decided to use the time to explore the attic rooms, which were out of bounds.

She remembered opening the door at the back of one of the dormitories and sneaking up the spiral staircase that led to the top of the four-storey house. She could still recall every detail: the musty smell, and the cobwebs that adorned the banisters like tinsel.

They opened the creaking wooden door and ducked to enter the first of what turned out to be three loft rooms. There was nothing but empty tea chests and some ancient suitcases, which also, disappointingly, turned out to be devoid of treasure.

They pressed on into the next room and then on further into the long room at the end of the house. The evening sun was pushing through cracks in the roof, stabbing the dark shadows in the house and spotlighting the spiders as they crept conspicuously over the rafters.

And then she felt it.

It was an overwhelming feeling of sadness. Unlike anything she'd felt before. Her heart sank and great teardrops began forming in her eyes. Her friend could see something had distressed her.

'Bex? What's wrong with you?'

'I don't know,' she sobbed. 'Something's wrong. But I can't say what it is. I just feel so sad. Do *you* feel it?'

'What d'ya mean?'

'Well I know this is going to sound stupid, but I feel sadness in here. Something's made me really upset.'

Her friend was looking scared. 'Stop messin' around, Rebecca. Stop it! It's not funny.'

'No, I mean it,' said Bex. 'I feel different, like I'm supposed to feel sorry for someone, but I don't know why, or who.'

And then she heard the voice.

It started off soft and low. It sounded like a child. Maybe a little boy. It was hard to make the words at first, but they sounded something like 'Stop them!'

'What was that?' she said.

'What?'

'That noise. Did you hear it?'

'No. What noise? Look, Bex, you're scaring me. I'm going back down.'

'No!' screamed Bex. 'Don't leave me! Stay! And *listen*.'

They waited again.

'Stop them!' came the voice.

'There!' Bex said. 'Hear that?'

Her friend looked scared and confused. 'I don't hear anything,' she said.

Bex felt so woeful. Deep sadness was running through her veins. But why?

She shouted at her friend again. '*Don't* pretend you can't hear, Julie!'

Her friend began to cry. She turned and made for the stairs at the far end.

But Bex remained where she was. She was transfixed. 'Go then!' she said. 'I'm staying here.'

There was definitely a voice calling to her. It was young and weak, but it conveyed passion and anger.

'Stop them!' it was saying. 'Please – someone stop the bombs. Stop the bombs. I wanna go home. I *really* wanna go home!'

The voice seemed so desperate. Such a heartfelt plea from a little boy.

She spun around and scoured the dark shadows in the room. For some reason she felt no fear. But she did feel alone. Like everyone else in the world was deaf and she was the only one who could hear properly.

'Stop them, please!' There it was again. It was definitely a child's voice. 'I wanna go back. I wanna be in London. And I want my dad to come home. *Now!*'

Was it a real person, hiding right here in the room? Or was it a ghost? Could it be, *really*? She hoped she wasn't going mad. Suddenly she was engulfed in a fear of being alone, not just alone in the attic now, but alone inside her head – seeing and hearing things that others couldn't.

But what about this talk of bombs? It unsettled her.

She tried listening in again, but she heard no more. Only the sound of the waves washing over the rocks way down below the cliffs outside.

She tiptoed out of the room and went downstairs.

She had some explaining to do when she got down. Her friend had run to the nearest teacher and told him what had happened.

'Rebecca!' said Mr Swainston, leader of the trip. 'What do you think you were doing up there?'

She apologised and said she'd been trying to play a trick on her friend. She knew it was wrong and promised she wouldn't do it again. No talk of ghosts in the house. It would upset everyone.

But secretly she knew she hadn't made it up. And she worried about it for the rest of the trip. Her friends said she was just in a mood, or homesick like a baby, but Bex knew there was something else going on. Something different to anything she'd ever experienced before.

It was only when she returned home from the trip, back to the safety of her bedroom, that she chose to research that old place.

It didn't take her long to discover it. The great house had once been used as a billet for dozens of evacuees during the war. They'd been evacuated from London to escape the Blitz.

The little boy she'd heard in the attic room could have been one of the kids who was sent away – away from the bombs – and wondering when he would return home, or if his father would be spared in the fighting overseas.

It sounded fantastical, but what other explanation was there? God knows she'd thought about it enough. Tried to imagine every other possibility. Perhaps it had been one of the boys on the trip, following the girls upstairs and trying to spook them.

But why those words? And why those feelings of fear and sadness that had run through her veins? How did that happen? How was it that she'd been able to feel such emotion just by being in a room? It had to have been the little boy's desperation after being ripped from his family and forced to live in the middle of nowhere. She'd *connected* with it somehow.

But if this first experience seemed impossible to believe, Bex then started to have more encounters of a similar kind. The old lady's voice in the hotel bedroom, the sound of singing in the empty church near her uncle's house, even the sudden burst of applause she'd heard from the empty auditorium when her school class had attended a backstage tour of the local theatre.

And every time she was the only one to hear the noises. The *only one*. It was like everyone else was deaf – but they weren't.

Just like in the tower at Micklegate. Only then it was an even sharper experience. It hadn't been just feelings or sounds or smells. Or a glimpse of an apparition even. It had been the whole scene she'd experienced. Like she was *actually* there. The place seemed recreated in her mind as it must have been back in history.

But why now?

'Bex? *Bex*?' Vorzek was unsettled by her silence at the end of the phone.

Bex drifted back into the present.

'I'm sorry, Dr Vorzek. It's been a weird day. I must have switched off. I keep doing that. I can't concentrate any more.'

'It's no wonder. You're tired, Rebecca,' said Vorzek. 'I shouldn't have sent you up there this morning – especially given that you had no sleep last night, worrying about Jud.'

Jud! Bex thought to herself. With all that had happened, she'd clean forgotten about his arrest.

'Oh no,' she said. 'What about Jud? What's happened? Is he going to be all right? Have they charged him with anything?'

'Calm yourself,' said Vorzek. 'He's no longer a suspect.'

'What? Why?' said Bex cautiously, unwilling to get her hopes up too soon. 'What's happened now?'

'There's been another incident at Westminster. While Jud was with us, so it couldn't have been him.'

Bex was relieved. She'd wanted so much to speak to him earlier. She'd even tried calling him on her way back from

Micklegate. If anyone would understand what it was like to experience the power of the paranormal, Jud would. But she'd been unable to raise him. She'd tried calling him again when she got to the hotel, but he'd not picked up. Probably still asleep.

'Is he back at the Houses of Parliament again? Is that why I can't raise him?'

'No,' said Vorzek.

'So where is he?'

Vorzek looked at her watch. 'I'd say about Peterborough by now.'

She laughed at Bex's confused silence. 'We thought you might like the company and support, so we've sent him up to York.'

'What time does he arrive?' said Bex, trying to hide her excitement.

'Some time after four. I've booked him a room at the same hotel as you. I'm sure he'll make contact with you when he arrives.'

Bex glanced at herself in the mirror across the room.

She was a mess! How could Jud see her like this?

And then she chided herself for caring so much. She decided to put it down to the ESP. Her emotions were wreaking havoc at the moment. No wonder she felt jittery at the thought of seeing Jud again. It wasn't anything personal. It was just the events of the day, the hypersensing, which had left her feeling exposed and vulnerable.

She'd have felt the same had anyone else been coming up.

Wouldn't she?

'Bex?' said Vorzek. 'Bex. You there?'

She'd drifted again.

'Sorry, Doctor. It's the experience. I don't know, my mind seems to be in overdrive. I'm all over the place!'

'Can we just quickly go over your readings, then I'll let you rest. We'll talk about your experience at Micklegate again when you're back.'

'Yes, of course,' said Bex. 'I stayed in the tower for a while longer. I mean I just wanted to get out, but I knew we'd need the readings.'

'And?' said Vorzek, trying to hide her impatience. At last they'd got to the science. The bit she'd been waiting for. She knew, like everyone did at the CRYPT, that the sensations agents felt through their ESP were valuable at every haunting, but unlike Bonati, Vorzek was especially interested in what was *measurable*. The data – results, readings on a scale – that was what Vorzek really wanted. She preferred to rely more on the power of science than the elusive powers of extrasensory perception. She was the person in charge of sourcing and managing the field equipment that supported every paranormal investigation. It was why she'd been given the nickname 'Q', from the Bond stories.

'I set up the Tri-Axis EMF meter straight away,' said Bex. 'I tell you, Doctor, the needle was off the scale. It turned out the electromagnetic energy in that room was higher than anything I'd ever seen.'

'And the Geiger counter?' asked Vorzek. 'What was the radiation like?'

'Again, very high readings. I moved the probe around the room. It was especially high nearest the window. The one I saw the severed head through.'

'OK,' said Vorzek. 'So there was real activity there.'

'And the electrostatic locator went berserk too, Doctor. I kept pressing the quick zero button to re-test, and the readings were just as high every time.'

'All this electrical activity goes some way to explaining your experiences, Bex.'

'Yeah, I suppose so. But the hypersensing? I mean, do you really think it could have created such an extreme experience?'

'You know I'm not the expert on ESP, Bex. I do the gadgets. You'll have to ask the professor about the touchy-feely stuff! But I do know there is evidence to suggest that a highly charged atmosphere can have a temporary effect on the neural patterns in your brain. It stands to reason that your natural receptors will have been sent into overdrive in those kinds of conditions.'

Bex felt a sudden surge of panic. 'But no lasting damage?'

'No. At least I think it's unlikely. The electromagnetic and electrostatic levels were high, I've no doubt – and this may have contributed to the hallucinations you experienced – but there's no way they were high enough, or your exposure lasted long enough, to cause any lasting damage. You'd have had to remain in the room for a much longer period. If anything, it might have done you some good.'

'What? How?'

'There's evidence to suggest that exposure to sudden changes in the magnetic field can sometimes have therapeutic qualities. You've not heard of TMS?'

'Nope.'

'Transcranial magnetic stimulation. It's a therapy used in some patients to treat depression. The strong magnetic field can sometimes interrupt habitual neural patterns and thus kick your brain out of bad habits, like negative thinking, depression, bipolar conditions and so on.'

'So it was actually *good* for me?'

'Well, I'm just saying it probably didn't do you any harm.'

'Probably?' said Bex.

'Yes. Don't get me wrong, Bex, exposure to extreme electromagnetic radiation over a long period of time can have damaging effects on the brain. This energy can be absorbed by anything capable of conducting electricity, and that includes nerves and neurons in your brain. So in theory you could soak it up. But I don't think the levels were high enough, or your exposure was long enough, to cause permanent damage. Remember, neither the professor, nor Mr Goode, nor any of us in this field of science have ever recorded levels of electromagnetic radiation from paranormal entities high enough to cause such health hazards. It's very unlikely. You'd be more likely to get greater shocks from your EM neutraliser. By the way, I take it you didn't use that?'

'No, I didn't Doctor. There wasn't time.'

'OK. Well, I suggest you get some rest. You've done well, Bex. I'm proud of you. Perhaps tomorrow you can interview some of the witnesses up there. What about the woman outside the churchyard, or the old man who saw the severed head?'

'Already on it. I've arranged to interview the lady who saw the headless figure later today. I'm hoping I can see the man from Micklegate tomorrow. He's out of intensive care, but I'm told he's still very weak.'

'Right. Well take it easy, Bex. Do you hear me? You've had a shock and your brain will need some down time.'

'Yeah.'

'I suggest you boil the kettle, make a cup of tea and then do some serious TV gawping. Best way to switch your brain off. A bit of mindless television. Doctor's orders!'

'If you say so,' said Bex. 'It's a tough job, but someone's got to do it.'

Vorzek rang off.

Bex was alone again. She sat on the bed. Then she lay down and stared at the ceiling. Then she sat up again and fiddled with the TV control.

She just couldn't settle.

She'd got too much energy. Whether it was the experiences at Micklegate, or the news that Jud was on his way up, or a heady cocktail of both, she wasn't sure, but one thing was certain, relaxation was going to be hard. Her senses were just too wired.

Mindless daytime television filled an otherwise silent room. It was a DIY programme in which a messianic presenter had changed the life of some hapless 'ordinary person' by painting their living room burgundy and replacing the rug.

She stood up. And paced the floor.

She looked at the clock. Jud was on his way, but there was still some time yet.

She went into the bathroom to shower and change, and put some make-up on.

There was no use denying it, she looked bloody awful in the mirror. There were bags under her eyes and she was still pale from the Micklegate experience.

She looked no better after the shower. She dressed, then picked up her make-up bag and started applying some eyeliner. The mirror had misted from the hot shower but was clearing gradually.

She switched from one eye to the other with the eyeliner pen. Then she took out her lipstick.

Wait a minute. *What was that?*

She blinked.

It was weird. Was it the light?

She looked up and saw the spotlights set into the ceiling above her. They hadn't changed.

She looked back again at the mirror.

My God, she'd never noticed that. Sixteen years she'd lived on this earth, and she'd never noticed how her nose turned to the left in certain lights. Were the patches of mist that remained on the glass distorting her face and playing tricks on her?

She stared at it. No, it wasn't a trick of the glass. Her nose genuinely looked different somehow.

Come to think of it, she'd never really noticed the mole on her left cheek – or was it her right? It was always difficult in a mirror. She raised a hand to her face to check which side it was.

Hang on. That's weird, she thought.

She looked down at her hand – perfectly normal. She raised it to the mirror again. It seemed smaller somehow, and paler. Much paler. She'd never noticed how clearly she could see the veins on the back of it. But when she looked at her real hand, instead of the reflection, it seemed normal again.

Now this *was* freaky!

She glanced again at the reflection of her face.

'Oh, *shit!*' she cried and ran out of the room.

She was panting now. She sat on the bed and tried to collect her thoughts.

No! You're doing it again! You're imagining things!

She felt angry with herself. With her senses. She wasn't going to fall for this again, but that feeling, that disorientating, lonely sensation was growing again.

No!

She marched purposefully towards the bathroom again.

She entered.

And there it was.

A different face. Same clothes, even the same hair – but her face had changed. It *wasn't* her.

Frantically she put her hands up to her face.

In the mirror they looked weaker, paler, and the veins were visible again.

She turned them round and looked at them in the flesh – normal.

One more glance at the mirror was enough.

Her eyes saw a different person looking straight back at her, and she screamed.

She fled the bathroom for the second time, grabbed her room key and her jacket and left the room.

She chose the stairs – remembering that the lift had a mirror. No more mirrors.

Arriving in the hotel lobby, she made straight for the automatic door into the street.

Down the steps and on to the pavement.

A quick glance up at the Minster, majestic and peaceful in the snow. Somehow the sight soothed her. She saw shoppers and commuters up ahead; taxis across the road, their drivers standing huddled together, smoke rising from someone's cigarette like a miniature chimney; a cyclist breezing by; two elderly ladies cautiously taking it steady on the icy pavement.

Normality washed over her like a second shower.

But she couldn't go back inside. Not yet.

Bex crossed the road and headed towards town. Fresh air and a brisk walk, that was all she needed. She'd be fine soon.

CHAPTER 23

WEDNESDAY 3 NOVEMBER: 3.26 P.M.

HOUSES OF PARLIAMENT, LONDON

Luc could see crowds of people – hundreds of them. All marching in the same direction. It was difficult to make out where they were. All he could see was some kind of ornate building in the background.

The figures were wailing. Their screams echoed around Luc's head. And he could hear words too. It was the same phrase repeated over and over again: *martyrs caritatis*.

But what made the spectacle so shocking was that the marching bodies were mutilated. Some had open wounds in their chests or stomachs, from which blood was pouring. Yet they marched onwards, tears falling from their grey, deathly faces.

And amongst them he'd seen a headless body too, its open neck gushing blood as its legs continued to march on like an automaton, swept along with the others on some kind of pilgrimage.

'Luc? Can you hear me, Luc?' Grace was whispering.

She was seconds away from calling for assistance when he slowly opened one eye.

The crowds of marching corpses had left Luc's brain. He saw Grace's gentle face – serene, kindly.

Grace continued to support his neck and stroke his forehead. She was so relieved to see him gaining consciousness again. But she didn't want to rush him. She knew all too well what could happen if you forced an agent out of a trance too quickly. It could take days to re-centre their emotions again. Episodes of extrasensory perception required careful managing, that was for sure. Bonati often compared it to the bends – that condition suffered by submariners and deep-sea divers, when a rise to the surface was too quick for the body to handle.

It was the same for the agents, at least emotionally.

He'd tell her in good time what had just happened. Better to keep him calm. Bring him out of his trance slowly.

Luc Dubois was a real asset to the CRYPT and they all knew it. Though he'd been living and studying in London when he was first recruited, his roots lay in France, where his parents ran a vast wine estate. His wealthy background had not been lost on his fellow agents. But no one had resented it. Somehow Luc was just too cool to dislike. Too classy. His grandparents had emigrated to France from Africa to escape a military coup. Though Luc rarely talked about it, there were rumours in the CRYPT that his family were royalty. Or had been.

And even Luc himself had regal qualities. There was something so reserved, so sophisticated about him. His dark skin, his striking brown eyes and his closely cropped black hair made him one of the most attractive agents in the group. 'Eye candy', as the girls secretly called him. When his looks were combined with that irresistible French accent of his, it meant the other guys in the CRYPT stood little chance.

Grace watched him as he began to orientate himself. He was back.

'What did you see?' she asked him gently.

He gradually replayed the strange images that had entered his mind at the point when he'd fainted. The marching corpses. What did it all mean?

Grace too had felt an eerie chill in the basement. Though she'd not seen the visions Luc had seen, she shared his belief that some great injustice was about to be avenged. But what? And when?

'Come on,' she said, helping him to his feet. She handed him his bag of equipment. 'Let's take a closer look at the body. You OK now?'

Luc nodded and approached the corpse with her. They set their backpacks down and within a few moments the corner of the room was filled with CRYPT equipment. They were leaving nothing to chance.

Luc glanced across at Grace, who began moving the Geiger probe up and down the wall just behind the mutilated corpse. She was bent awkwardly so as to avoid touching the body, though Luc saw her wince momentarily as she accidentally brushed up against the dead man's open chest.

He stared again at the corpse, so violently dispatched. A chill ran through him as he pictured the images that had flashed through his mind when he fainted. The overwhelming impression of crowds – hundreds, even thousands of bodies. All marching – somewhere. He wasn't clear where they were or where they were heading, though he was sure he'd made out some kind of elaborate building behind them. Could it have been Westminster?

The anger and the misery had touched him in ways he'd never experienced before.

There was a sudden burst of loud clicks from Grace's Geiger probe – showing that there were high levels of ionising radiation here. After further testing it was clear that the levels were most intense in the stretch of wall to the right of the corpse, near some large metal cabinets.

Why there?

Was there something inside? Grace went to open them. Her hand and arm jolted as a massive surge of static electricity jabbed into her.

'Whoa!'

Luc looked across from where he was standing at the other side of the bloodied corpse. 'You OK?'

'Yeah. It's just there's some massive radiation here. Come and see. Bring your electrostatic locator. The levels must be really high if I just got a shock from these doors.'

Luc moved to his bag, collected the locator and joined Grace at the metal cabinets. He pressed the 'quick zero' button to reset the machine. Quickly the needle rose, way past the safe level of 3,500 volts – 5000, 10,000, 20,000 volts. It reached the top level of 30,000 volts within seconds and looked like it could have climbed higher if hadn't reached the end of the detector's scale.

'You're right,' Luc said. 'These cabinets are alive with energy. Something is soaring through them.'

He threw her a pair of rubber gloves and put some on himself – specially designed insulators they'd brought with them to protect against high levels of static electricity. You never knew when you might need them.

Luc opened one of the cabinets. It wasn't locked – but there was nothing inside. The other was empty too. But the Geiger probe and the handheld Tri-Axis EMF meter both registered high energy spikes in this region.

There was undoubtedly radiation here. The needle on the EMF meter had settled on 153mG.

'We'll have to move them,' said Grace, determination written across her sweating brow. It was certainly warming up down in the basement.

'What, the cabinets?' said Luc incredulously. 'How?'

But she'd already started. Like a woman possessed, she was heaving her shoulder against the side of one of the cabinets.

'Do you sense something is behind there?' asked Luc, joining her.

'Don't you?'

'Well, it's hard to tell. But I'm convinced there is a real presence here. Something paranormal. There's a chance that whatever dispatched this guy so cruelly has not left yet.'

'Either that, or this is not the only body here,' suggested Grace.

'You think there's another?' said Luc.

Grace didn't answer but just kept pushing at the solid metal box.

'Easy, tiger!' said Luc.

'We've got to be quick,' said Grace, puffing. 'The others'll be back soon. Bonati said we'd only have a short while alone with the body. The staff here won't take kindly to us taking the room apart.'

They continued to heave at the first of the two giant cabinets.

'What the hell were these used for?' said Luc, panting.

'I don't know. I suspect for storing equipment in, or for housing some sort of machinery,' said Grace. 'Maybe linked to the air-conditioning in this place.'

'Well, they made them bomb-proof, that's for sure,' said Luc, pushing at one side with both hands.

After a few seconds the first cabinet was clear of the wall and Luc could see behind it.

Nothing.

Just plain wall and a lot of dust.

But the probe on the Geiger counter was now emitting a deafening series of clicks. The EMF meter was registering 170mG. Neither Luc nor Grace had ever seen a level like that other than in the SPA rooms, and that was simulated. This was for real.

They could both feel their hearts quickening, and it wasn't just from the exertion of moving the cabinet.

Now Luc threw himself at the second cabinet with the same determination Grace had shown. 'Come on!'

They pushed and shoved until eventually it was free on one side, where Grace was standing. She peered into the dark recess between the wall and the great metal box. Luc came round and joined her. Their eyes widened.

They saw the shape of a man.

But unless their eyes were tricking them, this guy was *within* the wall. They were looking at his side. They could see his ear and the nape of his neck – part of his left cheek was visible, even one eye. His body was half exposed too. But the other half was inside the wall – actually *inside*.

'But . . . how . . . ?' was all Grace could mutter.

'It's possible,' said Luc, nodding his head pityingly. 'When a dead man loses his spirit, he loses electrical energy too. In extreme cases, when other paranormal entities are present and they remove the spirit, the body is effectively reduced to plasma.'

'Non-conflict plasma?' said Grace.

'That's right. And non-conflict plasma can pass through walls. It's been known before. But it's rare.'

Grace was nodding. 'Yeah, that time at Greyfriars.'

'The woman dragged through the wall?'

'Exactly,' said Grace.

'So is this who I think it is?' said Luc.

They looked at each other in silence for a moment, chilled by the macabre atmosphere in the place.

'The missing engineer?' said Grace, quietly. 'Probably.'

'Well I tell you one thing, Grace. If it *is* Neil Jones, at least Jud is off the hook. There's no way a human could have done this. Not even an agent.'

'I agree,' said Grace. But she wasn't smiling – she was just staring at the wretched figure buried in the wall. 'But if it wasn't Jud or anyone else here – that leaves one question, doesn't it?'

'Yeah,' said Luc, ominously. 'Who the hell did this?'

CHAPTER 24

WEDNESDAY 3 NOVEMBER: 5.14 P.M.

PIMLICO, LONDON

'But why, master? *Why?* I don't understand.'

The spirit resisted the temptation to punish the man for such insolence. God knows he had the power to discipline him, like he had done so many times before. But times had changed. He needed the man now. More than ever. They both knew it was pointless resisting – pain could be meted out so quickly and with such devastating effects. The man's body was punctured with countless wounds – and then there were the savage burns that ran across his chest too, scars from the house fire years before.

But with the day of reckoning so close now – with the martyrs rising up and preparing – the spirit knew it was better to keep the man's love.

'Little one,' said the spirit. 'These things are beyond your comprehension. The spirit world is changing. The suffering that has blighted my brothers and sisters for so long will soon be avenged. We *will* see justice done.'

The man had heard this all before. So many times.

'But the murders?' he said. 'At the house. Why was it

necessary to kill again? And in such a brutal way. Why, master? We had nothing to gain from the killing, but much to lose. And it seems our plans have failed now.'

'Failed?' the spirit's voice came back. The man detected anger rising and he braced his body on the bed. '*Failed?*' it said again.

'Well, it seems our target is now innocent,' said the man feebly.

The spirit was quick to respond. 'Innocent? My friend, their meddlings with the spirit world have gone on too long. They could never be found *innocent.*'

'But our plan to disgrace them! It was working, master. We had the babies right where we wanted them. Especially the killer. How could he have done it now?'

The spirit tried to soothe the nerves of the little one. He hated to see him so frightened, so lost.

'Rest, my friend. Don't think on it. The children will be gone. We shall expose them for what they are. Fraudsters. Meddlers. We shall besmirch their name. The babies will be exposed. If not now, then soon.'

The man tried to find some solace in the spirit's words, but there was none to be had. It only made him worry more. The 'children', as he called them – the spirit had never granted them their real name of *agents* – would be all over Westminster now. And York.

The man knew all too well how the CRYPT worked – and how quickly, too.

It had been a risky strategy from the start. To involve a CRYPT agent directly – to actually bring one to the scene of a crime – in the faint hope that he could then be discredited, framed with a murder, was a plan not without risks. But it had been his idea. His baby. They could so easily have carried on and hoped that their plans never reached the attention of the CRYPT. Or at least hoped that by the time the agents were on the case, it would be too late for them to stop the great plan.

The man had resented the CRYPT from the very start. Their arrogance! Their stupid belief that they were the only ones who could reach out to the spirit world, when he'd been doing exactly that all his life!

Get the children involved and then mark their hands with blood, so they would never be allowed near the sacred site again – that was his plan. And it had been working. Until now.

'So who was it?' he shouted into the room.

Silence.

'Please, master, tell me! Who was it who was seen in the basement? Who did this for you?'

'For *us*,' the spirit corrected him. 'I have many close friends. Many spirits I can turn to. But once called, I cannot control them, my friend. They were wilful in life, and in death they have not changed. But the group is nearly complete. Soon we shall be together at last. To force the justice we seek. To make history.'

The man was no longer listening to this premature victory speech. He was hatching out a plan in his head.

If the plot to disgrace the CRYPT agents was no longer possible, given the second killing in the basement, he knew what he had to do. He had to deal with this himself. He *had* to keep them away from Westminster, just for two more days.

He had to silence the children.

As soon as the spirit left him, he began packing.

He'd be in York by nightfall.

CHAPTER 25

WEDNESDAY 3 NOVEMBER: 5.14 P.M.

THE CRYPT

The black, insect-like helicopter lowered itself on to the new pad now installed above the penthouse that Jason Goode called home these days. The treks from Battersea heliport had become frustrating for Goode, especially during rush hour, so he'd commissioned a new pad to be built just above his living room.

A few moments later, the blades were slowing and the door opened. Jason Goode stepped on to the new tarmac.

'Not a bad landing, Gary,' he said. 'Well done.' The pilot smiled.

'The new pad looks good too. Much easier.'

It was breezy up on the roof. Luckily Goode suffered no vertigo or agoraphobia. Which was just as well. He was standing thirty-eight floors above the street. On one of only a handful of buildings that towered so high over the capital.

The great architectural masterpiece, the design for which Goode himself was able to share some of the credit, was located on the banks of the Thames to the east of the city. Land was cheaper here. The place had been heavily bombed during the Second World War, and then the post-war closure of the great docks that once thrived here meant it was the perfect site for the new global headquarters of Goode Technology PLC. There had been nothing but an abandoned car park and a small stretch of poor grass here before the tower had been commissioned.

Soaring into the sky like some futuristic cone-shaped rocket, Goode Tower had already become a famous landmark, rivalling the Swiss Re Tower – or Gherkin, as it was known – to the west and the awesome new Strata Tower in Southwark to the south.

But although the presence of Goode Tower on the city's skyline could not exactly be hidden, no one knew of the secrets it so fiercely guarded below ground. Goode made sure of that.

He made for the lift door across the helipad and was relieved to escape the blustery wind that was clamouring to blow him off his own building.

Within a few moments he was inside the penthouse suite, and home. If that was what home was – he'd forgotten what the word meant. His wife was dead, his son lived 150 metres below him, disguised as someone else, and his castle – once the family home – remained only an occasional retreat. He couldn't even remember the last time he and Jamie had visited it together.

He poured himself a bourbon and Coke – a bit early perhaps, but it had been a long flight from Hong Kong and he needed a pick-me-up. In any case, he was still on Asian time. What would it be now? He'd lost track.

He was determined to find out what had been going on since he was last in London. The fragmented texts and cryptic emails he received whenever he was away were often more infuriating than not hearing anything at all. He'd tried to get hold of Bonati too, but they seemed to keep missing one another.

As for Jud, he'd tried to Skype him a few times from Hong Kong, but Jud wasn't accepting the call. Jason was never really sure if that was because his son was unavailable or unwilling to talk to him.

And the problem with Skype was the deafening silence that always came immediately after he'd ended the call. It was a sharp reminder that he was alone and his boy was thousands of miles away – beyond the reach of a hug. The face on the screen never compensated for the physical distance between them. It only made it worse.

There was no substitute for a real chat – face to face.

He was keen to see him now and called him on his mobile, hoping desperately that he was in the building.

No answer.

A few moments later he received a text in reply.

Mmm, I think I remember you. Don't tell me you're actually in the country?

Jason was at a loss to know how to respond. He tried keying in a few choice words about how it wasn't his fault that he was always travelling and how someone had to earn the money around here, but he soon deleted them. He tried again, being more conciliatory, but that just sounded cheesy and disingenuous. As usual he settled for the most diplomatic response – to pretend he hadn't received the text.

J's texts always hurt, there was no doubting that. He would never know, perhaps not until he had children of his own, what it meant to be an absent dad. How it robbed Jason of the right to have an opinion or show that he cared on those very rare times they were together. Absence – at least being away as much as Goode was – took away the opportunity to be close when you found yourselves together again. And yet whenever he travelled overseas, or even when he was in the country, he reserved the right to miss his own son. It was every father's right. And no matter how much Jud tried to shut his father out whenever he did bother to return – and to punish him for being away in the first place – he could never stop him from caring. Jason would always do that.

The phone on his glass desk by the window blurted into action.

'Ah!' the voice said. 'The weary traveller returns!'

'Giles, how're you doing? So what have I missed?'

Bonati had not been back long from his extraordinary experiences with Luc and Grace at Westminster; he'd been up all night trying to prevent Jason's own son from being charged with murder, so he hadn't slept since the night before last; he'd seen two dead bodies cruelly dispatched in ways not even Jason could have imagined, and he'd got agents falling apart around him.

'Well, Jason,' he said. 'How long have you got?'

'I think you'd better come up, Giles. Hungry?'

'Starving.'

CHAPTER 26

WEDNESDAY 3 NOVEMBER: 5.52 P.M.

ALL SAINTS CHURCH, YORK

Maureen poured another syrupy dab of Brasso on to her cloth and rubbed it into the already gleaming brass lectern. She loved the smell of it. She was sure – and her husband, the verger, had told her enough times – that it was bad for her, but she still continued to sniff away contentedly.

She moved to the pews that flanked the central aisle of All Saints and swapped cloths. A quick flick down each bench was all that was needed. It wasn't time for the 'deep clean', as she liked to call it – the fortnightly session in which Henry the Hoover accompanied her down each row. This was just the usual once-over that preceded evensong.

Seven o'clock kick-off, and the congregation would not start filing in until about 6.40. She had plenty of time.

That was if anyone turned up today. The *York Press* might have put paid to that now. Maureen didn't hold with the idea of ghosts. It was rubbish as far as she was concerned. The reports in the paper that morning of a severed head on Micklegate Bar and the headless body seen outside this very church had not deterred her from carrying out her job, business as usual. 'Bored reporters with nothing else to do but make up stories!' she'd said to her husband Clive over breakfast. He'd been more concerned about it, worried that the news reports would indeed affect the already falling congregation numbers. Either that or they would double in size, with all sorts of amateur ghost hunters pitching up, more interested in the supernatural than the Holy Spirit.

Either way, the church needed cleaning.

Once the central pews were dusted, she moved towards the back of the church. She had a system. Another quick flick over the benches at the back and then move across to the great elaborate font in the far corner. The ornate carvings might be pretty to look at, but Maureen knew they collected dust like nobody's business.

She set up the stepladder and began blowing into the cracks and crevices at the top of the ornate font hood, then swept the yellow cloth across it. She climbed down and slid the steps around to the other side. The metal feet of the thin aluminium ladder grated on the flagstones – an unpleasant noise that broke the silence inside the church.

It was particularly quiet at this time of day. A rare moment of calm for Maureen in an otherwise busy day. All Saints wasn't the only place she cleaned. Not by any means. There were the private houses she called on, and then the offices – they were always the early starters.

But cleaning All Saints had been something she'd done ever since Clive had become verger three years ago, at about the same time the previous cleaner left.

When she was satisfied that the font was clean, Maureen descended the stepladder and moved it towards the great west door.

The gothic arch housed two heavy oak doors, each one dressed with elaborate ironmongery.

Above the doors, fixed to the great stone arch, were some of the church's prized possessions: the great sword and gauntlets of the Earl of Northumberland, displayed for all to see (though most of the congregation missed them whenever they entered or exited this way).

She took her faithful cloth and gave the sword a quick wipe. It was a magnificent piece of weaponry. Lord knows how heavy it must have been to carry. Certainly the screws and brackets that held it in place now were almost as big as weapons themselves.

Then she began polishing the left gauntlet – the first in a pair of huge armoured gloves allegedly worn in battle by the brave Thomas Percy, 7th Earl of Northumberland.

She traced the shape of the hand with her cloth, whistling as she went.

And then she felt it.

A finger moved.

The shock sent her backwards, and as her weight shifted on the top step, the ladder wobbled beneath her. She clung on, praying it wouldn't give way. It held. She was all right.

She looked up again at the gauntlet.

'Don't be ridiculous!' she said aloud. The cotton cloth must have slipped over the shiny metal, creating the illusion that the glove had moved.

Come on! she told herself. Get a grip, Maureen! She half chuckled and looked forward to telling Clive what had happened – how her mind had played a trick on her.

The gauntlet coming to life! She knew what he'd say – *Been on the drink again, Maur?*

She resumed her polishing and moved across to the right gauntlet. She was just about to finish the quick rub over when it happened again.

And this time it was unmistakable. The forefinger and thumb moved. She felt their resistance against her own hand.

She shrieked and fell backwards. The ladder gave way this time, sending her crashing to the stone floor. She landed on her left hip and the pain was excruciating. But it wasn't the pain that made her go white with shock and start crying. It was the fact that above her the gloves were both moving now. With a wrench they broke free of the brackets holding them.

Two disembodied hands, encased in metal, moving freely. Was this some sort of nightmare? If it wasn't for the shooting pain in her hip, she might have thought she was dreaming.

But Maureen knew she wasn't. Was this talk of ghosts in the city really true?

Frantically she dragged herself away from the doorway.

She looked over her shoulder. The gauntlets had seized the sword and ripped it from its bracket.

And it was coming for her.

Convinced that either her heart would give way or the sword would silence her, Maureen tried to rise to her feet to get out of the church.

It was agony. She must have cracked or even broken her hip. She lay frozen with fear.

The sword, with the great iron gloves clasped around its hilt, swung left and right, as if commencing battle. Then it made for Maureen.

There was no way she could escape. The door was still many steps away – even running wouldn't have got her there in time, let alone the sluggish dragging that was all she could now muster.

The sword hovered close to her cheek.

She screamed and thrust at it with her naked hands. Bad idea.

She caught the edge with her left thumb. Blood instantly began to pour from it.

Quickly she pulled her hands back, held them tight to her face and shut her eyes to pray.

CHAPTER 27

WEDNESDAY 3 NOVEMBER: 6.17 P.M.

THE KING'S ARMS, YORK

Gabby and her friend Mel had sneaked an early doors drink at the King's Arms down on King's Staith. It was quiet, so they'd managed to grab a window seat. They watched the River Ouse roll its way past the ancient cobbled quayside and the trendy warehouse conversions on the far bank.

'So, what're we doing tonight, Gabs?' said Mel, sucking her drink through a chewed straw.

Gabby was peeling apart another beer mat, ripping off the layers of paper and rolling them up in her hand. Since smoking had been banned in pubs, she'd found dismantling cardboard beer mats was the only thing that kept her hands busy.

'Dunno,' she said.

'There's a band on at Fibbers,' said Mel. 'Might be good. Dunno how much it is to get in, though. Tony's going with Dave, I think.'

'Nah, not in the mood for live music.'

'Come on, Gabs! It's Wednesday. We're halfway there. It'll be Friday before you know it! We've gotta do something!'

'Yeah, s'pose so.'

'Well? Where are we going? We have to keep up the midweek tradition. Over the hump an' all that. It's the only thing that gets me through the week.'

'All right,' said Gabby. She was gazing wistfully out of the window at the bridge. Maybe it was time for a ciggie. 'Hey, look at this!' she said suddenly.

'What?'

'Come and see. Somethin's happening on the bridge.'

Mel switched to Gabby's side of the table to get a better view.

They could see a crowd forming in the middle of the bridge. They had their backs to the girls, facing upstream. Or were they actually looking at something on the road? It was hard to make out.

'Dunno,' said Mel. 'Has someone fallen over, maybe?'

'That's a lot of people to pick up an old granny!'

'Well I don't know, don't care either.' She moved back round to her own seat. 'D'you want another, or shall we go? I've got a great new top I wanna show you tonight. Did I tell you I got it from H and M last—'

'Hey, there's a flashing light now. I think it's the police,' said Gabby excitedly. 'Let's go and have a look!'

Mel rolled her eyes at Gabby. 'You know your problem, Gabs, you're so bloody nosy!'

With a loud slurping sound, they hoovered up their drinks and left the pub. As soon as they were outside, they could hear the police siren and the shouts from the swelling crowd that had now gathered up on the bridge.

Gabby began to run towards the stone steps that led up from the quayside.

'Hey, slow down!' shouted Mel. 'You'll slip over on the ice and it'll be you that attracts the crowd!'

They reached the top of the road and looked to their left.

A police car had parked right across the road, stopping the traffic, and blocking the girls' view of what was happening.

'What do you reckon? Is it an accident, d'you think?'

'Dunno. Come on, let's see if we can get nearer.'

They walked on to the bridge and joined the crowd. They saw a young police officer trying valiantly to hold people back. There was something on the ground; at least there must have been, due to the number of people crouching down. But the girls just couldn't see what was happening.

The sound of a second siren in the distance and then the sight of an ambulance racing towards them from the other side of the bridge confirmed their suspicions. Someone was in trouble.

'Come on,' said Mel. 'There's nothing we can do, and I'm not as bloodthirsty as you. Let's go.'

'No, wait a minute,' said Gabby. She'd spied the perfect vantage point for them both, up on the wall of the bridge, where they could hold on to a nearby lamp post.

'Follow me!' she said.

Reluctantly Mel trailed behind, and soon they were standing on the stone wall, behind them a thirty-foot drop into the icy-cold water.

'We must be mad!' said Mel. 'It's slippery up here.'

'Don't you wanna see what all the fuss is about?' said Gabby.

As the paramedics arrived, another police officer parted the crowd and they could finally see what was going on.

There was a girl – probably not much younger than them – lying on her back in the middle of the road.

But it wasn't the fact that she was lying there that shocked the crowd gathered around her; it was the fact that she was pushing and kicking and stabbing with her legs at anyone who tried to give her assistance.

'Oh no,' said Mel. 'I think she must be epileptic. I've got an uncle like that. It's OK – I mean, it looks a lot worse than it is – but she'll be exhausted when it's finished. The medics just need to keep everything out of her way and let her get on with it.'

'Get on with *what*?' said Gabby.

'The seizure. It's like a fit. It's when you get violent body movements that you can't control, triggered by impulses in the brain.'

'Ooh, listen to you, Dr Melanie!'

'Well I've seen my uncle have one. We were at a party. I remember it was horrid at the time, and then my auntie explained what was happening and that he was actually OK.'

They watched as the poor girl writhed about on the pavement. But there was something really weird about her. Mel was beginning to wonder if it really was a seizure.

As they watched her, they could see that her movements were not as wild as they'd first seemed. There was a pattern to them – and they were deliberate. Her arms and legs weren't flailing wildly, they were pushing upwards – almost like they were fighting against some imaginary obstacle.

The paramedics seemed to be at a loss. They'd cleared the area in the immediate vicinity of the girl, but then seemed unsure of what to do next. They'd tried talking to her, hoping to get a response. The girl's eyes were wide open, a fixed expression of terror written across her face. She wasn't answering their questions. She was just shouting now. Gabby and Mel listened in from their precarious perch on the bridge wall.

'Get it off,' the girl was yelling. 'No! Help me! Help me, please!'

It was a pitiful sight. Mel was welling up. It was so shocking to see. Neither of them, nor anyone else in the crowd, wanted to see this girl in such distress, but they couldn't stop watching. There's something inside the human condition, something resembling a morbid curiosity, that makes us stop and look at accidents and injuries. It holds a fascination, like motorists slowing down to see a crash on the other side of the motorway.

The crowd was still swelling. Everyone was talking to each other and shaking their heads.

'Do something!' Gabby yelled across at the paramedics and police officers. 'Why can't you help her? Give her a sedative or something, for God's sake!' She was ignored, but her cries had sparked something in others nearby and soon everyone was offering unwanted advice to the experts at the scene.

Meanwhile, the poor girl at the centre of the crowd stayed rooted to the ground, jabbing and kicking at whatever it was she thought was attacking her from above.

Her yells could be heard down on the riverbanks, where other drinkers now stood, looking up in confusion.

CHAPTER 28

WEDNESDAY 3 NOVEMBER: 6.41 P.M.

OUSE BRIDGE, YORK

If Bex had thought the experience in the tower room at Micklegate Bar was frightening, it was nothing but a gentle introduction to the nightmare that was now unfolding around her.

She pushed and kicked at the door as the guards lowered it on to her body.

'No!' she was crying. 'Get it off! *No!* Please!'

But the strange figures, dressed in some kind of military uniform from a bygone age – metal helmets and regal-looking tunics – continued to lower the huge oak door down towards her. Their faces were real, but expressionless and pale, like stone soldiers. There were two men at each end of the great oak slab. Where had it come from?

And why the hell was it being lowered on to her? What had she done? None of this made any sense. Had she slipped back into another time frame? Was she hypersensing again?

She yelled and protested with all her might, but it was no good.

Through her tears she gazed at the crowds who watched her. They too were dressed in clothes from another century – some in doublet and hose, other, less affluent figures in dowdy tunics and long leather waistcoats. Some were cheering the guards on, while others were daring to protest. They were shouting 'Leave her!' at the tops of their voices.

What the hell was this? In what realm was she now trapped?

Why or how this nightmare had struck, she could only wonder, but it was real. At least it *felt* real. Her back was already bleeding from the sharp chafing against the stony road as she wriggled and writhed to be free.

She felt a violent pull at her wrists above her head and arched her neck to look upwards.

A guard had grabbed her arms and was clamping them in irons. Huge metal manacles at the end of heavy chains now held her. She couldn't move.

A sharp pain in her shins told her that the same was happening to her legs. She arched her neck forwards, peered down to her feet and saw the great iron clasps.

She was locked in chains. The end was coming.

The great door was lowered even further, until it was touching her chest and face.

Still she screamed, but she was losing energy now. The hyper-sensing was draining her of life and her face had gone ghostly white. Her heart pounded so fast inside her ribcage she felt dizzy.

And then the first of the weights came.

A huge, burly guard appeared through the crowd of cheering onlookers, carrying a giant stone. He placed it on the door. The wood sank lower and lower onto Bex's body. Her chest felt so tight now.

She cried aloud for mercy. But her pleas were drowned out by the excited shouts from the bloodthirsty crowds. The protesters must have been moved on, as the only shouts she could now hear were calling for her death. A clear, repeated phrase, which chilled Bex to her core.

'Death to the traitor, death to the traitor!'

Suddenly a voice was speaking close into her ear. It was low and guttural, almost animal-like.

'Do you repent? Do you renounce your faith? Do you accept the sovereignty of the King?'

Bex could barely speak now. Another stone had been added. Her ribcage was moments from collapsing. Her nose and forehead had numbed under the colossal weight. Another stone and her skull would be smashed into splinters. She would be no more.

She was seconds away from yelling '*Yes, I repent!*' when another voice penetrated into her ear.

And she recognised it.

Somehow the familiarity of the voice, its smooth tone and the hand that was now gently holding her arm calmed her nerves.

There it was again. '*Bex.*'

Her eyes were still closed. She'd not wanted to open them any more. But as she lay there, the pain in her chest, the weight of the door and the tight clasp of the iron manacles were all, very slowly, diminishing.

She tried so hard to control her breathing again. There in the dark recesses of her head, she forced herself to ignore the cries of the crowd and the pushing and shoving from the guards. And slowly, these feelings faded.

Was she slipping away from the terrifying ordeal? Or was she *dying*?

Was she losing her faculties now? Was this what it felt like?

'*Bex!*' She heard it again. 'Wake up. Come on, wake up, Bex!'

She opened her eyes.

It was Jud. His brown eyes stared into hers. He looked so concerned. Was that a tear?

Bex blinked a few times. Had the door finally crushed her and this was what death felt like, filled only with the visions you wanted to see? Was she now a spirit?

She moved her hand up to her face. It was free of the iron clasps – and it was *real*.

She looked at Jud, who was now picking her up.

The feel of someone holding her again unsettled her for a moment. She suddenly kicked out in confusion.

'*Get off me!*' she said. Images of the guards returned to her mind and her heart was racing once again.

'It's OK. It's all right, Bex. It's over. I'm here now.'

She relaxed a little, though it was obvious to Jud that the experience was going to leave scars that would run deep within her. She would need some serious counselling. Whatever had happened to Bex up here, and how and why, would need to be answered in time, but first Jud knew they needed to get her well again. She looked dreadful.

He picked her up. He could feel her body relax – and her eye contact meant she was back. She smiled slowly, but then a frown came over her tired face.

'What's happening, Jud? What's wrong with me?'

'Don't worry, Bex. I don't think it's you. It's this place. It's reaching to you. We'll make sense of it. We'll find out what's causing this. But let's get you out of here first.'

The crowds of people, even the paramedics, were astonished by the recovery.

People dispersed from the bridge as quickly as they'd come to it. There was nothing to see now, no injury or crime or screaming victim. Nothing of any interest any more. Boring.

One of the paramedics, accompanied by a police officer, said, 'Let's get you in the ambulance, take you for some tests.'

Jud fought to keep her in his arms. 'No! I mean . . . don't worry. I know her well and she often suffers with these hallucinations. It's a condition she's had for a while and we're on it. I mean, she's getting treatment for it. I'll take her straight to her regular consultant now, don't worry.'

The police officer looked less convinced.

'What's your name, love?' he said to Bex.

'It's Rebecca De Verre,' she said.

'OK. And d'you know this guy, Rebecca?'

Bex smiled. 'I do,' she said.

'And you reckon you're OK now, do you?' said the paramedic, unconvinced.

'Honest,' said Bex. 'I'm fine. It happens all the time. It's a form of epilepsy.'

'Well, not one *I've* seen before,' said the other paramedic. 'You're coming with us. You need to get checked out.'

'No!' protested Bex. 'I said I'm fine.'

Jud was nodding. 'Really, you don't need to worry. I'll take it from here.'

The medics looked concerned. 'We can't force you to come with us,' said one, 'but you'd better get it checked out again. I mean, that was a nasty turn you had there. We couldn't reach you. I don't know where you'd gone inside that head of yours, but you weren't comin' out in a hurry. Back to the doctor today, I'd say. Now.'

She smiled and shrugged, though the paramedics' faces were anything but amused. The experience had shocked them almost as much as it had Bex.

Jud moved away, still supporting Bex in his arms. Once they were clear of the crowds on the bridge, he set her down on a wall near King's Staith.

'So?'

'So, what?' said Bex.

'So . . . pleased to see me?' he said.

'Just pleased to be alive!' Bex replied, but her smile said something more.

CHAPTER 29

WEDNESDAY 3 NOVEMBER: 7.48 P.M.

DEAN COURT HOTEL, YORK

Jud took another sip from his café mocha. It was probably one too many coffees for the day, but who cared? They'd got a long evening of research ahead of them.

He had accompanied Bex back to the hotel. After hearing about the ghostly face in the mirror, there was no way he was going to let her stay in the same room, so he arranged for a new room for her, and then one for him. A quick shower, a change of clothes and they were together again, huddled conspiratorially in a corner of the restaurant. The majesty of York Minster, floodlit and framed in snow, made one of the best views they'd ever seen. Its elaborate architecture, coupled with the serenity of the snowy Minster gardens next door, had helped to soothe Bex's nerves. She was beginning to feel human again, or nearly.

Her recovery from her ordeal on the bridge had seemed surprisingly quick. She had put it down to her determination to find out what caused the experience, though Jud had arrogantly suggested it was the manner in which she was rescued that had led to such speedy results.

But neither of them were under any illusions about the severity of what she'd been through during the course of the day. Nor were they blind to the possibility that there might be repercussions. Shock was a funny thing – the brain's own way of shielding itself from trauma. But it was often only a temporary defence. The relative calm that Bex presented now was deceptive, like undercurrents swirling beneath a seemingly calm surface. It was the deepest waters that made the least noise. Jud was playing it carefully.

He'd vowed to stay with her until they'd unearthed some answers, not only to the question of what was haunting York, but also to the strange sequence of events that had befallen the Houses of Parliament.

Grace had called Bex just as they were entering the hotel restaurant, and filled her in on the latest events down in the basement. It hardly seemed possible. But as Jud pointed out when Bex relayed the story to him, what Grace and Luc had found proved categorically that it must have been the work of ghosts.

Although Jud was off the hook as far as the police were concerned, he knew Bonati would be after him if they didn't come up with some answers – and soon. The case was already spiralling out of control.

'So,' he began, draining his coffee cup. 'Do you want to talk about it?'

His tone was patronising, though he hadn't meant it to be. 'What? Of course I want to bloody talk about it!' Bex replied. 'You think I'm going to break down or something?'

'OK.' Jud smiled and took out his iPad from a bag slung over his shoulder. 'So let's start at the beginning, if you're ready.' He opened the notes app and raised the keyboard. 'So, the tower. What was it called?'

'Micklegate Bar,' said Bex. 'It's one of four medieval gateways into the old city.

'OK, tell me what happened there this afternoon. I know the experience on the bridge was the worst you've had – and probably the worst I've seen – but I think we should take things in order to discover what the connections are.'

Bex agreed, though she was just as anxious to get some answers about what on earth Jud had been up to in the last twenty-four hours too.

She regaled him with the details. The experience had been so vivid, so real – at least to Bex's senses. The important questions were why did it happen, why now, and what did it mean?

'So, just talk me through your experience in that tower.'

'The hypersensing, you mean?'

Jud looked thoughtful. 'I've heard that word too. I've heard rumours that it can happen. But let's not jump to conclusions. It may have been hypersensing, but it may not. How did it begin?'

'Well, it was weird. I felt so much emotion as soon as I walked in,' she began. 'Not exactly anger as such, more like a feeling of . . .'

'Revenge?'

'Well, yes, but not an evil revenge. More like *suffering* and an overwhelming plea for justice.'

Jud could hardly believe what he was hearing.

'Bex, you realise you've just described exactly what I felt when I was in the cellar at Westminster.'

'Really?' said Bex.

'*Exactly* the same.'

The great Minster bells outside suddenly rang out to herald eight o'clock. It was a huge, resonating sound that almost shook the snowy window beside their table. Evening walkers were stopping and looking up at the great facade, bathed in orange floodlights. It was magical.

'Wow,' said Bex, getting excited now. 'Could there be a connection here? I mean, I know the two locations are two hundred and fifty miles apart, but shouldn't we be thinking about this maybe being the same case instead of two different ones?'

'Ghosts don't travel on public transport, Bex,' Jud said cheekily, hoping to get that smile going again. Bex looked exhausted. God knows what state her mind was in. She seemed lucid enough now, and the warm, sugary tea was obviously helping, but he feared her senses were in denial, delayed shock. He was bracing himself for the fallout sooner or later.

'No, I realise that, Jud,' she said without smiling.

'So what else? You've told me what you felt and then what you saw during the experience in the tower, but did you *hear* anything?'

Bex screwed her face up tight. There were cute wrinkles either side of her eyes.

'Well, I heard the sound of people shouting outside.'

'Anything before that,' said Jud. 'I mean, didn't you hear anything when you went into the tower? Sometimes it's the first sounds we hear that are the most important, before our imagination has had a chance to interpret and put its own spin on things.'

'Yeah, thanks for the lesson,' she snapped.

'Sorry. It's just that—'

'Wait a minute!' she interrupted, angrily. An elderly couple looked across from a neighbouring table. 'I hope you're not saying I made this stuff up, Jud. I mean, you're not saying it was all in my imagination, surely!'

'No, no. Definitely not, Bex.' He tried to sound as convincing as he could. He could see her temper was building. 'No, I just wondered what the first sounds were. Any voices, for example?'

Bex shook her head. The hypersensing – and she was sure that was what it was – had been so vivid it had overshadowed the moments that preceded it. The feelings of suffering and revenge had lasted throughout the experience, but other noises? She couldn't recall any.

'I can't think of anything. What about you, Jud. Did you hear anything or just feel the emotion at Westminster?' She was spooning an extra heap of sugar into her tea – she needed the energy right now, she was beginning to flag.

'Oh no, I heard something all right,' said Jud. The voice was still printed indelibly on his mind – he didn't need the notes on his iPad to remember it. 'I heard a kind of repeated phrase: "martyrs cari . . . ta . . . tis".'

Bex dropped the spoon. Sugar shot across the table like sand on a blustery day.

'My God, Jud. That's what I heard! In the tower. At Micklegate – when I first got there. I mean before the room went weird. Yes, I heard a voice – I swear that's what it said.'

They looked at each other. Had they made their first breakthrough?

Was there a connection here?

'What do you think it means, Jud?'

'Well, I Googled it when I was on the train coming up here. *Martyr* is obvious – someone who dies for their cause – but the word *caritatis* is harder to find. I've trawled through dozens of websites, in any number of languages, and I've seen it used, but I can't find its meaning. I think it has something to do with love and charity. Or the love of God.'

'Well,' said Bex, 'whatever it means, the fact that we both heard the same phrase means we've got a connection. Solve one mystery, we solve them both.'

'Yeah, sounds easy when you say it like that.'

Her phone sounded the familiar ping of a text arriving.

She quickly read it, as other diners turned and expressed their displeasure. It was from Vorzek:

How was the interview? What did the woman say?

'Oh no!' she said too loudly.

'What?'

'It's from Vorzek. I was supposed to be interviewing that woman today. With everything else that happened, I forgot.' She stood up, knocking the cutlery and making the cups wobble in their saucers.

'Hang on, Bex,' Jud said. 'There's nothing you can do about it now. You need to sit down and collect your thoughts. Vorzek can wait. The whole case can wait.'

Bex sat back in the chair, but she still looked worried. 'But I didn't even cancel the interview!'

'Who was it with?'

'You know, the woman who saw the headless figure outside the church.'

'Oh, right.' Jud knew who she was referring to. He'd had a brief conversation with Vorzek just before catching the train up to York. She'd given him a few details – just enough to explain why he was going up there in the first place, but not much more.

Little did he know that his arrival in the city would be so dramatic. He'd seen the same newspaper headline outside the station. Ghosts in the city!

He'd chosen to walk from the station to the hotel via Micklegate Bar. He wanted to see for himself the site where Bex was supposed to have had some sort of strange experience. Vorzek had called and filled Jud in during his long journey. And now he was anxious to see where it had happened.

The tower had been surrounded by police tape and the oak doors were bolted firmly shut. But Jud had been able to glance up at the great wall. He'd still got the newspaper, so he could see exactly where the severed head had been, from the picture on the front page. But he'd not seen or felt or heard anything.

The route from Micklegate Bar to the Dean Court Hotel, near the Minster, led Jud over Ouse Bridge. He'd surprised himself at how much of York he remembered.

Walking down Micklegate towards the river, he'd seen a crowd gathering.

His first reaction was that it might have been a street entertainer – the kind he saw regularly in the piazza at Covent Garden.

But it wasn't. And the shock when he finally saw what, or who, was causing the disturbance had chilled him to the core.

What might have happened had he not been there at the right time?

Where would Bex have ended up? Would the medics have sedated her right there on the bridge? It would have been the only way.

Might she still be caught in the place between the present and the past? Would the hallucination ever have ended for her?

He shuddered to think of it and then felt relieved to gaze at her now, slurping her tea and fumbling over a text in reply to Vorzek.

'What're you going to say?' he said.

'I dunno. What can I say? I was supposed to interview an eyewitness to a key haunting and I've failed to do it.'

'Bex, I think she'll understand that you were otherwise engaged!'

Bex shrugged. 'I know,' she said, 'but I just hate not delivering. Besides, if I say I've had another incident, she'll want me back at the CRYPT, no question.'

'Oh, so you'd rather stay here with me?' said Jud playfully.

'I'd rather stay here, yeah . . . to work on the case,' she added quickly. But Jud could see the flushing in her cheeks.

His own phone beeped, prompting another round of disapproving looks from their fellow diners.

He hurriedly read the words that flashed across the screen.

Seen the news? Call me. Bonati.

'Well?' said Bex.

'It's from the professor. He wants to know if we've seen the news.'

'What's happened now?'

Jud just shrugged his shoulders. 'I have a horrible feeling,' he said, 'that Bonati knows something we don't.'

They ran from the restaurant and made for Jud's room. Dinner would have to wait. Again.

CHAPTER 30

WEDNESDAY 3 NOVEMBER: 8.30 P.M.

NORTH YORKSHIRE POLICE HEADQUARTERS

FULFORD, YORK

'Ladies and gentlemen, if I can have your attention?'

Slowly the room fell silent. The reporters were eager to hear what the politician had to say. This was rapidly becoming a major story. There were representatives of most national newspapers in the room. Reporters from the local press felt a mixture of excitement and resentment at seeing so many of their peers. They were pleased to have broken the story of the hauntings before anyone down south had caught wind of it. But the large swathe of 'northern correspondents' that the national papers had hurriedly dispatched to the city now outnumbered the local reporters, and they were feeling territorial about it.

Simon Thacker cleared his throat and stared at the sea of cameras and faces ahead of him. He was no stranger to public speaking – he thrived on it – but it had been a busy couple of days. There was still so much to do at Westminster – the State Opening of Parliament was now just one day away, and his colleagues at both the Met and the House Authorities in Parliament had been incredulous when he'd said he was coming to York. But this was *his* city. His constituency. If his people were fearful right now, he wanted to be the one to calm them and give them the reassurance they needed. He not only spoke for the people of York as their democratically elected leader, he cared for them too.

'Well, thank you, everyone, for coming,' he began. 'As you will know, I am not only the Police Minister, I am also the Member of Parliament for this fine city. It is a city with a rich and famous history. But it is a city not without folk tales and legends.'

There was a rumble in the room. Reporters were getting excited; some had already planned their opening headline in tomorrow's edition.

'Such talk of ghosts is fun and appealing to many visitors. After all, this is one of the most historic cities in the world, so why shouldn't it have a few ghost stories?

'But these are what they are – stories. Fiction. I'm sorry to disappoint you, ladies and gentlemen – I know how tales of the supernatural can help you sell your newspapers. But it's gone far enough now. The residents in my constituency – the people I am so proud to represent – are fearful tonight. And there is no reason for it.

'If we let this nonsense about ghosts continue any further, who knows where it will lead? Fear can sweep through a city like a tidal wave.

'Let me tell you, it ends now. There are not, nor have there ever been, ghosts in York. That is the stuff of fiction.'

The reporters exploded into a frenzy of angry questioning.

'What of the recent incidents, Mr Thacker?'

'Have you not heard what's been happening?'

'When was the last time you were in your constituency, sir?'

'If you'll allow me to finish,' he shouted over the din, 'I said if you'll allow me to finish, I can prove there is no foundation in these stories.

'I have further developments for you tonight. It seems some of you may have been a little too quick to run a story and have jumped to the wrong conclusion. Let me explain . . .'

Jud and Bex watched from Jud's room. Thank goodness Bonati had called, thought Jud. If they'd missed this breaking news, they'd never have lived it down.

'Right, well the first incident, reported by someone with a very vivid imagination, involved a lady who said she'd seen a headless figure roaming around All Saints Church in the centre of the city. It's been alleged that the shock of such a sight caused her to slip, and she fell and struck her head heavily on the pavement. She received a nasty concussion.

'She was admitted to hospital and is now, I'm pleased to say, on the mend. My officers have interviewed the lady. She is clear that the sequence of events was quite different to those reported. She slipped on the icy pavement. She fell and struck her head. The blow caused her to lose consciousness for a short while, and she is certain that it was during this concussion that she hallucinated. She did *not* see a ghost. She was delusional due to the blow she received to the head.'

More chatter in the room. The reporters were clearly surprised and visibly disappointed. The story of a headless figure loose in the medieval city could have run and run.

'But it doesn't end there,' said Simon. 'May I turn your attention to the incident at Micklegate Bar – and the alleged sighting of a severed head on a spike.

'Well, the elderly man who is alleged to have witnessed the horror is now recovering in hospital after a mild heart attack that caused him to collapse just outside Micklegate Bar last night. We have interviewed him too. He and the doctors seeing to him feel that the vision was most likely to have been a hallucination brought on by a momentary starving of oxygen to the brain, caused by the heart attack. So, just like the lady at All Saints, this man collapsed first and hallucinated second. *Not*, ladies and gentlemen, the other way around. I'm sorry to disappoint you.'

There was a detectable lull in the room now. The accounts seemed boringly plausible.

But Jud and Bex, watching from the hotel room, were not so easily convinced.

'Wait a minute,' said Bex. 'I was there at Micklegate Bar. I saw the head myself. And I wasn't hallucinating. This is all lies!' Tears were appearing at the corners of her eyes, and she was making fists with her hands. Jud could see that the day's events had affected her more than she was admitting.

'Whoa!' he said. 'Slow down! You've had quite a day, Bex. I believe what you told me. But think about it. If Thacker wants to deny it all, that's fine with us. It keeps it off the front page. It means we can carry on without being interrupted. You *know* what the public's like. Look at the crowds we saw at Tyburn when the press got hold of that story.'

'OK, OK!' She sniffed her tears back, stood up and paced the floor. She gave him a stern glance. 'I understand. Just don't tell me to calm down, Jud. There's nothing worse than someone telling you to calm down. It always has the opposite effect.'

'I'm sorry.' Jud knew better than to argue with her any more. It was obvious that the day's events had left her more volatile than usual. The work they did could often leave agents emotionally fired up, or, in Jud's case, occasionally depressed. He should have expected it.

'Right, look at this,' he said, pleased to use the television as a distraction from what could have escalated into a full-blown row. 'The reporters are asking questions now, Bex.'

A woman had stood up in the conference room.

'Sarani Gadde, *York Press*. Mr Thacker, may I ask how it was that we were sent a photograph of the severed head displayed from the bar? I mean, an eyewitness saw it and photographed it, didn't he? How do you explain that?'

Simon did not look remotely fazed by the question. He'd been expecting it. 'Well, Sarani, you work for a paper, you'll be familiar with Photoshop,' he chuckled. 'Yes, there was a good Samaritan, you might say, who found the elderly gentleman and took him to hospital. On the way there, it seems the old man told the driver what he thought he had seen. And the man saw an opportunity. If he could manufacture a picture of the same vision – by digitally superimposing a disembodied head on to a shot of Micklegate Bar – then he could sell it to the press and make a nice tidy sum. After all, he had the old man to corroborate his story that he too had seen the ghostly head with his own eyes. So it was worth a try.

'And it worked a treat, it seems. He dashed home, created the photograph and contacted you guys . . . And you fell for it good and proper.'

The reporter sat down quickly. She felt embarrassed. If this was true, the opportunistic photographer had made a laughing stock of the paper – and of the other reporters in the room.

'Nice cover-up,' said Jud.

'What?'

'Well, I mean, you've gotta admire him. Sounds plausible, doesn't it – a great deal more likely than the *real* truth.'

'And it buys us time, I suppose,' said Bex. 'But who's dreaming this stuff up? I mean, who's pulling the strings? How far up the chain of command does this go?'

'Exactly,' said Jud. 'We're not the only ones trying to keep the hauntings covered up. So who else is behind this?'

'That's why we've got to speak to these witnesses. We've gotta find out if someone's been putting words in their mouths.'

'Of course,' said Jud. 'It's too late to see them now, we'll never get past the nurses. They'll probably both be asleep anyway. And you look done in, Bex. But first thing tomorrow morning we'll go. I can't help thinking the trail begins with them. We need to know if someone is really trying to squash this story, and then the question will be, are they covering it up to stop fear spreading across the city, like us, or because they've got some other reasons we don't know about?'

'Meaning?' said Bex.

'Well,' said Jud, 'I mean, is there someone who'd benefit by allowing the ghosts to flourish unnoticed?'

'That's what we've gotta find out,' said Bex. 'And quickly. The ghosts up here don't seem to have been violent so far. But they've caused some shocks and people are scared. I can feel it on the streets. And as for what happened to me . . . I'm scared, Jud. What if it happens again? And what does this *martyrs caritatis* mean? I don't like it.' A tear was escaping down her cheek.

'Slow down,' said Jud. 'You've had a real shock. Your emotions are still going to be all over the place. It would be weird if they weren't, to be honest. But if it does happen again, I'll be with you this time. I'm not leaving you alone until we get this sorted.'

Bex secretly hoped that would take a while. Such attention was rare.

CHAPTER 31

WEDNESDAY 3 NOVEMBER: 9.00 P.M.

THE CRYPT

It was time for some straight talking. Jason Goode had found it incredible that the police had been so quick to point the finger of blame at the CRYPT, and at Jud in particular. And why had this Braithwaite guy been taken off the case? Goode didn't believe the story about annual leave for one moment.

The only way to get at the truth was to locate someone on the inside.

And Bonati had known exactly who to call.

The lift reached the penthouse suite with a celebratory 'ting' and the officer stepped out.

'Ah, DCI Khan,' said a smiling Bonati, approaching from Jason Goode's suite. 'It's good to see you again. You well?'

Khan smiled. They had so much history now. The circumstances of his last visit here had been so very different. The Tyburn case had been a salutary lesson for Khan. To have kept his job was an unexpected bonus, but it hadn't come without strings.

Bonati and Goode had brokered the deal with M15. Despite his backhander dealings with the disgraced hotelier Lucien Zakis,

Khan would keep his position and even escape a custodial sentence provided he remained sympathetic to the CRYPT cause. If he wanted to be obstructive again, fine – he'd lose his post quicker.

But the Tyburn case had not only taught Khan the dangers of mixing with fraudulent millionaires, it had taught him something else too – that ghosts definitely existed and that the CRYPT was a very necessary and important element in the campaign to understand paranormal activity.

So when the call had come in earlier that evening from his old adversary Giles Bonati, Khan was surprisingly welcoming.

'Good to see you, Professor. I'm well, thanks.'

There was no point in raking over old ground. They both knew it was embarrassing for Khan, and there wasn't time anyway. They'd not invited him here for small talk. He was here for one reason alone – to find out if there was any truth in their suspicions that someone at Scotland Yard was after the CRYPT.

'It takes a rat to know a rat,' Goode had said when Bonati had first made the suggestion over dinner. But he knew all too well that Khan's detective skills were second to none – and it would be good to have them put to better use than serving the evil machinations of Zakis.

They entered the suite and Jason Goode rose to greet Khan. 'Thanks for coming, Detective Chief Inspector. Drink?'

'I don't,' said Khan.

'You *what?*' said Bonati.

'Listen, I wasn't going to mention Tyburn, but I wanted you to know that I saw it as an opportunity to clean up my act. I've ditched the drink and the cigarettes. Even got myself into a gym.'

'Blimey. Do you ever visit it?' said Bonati. He knew Jason Goode was still a fitness fanatic, but it had never rubbed off on the professor. He lived in his head most of the time, and used his body as a way of transporting his brain from one meeting to the next. He put his lean figure down to a high metabolism, and the simple fact that he rarely ate. But he did share Goode's love of curries, and the meal they'd just enjoyed would probably last him a couple of days.

'You're kidding,' laughed Khan. 'What do you think I am, a masochist? I've been once in three months. And then it nearly killed me!'

'Down to business,' said Goode. 'We have a special favour to ask.'

'Well I didn't think you'd invited me here just to enquire about my health.' He could smell the aroma of curry in the room. 'You might have saved me some food,' he said lightly. 'I could murder a good balti.'

'Well if you help us sort out our little problem, you can return here for the biggest balti you've ever had,' said Goode.

'It's a deal.' As if Khan had any choice. He knew full well that both the CRYPT and MI5 could make life difficult for him if ever he declined to help. That was the deal.

'Come on then,' he said, somewhat impatiently. 'Reveal all.'

They filled him in on the strange events at Westminster.

'It certainly sounds odd to me,' he said when they'd finished. 'I'd heard there were some pretty gruesome things kicking off down there, but it's not my territory – the boys at Special Ops 17 handle these sorts of cases. And they're rarely keen to involve us normal plods. I think it's Braithwaite's case, isn't it?'

'Well that's just it,' said Bonati. 'I don't understand it. He was assigned to be the lead investigator on it from the outset. I spoke to him on the telephone only last night. But he's disappeared. Apparently he's gone on holiday. His leave started today.'

'It's not unheard of,' said Khan. 'Even coppers are entitled to time off. Mind you, odd that he was taking on a new case just as he was about to go on holiday. It doesn't really make much sense.'

'That's what we thought,' said Goode.

'So you want me to see if Braithwaite really is on holiday?'

'Yes.'

'Is that it?'

'Well,' said Bonati. 'That and any other fishing around you can do while you're at it!'

CHAPTER 32

WEDNESDAY 3 NOVEMBER: 9.28 P.M.

THE SHAMBLES, YORK

Andy Hayes knew it was late, but there was still so much to do. It wasn't unusual – as a photographer, this was how he often spent his evenings, locked in his study, perfecting digital images from the day's shoots. And it had been a busy day. But as he'd often told his girlfriend, it was easier than in the old days, when, bathed in a red glow with the smell of chemicals wafting up his nose, he'd slosh each photo around in the tray and wait for the image to appear.

Today it was much quicker. It had to be. As the owner of Hayes Photographers, a studio in Britain's most picturesque street, Andy was in demand.

He opened up Aperture 3 on his giant iMac and began the slow but addictive job of refining the many images he'd taken during the day, sourcing the special backgrounds requested and cleaning up blemishes on faces so his customers would be happy.

He'd been staring at the screen for a couple of hours now and his eyes were tiring, but he knew he had to press on. He opened up the next batch – a couple from Washington DC, here on honeymoon. He loved taking shots of honeymooners – you could always see the excitement in their eyes and sense the chemistry between them.

He enlarged the first shot of the young couple, embraced in the usual newly-weds' pose against a smoky grey background.

Then he stopped. And sat back in his chair.

He stared at the screen incredulously.

There, behind the couple, just to the right of the girl, was the hazy outline of a third figure, shorter in stature than the couple, and slender too. It looked for all the world like it was dressed in some kind of priest's costume.

But it wasn't just the old robes that surprised Andy. It was the figure's face.

It was skeletal.

He'd been taking photos most of his adult life. He'd seen everything – all manner of anomalies, where images from one shot had become superimposed on to another. But he'd not taken any shots of this strange figure in priest's clothes. So how could he have become superimposed on to this photo?

And was his face *really* skeletal? Or was it a trick of the light?

A prickly shiver ran up the back of Andy's neck and across his head. His mouth gaped open.

He gazed at the gruesome image, which looked back at him from the screen. The romantic couple, smiling and gazing into each other's eyes. And there, just behind them, the skeletal face, its body wrapped in religious robes. Clear as anything. He wasn't imagining it.

Had someone doctored this image before he'd got to it? Was someone playing a trick on him?

He spun his chair around, expecting to find his girlfriend with a cheeky grin: *Surprise!*

Nothing.

He was suddenly acutely aware of the silence and the setting in which he found himself. With its wattle-and-daub walls and low-beamed ceiling, his studio was dark and atmospheric. He liked it that way. But tonight it was frightening. He gazed through the small shop to the dimly lit street beyond. The half-timbered houses just a few steps opposite, their leaded mullion windows revealing nothing but dark, empty rooms inside. Was he the only one still working on the street tonight?

Dare he turn back and look at the screen? He didn't want to see it again. But he knew he had to.

Slowly he inched the chair around.

And he screamed. It was a pitiful, childlike noise, the kind he used to make as a kid, awoken from a nightmare.

But this scream had not been prompted by the ghostly image on the computer screen. It was the figure emerging from the shadows behind his desk.

The priest was in the room.

CHAPTER 33

THURSDAY 4 NOVEMBER
7.41 A.M.

DEAN COURT HOTEL, YORK

Jud and Bex agreed to meet in the restaurant. The press conference had been on their minds for most of the night, and they were anxious to go to the hospital as early as possible to get the truth from the victims. Were they really mistaken? Could both apparitions just have been figments of their imagination? How come these things had happened on the same night anyway – coincidence?

And, most importantly of all, had someone else been to see them already? Had someone given them a script?

They sat at the same table as the night before. How different the city streets looked this morning. The snow was still clinging on, though much of it had turned to dirty sludge in the morning traffic. Early commuters were trudging their way past the window and delivery vans took turns to park up and offload their wares, to the deafening rattle of the sliding rear doors.

A cyclist tottered past, a winter fleece zipped up to her neck and frozen white knuckles clutching the cold metal handlebars.

And the great Minster, bathed in orange floodlights the night before, was now framed by a dark, ominous storm cloud.

There was a sense of foreboding in the air. You didn't have to be a CRYPT agent to feel it – like many dreary winter days when you kept your head down, got through the grind and looked forward to an evening gawping at the telly with the fire blazing.

'You all right?' said Jud.

'What? Yeah, fine. Why?'

'Well, I mean, after yesterday . . . It must have hit you hard, Bex. Don't underestimate the shock.'

'No,' said Bex, 'I don't think there's any chance of that. I was up most of the night. Felt wired.'

'You should've called me,' said Jud.

'Yeah, right. Would you have woken up? I've heard you snore. I called Grace instead.'

'Yeah?'

'And guess what?'

'What?'

'Luc had a weird episode down in Westminster. Might even have been hypersensing.'

'Really?'

'Yeah. And that's not all. Grace said they both heard something while they were down there. A strange voice, I mean.'

'Not "martyrs caritatis"!' said Jud.

She nodded.

'Bex, we've gotta solve this. There's such a strong connection. But we've got to find out what it all *means.*'

'We will. As soon as we've visited these victims. Can you see any taxis outside?'

Jud strained to look over her shoulder to the street outside. 'No, I'll order one. See you in the lobby in ten, then?'

'Fine,' said Bex. Jud had already ordered, received and devoured a full English breakfast before she'd finished her bowl of fresh fruit. It was the one thing she didn't like about Jud – the way he always rushed his food. One day, when this case was over and they'd been granted some time off, she would treat him to a proper meal out – and she'd force him to slow down and *taste* it.

She didn't hold out much hope, though. The one and only time they'd tried to grab a meal together, it had ended with them being chased at full speed through an underground car park by two assassins on motorbikes.

They just had no luck with meals. Last night was no different. After the text from Bonati, they'd rushed back to Jud's room and watched the news. Then they'd spent an hour trying to make sense of what was going on. The only connection they'd found in all of this was the whispering voice they'd both heard at the hauntings. Online searches using Jud's laptop had unearthed nothing conclusive, just confusing websites in which the word 'caritatis' was buried somewhere, so they'd vowed to go straight to the York Archives Library directly after visiting the hospital to find some answers. There had to be a connection between these hauntings – and experience told them the history books were always the best place to begin.

By the time they'd finished arguing and researching and hypothesising (without much evidence to go on), neither of them were in the mood for room service, so they went without.

Whether it was the press conference, or the events she'd experienced through the day, or a plain lack of food, Bex didn't know, but she'd been tired and short-tempered by the end of the evening. It had not been the welcome Jud had hoped for on his journey up to York.

Even Bex herself, as she'd sloped off to her room at ten thirty, had been disappointed by her mood. Everything would seem better in the morning, Jud had said, trying to hide his disappointment.

The new day had given them renewed energy. There was work to do, and Jud was in one of his 'let's save the world' moods. It wasn't just hunger that had made him rush his breakfast; he was keen to get to those victims, find the truth and figure out how to prevent more ghostly sightings in the city.

He necked his last drop of orange juice and stood up to leave.

'Right, see you in ten,' he said and made for the door.

Two minutes later he was in his bedroom.

He flicked on the television and then dialled reception to book a taxi to take them to the hospital.

'Hello, may I help you?' said the receptionist. 'Hello? Hello? Can I help you?'

Jud just stared at the TV screen in silence.

It was breakfast television, and a heavily made-up presenter had just said, 'And now for the news in your area.'

One second later, and an excited local presenter with a strong Yorkshire accent was announcing the headlines.

'Coming up this morning on *Look North*, our reporter James Baxter is in York, where reports are coming in of another inexplicable sighting. We ask the question, was it ghosts after all?'

There was a quick flash of a man standing in a narrow cobbled street, outside what looked like some kind of photography studio. Jud recognised the architecture and the close proximity of the buildings across the road. It had to be The Shambles.

'Er, sorry,' he said and quickly put the receiver down.

He rang Bex's mobile.

'My room, quick,' he said.

Moments later she was with him, staring in disbelief at the news reporter.

'Yes, thank you, Karen. Well, I'm here in the picturesque and, for the moment, tranquil setting of The Shambles, but I'm afraid the story belies the beauty of this place. Prepare yourself for a shock.'

'Just get on with it!' said Jud aloud, irritated by the reporter's smug introduction and poor attempt to build a sense of drama. This was obviously more exciting for him than the usual local news reports, and he was milking it.

'I'm here to meet Andy Hayes, of Hayes Photography. It's

here that last night Andy received quite a fright. Let's go in and meet him.'

The reporter went inside, followed by the camera crew. They entered a quaint studio of sorts, with a large screen to the right and an assortment of modern-looking stools and chairs. From the back of the room, near a desk, a man was approaching the camera. He looked suitably shattered.

The reporter continued his dramatic build-up.

'So, Andy, I gather that you received quite a shock last night. Tell us about it, please . . .'

Jud and Bex watched as the tired-looking photographer regaled viewers with the events of the night before – the strange image appearing in the background of the photograph, a copy of which he held up to show the reporter, and then the actual visitation by the same figure, right there in his studio.

It made compelling viewing, but Jud and Bex – like all the other viewers watching across Yorkshire – had stopped listening to the man's account. Their attention had been shifted elsewhere.

Behind both men, appearing from the shadows at the back of the studio, was a cloudy shape. It wasn't solid – the plasma from which it was formed was half translucent – but the swirling mist was forming a figure: the figure of a man.

Abruptly the picture pixelated and viewers were returned to the local news studio and a confused-looking presenter.

'Er . . . I'm sorry,' she said, her left hand reaching to her earpiece. 'Er . . . yes, it seems we've lost the picture, I'm afraid. Do forgive us, we'll try to regain the signal and return to York if we can later in the programme. In the meantime, the rest of the morning's news . . .'

Jud and Bex were speechless for a moment. Had everyone else seen what they'd just seen? If this news programme was being transmitted out across North Yorkshire, how many of its residents, waking up and getting themselves ready for work and school, would have been watching it?

It was unimaginable. A real-life haunting, caught on camera and beamed across the region.

Bex spoke first. 'They cut the signal. Someone obviously saw what we saw and stopped the transmission feed.'

Jud was nodding in agreement. 'And thank goodness. It's the last thing we need if we're going to get to the truth in this place. A public showing of a ghost is not exactly going to help a secret investigation, is it?'

'No. So do you think that was the figure this photographer guy was going on about? Is it the same one, do you think?'

'Well, yeah. Don't you?'

'I think so,' said Bex. 'If it wasn't on live TV, being transmitted to thousands of people across the area, I'd have found it quite funny. I mean, two guys discussing a ghost, and then it appears for us to see but they don't even notice.'

'Yeah,' said Jud, smiling. 'It's behind you!'

But their smiles were fleeting. They both knew full well that before the transmission had been cut they would not have been the only viewers to notice the figure. There would have been others. Many others. And all those people would now flock to The Shambles for a chance to see the ghost. All that human fear and excitement flowing through the street – entering the haunted rooms and filling them with energy.

How could they investigate this discreetly now? How could they take fair readings?

But Jud was in no mood for despondency. The sighting had only strengthened his resolve to get this cracked, and quickly.

'What do we do now?' said Bex.

'We carry on,' said Jud. 'We interview those witnesses. We find out who's silenced them. And why.'

'But what about the ghost? What about the—'

'Don't worry, we'll go straight there after we've seen those people. There's no need to rush round there now. If the ghost was violent, it would have killed last night while it had the chance

– but it didn't. I think it's here for a different reason. In any case, the place will be heaving with crowds after everyone saw it on the telly. The Shambles will be like Piccadilly Circus. I say we wait a while and visit discreetly later. Then we can interview the owner properly and take readings.'

As they left the room and made for the reception, Jud's phone beeped. It was Bonati. Jud knew exactly what he wanted. Answers. And right now, they had none.

Bonati would have to wait. At least for an hour.

CHAPTER 34

THURSDAY 4 NOVEMBER
7.58 A.M.

PEARMAN STREET, LAMBETH

DCI Khan was suspicious. The uncanny knack he had of sniffing out a scandal or a cover-up had been in overdrive during the night. Sitting at his faithful computer in his office, surrounded by half-drunk cups of coffee and empty Pot Noodles, he'd read as many notes as he could on the Westminster case, but there was so little to go on. Every investigation, no matter how small, had file notes that were constantly updated. Though it wasn't his department, Khan knew how to access everywhere. But there was surprisingly little on this case. Just a few patchy details about some lower-ranking officers attending a call at Westminster, and interviewing a suspect after reports of an engineer going missing. Khan saw no mention of any intruder earlier in the day.

And why was there nothing from Braithwaite? No notes, no records of interviews or telephone calls. Khan knew the DCS had been involved in the case from the start – he'd contacted Bonati after all. But there was no evidence of his involvement.

Questions to the few colleagues he could raise at that time of night had ended in dead ends too. The answer everyone had given was the same: 'I heard he was on holiday.'

He'd tried to call Braithwaite at home, and on his mobile, but had received no response. It was perfectly possible that he'd gone away, and it was equally possible that he'd turned his phone off – who could blame him? Khan knew what it felt like to have your holiday disturbed.

But something didn't feel right.

He'd retrieved the DCS's home address from the records, and after returning home for the briefest sleep on record, he'd headed over to Pearman Street first thing.

The lights weren't on. It didn't look like anyone was at home. So maybe he was away? Suddenly Khan felt stupid for worrying so much.

He tried the bell.

Nothing.

He turned to leave, but decided to just try the door knocker instead. Maybe the bell was faulty.

He held the large brass knocker and brought it down on the green-painted door.

He was surprised to find that it swung open. Had it been ajar all night? Or had Braithwaite left in a hurry that morning – perhaps he'd not pulled it shut behind him. Still, seemed odd.

Tentatively he pushed the door further. The hallway looked normal. The phone was on the neatly polished mahogany side table. But was that Braithwaite's wallet and keys next to it?

Now that *was* odd.

Why would Braithwaite go away and leave those behind?

'John?' shouted Khan. 'Are you there?'

Silence.

He walked past the living room. Everything looked normal. No sign of any burglary – and what burglar would miss the wallet, anyway?

'John?' he shouted again.

Nothing.

After sweeping through the kitchen and dining room at the

rear of the house, he returned to the hallway and climbed the stairs. There was sweat forming on his palms and he became aware of that familiar wrench in his ulcerated stomach. Something had pricked his nerves in this place. The house just didn't feel right. He'd been hanging around with the CRYPT agents too long, he thought to himself, and dismissed a growing sense of foreboding.

At the top of the stairs he began trying the rooms. Braithwaite clearly lived alone – just spare rooms and a study. The final door led to a master bedroom at the front of the house.

He peered round the door and saw Braithwaite. Fast asleep.

He walked around the bed towards the window and was about to open the curtains in an effort to stir him when he noticed something on the carpet.

Was that a stain of some kind?

He turned and stared at Braithwaite.

The bullet hole was clean, just a small puncture wound on his right temple, but a steady stream of blood had leaked over the white linen and dripped on to the floor, forming a giant congealed puddle on the beige carpet.

CHAPTER 35

THURSDAY 4 NOVEMBER:
8.28 A.M.

YORK GENERAL HOSPITAL

Jud and Bex ran into the hospital foyer. A few quick minutes at the desk was all it took.

'I'm sorry, young man,' said the receptionist. 'I know the guy you're referring to. We all do. He became a bit of a celebrity, I can tell you. And the woman too. We've had reporters and police officers and you name it coming in to interview them. But they've gone, I'm afraid.'

'They've what?' Jud and Bex said together.

'They've both been discharged. There were taxis for them. Took them home.'

'So they've recovered, then?'

'I don't know. I'm not their doctor, am I? But if a patient gets discharged, it's usually because they've recovered, don't you think?' she said, sarcastically.

Who were these stroppy teenagers anyway? She was getting fed up with their pushy questions.

'Can you give us their addresses?' said Jud as politely as he could manage. The woman's attitude was beginning to bug him.

'Certainly not!' she said.

There was nothing for it; Jud knew what he had to do. His MI5 card was in his wallet – where it was supposed to remain except in emergencies. But this was an emergency. He flashed it in front of the receptionist and told her that all it would take was a phone call and she'd be forced to cooperate.

'OK, OK,' she said, unable to hide her surprise. MI5? They looked more like school kids, this pair.

'Look,' she continued. 'We don't keep patients' personal records down here. You'll have to go up to the wards where they were treated. You'll need to ask the staff up there.'

'And go through the same rigmarole with them? Spend another ten minutes trying to persuade them to cooperate, you mean?' said Jud rudely. 'Sorry. No time for that. You'll have to make the necessary phone calls from here. And quickly.'

'Oh, and can you book a taxi for us as well?' Bex added. 'Same company if you can. We'll have some questions for them.'

Now the woman looked angry, but she knew very well that the situation was rapidly falling out of her control. And they seemed authentic enough – you only had to look at the determination in their faces, even if they *were* young.

With a roll of her eyes she picked up the receiver and made the calls. A few moments later she handed them a piece of paper with a couple of addresses scribbled on it, and the name of a taxi company.

'There you are,' she said reluctantly.

'Thank you,' said Bex.

A couple of minutes later a taxi drew up outside. They could see it was a different company.

'Bex, tell the driver to wait a second, will you?' Jud ran inside again.

'It's a different company!' he said to the receptionist, who looked anything but pleased to see him again.

'What?' she said, sounding irritated.

'We asked you to use the *same* taxi company as the one that picked up the patients last night – but it's not.'

The receptionist looked bored. 'What? Oh, yeah,' she said casually. 'Well they weren't picking up the phone. Couldn't get hold of 'em, could I?'

'But we've questions to ask them,' said Jud angrily.

'So? Call 'em yourself. Look, I've had enough of—'

'Oh forget it!' interrupted Jud, heading for the doors again. He'd try and call them himself from the taxi.

Twenty minutes later, and after several failed attempts to raise the other taxi company, Jud and Bex were pulling up outside the house of Fiona Peters.

Her husband came to the door.

'Yes?'

'We'd like to speak to Fiona Peters, please. Your wife?'

David looked puzzled, and then worried.

'Fi? She's in hospital. What do you want? Who are you? Not bloody reporters!' He went to shut the door, but Jud managed to place his foot in the way. The door bounced off his boot, nearly hitting David in the face.

'Hey! What do you think you're playing at, mate? What the hell is this? I said who are you, and what do you want with my wife?'

'It's OK,' said Bex kindly. 'We're from the police. May we come in for a moment?'

'Oh yeah? Got some badges, then?'

It was Bex's turn. She flashed her MI5 card in David's face. It gave no details about the CRYPT – just the official crest and the words SECURITY SERVICES across the middle. Her name and photograph were there too. It was obviously the real thing.

'And you?' he said to Jud, still not fully convinced.

He showed his card. 'Look, sir. I have to tell you that your wife was discharged from hospital late last night. Are you saying she's not here?'

David went pale. 'What? She's left? Where's she gone? Who went to collect her?'

'Apparently she was collected by a taxi driver. I think the hospital assumed you had arranged it.

Bex shot Jud a stern look. She was angry that he'd chosen to break the news like this, on the doorstep. Typical Jud. Always impatient to get to the truth.

'I can see this is very worrying for you, Mr Peters,' she said. 'But may we come in and talk to you? We're here to help, but we'll need to ask you some questions. I'm sure there's a reasonable explanation. There usually is. But first we need to find out when you last saw her and what kind of state she was in.'

David was shaking his head. Beyond him, through the hallway, Bex could see two boys dressed in school uniform.

'Who is it, Dad?' said one. 'Is it about Mum?'

David turned quickly and said, 'Er . . . no, Jason. Don't worry. It's nothing, son. Go and get your things ready for school. I'll be up in a minute.'

He opened the door wider and gestured to them to come in.

But Jud remained outside and beckoned to Bex for a quick word.

'Look, it's a waste of time if we both do this. We need to call Bonati as soon as possible and get a plan together. I'll go over to the old man's house now and meet you back at the hotel in an hour.'

'OK,' agreed Bex

Jud disappeared down the drive to the waiting taxi as Bex nervously followed David down the hall, wondering what on earth she could say to comfort him.

CHAPTER 36

THURSDAY 4 NOVEMBER:
10.02 A.M.

DEAN COURT HOTEL, YORK

Jud walked up the steps into the hotel foyer. Bex was sitting in one of the leather armchairs waiting for him.

'Well?' she said.

He shook his head. 'Got there. No one in the house. Spoke to the woman next door. She said the old boy was in hospital. I said he'd been discharged and was supposed to have come home. She said no one had been home last night or this morning. And she looked like the kind who'd know. A real curtain-twitcher. Up at the window at the slightest noise, keeping tabs on everyone. If she says he hasn't been home, then he hasn't been home.'

'This is weird,' said Bex. 'Mr Peters confirmed that his wife hadn't told him she was coming home. In fact last time they spoke on the phone, she'd given no indication she was coming out. He'd presumed it might be later today.'

'And what did he make of the haunting? Did he believe she'd seen something?'

'He wasn't sure. But he said it was unlike her to have made something up for attention. He said she isn't like that. If she said she saw a ghost then he thinks she must have done. Apparently she seemed really shocked when it first happened.'

'And now,' said Jud, 'the two key witnesses have gone missing.'

'Vanished.'

'What about the third one? This person who was supposed to have picked up the old man and carted him off to hospital. The one they said had made up the photograph and sold it to the press. We need to get to see him.'

'But how?' said Bex. 'We don't even know who he is.'

'The police will know. We have to get over to Police HQ and ask some questions. They might not even know about the missing people yet.'

'Oh, they will now,' said Bex. 'Mr Peters was ringing as I left. I told him to leave it to us, but he wanted to report it himself. Said he'd not rest till every police officer in York was looking for her.'

'Who can blame him?' said Jud.

'So is it The Shambles next, or the York Archives Library?' said Bex.

'I think we need to call Bonati before we do anything else – fill him in.'

'Excuse me, Mr Lester?' A hotel receptionist had come over, clutching a piece of paper.

'Yes?'

'There's a telephone message for you.'

'Ah, talk of the devil!' he said to Bex as he took the paper. 'Hang on,' he said, reading the message. 'It's not Bonati. It's from that politician, you know, the one we saw on the news. Thacker. Said he was the York MP, didn't he?'

'Yeah. What does he want?' said Bex.

'How do I know?' said Jud. He rose and walked outside with his mobile.

A few minutes later he returned, looking confused.

'Well?' said Bex anxiously.

'He says he wants to meet me. This afternoon. Says he can help – pull some strings and give us the support we need.'

'Great.'

'It's his city. He sounded quite concerned, actually. Said he's worried the press are going to whip this thing up even more and get the public terrified.'

'Well that's what they do, Jud. Do you know what's in the paper this morning? Have you seen one?' said Bex.

'When? Haven't had a chance! Have you?'

'No,' she said, rising and walking to the reception desk, where there was a pile of complimentary *York Press* copies.

The front page read: WOMAN ATTACKED BY GHOSTLY HANDS.

There was a photograph of a middle-aged woman standing in what looked like a church, and a smaller shot of a large pair of metal gauntlets and a sword.

'This is mad,' said Jud as Bex flashed the front page at him. 'The city's alive with it. It's almost like it was planned. There's a link, Bex. There always is. There's a connection between these hauntings. We just haven't found it yet.'

'Well why don't you go to The Shambles and I'll do All Saints? Then we can meet at the Archives Library and compare notes. Hopefully find a connection at last.'

Jud was shaking his head. 'No, we can't take the risk, Bex. I think you should give the hauntings a miss today.'

'Don't be ridiculous.' Bex was getting angry. Residents in the hotel were glancing over. Jud recognised some of the faces from the restaurant last night. It was obvious they weren't impressed.

He tried to keep his voice down in the hope that Bex would too. 'Listen,' he whispered. 'Neither of us know why, but there's something here in the city that is affecting you, I'm sure of it. Something's reaching out to you. Look at what happened at Micklegate – and on the bridge. I mean, you were delirious, Bex.

Who knows what'll happen at the church. I can't let you take that risk.'

'You can't *let* me? Oh, so you're assuming authority now, are you? Banning me from taking readings and visiting sites?' snapped Bex, refusing to take Jud's cue and speak in hushed tones. 'Or are you taking me off the case completely, *boss?*'

'No. That's not what I'm saying, Bex, and you know it. It's just that since you arrived here, your senses have gone into overdrive. Surely you can see that. Don't you want to stay safe?'

'Of course I do,' she said in a resigned tone. She knew Jud was right. She had indeed felt strange ever since that incident at Micklegate, and the weird experience in the hotel room, and then the terrifying episode on the bridge. 'But I'm not going to stand back for long. I'm not just a researcher, Jud.'

'Bex, I know that. But you understand how important researching is. It's not like you'll be doing nothing. You've got lots to go on now and so you should be able to find out some real connections. I'll join you there as soon as I can.'

She misinterpreted his softer tone. 'Don't patronise me, Jud. I'm an agent too, remember that. The same agent who has saved your life in the past. Or had you forgotten?'

'Of course I hadn't. No one, least of all me, is saying you're being cowardly about this, Bex! But I've just got a funny feeling that the spirits are talking to you particularly. I don't know why, any more than you do, but we've got to keep you away from the sites that are seeing most paranormal activity. Just for today at least.'

Bex looked unhappy about it, but deep down she knew it was the right thing. She sat down again. 'OK, so what about the missing witnesses? What are we going to do about them?'

'Well, Peters is calling the York police. But you could call Bonati. He'll brief MI5 and take it from there.'

He stood up. 'I'm going to get the instruments from my room. I dread to think how many people are going to be flocking to these sites today, given the press coverage, but I've gotta try. I'll come and see you before I go to see Thacker.'

He stood up and went off to his room.

Bex remained in the quiet corner of the lobby and called Bonati as agreed.

'Sir?'

'Ah, Bex. I was just about to call you. Are you safe? Are you OK?'

'Not you as well, sir! I'm fine,' she said.

'What?'

'Oh, nothing. I was just calling in to give you another update.'

'Yes, I've heard from Vorzek about your experience at Micklegate.'

'That's nothing,' she said. 'I haven't told you what happened on Ouse Bridge.'

She filled the professor in on the latest details and he listened patiently: the bridge incident, the missing witnesses, the ghost in The Shambles, and this mystery of the moving gloves and sword at All Saints.

Bonati interrupted her when she got to the witnesses.

'So you say they were discharged from hospital but never made it home? They're actually missing?'

'That's right. We've checked both addresses and they've not been seen since last night.'

'This is serious, Bex. Leave it with me. I'll get on to my contacts at MI5 and the Met. We've got to find those people, and fast. They may hold the key to all of this. Call me again later. You focus on the hauntings, leave the missing persons to me. And Bex?'

'Yeah?'

'Stay safe.'

'I'll try, sir.'

She rang off just as Jud was coming down from his room.

'Bonati?' he said.

She nodded.

'Well?'

'He couldn't believe the witnesses had disappeared. He'd not heard. Says he'll get on to his contacts straight away. He wants us to focus on the hauntings now – and find some answers.'

'That's exactly what we're going to do, Bex. Bonati won't let us back into the CRYPT until we've solved this!'

He made for the door. Bex watched him leap down the steps and head off in the direction of The Shambles. His dark hair was matted and greasy, there was stubble on his chin and his jeans and jacket were crinkled from living out of a suitcase – but he still looked good. How do some guys do that? she thought.

He was so energetic. So focused. She'd never met anyone quite like him. Not even the other agents at the CRYPT – no one was as intensely focused or as hard-working as Jud.

All he ever talked about was work, if he spoke at all. He rarely sat around long enough to talk to anyone, not socially. No one knew much about him; or at least Bex didn't. He was an agent – that was it. How, when or why he had joined the agency, no one really stopped to question. It just seemed like the natural place for him to be.

But occasionally, just occasionally, she'd see through the tough, dynamic exterior, past the secrecy and the stand-offish reputation, and look deeper inside him.

Why was he so intriguing? Bex couldn't work it out.

Maybe it was this sense of mystery that she liked most about him.

CHAPTER 37

THURSDAY 4 NOVEMBER: 10.07 A.M.

THE CRYPT

'Will someone tell me what's going on? And, more to the point, what we're doing about it.'

Jason Goode looked mad. It was unusual for him to lose his composure, but then it was unusual for a CRYPT case to be changing so quickly, and involve so many hauntings, without anyone having even so much as an inkling as to what was behind it all. Bonati had filled him in on the news from Bex and Jud in York – and things were getting stranger by the minute.

And now this news from Khan. Braithwaite had been murdered in his bed.

Bonati shifted uncomfortably in his chair. The night he'd spent on the plastic furniture in Scotland Yard's waiting room was having repercussions: his back had seized up.

'Look, Jason, I've got as many agents on this as I can spare.'

'Yeah? And what are they doing? Do you know? What have they found?'

'Well, er . . .'

'Exactly.'

Khan, seated at the other side of the lavish penthouse office, tried to avert his gaze towards the window. He took no pleasure in witnessing this spat between the two CRYPT leaders. He shared Goode's frustrations, but he knew very well how difficult this case was becoming. Precisely because it spanned two cities and the hauntings seemed to be happening virtually every hour with no obvious pattern or connection.

Relaying the news of Braithwaite's brutal murder had only served to fuel tempers in the room. But they had to know.

'Look,' said Bonati, wincing again as he repositioned himself in the chair, 'we have to separate fact from fiction; we've got to distinguish between what the public is being told and what's really going on here. We need to know who's lying and for what purpose.'

Khan chipped in. 'Believe me, Professor, I've got the top people working on this back at the Yard. The killing of any police officer, let alone such a senior one, is about as serious as it can get. Braithwaite's house is now being pored over by forensics, as is the basement at Westminster. And we've got the place surrounded by officers from Special Ops. It's safe as houses now.'

'And what about tomorrow?' said Bonati.

'Tomorrow?' said Khan.

'The State Opening! Only the day when the entire parliamentary body, and the royal family, and every dignitary you can pull out of the woodwork will be descending on Westminster. And meanwhile, we've got a ghost still on the loose underground, looking for his next victim I've no doubt.'

'Well that's just it,' said Khan, looking red-faced. 'The House Authorities – and God knows they seem to own the place – are saying there's *no* ghost.'

'Well you'd expect them to say that publicly, wouldn't you,' said Goode. 'But privately?'

'Publicly they're trying not to say anything at all – at least for the moment. Trying to bury the story until after the State

Opening, I guess. And privately it's the same. They're denying there's any paranormal activity at work.'

Bonati was incredulous. 'But I was there!' he said. 'I saw what happened to the officer. And the civil servants were there too. I met Black Rod down in the basement! How can they say there's no ghost?'

Khan shook his head. 'They're saying it was the work of a human, not a ghost, Professor.'

'Oh, come on! Don't tell me – Jud, I suppose!'

'No, no. They know it couldn't have been Jud. Quite why he was embroiled in it at the beginning I don't know – though I mean to find out, believe me. But they're saying there's nothing paranormal going on down there. No ghosts.'

'But the engineer!' shouted Bonati. 'The one Luc and Grace found. He was half dragged into the wall, for goodness' sake! How could a human have possibly done that to him?'

'According to my men on the inside,' said Khan, 'the House Authorities, including Black Rod, haven't seen the engineer.'

'They *what?*'

'No one from the House has seen his body. The place was sealed off by Special Ops just after you left with your agents. No civilians have been allowed down there. The order came from the very top for complete secrecy.'

'From the very top?' said Goode. 'You're talking about the PM, yeah?'

'No. As far as I can tell – and you have to understand I'm not on the inside here – Special Ops are getting their instructions direct from the Police Minister.'

'Simon Thacker?' said Bonati.

'Exactly.'

'Who, I assume,' said Goode, 'is so bloody paranoid about everything running smoothly tomorrow that he doesn't want to upset the apple cart now. Typical politician. Doesn't want his own head to roll if there's a scandal. Wants to play it down, I suppose.'

'Yeah, I guess,' said Khan. 'Let's face it, if this thing gets into the public domain – I mean a security breach like this – who'll take the rap? It'll run all the way to the top of the Met and beyond – and that means the minister, ultimately.'

Jason Goode was staring out of the window now. The great skyline of the city unfolded before him – below him. Offices and banks and government buildings. All filled with upwardly mobile, ambitious people. 'It's always the same with you Brits,' he said. 'It's all about ass-covering, isn't it. I mean, just protecting your own jobs!'

'Whoa, slow down there, Jason!' snapped Bonati. 'Let's not paint every one of us with the same brush, shall we? We're not all just concerned about our own careers.'

'No?' said Goode. 'Just the politicians, then.'

'But this doesn't get us anywhere, does it,' said the professor, who was rapidly getting fed up with this squabbling. His old friend was doing his usual trick of throwing his weight around, trying to be 'hands on' and involved. He did that whenever he'd been away for a while. He always came back and wanted to show them all who was boss, and how much he cared, before jetting off again and leaving them all to it. 'We need to get everyone together, and fast,' he said.

'You're right, Giles. This afternoon, is that feasible?'

Bonati nodded. 'Should be. We've got a dozen cases on the go at the moment, but this one is slipping out of our hands and we need to get a grip.' He turned to Khan. 'What do you think? Will the investigation wait until then? Nothing's going to happen between now and then, is it?'

'I don't see how it can – we've got more officers at Parliament than they've got politicians. The place is bomb-proof.'

'Yes,' said Bonati. 'But is it ghost-proof? That's the question.'

'OK,' said Jason. 'I've got appointments now, but I wanna be in on this. So let's meet at three. Get hold of Jud and Bex in York. We'll patch them into the video link. Get Luc and Grace up here too. They came with you to the basement the second time – they should help shed some light on this. And bring Vorzek too. She's got a good, logical brain.'

Khan rose to leave the room.

'And you, Khan. Don't go too far. We need you on this too! Hey, after Tyburn, you're one of us now. You're on the side of the good guys!'

'At last,' said Bonati drily.

The phone rang on Goode's giant glass desk.

'Yeah? OK, tell them I'm coming.' He turned to the two men. 'Sorry, gentlemen, I've gotta go. See you this afternoon. And believe me . . . I want some answers.'

CHAPTER 38

THURSDAY 4 NOVEMBER: 10.18 A.M.

HOUSES OF PARLIAMENT, LONDON

Brigadier Geoffrey Farlington marched purposefully across Central Lobby and on towards the Lower Waiting Room, which housed the committee stairs. Excited chatter echoed up to the vaulted stone ceilings that towered over the heads of the politicians, making them look tiny and insignificant. The larger–than–life statues of former prime ministers and elderly statesmen peered down in disappointment at their twenty-first-century counterparts.

The place was buzzing with activity as usual, but there was an extra sense of urgency about the movements and conversations that filled the great octagonal chamber at the centre of the Palace of Westminster. MPs, peers and House Authorities all anxiously preparing for the great pomp and circumstance the next day would bring.

There was no other occasion like the State Opening of Parliament. It was the single day in the year when the Queen, her lords, MPs, senior judges and foreign diplomats all assembled in one place to symbolise the start of the next parliamentary session.

The air was alive with expectation already. Various parties were rehearsing their duties and speeches. No one, least of all the

Black Rod, wanted to see mistakes occur. The whole thing had to be run with military precision.

Once the Queen arrived at the Sovereign's Entrance, climbed the Royal Staircase lined with soldiers in full ceremonial dress, and entered the Robing Room to don her state robes and crown, the day would have begun and nothing could stop it. Get the planning wrong and you risked breaking a tradition centuries old.

Black Rod, like other senior members of the House Authorities, would not tolerate mistakes – in terms of organisation, presentation and the ceremonial procedure. It had to work like clockwork. Her Majesty expected nothing less.

The incidents underground had caused much activity, yet the peers and MPs were going about their business blissfully unaware of the frantic work being done beneath them. There was a particularly heavy police presence noticeable at ground level too – officers at just about every turn – but few people questioned it; everyone knew it was quite normal to raise security levels in the run-up to the State Opening.

The brigadier understood the need for secrecy. A scandal like this could rock the very foundations of the place and would undoubtedly cause the postponement of the State Opening. With such a breach of security, there would be those who'd doubtless say it was no longer safe to have every aspect of the British constitution in one place. They'd call to change the tradition, modify it, like everything else in the country.

It had always seemed risky, but tradition was a strong driving force. There was no way Black Rod would allow the situation underground to jeopardise the plans above ground.

But even the brigadier had been surprised by the level of secrecy. Since the body of the police officer had been found in the large storage area buried deep underground, that section of the basement had been sealed off – to everyone. Even to him and his security staff.

The only personnel allowed down there were members of the Special Operations 17.

Black Rod had been informed there was a second corpse down there. The body of engineer Neil Jones had been located apparently close to where the officer was found. But neither he nor his staff had seen it.

All that was coming out of Special Ops was that a second corpse had been discovered and forensics required total isolation so the crime scene was not contaminated or altered in any way.

What Black Rod had found particularly strange was the blanket ban on any talk of ghosts. The Police Minister, Simon Thacker, had said that he and his senior officers at the Met were now convinced that the paranormal could be ruled out. This was the work of humans only. The Palace of Westminster was not, and had never been, haunted.

The brigadier remembered so vividly the security guard bursting into yesterday's meeting saying that he'd seen a ghost. Was he mistaken?

Apparently so.

But if the police were willing to put a lid on rumours of ghosts in the place, then so was he. There was enough to worry about as it was, and a spectral cloud hanging over the place the day before the State Opening was exactly what he didn't want.

He climbed the staircase leading to the labyrinth of committee rooms and offices that occupied so much of the palace. The serenity and majesty of the great state rooms and lobbies on the ground floor stood in stark contrast to the modern, ordinary-looking committee rooms that ran the length and breadth of the place upstairs.

Locating the room he'd reserved for the morning's meeting with staff, Black Rod opened the door and swept in.

'Sorry I'm late, ladies and gentlemen.'

He offered no excuse. He didn't need to. This was his meeting, his staff, and with Simon Thacker caught up on some urgent business in York, at last he would have the planning committee to himself without the meddling minister.

'So, let's go through each department in turn, shall we?'

They romped through the agenda, with each representative from the various departments proudly claiming that all preparations were in place and everything was on schedule. When it came to the turn of the security chiefs, the atmosphere became understandably tense. Officers from the Royalty and Diplomatic Protection Department, including some from the Royalty Protection Squad and the Special Escort Group, were in combative mood.

The senior SO17 officer from Scotland Yard had received his brief from the Police Minister by phone that morning. He wasn't going to be drawn from the script that Thacker had given him. Everything was under control. It was true that serious crimes had been committed in the basement, and investigations were ongoing, but the crime scene had been sealed off, and Special Ops officers were stationed throughout the building. Police presence in the place was the heaviest it had ever been. The perpetrator – whoever he might be – had clearly fled the premises. And the building was now safe. Additional officers had also been drafted in to assist with the usual security checks and searches that took place at all entrances and exits across the site.

The place was a fortress.

'But what about the Yeomen of the Guard?' said Black Rod to the officers when they'd finished their boasting about how bomb-proof the building was. 'How will they be able to carry out the traditional search first thing in the morning if part of the basement is sealed off?'

Some of the officers rolled their eyes and smirked.

The four-hundred-year-old tradition, carried out every year since the days of the Gunpowder Plot, saw members of the Yeomen of the Guard conduct a ceremonial search of Parliament prior to the Queen's arrival. Very few of the real security forces took it seriously, it was just another bizarre custom during a whole day of pomp and ceremony.

'Brigadier, with so many real security forces in the building, it is unlikely the ceremonial Yeomen will uncover any surprises!' said an officer from Special Ops.

'OK. But you know how Her Majesty is particular about these traditions. She will ask me if the Yeomen have searched the place and I shall need to tell her they have. I cannot exactly say, "Well, Your Majesty, they've searched some of the basement, but not the part directly beneath you, ma'am."'

'Because that part is sealed off with a dozen armed police with live rounds standing by,' said an officer. 'You can tell her that!'

'And the Queen's speech, Brigadier?' said one of the civil servants, keen to avert another head-to-head between the House staff and the security forces. 'All set, are we? PM happy?'

'Yes, I think so.'

'Any surprises this year?'

'Oh come on, Jonathan,' said Black Rod. 'You know as well as I do that the entire thing has already been dissected in the press. But no, not really, from what I read over breakfast. There's the thorny issue of the wretched Act of Settlement. Everyone was so sure it was going to be repealed this year – the new Bill was going to reverse it, but it's been thrown out.'

'Pity,' said another member of staff. 'I mean, why on earth that Act has been allowed to continue all these years, I don't know!'

The 1701 Act of Settlement had always been a controversial issue in Parliament, to say the least. There were many MPs who thought it was out of date and permitted the kind of prejudice normally illegal in Britain to continue unnoticed.

It was a three-hundred-year-old law that excluded any Roman Catholic from succeeding to the throne. Under the Act, any Protestant in line to the throne who converted to Catholicism, or even married a Roman Catholic, could not become king or queen.

The Act had come close to being revoked several times over the years, but somehow it had always remained. A new Bill had been talked about recently, which would see the anti-Roman Catholic law scrapped once and for all, but it had not been popular enough to make it into the Queen's speech for the next Parliamentary session, which meant the Act lived to fight another day. Again. Quite why the MPs never found it in themselves to scrap the Act no one knew. They all criticised it publicly, but when it came to voting, they lost their bottle it seemed. Of course, some staff at the House, including Black Rod, harboured suspicions that there was always pressure from key Protestant MPs and perhaps even members of the royal household.

No one was immune to persuasion, it seemed.

'I agree,' said the brigadier. 'It does seem strange that the Act has survived. It's odd, isn't it? I mean, we think we live in a modern and fair society, and yet in many ways we still don't.'

There were several people in the room who saw the irony in what the brigadier had said, given that he enjoyed the title of Gentleman Usher of the Black Rod, and all the privileges the office brought. But they decided that now was not the time, and Farlington looked in no mood for jokes.

The sordid business below ground had clearly unsettled him. As the person responsible for the day-to-day running of the House of Lords, the last twenty-four hours had been particularly stressful for him, given that the macabre incidents had happened just below the upper chamber.

'Will the Police Minister be joining us?' said Janice, the newest member of Black Rod's team and the one who'd asked so many questions at the previous gathering. 'I thought after yesterday's meeting he was taking a special interest in all this, Brigadier. Giving us his personal attention. That didn't last long, then!'

'I think the minister is a very busy man, Janice,' said Black Rod, giving her the kind of look a head teacher gives an errant pupil. 'Well, if there's nothing else, may I suggest we adjourn and agree to meet back here later this afternoon for the final run-through – give us a chance to dot any i's and cross any t's. I hope very much we shall be joined at that juncture by a member of the Cabinet, but we'll see. What shall we say: six o'clock, everyone?'

They nodded obligingly, as if they had a choice.

CHAPTER 39

THURSDAY 4 NOVEMBER:
10.39 A.M.

THE SHAMBLES, YORK

The Shambles was a hive of activity. Television vans and police cars lined the kerbside in Petergate and Colliergate. The ancient cobbles heaved under the strain of so much stationary traffic. You couldn't move for people, either.

The television coverage, the newspaper articles and, most of all, the city's grapevine of gossip and scandal had combined to create huge interest in this ancient corner of York. At the Caffè Nero on the corner of St Andrewgate, business was booming.

But Jud had not made it to The Shambles. Not yet.

He was still sitting on a bench just a few minutes' walk from the place.

Walking from the hotel earlier, he'd taken a detour around the Minster gardens, keen to relieve those happier times when he and his school friend Charlie would sit eating ice cream in the shadow of the great cathedral. And then on towards the walled garden outside the Treasurer's House. The cosy courtyard where they used to sit and scoff hog-roast baguettes and caramel slices from the shop around the corner. It seemed like yesterday.

He recalled one summer when his parents actually came to

York. They'd been in London at some IT conference. Jud had been shipped off to Charlie's place up north at the beginning of the holidays, but his father had decided they'd surprise him. Jud could vividly remember his phone call from the train. And then he and Charlie running across town to the station. Standing on the bridge over Platform 5. Watching the train pull in. Seeing his parents again – for the first time in three months.

He gazed at the Treasurer's House. Nothing had changed. It still looked so beautiful, so peaceful. He glanced up at the great Minster beyond. Solid. Steadfast.

If only his life had remained so constant.

His mother was gone. His father was a virtual stranger these days, and Charlie, his closest friend at school, had been forbidden from contacting Jud ever again after his conviction. What parent would allow their son to mix with a murderer?

It would never be possible to see Charlie again, just as he could never see any of the old school crowd. As far as they were concerned, Jamie was still inside a young offenders' institution, where he would remain for many years yet.

If only he could see the gang again. Find out what they were doing now. Catch up on old times. Swap stories. But he was a nonentity now; he didn't exist. No history, no family, no friends – save the fellow agents at the CRYPT. It had all been obliterated.

He'd been so looking forward to returning to York. But why? Sitting in the same old haunts as before, he knew now the error of coming here. He'd vowed once never to go back to any of his favourite places ever again. He should've kept to it.

It was just too painful.

He was, and would always be, a ghost – like the spirits he investigated, stuck forever in the realm between life and death. He was alive – and yet he had no life. He was visible, but invisible. His past obliterated.

He suddenly felt like he was floating. All at sea. We anchor ourselves by the friends we keep, the stories we tell and the memories we share. But he had none of that.

With a deep sigh that sent cold air rattling down his throat and brought a shiver inside, Jud rose from the wet bench and left the walled garden. His black jeans and black padded jacket cut a sharp contrast against the snow-covered walls.

A few moments later he was trudging through the sludge along Petergate. People passed him but he felt he wasn't there. He saw friends, couples, lovers. Laughing and joking, stopping to buy gifts for families back home.

The police cars and television vans came into view as he turned the corner.

The press conference held by Thacker at the police head-quarters in Fulford had obviously done nothing to curb people's enthusiasm and excitement. Or fear. The place was crowded already.

And it was obvious to Jud, walking through the city's streets, that there was real tension in the air. This was exactly what he'd hoped to avoid. Such a concentrated release of emotion in one area would only serve to energise whatever spirits were still roaming the streets of the city. Who knew what the day would bring?

He pushed his way through the crowds towards the world-famous Shambles, hiding in the corner of the square. It really was like something out of a history textbook. The buildings didn't seem real – more like an artist's clichéd impression of what a half-timbered street might have looked like in Tudor times. The wattle-and-daub frontages, the narrow cobbled road squeezed between them, its crude drainage system still visible down the centre. In places, the first and second floors of the buildings were just an arm's length away from those on the other side of the street. If you leaned out of a window, you could shake hands with the people opposite.

It was just as Jud had remembered. But he shrugged off any

memories and walked on, towards Hayes Photographers, halfway down the street. It was surrounded by reporters and police officers and anxious onlookers.

He flashed his MI5 card to an officer in the doorway of the shop and entered. There was just no way he was going to be able to take readings here, or attempt to use his ESP. The place was crammed full of hungry hacks, all keen to get a new angle on the story from a dazed-looking Hayes, trapped in the corner.

He'd given his account more than a dozen times so far to reporters, each time showing them exactly where he'd been sitting and where the ghostly priest had appeared.

Jud could see the giant iMac screen displaying a photograph of a young couple embracing, with a strange figure in the background. He recognised it from the news bulletin earlier.

'Excuse me, sir,' he said, pushing his way through the bodies. 'Jud Lester, crime scene investigator. May I have a word?'

There was a rumble of objection from reporters who were still queuing to interview the witness, but a police officer gestured for them to let Jud through.

'Yes?' said Andy Hayes. 'How can I help?'

'Can you tell me about the history of this building?'

'What? Don't you want to know about the ghost?'

'I think the whole world knows about the ghost now, Mr Hayes,' said Jud. 'I was more interested in the building, sir. Just wondered if it had any connection to priests?'

Hayes looked at him incredulously.

'You know, you're the first person to bother asking that. It's probably just coincidence, though.'

'What is?' said Jud.

'What this place was used for hundreds of years ago.'

'Yes?' said Jud, trying to hide his impatience. Reporters were pushing him closer to Hayes. He could feel the sinews in his arm tensing and his knuckles were closing to a fist.

'You'll be surprised!' said Hayes.

Just bloody tell me! thought Jud. 'Oh, right,' he said with a fake smile.

'Yeah,' said Hayes. 'This place was used to hide priests, you see. The Catholic recusants – the ones who refused to accept Protestant beliefs. You know, the ones who died as martyrs.'

Jud stared wide-eyed at the man.

'Did you just say *martyrs?*'

CHAPTER 40

THURSDAY 4 NOVEMBER: 11.30 A.M.

YORK ARCHIVES LIBRARY

The dust in the York Archives Library was playing havoc with Bex's allergies. She'd suffered from asthma since she was a little kid, but had kept it pretty much under control – apart from when she was in dusty places like this. The old wooden bookshelves and the fine collections of leatherbound books might have looked impressive, but they left Bex sneezing and wheezing. Her dark, piercing eyes were now red and watery where she'd been rubbing dust into them ever since she'd arrived an hour ago. She'd scraped her long black hair back in a scruffy knot. She'd tried to look inconspicuous but she couldn't hide her beauty. And the erratic sneezing didn't help. It only made her cuter. She'd noticed a few male students across the room eyeing her up earlier. Perhaps they thought she was there researching for a college assignment too.

She sniffed again, but the dust from the books in front of her tickled her nose.

One of the many reasons why she loved living at the CRYPT was because it was so clinical – so ultra-modern. She preferred it that way. Other agents had said they loved the funky decor and the modern furniture. Bex just loved the fact that she never wheezed or sneezed at the CRYPT. Not once.

She took a discreet puff of her Ventolin inhaler, wiped her nose and carried on searching through the contents page of the next great tome on the table: *The Walls and Bars of York*.

She found the chapter on Micklegate Bar and began scanning the pages. It had had a bloody history, to say the least.

Her eye caught the phrase 'traitors' heads' and she quickly flicked down the page.

It was clear that the bar had displayed many severed heads over the years – as a deterrent to would-be criminals and dissenters. Bex read down the list of people who'd been executed and had their head displayed: Lord Scrope, Lord Treasurer of England; Richard, Duke of York; the Earl of Devon; Thomas Percy, 7th Earl of Northumberland . . .

Wait.

She stopped. The entry for the Earl of Northumberland had caught her eye. It read: 'Executed for his part in the Rising of the North, an attempt by Roman Catholic nobles to depose the Protestant Queen Elizabeth I; beheaded in 1572 outside All Saints Pavement Church, York.'

All Saints?

Wasn't that the location where Fiona Peters claimed to have seen the headless man?

She looked up. Readers were quietly sifting though books and scribbling on notepads. The place was tranquil, but she could feel that her heart had sped up in excitement.

Had she found it? Was this the link?

It was a connection, but not the whole story. Not by any means.

Quickly she moved to her MacBook and Googled All Saints Pavement Church, York.

Another click and she couldn't believe what she was reading: 'The church houses the helmet, sword and gauntlets of Thomas Percy, 7th Earl of Northumberland, who was beheaded outside this church without trial in 1572 for his part in the Catholic uprising of 1569.

'It is said that Percy made a speech moments before his death – a rousing confession of his Catholic faith, which may have inspired the young Margaret Clitherow, one of York's most famous Catholic martyrs.'

The last word rang around her head, just as it had done in Micklegate Bar.

This was getting weird. The connections were too strong. It couldn't have been a coincidence. She and Jud had both heard the word *martyrs* in the haunted locations.

But who was Margaret Clitherow?

Bex Googled her name and saw there were hundreds of entries.

If the research into Thomas Percy had been surprising, it was nothing compared to what she read when she clicked on the first entry.

Margaret Clitherow was executed for her Catholic sympathies and for providing shelter for Catholic priests. She was taken to Ouse Bridge in York, where she suffered '*peine forte et dure*'.

She was pressed to death.

Bex let out a sigh. Others in the room heard it and looked up. She quickly coughed, and sneezed, as if to cover it up.

She just couldn't believe what she was reading. Was this really what she had experienced on Ouse Bridge? Had Margaret Clitherow reached out to her? Had her extrasensory perception been that strong?

She felt such a strange mixture of emotions now. Excitement that she was making sense of what was happening in the city – what had happened to her. But fear, too. Where was this leading?

And a growing sadness was beginning to take hold of her. The thought of that poor woman, enduring such a horrific execution. And for what? For being a Catholic? For putting her faith ahead of her monarch?

This was brutal – and wrong. She began to understand the feelings she'd experienced in Micklegate Bar. All the resentment and pain and suffering. The anger.

She had an awful sense of foreboding. An almost tangible feeling that something even worse was round the corner. Something was building.

Wasn't that what Grace had said Luc felt in Westminster too?

Bex knew, deep down, that this was not the end of it. Not by a long way.

She read on.

Margaret Clitherow was crushed when the sheriffs placed a large piece of wood on her body and steadily applied weights until she was dead. The piece of wood used was her very own front door, the same door she'd used to welcome Catholic priests to her house in The Shambles.

The Shambles.

The priest!

'Oh no!' Bex cried. She didn't look up, but now she knew everyone was staring at her. In her peripheral vision she could see someone approaching her.

'Are you OK, love?' It was one of the librarians.

'Oh, er . . . yeah. I'm sorry,' she said. 'It's just I, er . . . suddenly remembered I'm supposed to be somewhere. Sorry.'

The librarian gave her a quizzical look and then walked back to her desk near the door. It wasn't the first time they'd had a crackpot in there, and she knew it wouldn't be the last. But she kept a beady eye on Bex for the rest of her time there.

Bex looked up from her MacBook and tried to think. A young man with floppy hair and fashionably geekish glasses across the table attempted a subtle glance at her, but she ignored it.

Come on! *Think!* If the city was being visited by the ghosts of Catholic martyrs, then why now. Why here especially?

And what about London? Had this anything to do with Westminster at all?

She remembered that Jud had said he had heard the words 'martyrs caritatis' down in the basement at Westminster. And now she knew that Grace and Luc had also heard it, the connection was undeniable. They'd felt the same feelings of suffering and revenge too.

But why Westminster?

And why now?

The same questions were whizzing around her head.

She decided it was best to find out more about Margaret Clitherow and the Catholic martyrs.

She got up and walked to the desk, and asked the librarian if she could find some books on Margaret Clitherow.

'I thought you said you'd got to go?' the woman said.

'Er . . . no. It's too late now. I, er, I might as well stay,' said Bex.

'I see,' said the librarian, nodding but rolling her eyes at the same time. She walked off reluctantly in the direction of the wooden drawers that housed the card reference system.

Bex returned to her table.

A few minutes later the librarian returned with several books and pamphlets: *Catholic Recusants in York*; *Margaret Clitherow – York's Catholic Martyr*; *The Life of Saint Margaret Clitherow*.

Bex began reading. She was halfway through skimming the second book when she saw it.

It was a small paragraph at the top of the right-hand page.

'Like many of her fellow martyrs caritatis, Margaret Clitherow refused to enter a plea at her trial, believing that she would be judged by God and God alone.'

Martyrs caritatis.

That was it. The words Bex had heard. And the other agents too.

Years of studying Latin at school had given her a nagging feeling that this 'caritatis' word had something to do with '*caritas*', which she knew meant kindness or charity. Martyrs was not

Latin, she knew that, but when put with the word caritatis, it must mean people who died for Christian charity – for their love of God.

It was coming together.

So the ghosts of Catholic martyrs were stirring across York. At the same time, similar hauntings were being reported down in London. But why on earth were the ghosts stirring *now*?

She may only have been at the CRYPT for a few months, but Bex knew that every spirit returned for a reason. There was always a trigger – something that pricked an emotion, raising the intensity of the plasma that surrounded the ghosts and bringing them back into the visible world.

There was no doubt whatsoever that these ghosts might never have rested in peace, given the appalling persecution they suffered in life. But why return now? Why four hundred years later?

She searched online for 'moves against Catholics'. Most of the entries related to events in history, but there was one that stood out. It referred to a news item from just a few years before.

On further reading, Bex noticed it concerned something called the Act of Settlement.

She read on.

'ATTEMPT TO ABOLISH THE 1701 ACT OF SETTLE-MENT IS BLOCKED BY JUSTICE MINISTER.

'The Act, which bans any Roman Catholic from becoming head of state and prohibits a monarch from marrying a Roman Catholic, came the closest it has ever come to being scrapped this year. MPs were poised to vote in a new Bill that would repeal this discriminatory law – until justice minster Brian Maxwell got his hands on it. Maxwell found inconsistencies in the new Bill and has said it is not lawful. His intervention will put back any hopes of abolishing the Act by several months at least, while the lawyers and judges and the church leaders start their wrangling again. It is unlikely to be passed in this year's parliamentary session. The fact that the controversial Act has come this close to being scrapped but has still clung on suggests to some that it may be with us for ever.'

Bex was curious now. Who was this Brian Maxwell, and why was he so opposed to scrapping the Act? It clearly discriminated against Roman Catholics, so why would anyone want to keep it? she thought to herself.

She began searching for entries on Brian Maxwell and was amazed to find that he was MP for York. At least he *was*.

Maxwell died in a house fire not long after he opposed the new Bill. The Act of Settlement survived, but Maxwell didn't, it seemed.

Coincidence?

Bex got up and went to the librarian again. She was on the scent of something. More research was needed. She tried to stifle a sneeze as she brushed past other visitors buried in books, but it came out as a snort instead.

She reached the desk and asked the assistant, 'Do you have archived back issues of the *York Press*?'

'Yes, of course. This way, please.'

Bex followed the woman to a set of large computer screens.

'You can search the archive here. Once you get your reference, come and let me know and I'll retrieve the newspaper for you.'

'Thank you,' said Bex, smiling and doing her best to convince the woman that she really wasn't a crackpot, despite her earlier outburst.

A few moments later she was back at the table, reading the old copies of the *Press*.

One story caught her eye: 'POLICE REJECT THEORIES OF ARSON'.

She quickly discovered that the house fire that had killed Brian Maxwell was said to have been caused by a gas leak from a faulty appliance inside the house. However, there were those at the time who harboured suspicions that the fire may have been started deliberately. Police rejected any suggestion of arson:

Maxwell was found to have suffered accidental death, caused by the gas explosion, and no criminal investigation was undertaken.

But Bex could see there were those who didn't believe that it was an accident.

She had to go there. She had to see for herself. Maybe pick up some vibe. There was no question she had the gift to witness something – recent events had confirmed that – so it was worth a try.

The address was mentioned in the papers. The house had been in the Huntington area of York. It was unlikely there was anything left of the original building now, given the severity of the fire reported in the stories, but Bex felt it was still worth going there. Once her curiosity had been pricked, there was no holding her back – it had to be satisfied.

She tidied up her things, returned the newspapers and much to the disappointment of the young men in the room, left the building and headed straight for the taxi rank outside.

CHAPTER 41

THURSDAY 4 NOVEMBER: 12.33 P.M.

THE STRAND, LONDON

Rosa Merriwell had been a legal secretary for more than thirty years. She knew more about the law than most of the young partners at Mason Bawthwicke put together, even if she did earn a fraction of their salaries.

She had seen the young lawyers come and go, but her boss, Di Bawthwicke, celebrated London solicitor and much-respected name in the Law Society, had been there since the very beginning. Rosa respected Di – everyone did, even the young hotshots who thought they knew it all. You crossed her at your peril. Di was practising law when the youngsters were still at school choosing their GCSEs.

And Di respected Rosa too. She depended on her. No matter how busy she was, no matter how many files Di had given her to work on, Rosa was a rock. She was always well presented, dressed in smart skirts and tops, just a hint of make-up and her greying hair tied into a neat bun. It was a running joke throughout the practice that Di would not be the lawyer she was if it wasn't for her faithful Rosa.

It was lunchtime, and most of the partners were either out dining yet again with a client or locked away in the partners' boardroom in a 'meeting'. Rosa knew full well what that actually meant. Sitting at the newly commissioned bespoke cherrywood table, reading the *Financial Times* and sharing a particularly piquant bottle of Pinot Grigio.

But there were times, of course, when things became busy. Cases often collided, creating deadlines that coincided and prevented partners from returning to their families for two or three days on the trot. It was just the way life was. How else did they earn their six-figure salaries?

But today wasn't one of those days for the City firm of commercial lawyers. Today was a sane day, a day when they could catch up on paperwork and get that crossword done and go for those 'important' meetings at the bistros and clubs down on the Strand and Fleet Street.

There were few staff left in the building this lunchtime. But, as ever, Rosa remained in the office. Di had given her a special job today. There were cases now settled that needed archiving. Take the folders down to the cellars and put them away.

Rosa was very particular about the archive. She'd been in charge of the indexing down there for some years now, and it was her domain. Junior secretaries had often tried to do her job for her, when their own bosses had asked for a file from down below, but they'd not lasted long before the large-framed, grey-haired Rosa had got wind of it and grilled them as a headmistress might interrogate guilty-looking schoolgirls.

She descended the stone steps at the back of the stately Georgian townhouse, her left arm clutching a huge bundle of folders and ring binders.

She flicked the light switch outside the large, thick door. She turned the key and opened it.

The smell of dust filled her nostrils. She loved that musty odour. It spoke of history, of tradition – it reminded her she was working for a long-established firm, not some newly formed outfit of young lawyers fresh out of law school.

She waited for the neon strip lights to stop flickering and hold. Then she placed the large bundle of files on the small table in the centre of the cellar. The walls were lined with metal cabinets, each one filled with similar files, arranged alphabetically. Rosa's was a tight ship. No clerical errors here.

She busily placed the top few files in the correct places on the shelves.

The next one was for former client Christopher Wall. The 'W' section was through the main lobby and out in the back room, deeper into the vast labyrinth of cellars that ran the length of the building.

She flicked another switch on the wall and waited again for the lights to flicker and come on.

They didn't. Curse those bulbs!

Luckily there was just enough light to see by from the great strip lights lining the main lobby and casting rays into the shadows of the back rooms. Rosa moved in further, scanning the shelves for 'W'.

She'd not got far beyond 'T' when she dropped the folder in her hand.

And screamed.

It was a loud, terrified cry, but there was no way her colleagues would hear it on the floors above her. The walls and floors were thick, and the rooms were lined with so much paperwork that any noise was instantly deadened.

There, beyond the cabinets and shelves, in the corner of the back room, was the old boardroom table – abandoned ever since the partners had treated themselves to the new cherry-wood table, though Di could not bring herself to dispose of it altogether.

And seated around the table, hunched in a conspiratorial huddle, were four figures. It was too dark to make out their faces.

But their bodies loomed large in the dusky light. And the sight had shocked Rosa to her core. She tried to turn around and flee, but the sound of her scream had brought the same shock to the ghosts.

And one was approaching her now.

As she tried to escape, it pinned her to the cabinet, its head falling uncontrollably towards hers.

Rosa could see its face now. It was the ugliest thing she'd ever witnessed. Sunken eyes, a sharp, bony nose and a straggly beard that gave it a wild, vagrant look. Its breath was like pungent sulphur.

But it wasn't just the face particularly that frightened Rosa, though its rank appearance repelled her and the way its head fell limply on to its shoulders seemed abnormal. It was the neck – or lack of it. Close up like this, she could see that the figure's head was attached to its body by just a thin sinew of muscle on its left side. A large portion of the neck was not there. Just a gaping hole, leaking black, congealed blood that poured down its chest in a never-ending stream. Now Rosa's shoes were covered. And her skirt.

She pushed at the strange body that engulfed her, kicked and screamed. Jabbed it with her hands, but she was too weak.

As the ghost leaned in to her, its head flopped closer and collided with the bridge of her nose, sending a sharp pain through her skull and making her already tear-filled eyes sting.

She screamed again and tried to free herself, but it was no use.

She could see over the ghost's shoulder that the other figures were rising too. And approaching her.

Each one emitted a strange reddish glow, which gave them a demonic appearance. Rosa was terrified.

She closed her eyes. She could feel the ghost's claw-like hand around her neck, and another at her right arm. She felt a soaring pain in her wrist as the ghost pressed its bony fingers into her veins. Its head had flopped on to her shoulder now and buried itself in her neck.

And then she felt the teeth.

The pain was excruciating. She was unable to speak any more. She tried, but no sound came out. Energy was leaving her, along with her blood. She struggled to resist the ghost's onslaught, but her body was going limp in its clutches.

The other figures in the room had come even closer, but they were not after Rosa. They grabbed her attacker and began wrestling with him. Strange, glowing bodies all tussling and falling to the ground. Writhing around in a ferocious melee.

Rosa was free of the ghost now, but when she tried to make for the door, her legs gave way. She was bleeding badly. The puncture wound in her neck was serious. Very serious.

She felt faint and sank to the floor near the mass of ghostly bodies, her eyes fixed with a terrified expression. The sight was abhorrent. The figures were still jabbing into one another. Dark, congealed blood was leaking from the face of her attacker as the others lashed out at him.

But as they fought, the strange aura that had seemed so intense around them, like a glowing plasma, was gradually fading.

Energy was draining from them.

Rosa, too, was slipping away. Life was leaving her, and she knew it, bathed in her own blood.

She tried to rise but fell back again on to the hard stone floor.

Her hand was drenched in blood. As she lay crumpled in the corner, she pressed a bloodied finger to the wall beside her and began writing a message.

CHAPTER 42

THURSDAY 4 NOVEMBER: 1.01 P.M.

HUNTINGTON, YORK

The car pulled up slowly at the kerbside. Fortunately the taxi driver was a local man and had been able to shed more light on the story during their journey over there. Bex had said she was a local writer, working on a new book on York politicians. And he'd bought it.

'Oh yeah, the Maxwell case. There was always somethin' fishy about that, you know.'

'In what way?' said Bex.

'Well,' the driver continued, 'I don't know much about the facts, but I do know that there were rumours in the city that the fire that killed him had been started deliberately.'

'So why didn't the police investigate it?'

'Well that's just it. We all wondered why. They said they'd had experts on it – you know, crime scene people and specialists in gas appliances. They'd been convinced that the fire had started by accident.'

'So why the rumours?' said Bex. 'Why didn't people accept that?'

'Dunno. I guess he was quite a famous bloke, you know. Everyone knew him. Maybe it just seemed weird that a man like that was there one minute and gone the next. Maybe people thought he was famous enough to have enemies or somethin'. You know what the conspiracy theorists are like. Always after a scandal.'

Bex wasn't convinced. For there to have been a rumour of foul play at all, someone must have seen or heard something. There must have been more to it than just theories.

And now here she was, pulled up outside what must have been the MP's house. The windows were boarded up and the door had a metal plate across the top where a small window would have been. The garden looked like it had been abandoned. Weeds grew up through cracks in the block paving, and the flower bed beneath the large bay window at the front was nothing but a tangle of dense, thorny brambles.

'It's a sad place,' she said.

'That one is, yes, but they did a grand job doing up Maxwell's house – looks like new now,' said the driver.

Bex peered through the taxi window again.

He was right. The house she had been looking at had no number, but the one next to it had a large, ornately painted '43' on the porch wall.

And though it was in the same style as the Victorian houses in the street, it certainly looked like a new build. The bricks were cleaner, the roof tiles were unstained and the painted woodwork around the doors and windows looked fresher.

This was a new house. The previous fire must have swallowed up the whole building, with the MP inside it. He couldn't have stood a chance.

'Well that's weird,' Bex said to the driver. 'I mean, you'd have thought it was the house next door, surely. Look at it!'

The driver was nodding. 'Yeah, well, it takes all sorts, I suppose. I don't know why it's like that.'

She asked him to wait a few minutes. He was happy to do so. The meter was running and he could go back to his paper.

Bex got out and walked towards number 43. She had to be careful. It was obviously inhabited, and it was unlikely that the new residents would be happy to be reminded that they were living on the site of a crematorium. Quite what the atmosphere inside was like, she could only imagine. It might have looked like an impressive family home – she could see small bikes discarded in the front garden – but what about the vibes left behind by the previous owners? But then not everyone was like Bex.

She couldn't feel much outside. She detected no emotion, despite her senses being on 'receive'.

She turned as she heard footsteps behind her. Slow trudges through the snow.

An elderly lady – far too elderly to be out in the cold snowy weather – was slowly pushing an old-fashioned shopping trolley towards her. Her face was wrapped up in a headscarf and she was wearing a sheepskin coat that must have weighed as much as her.

She was staring at Bex. Really staring at her, and her face showed a stern expression.

Bex quickly averted her gaze and moved into the road to let the old woman pass by. But she didn't.

She stopped.

'Yes?' she said in a voice that carried too much anger and energy for one so old and frail. It took Bex by surprise.

'Er . . . I beg your pardon. Is everything OK?' She tried to speak kindly.

The woman looked angry. 'What d'you mean, is everything OK? What're you after, eh? What d'you want?'

'I'm sorry,' said Bex. 'I . . . er . . . I don't want anything. It's fine. I wasn't waiting to speak to you.'

'No,' said the woman. 'Then why're you standing here, huh?'

'Oh, I'm so sorry. You live here, do you? Well, I didn't mean to cause offence. I . . . er . . . was just—'

'No! Of course I don't live here,' the old woman interrupted, which was lucky, as Bex had no idea what she was going to say to her next. 'I live next door.' She was pointing in the direction of the abandoned-looking house to the right.

Bex found it hard to hide her surprise. That anyone should want to live in such a hostile-looking place, boarded up like that, seemed incredible.

'So why are you here, young lady? Are you friends of the Jacobs?' the old woman said.

'No,' said Bex, and then suddenly wished she'd said yes. The Jacobs must be the family living in the newly restored house. It might have explained why she'd been seen loitering outside.

'So? What're you doing?' Bex noticed that it wasn't anger especially that was shaping her face, it was fear. This woman was frightened. Her stern expression didn't fool Bex. She could tell there was anxiety in the old woman's voice. Her hands had begun to tremble.

Bex was stumped. What should she say? She had to reassure her that she wasn't here to cause trouble, or rob her or something. Perhaps honesty was the best policy.

She said, 'No, I'm not a friend of the family. But I *am* interested in the house. I'm researching the life of the previous inhabitant. Brian Max—'

'What?' Now real fear had brought a croak to the woman's voice and a wateriness to her old eyes. Her lips moved the way people's did when they were emotional. She was shaking too.

'Look,' said Bex kindly. 'I didn't mean to upset you, but I think I have. I'll go. I'll leave you in peace.' She said it softly and in as unthreatening a way as she could manage. Her deep brown eyes were peaceful and kind. There was a compassion to her that settled the old woman's nerves slightly.

She hadn't moved, but just stared at Bex, her heavily painted eyebrows moving as she thought. Her cheeks were rouge with too much make-up. The way some old ladies wear it.

After a few awkward seconds – during which Bex tried to avoid the old woman's gaze by staring at the kerb and taking a sudden interest in kicking a stone – the woman broke into a more kindly expression.

'There's something about you,' she said slowly. 'You're not from the police, are you?'

'The police?' said Bex. 'No!' It was a kind of half-truth, but she felt awful for saying it. She certainly wasn't a writer, though. Gaining the old lady's trust felt good, but not if it was based on a lie.

There was no way she was going to tell her what she really did, though. She looked like the kind of person who'd scream if Bex told her she was a ghost-hunter.

'And you're here to find out about the fire, are you?'

'Yes. Do you know much about it? Were you living here when it happened?' said Bex gently, keen not to offend.

The old lady stared straight into her eyes. Bex could see she was troubled. She could only imagine what lay behind that gaze.

'Know about it?' said the old woman, now breaking into a whisper. She came even closer. Bex could smell her perfume. That familiar smell – why do old ladies always wear the same lavender perfume? she thought. 'Know about it? Of course I know about it . . . and I know who did it, too.'

Bex couldn't believe what she was hearing. Either this woman was a few screws loose, or she knew something and had chosen to bury it, or had not been listened to. A whole myriad of possibilities flew through her brain. Either way, she needed to speak with this woman. But not here. She could see the woman was being secretive. She was now looking around her, peering into the car at the driver and twitching nervously. Her eyes were darting backwards and forwards and she was stooping even lower. Withdrawing into herself.

This woman was paranoid. That was obvious.

'And I'll tell you,' she whispered. 'But not here. You don't know who's listening outside. The street has ears . . . and eyes. It knows things. It's not safe. Not any more. They're after me.'

'Who are?' said Bex.

'They are.' She was glancing around the street, but at nothing in particular. She was clearly delusional. 'All of them. Because of what I know. What I saw. That night.' Her voice was becoming a croaky, ghostly sort of whisper now.

But Bex wasn't frightened; she'd been through enough the last few days to cope with a slightly spooky old lady.

'Come in and I'll tell you,' the woman said. Bex turned to the driver, who lowered the window nearest to her. 'Can you wait another ten minutes?' she asked sweetly. 'I *will* pay you, of course.'

'Fine with me, love,' he said. It was better to be doing the crossword here, with the meter running, than back at the taxi rank, earning nothing. He shut his window again and went back to 4 down – still couldn't get it.

Bex followed the old woman up the garden path, strewn with weeds and decomposing leaves.

It took her hostess a good five minutes to locate her keys and then unlock the various locks that lined the right-hand side of the door, top to bottom.

Clearly this woman had security issues.

And then they were inside. The hallway was surprisingly tidy and clean. From the outside of the house, Bex had had the distinct impression that the inside was going to be just as unkempt. But it wasn't. Quite the reverse. This woman was as house-proud as Bex's own grandmother – and *she* was as house-proud as they came.

So why the boards and the locks and the abandoned garden? Bex had to ask – but decided to wait a while. Too many questions might unsettle the woman even more. From the look of the security system outside, the house didn't see many guests these days, and she felt too privileged to upset her so soon after coming inside.

But she noticed a visible change in the old lady's demeanour once the door was shut. She seemed more relaxed as she tottered into the kitchen at the back of the house and set her shopping trolley down.

A little while later she returned with a tray of drinks.

'You'll have some orange squash then, my love? And I've got some Garibaldis, too.'

'Lovely,' said Bex, smiling.

They went into the front room. Like so many front rooms in the houses of the elderly, it was pristine. Never used, always saved for when they had 'company', which in this case was hardly ever.

There were two floral armchairs, a coffee table covered with a large white lace doily and in the window a well-polished table with four chairs neatly tucked underneath. Above them, the chandelier struggled to cope with the darkness of the room, caused by the boards fixed to the windows outside. The shade gave the place a melancholy air – lonely and forgotten.

'You'll have to forgive the boards,' the woman said, seeing Bex's puzzled face as she gazed towards the windows. 'You see, when you know something as I do, it can keep you prisoner. What I know could bring trouble on a lot of people. So I have enemies. Lots of enemies. Hundreds, thousands. They're all out there. But I'm safe in here.

'I go out sometimes, but I wrap up and I keep my head down. I'm marked by where I live, you see. My address is my prison.'

Bex was trying hard to understand what she was rambling on about, but until or unless she was going to share whatever her secret was, she could only nod her head and smile politely – and hope to get out of there as soon as she could. She sensed she was this woman's first visitor in a *very* long time.

She sat down in the chair opposite her and reached for the plastic glass of weak orange squash. She was thirsty from sitting for so long in the dusty library. Hungry too, though the currant-filled Garibaldis looked anything but appetising. Were they even fresh? She decided to risk it.

The old lady sat back in her chair and began. Bex noticed she had changed her zip-up boots for pink furry slippers.

'So, you're interested in the old man's murder, then?'

Murder? Bex wished she'd paid the taxi driver and told him to move on. This was going to be a long visit.

CHAPTER 43

THURSDAY 4 NOVEMBER: 1.44 P.M.

YORK CONSERVATIVE HEADQUARTERS

ACOMB, YORK

Jud walked up the steps and pressed the metal buzzer on the right of the great black door. The polished brass plaque read 'Conservative Party, York'.

'Can I help you?' a voice crackled through the speaker.

'Yes, it's Jud Lester. I'm here to meet Mr Thacker?'

'Come in.' The door buzzed and Jud pushed it open.

The hallway was a grand affair with black and white marble tiles on the floor and two large urns flanking the staircase that spiralled upwards.

To his left, Jud saw an open door and a smartly dressed lady sitting behind a polished wooden counter. Sunlight was pushing through Venetian blinds, giving her tweed suit a distinctly striped look.

'Good afternoon, Mr Lester, do take a seat.' The woman was smiling and pointing to a comfortable-looking leather sofa in the corner of the reception room.

'Thank you,' said Jud, reaching for a magazine and sitting down.

'Mr Thacker won't be long. He's gone for his usual lunchtime run, I'm afraid.'

'Oh, right.'

'I said to him it was too cold to be running about in a T-shirt and tracksuit, but he won't be told. Got too much energy, has our Mr Thacker!'

'I see.'

'Yes. He's always been like that. I remember when he used to come here as a lad. Bounding about all keen, you know. He used to help us on campaigns. Could fold and stuff envelopes faster than anyone in the building! Then he'd insist on racing us all up and down the stairs.'

'Great.' Jud smiled non-committally. What was this? Thacker's life story? She was obviously one of those women who had to chat – to anyone, about anything. It must have been a quiet day for the York Conservatives until now. She seemed in overdrive.

When she wasn't talking, there was a reassuring tick from the grandfather clock which stood between the two large sash windows. Other than that, silence.

No wonder she likes to chat, thought Jud. I'd go mad working in a place like this.

A few monotonous minutes later, and some pointless facts about the way the office was manned, where she liked to buy her sandwiches and why Thacker was the best boss she'd had so far, Jud heard the door go.

'Ah, it's the man himself,' said the receptionist. A guy in his thirties walked in, panting.

He was handsome and fit, with a friendly face. Just what every party secretary wanted in their Member for Parliament, Jud thought. He had a shock of blond hair, neatly combed but darker in places where the sweat had run.

Jud stood up to shake his outstretched hand.

'So, we meet at last! I'm Simon Thacker.'

'Jud Lester. Good to meet you.'

Thacker smiled and rubbed the back of his neck. 'Do forgive the attire,' he said. 'I was expecting you at two o'clock, but I'm glad you made it.'

Jud glanced quickly at the clock over his shoulder. Thacker was right; he was early. He smiled and said, 'No, forgive me for being early. I'm happy to sit and wait if you wish to freshen up or something.'

'No, no,' said Thacker. 'If you don't mind the tracksuit, then I'm happy. It's more comfortable, to be honest. I suggest we go straight on up, shall we?' He was warm from his run. His face was reddening now, as it often did when he first arrived back from the cold air outside. He pulled out the neck of his T-shirt and flapped it a little to create a miniature breeze, which cooled him momentarily, revealing an unusual scar at his neck. It rose up from his chest, like the kind you saw when someone had been scalded.

Thacker's office was spacious, but not grand. There was a large reproduction Georgian-style desk in the centre, with matching cabinets behind. A leather sofa ran along the front wall, under the windows. There was a polished table and chairs to Jud's left.

Thacker obviously ran a tight ship, or perhaps it was the overly efficient lady downstairs who did the tidying.

'Please sit down, Mr Lester,' said his host, wiping his face and hair with a hand towel from a peg behind the door.

Jud sat in a chair near the desk as Thacker walked round and sat opposite him.

'So!'

Jud looked puzzled. 'So?'

'Well,' continued Thacker, 'I mean to say – it's been a strange time, what?'

'It has, sir, yes. I take it you're up to speed with all the latest developments in the case?'

'I think so,' said Thacker. 'My guys at the Met are on the ball most of the time. We've got officers stationed throughout Westminster, and I know the force up here are working flat out to try to keep pace with the developments as they break. I tell you, it's certainly the strangest investigation I've seen.'

Jud looked pensive for a moment. 'So do you think the events are connected in some way, Mr Thacker?'

'How do you mean?'

'Well, you said it's the strangest investigation. Do you mean that what's been happening in York and London is part of the same case?' said Jud, watching his reaction.

'Er, well, I mean, I don't know. You asked if I'm up to speed with the latest developments in the case, so I assumed you meant the two locations were connected. Though I don't know how they could be.'

'Well it's too early to say, isn't it?' said Jud.

There was something in Thacker's demeanour that was nervous. Jud was unsure why he'd been invited. He'd presumed that as Police Minister, Thacker was fully aware of who he was and for whom he worked. But quite why he wanted to see him now, he really didn't know. The press conference on the television last night, which had been filmed, Jud presumed, at the York police headquarters, had been astonishing. Thacker's public denial that there were any ghosts, whilst helpful for the CRYPT, seemed strange to say the least. Jud wanted to grill him, but decided it was better to wait until he brought up the subject.

'I'll cut to the chase, if I may.' Thacker must have sensed Jud's impatience to know the reason for his visit. 'I wanted to apologise in person for the way you were treated down at Westminster. I understand from my colleagues at Scotland Yard that you were arrested and questioned over the alleged disappearance of the engineer.'

'Oh, yes,' said Jud, deliberately keeping quiet to see where this was leading.

'Well, I mean to say – you were treated pretty appallingly, and I've already launched an internal inquiry to ask some serious questions. When the engineer's body was found – close to the site of the unfortunate police officer – it seemed clear to everyone that you could not have been involved.'

'Oh, right. Well thanks.'

'Seriously, young man. I value your work and I shudder to think what kind of impression you must have drawn about the force from the way they treated you. I can only say the young officers concerned have already been spoken to and their – shall we say – overzealous investigation style will be kept in check from now on.'

'Thank you, Mr Thacker,' said Jud. 'I appreciate you taking time out of your busy schedule to see me. I've no doubt things are hectic right now.'

'Yes, they are rather, but that's the way it is these days.'

'And the press conference last night – that must have been a bit of a scrum for you.'

'Oh, you watched it?' said Thacker.

'I did,' said Jud. 'And I wanted to thank you for setting the public's mind at rest and deflecting fears of ghosts. It's always helpful to do that from the outset.'

'Well, it's easy to do when it's true, of course. There are no ghosts involved.'

'What?' Jud couldn't hide his surprise. 'You believe there are no ghosts at work here? It's all in the minds of the witnesses?'

Thacker smiled. 'Yes, exactly. Look, I know that you and your fellow agents at the CRYPT do a wonderful job. I've followed your work for some time, and I must say your courage is matched by your expertise in what you do. I have no doubt that you have witnessed some real paranormal activity in the past.'

'But?' Jud sensed it was coming.

'But on this occasion, I genuinely believe you're wrong.'

'OK,' said Jud. 'Go on.'

'Well. I've been advised - and you'll appreciate I can only go on the advice I'm given; I can't physically be at every crime scene myself, of course - that in every case so far, the witnesses have been somewhat deluded in what they claim to have seen.'

Jud looked carefully at Thacker before he spoke. There was so much he could say. How he personally had wrestled with a ghost in the basement at Westminster, how he'd seen with his own eyes the effect that the paranormal activity here in York was having on Bex, how some of the witnesses he was referring to had now mysteriously vanished. But Thacker was hard to read. Did he know about this? Was he behind the lies and the cover-up? It seemed unlikely. But Jud decided it was better to play his cards close to his chest for now.

Thacker appeared energetic and engaging, articulate and driven - but he still seemed, like so many politicians, a little wet behind the ears. Jud suspected that this guy knew a lot less than he himself did about the truth of what was going on here.

So who was pulling his strings? Or at least, who was feeding him the false information and giving him the script for the press conferences?

'Well,' said Jud, 'I must say, though I respect what you're saying, and I also understand your need to play down any notion of ghosts - we all know what that can do to the public - I just don't share your view that this is all the work of humans. My research up here too has shown me that there must be something supernatural at work.'

'Well, I tell you what. If you're right, then I'm very glad indeed that we have guys like you around! I'm advised by everyone at the Yard and at Parliament that this has nothing to do with anything paranormal. But as Police Minister, I am at liberty to employ whoever's services I want, and I have no objection - no objection whatsoever - to you guys continuing your research. And I'll do all I can to assist you.'

'Does this mean we can return to Westminster?' said Jud, directly.

'Ah, that's a good question. You know what's happening tomorrow, don't you?'

'Yes,' said Jud. 'It's the State Opening of Parliament.'

'Exactly,' said Simon. 'Now what that means – and I know you won't like this – is that CRYPT work is going to have to be put on hold, just for twenty-four hours. We've sealed off the basement to all visitors, and I'm afraid that includes you guys.'

'But—'

'I know you won't like that. I wouldn't either,' said Thacker warmly. 'But you see, any talk of ghosts will run right round the halls of Westminster like wildfire. It will eclipse the ceremony tomorrow – might even sabotage it. And we can't have that. Her Majesty won't allow anything – *anything* – to halt proceedings. The State Opening *must* go ahead. I'm sure you know how much is riding on it. It's the beginning of the next parliamentary session. The Queen's speech proposes all the new bills for the coming year. We simply can't not hold it.'

Jud could only guess how frustrated Bonati and the guys down in London must be, to be shut out of the cellars beneath Parliament, even for a day, when there was so much paranormal activity down there, but Thacker sounded genuine enough.

'So, how about we agree, right here, that you'll give me twenty-four hours and then continue your investigations – you'll have access to as many areas as you wish, including the basement at Westminster.'

Something was troubling Jud, and he had to mention it before he agreed to a halt in the investigation.

'Mr Thacker,' he said tentatively, 'can I ask you a question?'

'Yes, of course!'

'Did you say you have spoken personally to the witnesses up here, or you've been advised by others who have?'

'No, I haven't seen them myself. I mean, frankly I really

shouldn't be up here at all today. There is so much to do in London for tomorrow. But I spoke with the PM and we both agreed that the people of York needed some reassurance from their MP. This whole ghost thing has really unsettled folk – and God knows the press like to whip up a story like this. We felt it was worth me dashing up last night to hold that press conference. I heard that you were up here too, so I thought I'd catch up with you. I'm due back this afternoon. There's a meeting at Westminster this evening that I really can't miss.'

'So you haven't seen the witnesses yourself? I mean the people who claimed they saw ghosts here in York?'

'No. I've been advised by people who have, though. York police have interviewed them.'

'Oh. I see,' said Jud. 'Well, can I share something with you, Mr Thacker?'

'You must call me Simon!'

'OK, Simon. Well, another agent and I have been trying to contact them today, and it seems they've vanished.'

'What? Vanished? What do you mean?' said Thacker, looking genuinely concerned.

'They were discharged from hospital last night, but it seems they didn't return home.'

'How do you know? Have you checked?' said Thacker.

'Yes.'

'What, you mean you've been to their houses?'

'Yes, exactly,' said Jud. 'No one has seen them.'

Thacker looked pensive. He rubbed his neck and then ran his hands through his blond hair. 'That is weird. I can see why you're concerned. OK. Leave it with me. I'll speak to the police up here and find out what's going on. I'm sure there's a rational explanation, of course. People often take time out when they return from hospital – sometimes the shock of an injury does funny things to them. They need a break. Time out. But it does seem strange.'

'Well, I should think the police are on to it already,' said Jud.

'Oh, I'm sure they are. Have their families reported them missing?'

'Fiona Peters' husband certainly has. I don't think the old man had any relatives, but his neighbour seemed concerned.'

'OK,' said Thacker. Then he looked at Jud thoughtfully. 'So, tell me. I've always wondered. Why does a bright kid like you want to get mixed up with ghosts?'

Jud shrugged. 'I don't know. It's just something I've always been interested in.' He wasn't about to go into detail. This was not the time or place, and though friendly enough, this guy wasn't even from MI5. Who knows, by next election he might be voted out anyway.

'Oh, I see. And you like history, I presume? I mean, you must do, with all the research you guys do.'

'Yes, I love it. Always have. York is a particularly great place.' Jud was pleased to be off the subject of ghost-hunting so quickly.

'Want a quick tour?' said Thacker.

'I beg your pardon?'

'Well, I've a got a few moments to kill before my train later this afternoon. I can show you some fascinating places if you like. I've lived in York all my life.'

'Sounds great, but I've really got to get back to the hotel. I'll be returning to London later too.'

'OK, maybe next time,' said Thacker. 'I tell you what. I need to go into town anyway, I'll walk back to the hotel with you. Perhaps I can give you a guided tour on the way!' He got up, smiling and took a fleece jacket from the back of his door.

It seemed surprising to Jud that an MP, and a minister at that, should be so free with his time, but why not?

'OK. Great,' he said.

Poppleton Road was a few minutes' walk from the town centre, but the cold weather had abated for a short while and the snow-covered buildings and pavements made it a pleasant stroll.

They walked on into Holgate Road, where the great metal road bridge loomed ahead, crossing the railway line. Thacker was a font of all knowledge about York's history, it seemed. Jud was quite interested as the MP regaled him with some of the more interesting ghost stories that helped to give the place the unusual title of Europe's most haunted city.

As they crossed the railway line, Thacker indicated that he knew a short cut down Dalton Terrace.

'I've been coming down this road for years,' he said. 'Ever since I was a boy. My church is down here, you see. Now there's an interesting place, if you like your English history!'

They walked on, and Jud could see the giant building ahead of him. Though it was fairly modern in style, it was obvious that it was a significant building. It was the name that struck him as soon as he saw it. The English Martyrs Roman Catholic Church.

'Now that's interesting,' he said. 'Tell me about it.'

'I can do more than that; I'll show you around if you like,' said Thacker.

'Lead the way,' said Jud.

CHAPTER 44

THURSDAY 4 NOVEMBER: 2.16 P.M.

HUNTINGTON, YORK

'I can't believe it,' said Bex. 'I mean, it's not that I think you're mistaken, I'm sorry. It's just that it's so incredible.'

She had listened intently to the old lady as she'd slowly regaled her with her secret, pausing to clear her throat, fill up her teacup and visit the lavatory, in that order.

Bex had been in the house for more than an hour now, but she was still far from ready to leave. It was just too intriguing.

If any of what the woman was saying was true, of course. There was always the possibility that it wasn't and her hostess was delusional, or crying out for attention, or suffering from the onset of dementia. But she just didn't seem that way to Bex. The old lady was as sharp as pin – slow and steady with her movements maybe, but mentally she had all her faculties, and then some.

'I know,' she said quietly. 'And that's why no one believed me at the time, or has since.'

Bex was truly astonished. She was having trouble taking it all in, and that was rare for Bex. She was brave and sassy and bright. There was very little that stumped her and left her speechless, but this had.

'So let me get this straight – and I'm sorry to go through it again, but I may have missed something – you saw an intruder the night Mr Maxwell died in the fire next door?'

'Yes. Like I said, dear, I saw him enter, and I saw him leave.'

'And when he left, the place was alight?' said Bex, trying to clarify.

'Yes. And so was he.'

'Yeah, you said you saw flames on his jumper, right?'

'That's right, my dear. He launched himself on to the wet grass, trying to put out the fire, I suppose. Must have been agony for him. Good. Served him right. I can't believe what he did to Brian. When I think what—'

'Yes. I'm sorry,' interrupted Bex. She could see the memories were painful for the old lady and tears had reappeared at the edges of her grey eyes.

She still hadn't introduced herself properly – all part of her secrecy, Bex supposed, but it meant she couldn't even use the old lady's name to comfort her now. 'Look, I don't want to cause you upset again,' she said gently. 'Tell me about the intruder. What did he do next?'

Her hostess retrieved a screwed-up tissue from her sleeve and dabbed her eyes with it.

'Well, dear, after trying to get some relief from the wet ground, he stood up and made straight for the bushes across the road. There's a footpath that leads to a park opposite. I imagine that's where he fled to, and then who knows where?'

'OK. And you're absolutely certain you saw his face?'

'My dear. I know what you're doing. You're asking me to repeat everything to see if my story is the same each time. It's the only way you'll decide whether I'm dotty or not. If I tell you differently this time, you'll think I'm losing my marbles and my evidence will be useless. I've been here before, you know. No one believed me five years ago. That's why nothing happened to him.'

'So that's why there was no investigation?'

'Exactly. The coroner said it was accidental death – caused by a gas explosion. They said one of Brian's appliances was leaking or something. No one believed me. But *he knows*.'

'He knows *what?*' What was she talking about now? Bex thought to herself.

'He knows I saw him.'

'Oh, so he saw you looking out of the window that night?'

'I can't be sure. He didn't stop to face me. But I'd be surprised if he hadn't spied me from the bushes.' Bex noticed she was twitching nervously now and glancing up at the darkened windows. This woman really was a prisoner in her own home. Bex wondered whether her trip out earlier had been her first for a while.

'He could have seen me,' she continued. 'He could have. And he could come back.'

'And you're sure about his identity?' said Bex.

'Look, I don't know how many times I have to say this. *Yes*, I'm sure! I saw his face then, just as I saw his face last night on the television. And just as I saw his face the night of the election.'

'So it really was him? No question?' Bex knew she was being annoying, but it was just too weird for words.

'Yes! Now please don't ask me any more. If you don't believe me, just like everyone else, then fine, don't. But I'm telling you, the man I saw that night, the man who *murdered* our MP, was the same man who took his job . . .

'Simon Thacker.'

CHAPTER 45

THURSDAY 4 NOVEMBER: 2.31 P.M.

ENGLISH MARTYRS ROMAN CATHOLIC CHURCH, YORK

'It's a beautiful church,' said Jud. 'I can see why you worship here, certainly.'

'Thank you,' said Thacker. 'We're proud of our community too. We have a loyal congregation.' He smiled warmly. 'This place is important to me. I suppose it's where I first thought of becoming a politician. To serve God by serving the people.' He pointed to the pews at the front. 'Do sit down, by all means.'

'Well,' said Jud, 'I think I probably need to get going, if you don't mind.'

'Oh, nonsense,' said Thacker. 'That's just the problem these days, don't you think? The way no one ever has time to sit and take stock. Always rushing about, in and out of meetings, dashing here and there. I mean, look at me! I'm not even supposed to be here right now. I should be in London, preparing for tomorrow's big day.'

'I understand,' said Jud. 'Well perhaps we'd better—'

'And what a day it will be!' interrupted Thacker, pacing up and down the central aisle like the owner of the place. 'A day when our great nation comes together to celebrate democracy and our allegiance to God and to the Queen.'

'Well, quite.'

'A day when at last we shall see justice.'

'What?' Jud was feeling confused. What was this guy talking about? He sensed he was one of those career politicians, high on the thrill of being in Parliament.

Jud's phone beeped. He fished it from his pocket and stared at the screen.

'Have you ever watched the State Opening, Mr Lester? I expect you'll have seen it on television.'

It was a text. From Bex.

'But you really can't appreciate the splendour from your living room. I mean you need to be there, in the flesh.'

Jud froze. The text read: **If you're with Thacker – GET OUT NOW!**

He looked up at Thacker, who had stopped, turned and was now looking at him quizzically.

'Problem?' he said.

'What? Er . . . no, it's nothing. Sorry, you were saying?'

'Oh. Well, I mean, I was saying how important a day tomorrow will be. A day when . . . Hey, where are you going, Lester?'

Jud had risen and was walking to the door.

'I thought I said we need to take time out now and again, what? Why the hurry?' Thacker was walking briskly towards him now.

The door was still some distance away, further down the central aisle and to the right.

Jud turned. 'I'm sorry, Mr Thacker. I really must get going. Something's come up, you see.' He kept walking.

Thacker moved swiftly. He was at the door before Jud and stood in front of it.

Jud saw him remove something from his jacket. What was that? He had a suspicion, but he couldn't be sure. Thacker's sleight of hand had been too quick, and whatever he'd removed was now hidden in the back pocket of his tracksuit as he leaned casually against the doorway.

'Oh, come on, Lester. I haven't shown you the altar yet. Or the choir stalls!'

'No, I really must get going,' Jud said, as politely as he could. He moved to turn the handle of the great door, but Thacker was having none of it. He pushed Jud backwards against a display stand, sending it crashing to the floor.

'I'm so sorry, I can't let you go anywhere.' Thacker spoke calmly, but the colour of his face belied his attempt to stay in control. He looked redder than he had after his run. And beads of sweat were appearing at his forehead, despite the cool air inside the church.

Jud steadied himself and saw that Thacker's hand was reaching to his back pocket again. He couldn't take any chances. He had to strike now.

He launched himself at the MP, catching him by surprise. The force caused Thacker's head to strike the solid oak door behind him and he slipped to the ground.

Jud quickly kicked him in the face, hard and solid. Thacker's lip burst almost instantly into a pulpy dribble. Red splattered across his face and on to Jud's boot.

'You bastard! You meddling little shit. Time to join your spirit friends, Lester.'

Jud had been right. It *was* a gun. A Glock 17 9mm. But Thacker had misjudged him. He'd not appreciated how fast Jud could move. He pressed the MP's gun hand to the ground with his foot and then stamped savagely on his knuckles. Thacker's grip released and the gun fell on to the flagstones. There was no time to stoop and pick it up – Thacker would reach it first – so Jud hoofed it towards the corner of the church with his boot. The metal scraped across the hard floor.

Thacker was no match for Jud. He was weak and tired – *so*

tired. Why hadn't he dispatched the kid while he had the chance? He could've taken him out in his office, or on the way here, or in the pews. Why did he wait?

The text had taken him by surprise. Who could possibly have tipped Lester off, and how?

Thacker staggered to his feet and watched his target sprint out of the churchyard and down the road. There was no point in trying to shoot. He'd never hit him from this distance. He shouted in desperation, 'You can't stop it now! You can't stop the Master. He will have his revenge! Justice will come tomorrow . . . for the martyrs. *And you can't stop it!*'

Jud didn't even look back. He just kept on running.

Thacker slumped to the floor in the entrance. His jaw and his lips and his hand were in agony – but it was nothing compared to the punishment he knew he'd soon be facing.

From the master.

CHAPTER 46

THURSDAY 4 NOVEMBER: 2.58 P.M.

DEAN COURT HOTEL, YORK

Jud ran up the steps and entered the hotel lobby. The receptionist noticed that he was panting.

'Are you OK, sir?'

'Yes, yes, I'm fine, thank you,' he said, offering no explanation for his condition.

'I'm glad you're here,' she continued. 'Your colleague asked me to inform her if I saw you. I think she is keen to catch you, sir. Shall I tell her you're here?'

'Don't worry,' he said. 'I'll go and see her now. Room 43, wasn't it?'

'Yes, sir. Can I get you any refreshments? Some tea, perhaps?' She had decided he looked like he needed that age-old English remedy for anything – a good cuppa.

'Yes, please. Tea would be perfect. Can you send tea for two up to Room 43. Thank you.'

'Righto, sir. I think some biscuits, too. I'll bet you haven't eaten!'

She was so right.

A few moments later Bex opened the door and smiled with relief.

'It's good to see you're safe, Jud,' she said. 'When I had no reply to my text, I rang the York Conservatives' office. I thought you'd still be there, but the lady said you'd gone out for a walk with Thacker. I can't tell you what I've been thinking. I was just about to set off and try to find you, but York is a big place and—'

'It's OK,' said Jud. She was speaking so quickly. Part of him thought it was charming to see her in a fluster like this. 'Can I come in?' he said gently.

'Oh, er . . . yes, of course!' She turned back into the room and Jud followed her. 'Actually, have you heard from Bonati?'

'No, why?'

'Well, we're supposed to be meeting up for a video conference call.' She looked at her watch. 'Any minute now.'

The room was a mess. Jud had always harboured a suspicion that girls, in their natural habitat, were messy creatures. Messier than boys, in fact.

He wasn't sure if this was true, it was just a hunch, but if Bex was anything to go by – then his theory was right. There were clothes on the floor, half-eaten biscuits on the dressing table and the television cabinet, a discarded Coke can by the bed and a laptop on the chair, which was also strewn with clothes. It looked like she'd been dossing here for weeks.

He tried to hide any sense that he was judging her – he most certainly wasn't. Any comment he made would be hypocritical, to say the least; his room back at the CRYPT was a pit. Besides, there was something charming about the mess. It showed she was kooky – and every guy liked kooky.

'So,' Bex said, sitting on the edge of the bed, trying to regain her composure after seeming so pleased to see him at the door, 'tell me! What happened?'

Her phone blurted out an unwelcome shrill ring. 'That'll be Bonati,' she said.

'Bex?' said Bonati, clearly agitated.

'Yes, sir.'

'Are you online? We've been trying to raise you. We said three o'clock, did we not?'

'I'm sorry, sir. I'm just setting it up now. Jud's here too.'

'Oh good,' said Bonati.

'Tell him I've been in the pub all morning and left my phone there!' Jud whispered cheekily. 'No, tell him I've been at the cinema so I had to turn it off.'

'*No!*' mouthed Bex. She was trying to give him an admonishing look, but she couldn't prevent her lips from curving into a wry smile. 'What was that, Professor? Sorry?'

'Are you online now?' said Bonati impatiently.

'Yes, yes, indeed, sir. I'm just logging into the site now. You'll see us in a second.'

The CRYPT operated their own secure web-conferencing system that was light years ahead of commercial online services. It helped having the owner of Goode Technology PLC, as their founder. If there was one thing Goode liked, it was clear, fast and efficient multi-party conferencing. He was holding online meetings before anyone. How else could he keep tabs on his executives across the world? Goode Technology PLC now had offices on every continent, and each one required regular 'stir-frying', as he called it. The giant screen in his office, and in every office he'd used for years now, regularly projected the faces of his top people, no matter how many thousands of miles away they were – and no matter what time of day it was. When Goode wanted to catch up with his top execs, that was what he did.

And his beloved CRYPT had the very latest technology available. State of the art. The clarity and speed of the images made it seem like Goode was in the room with you – which was the whole idea.

Within a few seconds, Bex's screen was divided into several mini-screens. She and Jud saw Bonati in one corner, obviously in his office. Then there was Dr Vorzek, and Grace and Luc too, sharing her screen. In another screen was Jason Goode, framed by the vast windows of his penthouse, which overlooked the London skyline. DCI Khan was in another screen – he'd had to return to Scotland Yard, but Goode had made sure he'd taken a Goode Technology laptop with him. It looked like he was in what must have been his own cramped office – such a contrast to the room in which Goode was sitting. Jud and Bex saw themselves in a smaller box at the bottom of the screen too.

Goode began.

'So, our northern travellers are still alive, then! Good to see you've not been devoured by ghosts just yet. If you believe the media, you'd think the city was awash with them!'

'Yeah, we're here,' said Jud, casually. It had been so long since he'd seen his father, but he wasn't about to let on that he was pleased to see him now, and with everyone else there it was hardly possible anyway.

But he couldn't deny it, he felt a real need to say simply, 'Hi, Dad.' Those words were so rarely possible. Such a simple phrase, that most people took for granted, but one that Jud could hardly ever utter.

'Good to see you, J,' piped up Bonati. He could tell – even at this distance – that there was an atmosphere between Jason and his son, an awkward formality. Now was not the time. He decided to rescue them both by leading the conversation.

'So, I'm sure we've all got progress updates to share. It's been a frantic time, for sure. Shall we begin with our agents in York?'

'Go for it,' said Goode, smiling. He too felt a keen need to greet his son properly. He would – soon. He'd make it up to him. He'd meet him in the lower car park and whiz him off to some decent eatery in town as soon as he was able. Somewhere quiet where they could catch up properly. Maybe the Ivy this time.

Bex kicked off. 'Well, it's good to see everyone, and thank you, Professor. I'll be glad to start.'

Jud was sniggering. He always found it amusing how Bex spoke so formally in these conferences. Some people had their 'telephone voice'. This was hers.

'I don't know how much everyone is aware of,' she began, 'but there's no doubt the paranormal activity up here is as great as anything we've seen before. The emotions we've both experienced have been so powerful. Too powerful in my case.'

'How're you feeling now?' said Vorzek. She remembered her previous chat with Bex, just after she'd been to Micklegate Bar.

'I'm fine, thanks, Doctor,' said Bex. 'But so much more has happened since we last spoke. I really need to tell you about my experiences on Ouse Bridge. And all the research we've done up here. We think we've found a connection. A link. But more on that soon – there's something much more pressing.' She turned to look at Jud, sitting on a chair he'd pulled up alongside her at the dressing table. 'I think Jud should explain.'

'Go on,' said Bonati.

Jud took up the long and complicated story of how and why Thacker had just pulled a gun on him. Bex contributed to the story, sharing the research she'd done at the York Archives. They covered everything: the Earl of Northumberland, his headless body in the graveyard at All Saints and what was probably his severed head on the spike at the tower; Bex's hypersensing experience at Micklegate; the priest in The Shambles; the strange experience on Ouse Bridge, which could only have been a deep empathic connection to Margaret Clitherow; and the frankly unbelievable story of the man seen outside Brian Maxwell's house the night he died.

Simon Thacker.

When they'd finally finished, the assembled people in the screens just stared at them for a few seconds. No one said anything. It was almost like they were waiting to see who was going to speak first.

'My God,' whispered Bex to Jud. 'Don't they believe us?'

Bonati heard the whisper. 'I'm sorry, Bex. I have a feeling we're all rather in shock.' Other heads were nodding.

'Right, that's it,' said Jason Goode. 'We're coming to get you outta there. I'm not taking any more chances.'

Bonati could see from his friend's face that there was no point in arguing. He knew, better than anyone, how protective Jason was of Jud. And though he couldn't show it publicly, Jud's story had obviously shaken him. The professor could see it – and so could Jud.

'No, it's OK,' said Jud. He hated it when his father went all protective like this. He only did it when he'd been out of the country for a while. He always panicked about Jud's safety when he came back. He wanted him close in the building, where he could see him, talk to him.

'I think Mr Goode's right, Jud,' chipped in Luc. 'It's not safe for you up there. Besides, we never did finish that movie, did we?'

Both boys smiled. The night Jud was sent to Westminster seemed light years away now.

'Seriously, Jud,' said Goode. 'I'm sorry, but when a member of the CRYPT is threatened with a gun, we pull them home. End of story. You don't know where this Thacker is. I'm dispatching the chopper now. It'll be with you in sixty minutes. You're coming home.'

Bonati agreed. 'You're better here with us, J. Your time in York is over, at least for now. Until the chopper arrives, stay in the room, keep the door locked. Khan, can you get a police escort organised?'

'Yeah, sure. I'll speak to the Chief Superintendent in York myself. He'll hand-pick the officers who come to get you. We'll keep Thacker out of this, I'll make sure of it. And I'll get their names to you so you know you're safe.'

'So we know we're *safe*?' said Jud. 'What're you not telling us, Inspector?'

Khan looked pensive. 'Well, I wasn't going to mention this until I'd heard everything you'd got to say first. I didn't want it to influence your theories. I wanted to draw my own conclusions, but I'll tell you now I have some news on the missing witnesses.'

'*What?*' said Bex. 'You mean the woman who saw the headless figure?'

'And the old man at Micklegate?' added Jud.

Khan was nodding his head slowly on screen. He looked mournful. 'Yes. I'm sorry to say it, everyone, but it seems they were arrested.'

'*Arrested?*' said Grace.

'Yes. Two officers picked them up, arranged for them to be discharged from hospital and took them to the cells at a local station, where they spent the night.'

'This is incredible,' said Jud. 'On what charge?'

'Details are patchy, Jud. You'll have to appreciate I wasn't there, but I've done some fishing around. When the woman's husband reported his wife missing, all units up there were notified, and that's when it came to light that they were being held. On suspicion of wasting police time, I think.'

'My God. So they're home now?' said Bex.

'Yes.'

'And who ordered their arrest, Khan?' asked Bonati, intrigued.

'The Chief Superintendent says he's looked into it and the police officers concerned said they'd received instructions from a superior officer. But the weird thing is, there's no senior officer who claims to have sanctioned it.'

'So they made that up?' said Luc.

'It would seem so.'

'My guess is they were told to do it by Thacker,' said Bex.

'It's not impossible,' said Khan.

'Well, we'll await developments on that score,' said Bonati. 'Keep us posted, Inspector.'

'So where's the chopper going to land?' asked Goode, still anxious to get his agents home.

'It can put down at York racecourse,' said Bonati. 'There'll be no meetings there in this weather. Vorzek, can you get it organised now?'

'Yes, Professor,' she said grudgingly. She didn't want to miss anything, but she shared their desire to get Jud and Bex home. 'I'll get straight on to it. Back to you shortly.'

'I think you've both earned your wages up there,' said Goode. 'I want you back here now.'

There was no point in arguing. They had an hour.

Bonati continued with the meeting. 'The extreme level of emotion you've experienced is strange enough, and the research into the Earl of Northumberland, that was good work, Bex. The priests hiding in The Shambles too. Good strong links to Margaret Clitherow and these Catholic martyrs ... But *Simon Thacker*? Even if it *was* him behind these wrongful arrests, is he a murderer? I mean, that's extraordinary.

'Let's say the old woman wasn't mistaken, or deluded, or paranoid, and she *did* see a man leaving the house, and it *was* Simon Thacker. The problem I have is, none of this tells us why there are ghosts in London, does it? Where's the connection to the atrocities down here?'

'I'm afraid it's happened again,' said Khan. 'There's been another incident just this afternoon. You tell me if it's related.'

'Go on,' replied Bonati.

'A woman was found dead in the cellar of a firm of solicitors on the Strand.'

'And why do you think it might be relevant, Inspector?' said the professor.

'She sustained fatal injuries to her neck and wrist. It seems she'd bled to death. I understand her boss found her body. She was the one who reported it. My men said it was a complete mess when they arrived.

'It seems,' continued Khan, 'that she'd tried to write a message. The poor woman was drenched in her own blood and she'd tried to write on the wall with it.'

'Khan, that's horrendous,' said Bonati. 'What did the message say?'

The inspector spoke in a quiet, ominous tone. 'Just two words, Professor: "ghosts here".'

There was silence for a while.

'I'm afraid that's not all,' said Khan slowly. 'Forensics have said the puncture wound to her neck was unlikely to have been caused by a knife or any other kind of improvised weapon.'

'Why?' asked Bonati. 'Why do they say that?'

'Because of the teeth marks they found,' said Khan.

No one said anything for a moment. There was a chill descending over Jud and Bex.

Then Bonati spoke ominously. 'It *has* happened before. Ghosts can sometimes devour human flesh in an attempt to find strength. It seems some spirits may believe they can suck the energy out of us while we're alive. It's a terrifying thought, and I hope to God it didn't happen to this woman.'

'Or when they're angered,' added Goode. 'Who knows, some might do it for revenge. Punishment against the human who disturbed them.'

'But there's nothing that links any possible ghost there to this case, is there?' asked Jud.

'You tell me,' said Khan. 'It only happened this afternoon – reports came in just a short while ago. I suggest you get someone, down there asap, though, Professor. Who knows, they might feel something, or record some levels, or whatever it is you guys do.'

'Good idea,' said Bonati. 'We'll get straight over there once we've finished. Stay online, Khan, and I'll get some details from you.'

'Will do. Can I put a question to Jud first?'

'Go on.'

'This gun, said Khan. 'The one you said Thacker was holding in the church up there?'

'Yeah, what about it?'

'Well, I just wondered. I don't suppose you could tell the make, could you? I mean, I know you guys don't exactly use ordinary weapons, but I was just curious.'

'It was a Glock 17,' said Jud instantly. 'Nine millimetre.'

Jud knew his guns. He'd read enough military stories and magazines to recognise what type of pistol it was.

'Oh, right.' said Khan pensively.

'Why do you ask?' said Bonati.

'Well, you know about DCS Braithwaite?'

'Yes,' said Bonati and Goode.

'No!' shouted everyone else. 'What about him?'

'I'm sorry, everyone,' said Khan. 'I wasn't sure what you'd been told. I'm afraid to report that I found his body this morning. He'd been shot dead at his home in Lambeth. Bullet through the head. Ballistics have been on it. They found the bullet.

'It was from a Glock 17, nine millimetre.'

CHAPTER 47

THURSDAY 4 NOVEMBER: 3.41 P.M.

YORK TO LONDON TRAIN

Simon Thacker pulled his hoodie tight around his head and kept his face buried in his newspaper. His jawbone was still sore where the meddling kid had socked him. His lips were badly swollen and the knuckles on his gun hand were inflamed too.

But the worst injury was to his nose. He'd mopped up the blood with a handkerchief, but the bridge of his nose had swollen massively and he looked like a boxer after twelve rounds.

Luckily there had been no one in the church when he'd taken Jud in there. And no one came in after. He'd been able to slope away.

But where? He couldn't return to his constituency office. Lorraine at reception would have fussed all over him. He would have had to make up some crappy excuse – fallen over in the snow or something. She would have insisted he went to A&E – probably driven him there herself.

And this would all have wasted time – time he didn't have. No doubt Jud would have told the police by now. There was probably a manhunt on.

The only solution was to get the hell out of York, back to

London and disappear amongst the millions. He couldn't return to his flat. He knew that. He needed time to think.

Luckily he'd found a quiet carriage. Just one other person – a middle-aged man in a pinstripe. He'd looked Thacker up and down when he'd first boarded. Probably thought he was about to mug him, given the state of his face and the hoodie over his head.

Thacker had slumped into a seat and stayed there motionless. Luckily a discarded newspaper lay on the seat next to him and he'd grabbed it to cover his face.

By some amazing stroke of luck, his wallet was still in his jogging pants, so he'd been able to buy a ticket from the machine before boarding.

The guard was doing the rounds. He approached his seat. Without looking up, Thacker handed the ticket to him and he duly stamped it. Then he was gone.

It was twenty minutes in when he heard it.

At first it was just a whisper, almost undetectable. But Thacker was used to it. He knew the signs. It wasn't just the voice in his head, it was the prickly sensations down his neck, the tingling across his scalp and the palpitations in his chest that told him the master was coming.

He knew he'd have to face him soon. There was no chance he'd get away with such a failure. But not here. Not now.

He'd often wondered if the master could see him, watch him wherever he went. He just didn't know.

Had he seen him in the church? Had he seen him mess up so badly?

Perhaps he hadn't. Perhaps he could keep it under wraps.

But the problem – and it had been beating in his brain since leaving the church – was that he was unable to assist the master in carrying out the plan. How could he be there at the State Opening now?

Everything had changed.

How could the master's dream be realised? All the plans, the sacrifices along the way. For what?

God knows, he and the master had planned it long enough. For years they'd rehearsed it all. The master, and his so-called friends, would wreak havoc in Parliament. There would be bloodshed, there was no escaping that, but Thacker had managed to persuade the master that to take out the monarch and her faithful government in one blow – just like they'd planned to do all those years ago – would not work. Not in this day and age.

So the 'friends' were going to swoop into the House of Lords and whip up those present into a frenzy of fear – maim and injure if necessary, but no deaths. Thacker had pleaded for that. And the master had promised.

When the dignitaries were at screaming point, Thacker would step in. Speak to the ghosts – calm them. Reason with them. Bargain with them for the monarch to be spared. He would be hailed a hero. The packed house would be in awe.

And then the deal. The documents were ready. Thacker had spent so long preparing them. The Bill that would see the Act of Settlement abolished once and for all was drafted. Everything was ready – and hidden securely in Thacker's flat.

All he'd needed to do was pitch up at Parliament tomorrow, wait for the ghosts to make their demands, and then produce what they wanted.

The Queen would have signed, the Bill would have been made law and the course of English history would be changed for ever.

Roman Catholics would enjoy the same rights as Protestants. If the monarch wanted to marry a Catholic, or convert to Catholicism in their own right, they could. At last.

And the master would rest easy. He'd promised that. Thacker would get his life back – a life, until now, that had been shaped by another. And all for this moment.

But Thacker's failure in the church had changed everything. He would be arrested the moment he turned up at Westminster. How could he attend?

And the voice was growing stronger in his head.

'Not now, master,' he whispered. 'Soon. I beg of you. I will talk to you soon. Leave me until then.'

It was no use. The pain was starting in his leg. He grabbed his thigh. It was agony, like someone was driving a dagger right into his flesh, and turning and moving it, causing all the muscles and sinews to twist and rip and haemorrhage.

He could already feel the dampness of his own blood seeping through his trousers and on to the grey seat beneath him.

'Oh God,' he whispered. 'Not here. Not now. Have mercy, master . . . please!'

He screwed his face into his chest and willed the master away. He was rocking uncontrollably now. He knew it was no nightmare – no dream. It was starting already. He'd not even had the chance to explain himself. To plead.

Writhing in pain, he shuffled to his feet. The man behind him looked anxious.

'You OK, mate?' he said desperately. 'Do you want me to get some help?'

Thacker turned half in his direction and just shook his head. This was one problem no one could save him from. The spirits were impervious to human meddling. He could have been in the safety of a police cell, or in the middle of a hospital ward, or surrounded by bodyguards in an armoured car – it would have made no difference at all. No physical protection could save him now.

The only thing he could do was plead. Appeal to the master's conscience. They'd been together for so long now, surely the master would listen just one more time, before passing his sentence.

He was heading for the only place he could find privacy – the toilet. The electronic door swung open. He staggered inside and pressed the button to close it. It swung shut again.

Another stabbing surge at his leg. And now one to his stomach. Like a vicious blow to the gut, but one that he knew would bleed before it bruised. And it would keep bleeding this time.

He fell on to the toilet seat.

'Master!' he shouted.

Nothing. Only pain.

'Master, hear me! I tried. I only wanted to protect you. They would have stopped us. They would have used their machines. Your energy would have left you slowly. They can do that.'

Another sharp puncture, to his shoulder this time. 'Aagh! Please. No more! You've made your point. You are angry, master, I know. I have failed you, but we are family, you and I. We are like brothers. We are bound together in—'

He stopped. His peripheral vision had caught something.

In the metal mirror over the tiny sink to his left.

He slowly turned his head. His eyes widened in fear. He let out a shrill scream. But the electronic door was thick and airtight. There was no way he'd be heard.

A face was pushing its way through the mirror, just like before – back at his flat, in the ceiling. There was a strange glow that sent tiny red beams like daggers across the mirrored surface. And in the centre, the same face he'd seen before. The same horrific vision. The sickly pale skin. The black straggly hair. And those eyes – white as marble, devoid of pupils. But they flickered from side to side. They were alive.

There was still no body. The spirit was still too weak for that. Just his head appeared, stretched and twisted. Writhing around uncontrollably, as though its muscles had a mind of their own.

Then the ghost opened his blackened, cracked lips.

'You've failed me, little one. You decided to take matters into your own hands.'

'But master, I—'

'You didn't trust me. You didn't believe it was possible.'

'I did, I did! But I wanted to—'

'*Silence!* You did not trust me when I told you to forget the babies at the CRYPT. They are of no consequence to us. We are bigger than them, stronger. We have power now – more than they could ever take away from us. But you thought you'd silence them yourself. And you failed. And now you have revealed yourself to them. You cannot return. You have jeopardised our plans. Tomorrow we shall have to proceed without you.'

'Aagh! Master, please!' Another stab, in his chest. Blood was leaking from his punctured body. He was already feeling faint. He saw his own face in the mirror – sickly white, except for the bloodied, swollen mass that was once his nose.

Another blow – to the neck. It struck an artery.

The metal mirror was splattered. The ghost's face was fading beneath the red splashes. He'd done his job. The little one was punished.

He was no longer needed. Surplus. He'd failed. The spirit had invested so much time and love and guidance. And for what? He was weak and pathetic, like all the others.

He deserved to die.

Thacker fell to the floor. He was haemorrhaging from so many parts of his wrecked body. The floor was covered. He made one last effort to rise and reach the button to open the door, but he was too weak now. He was dizzy. The room went dark as he keeled over. His head struck the stained metal toilet and he was no more.

It was another six minutes before anyone came past. The man in the pinstripe had been concerned that his fellow passenger had still not returned. Was he all right?

He left his seat and made his way towards the toilet. The carriage doors slid aside and he gasped in horror.

Though the toilet door remained shut, blood was seeping

through the gap that ran along the base of it, pouring across the corridor.

He steadied himself against the wall, held a handkerchief to his mouth with one hand and pressed the emergency alarm with the other.

CHAPTER 48

THURSDAY 4 NOVEMBER: 3.51 P.M.

CRYPT VIDEO CONFERENCE

Jud knew it was the same gun. 'Shit, he really would have used it on me,' he said into his screen anxiously. 'Sorry, everyone. It's just that if that bullet was from Thacker's Glock 17 then, well, I mean, where the hell is this leading?'

'There's something that connects Thacker to all this, and it's more than the gun, I can feel it. But *what*?' said Bonati.

'Good question,' chipped in Goode. 'And what is the connection between the ghosts in York and those in London anyway? I mean, we still haven't solved that yet, have we?'

'Well,' said Luc. 'We've got the words that we've all heard at the hauntings. I mean the martyrs caritatis phrase.'

Bex spoke up. 'It's a phrase I saw in a book at the library. So I looked it up. It comes from *caritas* which is Latin for kindness or charity, I think. The term means something like "people who died for love" – or for God.'

'And that in turn links us back to this Margaret Clitherow and the priests she was hiding up there in York,' said Vorzek, who'd now returned from organising the helicopter. It would be well on its way now. Since the installation of the new helipad on the rooftop of the building, emergency sorties like this were easy.

'Exactly,' said Bex. 'Margaret Clitherow was giving shelter to priests from Europe.'

'But why now?' said Khan. 'And why Westminster? That's what I want to know. I mean, it's going to be bad enough telling the Palace that a member of Her Majesty's Government is a murderer. If she hears there's ghosts at the Houses of Parliament too, there'll be fireworks, I can tell you.'

Jud suddenly gasped. '*What* did you just say?'

'Huh? I said it's bad enough that I've got to—'

'No. After that. You said *fireworks*,' said Jud hurriedly.

'Yeah. I mean there'll be serious trouble if she has to postpone tomorrow. The State Opening. She'll never—'

'That's it!' Jud shouted into his screen.

There was silence.

'Fireworks! What is it we remember on Bonfire Night?' he asked.

'Well, it's Guy Fawkes Night, isn't it,' said Grace. 'It's when we remember . . . Oh my God.'

Grace echoed what everyone else was thinking.

Bex spoke first.

'The Gunpowder Plot was an attempt by those who sympathised with what was happening to the Roman Catholics at the time. They were being persecuted, weren't they? The plotters wanted justice, I suppose.'

Vorzek joined in. 'Yes. It was their intention to take out the Protestant monarch and so return the country to Papal rule.'

'And it was to happen at the State Opening of Parliament,' said Jud, ominously.

'Now wait a minute, everyone,' said Bonati. 'Let's not get carried away here. None of what's happened links us definitively to the Gunpowder Plot. This is pure conjecture.'

'Do you think so, sir?' said Bex. 'I'm not so sure. From what I know of Guy Fawkes – I mean, what I studied at school – he was from York, wasn't he?'

'Yes,' said Jud. 'There's that pub down the road, isn't there, Bex? It's the Guy Fawkes Inn – the house he was born in!'

'I don't know,' said Bonati. 'I'm a scientist, not a historian. We need much more evidence than this.'

Jud was already on it. He'd taken out his iPad and started searching for Guy Fawkes entries. Within moments he'd found something. He read it to the assembled group.

'Listen to this: Fawkes grew up in York, where, as a teenager, he witnessed the cruel treatment of Catholic recusants in the city, including the brutal execution of Margaret Clitherow.'

The name shocked everyone. For there to be such a strong link between the various ghosts appearing was more than coincidence, and they all knew it. There was a surge of energy rising from everyone in the meeting and combining in the ether. Jud's words had just changed everything.

Goode said, 'So Guy Fawkes and his fellow plotters had seen the injustice in the way Catholics were being treated and chose to take the law into their own hands?'

'And return a Catholic monarch to the throne. Yes!' said Bex.

'Luc?' said Jud. 'You OK?' He could see on the screen that Luc had put his head into his hands. He looked up slowly.

'Yeah, I'm fine. It's just . . . well, it's just I'm now beginning to understand what I saw in that basement in Westminster. I saw it, Jud. I saw them. All those bodies marching. And the sighs and the wails. The suffering in their faces. They were Catholic martyrs, I know it.'

Everyone glanced at their screens in silence for a moment, filled with a sense of dread as to what they'd uncovered here.

'Mr Goode is right,' said Bex. 'That's exactly how the Gunpowder Plot came about. It was a gang of devout Roman Catholics who believed the solution was to rid the country of the

Protestant king and his government. Basically, they were going to blow them all up.'

'Yeah, and it wasn't the first uprising, was it, Bex,' said Jud.

'No, it wasn't.' She remembered her research again. 'I've found out that Thomas Percy, 7th Earl of Northumberland, had led a rising against the Protestant faith years before. It was called the Rising of the North.'

'And what's so special about Thomas Percy?' asked Grace.

'Good question,' said Bex. 'I'll tell you. He was beheaded outside All Saints Church in York.'

'That's right,' said Jud. 'We believe it was his ghost outside the same church the other night. And I'll bet it was his severed head that was seen at Micklegate Bar.'

'And I've just realised,' said Khan. 'If my history's right – and it's been a long time since I read a history book – didn't Fawkes and his men rent a house near Westminster? Isn't that where they stored the gunpowder or something? I'll wager a bet with you it was in a house in the Strand – where a certain solicitor's is today!'

'Of course!' said Bex. 'I think it was! That poor woman at the lawyer's office must've actually disturbed the conspirators. I can't believe it!'

Bonati was still silent. He was just as struck by the revelations that were unfolding, but he was still troubled.

'Look,' he said. 'This might – and I stress *might* – explain why we've seen ghosts rising up, why you've all heard the phrase "martyrs caritatis" at different hauntings and so on . . .'

'But?' said Jud. He could always sense when there was a 'but' coming.

'But,' continued Bonati, 'it does *not* explain the actions of Simon Thacker, or why any of this has come about *now*. I mean, the Gunpowder Plot happened four hundred years ago, for goodness' sake!'

'OK,' said Jason Goode. 'Let's focus our minds on Thacker

first. I take it he's still on the loose. Is the helicopter dispatched, by the way? I want these agents home!'

'Yes,' said Vorzek. 'It'll be in York soon.'

'And the police escort?'

'Yes,' said Khan. 'Already done it. They're on their way to the hotel.'

'Thanks, everyone,' said Jud. 'But the answer to Mr Goode's question about Thacker is, I don't know. I've only just returned – I mean literally in the last few minutes – from the church. I reckon he'll have left the city by now – he won't have hung around looking for me. I'm sure he'll have assumed I've told the police, and fled.'

'He *owns* the police,' said Bex.

'Not quite,' said Khan. 'The Commissioner down here is absolutely determined to root out whoever killed Braithwaite, and believe me, he won't rule out any suspects. As soon as I've finished here, I'll be giving him your evidence, and I've no doubt he'll instigate a nationwide search. Don't you worry, we'll get him.'

'But why Thacker?' said Goode. 'Why *him*? Is he even a Catholic, for starters?'

'Yes, sir,' replied Jud quickly. 'I haven't told you the name of his church – The English Martyrs Roman Catholic Church.'

'OK,' said Goode. 'But listen, everybody, we're all in no doubt, aren't we, that from the martyrs way back then to their Catholic descendants today, *none* of them would commit harm like this. Let's not start a witch-hunt here. They're God-fearing people. Thacker is working alone!'

'Or at least his accomplices may not be alive, put it that way,' said Jud.

'Wait a minute,' said Vorzek. 'Are you really suggesting he is collaborating with ghosts?'

'Unlikely' said Bonati.

They fell silent again. Could it *really* be true? Could a grown man have retained his extrasensory perception all the way into adulthood?

Goode was less hasty to refute such an idea. 'The only way I would say it *was* possible was if a spirit had been in direct communication with the man from an early age. As a partner through life, if you like. Plausible, Giles?'

Bonati was unsure. 'I don't know, Jason. It's not impossible, I suppose. If the bonds between man and spirit were strong enough, then who knows?'

'Wait a minute!' said Jud suddenly. 'When I left the church just now – when I was running down the path – I heard Thacker say something. What was it?' He was closing his eyes now, focusing hard.

'I know, that's it. It didn't mean anything at the time, but I'm sure he was shouting something about "the master".'

'So maybe this Thacker is a pawn in the game,' said Goode. 'Poor guy. He's being used. He's not the real force behind all this.'

'So, who is the master?' said Grace.

CHAPTER 49

THURSDAY 4 NOVEMBER: 4.16 P.M.

BLACK ROD'S PRIVATE RESIDENCE, WESTMINSTER

Brigadier Geoffrey Farlington was having a manic day, but then what did he expect? He'd seen so many State Openings, but they never got any easier. It always came down to the reliability of his staff. He was a hopeless delegator. Everyone said so. But then, in Farlington's arrogant opinion, if you wanted something done quickly and efficiently and up to your own exacting standards, then nine times out of ten you had to do it yourself. There was no point in trusting a minion to do it.

Besides, it was his head on the block if things went awry – he was the one who'd have to face Her Majesty if there was a hitch in the proceedings.

Much of the day was spent doing the final checks – touring the building, meeting staff, seeing for himself if they'd done their job properly, and redoing it if they hadn't. It wasn't until four o'clock that he realised he'd not eaten since breakfast at six. He had two hours until the next meeting – the 'round-up' as he called it.

There was time to nip back to his apartment, catch up with Susie, his wife, and see if he could persuade her to rustle something up for him. The round-up might go on late, and then there was a myriad of things to do that evening, including the final meeting with his closest staff, the Yeoman Usher of the Black Rod – his deputy – the Staff Superintendent, the Principal Doorkeeper and his deputy, and the Chief Admin Officer.

He was going to need some sustenance to see him through.

Luckily, Farlington's London residence was close to the House. He slipped out of the doors that led into Black Rod's Garden – a private entrance used by just a few of the House Authorities at Westminster.

A brisk twenty-minute walk and he was at the mansion block of grand apartments in Great Peter Street. The Georgian facade was elegant but not ostentatious. Farlington's flat on the sixth floor overlooked Millbank and the beautiful oaks of the Victoria Tower Gardens across the road.

Through the lobby, with its grand mahogany staircase, red carpet and giant pot plants, to the old Victorian lift. He pulled the rattling brass cage to one side, stepped in and then closed it again. The pulleys lurched into action and the old metal box slowly juddered skywards, revealing walls and floors, windows and doors. The brigadier preferred these old-fashioned lifts – at least you could see out of them. He hated those modern coffin-like boxes that surrounded you these days. He always feared getting trapped inside one, with not even so much as a window to the world outside. Soon he heard the very pleasing ring that heralded his arrival at the sixth floor.

He stepped out and marched across the blue paisley carpet to his own door, whistling as he went – the old and much-derided signal to his neighbours that the 'whistling brigadier', as they called him, was back in the building. His whistling was well known throughout Parliament as well as in the great mansion block.

He rang the bell. No answer. It wasn't unusual. Susie was probably in town somewhere, and in any case he hadn't told her he was coming home.

He located his key buried deep inside his leather briefcase and opened the door.

Peace at last.

He went through to the kitchen and began a clumsy attempt at preparing a salmon sandwich with cottage cheese and rocket. He wasn't a cook of any description, except 'awful'. But he managed it.

He carried his plate, and a cooling glass of gin and tonic that he'd rustled up with a great deal more skill and practice than he'd shown when preparing the food, into the main drawing room. The great leafless oaks in the park opposite, and the darkening skies behind them, gave the windows an eerie quality.

Black Rod was relieved in some ways to find the apartment empty. Moments like these were so rare, when he could truly be alone with his thoughts – and Radio 4. He placed his food and drink on the mahogany coffee table and switched on the radio on the shelf behind his favourite chair.

It didn't take long for him to fall asleep after he'd eaten. Whether it was the food, the gin, the hectic pace of life at Westminster or a combination of all three he wasn't sure, but his tired eyes had closed at some stage.

It was the key in the latch that woke him now.

And the familiar voice of his darling wife. She'd seen his briefcase by the door – his well-worn doctor's-style Gladstone bag. She knew he was back.

'Geoffrey?'

He opened his eyes with a jolt. His head felt heavy, and he'd fallen asleep in an awkward position in the chair, so his neck was now stiff and sore. The gin had been a silly idea. It had wiped him out and brought on a heavy sleep at the wrong time in the day. He was disorientated and his head felt as fragile as glass. It had been the first drink of any kind he'd had since breakfast. He chided himself for not taking enough fluids.

'I'm here,' he managed, with a croaky voice.

She entered the room. 'What're you doing home, Geoffrey? Are you all right?'

'What? Oh yes, I'm fine. I had a slight gap in appointments and realised I'd not eaten anything. I thought I'd pop back and grab a bite before I head back again at six.'

'Did you say *six*?' said Susie.

'Yes,' said Farlington, rubbing his watery eyes and rotating his painful neck.

'But it's six twenty, darling!'

'My God, how long have I been asleep? I don't believe it!'

He rose shakily to his feet.

'Whoa, steady there, darling,' said Susie as she went to catch him. He'd lost his balance. 'Sit down and try again.'

'I'm sorry,' he said, rubbing his head. 'I tell you, that was a deeper sleep than I thought. I reckon that gin must've knocked me out.'

His wife rolled her eyes and tutted at him.

'Well I hardly drink at all, Suze. It was only a small gin. I mean, how often do I have that?'

'That's just the problem, you don't drink enough! Water, I mean. How many times have I told you to drink more fluids! You're not getting any younger, Geoffrey. Your body needs water, like an engine needs oil.'

'Before it seizes up, you mean?'

'Exactly,' said Susie. 'You've got to slow down.'

'I thought I had just slowed down by resting in the chair, and now I feel bloody awful,' he said. 'If that's what slowing down does to you, you can forget it!'

'You know what I mean,' said his wife. She looked at his face. 'You look pale, Geoffrey. You've been overdoing it, haven't you?'

He stood up again, keeping his balance this time.

'Oh, don't fuss, Suze,' he said. 'Right, I've got to go. I'm late already, and I was late this morning too. I'll be getting a reputation.'

Susie knew how much of a stickler he was for being on time – it was his army background. All those years on manoeuvres.

She ran to the kitchen, poured a glass of water and came back with it, blocking the doorway. 'You're not leaving until you drink this. All of it!'

'OK.' He smiled. He gulped large mouthfuls down and tipped his head backwards to finish the glass.

The room spun again and he had to grab Susie's arm before he fell.

'Geoffrey? Are you sure you're all right?'

'What? Er . . . yes. Yes, of course. I tell you, I don't know what was in that gin. I feel bloody weird, Suze. But I'll be OK.'

He regained his posture and walked past her to the door. He picked up his briefcase and went out into the hall.

'Don't be late!' Susie whispered from the doorway. She hated holding conversations outside, where the neighbours could hear. But she stayed to watch him trudge slowly down the corridor. He'd been working too hard, no question.

And then she noticed something else.

He wasn't whistling. Poor darling, she said to herself. He needs a day off.

The metal lift rattled up and the brigadier clasped the brass handle and swung the cage across. He stepped in.

The motion of the lift lowering again brought a sickness to his stomach.

Was it the salmon? Perhaps that was it. A bit of dodgy fish – bringing a temperature and a heavy head when he awoke.

It might explain the dreams, too. Sitting in that chair, he'd seen such weird images. He could picture them now, as if he were still asleep. He knew he wasn't – he'd seen Susie after all – but the things he'd seen whilst sleeping had been so vivid. And disturbing.

He'd dreamt of a face.

It was pale and sickly and gaunt. Did it have black hair? Yes, that was it. Jet black. He could see it now, just like in his dream. The eyes were the most haunting thing of all – pearly white with no pupils.

Wait a minute.

'Jesus! Am I dreaming again?' He slumped against the metal wall of the lift.

It was like he'd drifted off once more. A micro-sleep – a millisecond's worth of dreaming. The face seemed so real again. Had he closed his eyes? He must have done.

He stood upright, coughed and shook his head.

Come on! he said to himself. *Get a grip.*

The lift was moving slowly down the floors with a reassuring grind. No, he wasn't asleep again. He was awake. Maybe he'd let his mind drift, but he was now in control.

'Lay off the gin,' he said out loud.

Then the lift stopped.

Was he between floors?

The gaps between the bars of the cage revealed nothing but concrete walls.

Where the hell was he?

He pressed the emergency button. There was a spark – a little arc of light that jumped from the buzzer to the metal wall of the lift. Then a fizzle.

The emergency button had died.

The light above his head flickered momentarily, but stayed on. 'Oh, come on!' said the brigadier. 'Give me a break!'

He pressed the button again but nothing happened. No ringing or buzzing. Nothing.

He felt alone. Years in the army had prepared him for crises of all kinds. He was as tough as they came. Except for his one weakness.

Claustrophobia.

He could feel his heart speeding up, though he was trying to talk himself down. Like so many soldiers, he'd learned ways of persuading himself out of fear. Rate your panic on a scale of one to ten. If it's as high as a nine or a ten, see if you can talk yourself down to an eight. All you have to do is breathe slowly and deeply and distract your mind. Problem solved. That was usually the way out of it. Harness the ferocious power of the imagination – which usually went into overdrive in these situations, conjuring up the very worst-case scenarios possible and bringing on the panic attacks – and use it to focus on the very practical task of finding a way out.

He breathed deeply. He was at a seven already. And rising.

Pop. The light bulb burst.

And he was at a ten. It was the most afraid he'd been in years. Trapped. No way of ringing the alarm. No way of signalling someone.

Come on, he said to himself. *You can do this.*

He knew someone would be there shortly.

And then he realised. His mobile phone. Of course! He could call Suze, who'd get help. He had a torch app on his phone too.

He fished around in the pitch black for his briefcase. The phone was buried inside it; he hated carrying it with him – it made his pocket bulge and his suit look shabby. Same as his wallet, and his specs. All buried in the dark recesses of his bag.

He stooped to sweep the floor of the lift for the bag.

Where *was* the bloody thing!

As he fumbled for it on the floor, he failed to notice what was happening above him.

The roof of the lift was altering.

Tiny sparks were flying, and there was a kind of glow appearing in the centre.

It was reddish in colour.

Farlington noticed the faint light casting shadows on the floor by his feet. He looked up.

The face of the spirit was bursting through the ceiling above him.

He recognised it instantly and fell to his knees.

He buried his own face in his hands.

What was happening to him? Was he dreaming again? Was he back in his armchair in the drawing room?

He raised his head and parted his hands nervously.

'No! Leave me! Go away!' he bawled at the apparition. His voice was deep and commanding. Anyone at Westminster would have followed his instructions to the letter.

But not the spirit. Not the master.

The ghost of Guy Fawkes had no respect for the authority of Black Rod. The brigadier could lord it up at Westminster with his archaic titles of office and his pompous attitude, but here, right now, it meant nothing.

Dignitaries like him were exactly who Fawkes despised the most. They thought they ruled the people – not served them. Four hundred years and nothing had changed. Black Rod! Still the same ridiculous titles and badges and honours – the ceremonies of the elite. And their *laws*. How he hated their laws.

But soon, soon it would all change. And the one law he'd spent so long despising would finally be buried.

He didn't need to bellow. Didn't even need to shout. This pitiful man was now cowering on the floor. His pompous ranting had been silenced. Farlington had been so shocked by the spirit's eyes. Lifeless, colourless spheres that now danced about the lift.

The spirit just whispered.

'You know me, then.'

'I've seen your face. In a dream. What is happening? Why can I hear you? Oh God, oh God – leave me!' He'd put his hands to his head and was shaking it left to right, as if to shake himself out of a stupor. He knew this couldn't be real. But when would he wake up?

'*Susie!*' he shouted.

'She can't hear you now,' said Fawkes. 'It's just you and me.'

'Leave me,' pleaded Black Rod. 'Please.'

'I came to you in your sleep. The task is almost done.'

'Task? *What* task?' said Farlington desperately.

He had a sense of foreboding. The spirit's face was the most pitiful thing he'd seen. Tragic, wretched. As though it had been callously beaten and then abandoned for dead. But it was those eyes that chilled him to the bone. So lifeless, like a statue's, and yet moving.

The face broke free from the roof of the lift and floated like glowing plasma towards Black Rod. Nearer, until it was nearly touching his own face. Farlington could almost see through it. The lift was glowing too. Sparks were dancing up the metal bars that formed the cage around him. It was as though he was a guinea pig inside some futuristic laboratory.

He could feel a terrible tingling at the back of his neck now. It was more real than the goose bumps of fear – and it was spreading over his skull. Prickly and jabbing, like a million tiny pinpricks across his head.

And the pain inside was growing. The hangover he'd awoken with had not abated, only worsened. It felt as though his head was being squeezed. The pinpricks had grown to actual stabbing pains.

'You will be useful to me,' said Fawkes. 'I am too weak to appear in body. I have tried – for so long now, I have tried to appear as I once was. But alas, I have always lacked the energy. My death was so painful. So barbaric. It almost robbed me of my spirit entirely. But I lived on.

'And now I shall return – with your help.'

Black Rod's face was frozen with terror. *Real* terror. He couldn't move, he couldn't breathe, he couldn't do anything. His body was rigid with fear.

And then he felt it.

He was *changing*.

His thoughts, his emotions, they were altering. His fears – they were ebbing away.

Had he been himself, he would have questioned what was happening. He would have struggled and fought, protested physically and mentally against the violation that was happening to him.

But he was no longer himself. The spirit – the soul – the thing that makes us who we are inside was *altering*. And he couldn't stop it.

The spectral face was disappearing from view. Moving into him. Feeding on his fear.

The spirit of Guy Fawkes was *inside* Black Rod.

CHAPTER 50

THURSDAY 4 NOVEMBER: 6.41 P.M.

THE CRYPT HELICOPTER – EN ROUTE TO LONDON

'So where do you think Thacker is now?' said Bex into her headset.

'Who knows?' said Jud, gazing down at the rooftops and gardens that swept past below.

The black Squirrel HT1 dipped sharply forward and accelerated again. The pilot had been told to make the journey quick. But this was ridiculous.

'How long till we're in London, Gary?' said Jud.

'Twenty minutes or so,' said Gary.

'Blimey, that's good going!'

'Dr Vorzek said she wanted you back quickly. So that's what I'm doing.'

'We're headed for the new pad on the CRYPT, yeah?'

'No,' said Gary.

'What? Why? Where're we going, then?' said Bex, a sudden panic entering her voice.

'Don't worry,' said Gary. 'It's all sorted. There's been a change of plan. Bonati wants you at Westminster. They're all there now. We'll be landing on Parliament Square.'

'Yay!' said Bex. 'Bring it on!' She liked to make an entrance.

Jud was not so sure. 'Why? It's not exactly subtle.'

'Well that's my orders, Jud. And you know Bonati. You don't say no to him.'

Sure enough, a few minutes later the low-rise houses and factories of the London suburbs faded and were replaced by the great skyline of central London. They could see the sharp spires of Westminster. Snow was lingering on rooftops, giving the whole place a fairy-tale look.

Khan had done his job properly. He had organised the police escort up in York – they'd taken Jud and Bex straight to the racecourse as planned – while here in London he had arranged for Parliament Square to be cleared. There were just a few police cars at the corners of the vast expanse of snow-covered grass.

The Squirrel gently lowered itself. The trees that lined the roads bent and bowed as the force of the rotary blades swirled the air around. Onlookers had stopped to peer.

Who *was* this? Was it the PM, or some royal dignitary? Cameras were at the ready, but they were quickly replaced in bags as police kept a tight rein on security.

And then they were down.

Moments later, Jud and Bex were running across the square towards the great Palace of Westminster.

Bonati met them at the main gates.

'Well done. Good to see you both.'

'Why here, sir? I thought you wanted us back at the CRYPT?'

'That was the plan, but there's no time.'

'Why? What's happened now?' said Bex anxiously.

'Nothing, not here at least. But we're convinced something will. Security are all over this place, but I've finally managed to get access to the basement. That's where the others are now. Come on.' He led them past the security guards and around the front facade of the building to the private entrance of Black Rod's Garden. Another security check and they were inside.

Jud and Bex could see that the place was crawling with police officers.

'Have we missed something, sir? Has something else happened since the conference?' Jud said, trying to keep pace with the professor as he walked briskly down the long corridor towards the lifts that would take them down to the basement.

'You bet it has,' said the professor. 'It's Thacker.'

'*Thacker?*' they said in unison.

'Yes. Keep your voices down!' said Bonati. He waited until the lift doors had opened and they were inside before he spoke again.

'Thacker was found dead on a train bound for London. Bled to death. His body was in a mess by all accounts.'

'No wonder the place is crawling with officers,' said Jud. 'The minister responsible for security found dead the day before the State Opening. Doesn't look good, does it?'

'Exactly. First DCS Braithwaite, now Thacker. I tell you, we can't keep this under wraps any more. Whoever found Thacker didn't just tell the police, they told the press too.'

'Oh no,' said Bex. 'I can only imagine the headlines in the morning.'

'Is the State Opening still going ahead, sir?'

'Absolutely. There's no way Her Majesty will postpone it. And why? If there's a serious security threat today, there'll be one tomorrow, and the next day. When can you ever say there won't be these days? But you can't stop democracy. The Queen and Parliament are agreed on that one. They refuse to let this change their plans. But there's something else I haven't told you.'

'Yeah?'

'Black Rod's gone missing.'

'What?' said Jud incredulously. 'But he's—'

'In charge of security for tomorrow's ceremony, yes, I *know*! The search is on.'

'So it's going to be a long night, sir?'

'Don't tell me,' said Bex. 'Vigil in the basement?'

'Exactly,' said Bonati as the lift doors swung open.

'Welcome to the new underground headquarters of the CRYPT, for the next twenty-four hours anyway. Follow me.'

CHAPTER 51

THURSDAY 4 NOVEMBER:
7.03 P.M.

CRYPT EMERGENCY HQ, HOUSES
OF PARLIAMENT, LONDON

Jud and Bex could hardly believe their eyes. There were more agents than they'd ever seen in one place. Instruments were set up everywhere, people were making recordings and taking readings, Vorzek was camped out in a corner, surrounded by laptops.

'Is this everyone, sir?' said Jud.

'Nearly. I've asked Luc and Grace to get over to the building at the Strand where the woman was found. And the PM has requested that we station some agents at Downing Street, and at the Palace too.'

'Buckingham Palace?' said Bex, astonished.

'Yes. MI5 are throwing everything at this one. I mean, do *you* know where the next haunting will be?'

'No. But we know the targets, I suppose,' said Jud.

'That's right. Anyone with a leading role tomorrow. I tell you, Jud, this may be the biggest case we ever do.'

'But sir,' said Jud. 'I don't understand. Are you saying that the Palace and the PM are all on board with our theory now?

Do they actually believe the place is under threat? I mean, from ghosts.'

'Yes, exactly,' said Bonati. 'I know we've had our difficulties in the past, trying to persuade others to take paranormal activity seriously. But that was before. We know now that it was Thacker who was covering up what happened down here in the basement. The gruesome state of the bodies. I saw them, Luc and Grace saw them. You saw one of the ghosts yourself, J!'

'I know, sir, but I just can't believe we've got their support now.'

'*Believe it!*' said the professor. 'Think about it: once the PM learned the real truth about what happened down here – and not some bullshit spun by Thacker – he wanted us on the case straight away. As did Her Majesty.'

'The Queen?' said Bex. 'So the CRYPT operates by royal appointment now.'

'Don't push your luck, Rebecca,' said Bonati. 'There's work to do.' But Bex could see that even the professor was excited to have been given such a green light.

'And what about the press?' said Jud, ominously. He was not sharing their excitement. For him, such a high-profile case could only mean one thing. Publicity. And that was his worst enemy. He preferred a life in the shadows.

'Don't worry, J,' said Bonati. 'DCS Khan is on it. He's holding a press conference this evening. We've already written his script. Serious security risk, yes, but no mention of ghosts. The information Scotland Yard have received has led them to take extra precautionary measures here at Westminster to ensure the smooth running of tomorrow's State Opening. You get the gist. The public won't know the cause of the threat.'

'You reckon?' said Jud, unconvinced.

'Well, we'll see,' said Bonati.

'And Mr Goode? Where's he?' said Jud, trying to hide his interest.

Bonati allowed himself a small smile. 'He's here too, J. Just returned from Downing Street. Let's tell him you're here, shall we.'

CHAPTER 52

THURSDAY 4 NOVEMBER: 7.21 P.M.

THE STRAND, LONDON

CRYPT agents Grace and Luc needed to keep strong. This made three corpses in two days. Grace had looked deathly white since seeing Rosa's body, and Luc too had been speechless at first. The residue of emotion that lingered in the room was almost tangible, though their senses had barely recovered from the experiences at Westminster.

Since Di Bawthwicke had made her awful discovery at lunchtime, staff had been evacuated and the place was now awash with forensics and police officers. The building had been cordoned off. Khan had been keen to keep the nature of the killing under wraps. The press would have had a field day if they'd known the true extent of the injuries sustained. And as for the message on the wall, it didn't bear thinking about what kinds of headlines that would produce.

But Grace and Luc had seen the body. And it had tugged at their emotions greatly. Both had shed a tear on seeing the woman in such a state, with a terrified expression etched on her face.

The poor woman's remains lay on the floor of the old cellar, in a pool of her own blood. The stack of files she'd so meticulously prepared for archiving lay strewn across the floor, also stained in red.

This had been her domain, her little empire of carefully ordered case notes and folders – but it now served as her tomb.

'How can ghosts do this?' Grace had said as she'd entered the room.

'And why?' said Luc. He too had been shocked by the sight. It was hard not to be. Even the forensics had found it difficult.

This was a real woman, after all. A person – and a much-loved one, judging by the reactions of the staff as they'd left the building in tears.

Luc had managed to persuade the officers in the cellar to give them a few moments alone with the corpse – to check for residues of emotion. To take readings. To see, above all, if there was a chance the ghosts would return.

The video conference earlier had been a productive one, and it had led to Bonati and his team researching the locations where Guy Fawkes and his team of plotters had camped out in the run-up to the State Opening. It seemed that they'd used several different places across London, including this house on the Strand. If only the victim had lived; if only she'd been able to tell them what she'd seen. Had the gang been here today? Had she really seen the Gunpowder Plotters? Grace and Luc could only wonder what sights and sounds had flashed past her eyes in those dying moments. And the pain. Unimaginable.

But now they had a job to do. There was no point in moping. Bonati had sent them there because he trusted them and knew they would cope – after enduring the scenes at Westminster, he knew they'd be tough enough for this. And now they had to get something concrete to report back to him beyond the revulsion they felt.

From the moment they'd entered the cellar, both agents had been able to detect high levels of emotion in the atmosphere. And once the forensics and police officers had left them alone, their extrasensory perception had gone into overdrive – again.

It was different here. The feelings of revenge and suffering they'd detected at Westminster were replaced with a vivid sense of anger. And scheming. There was an overwhelming feeling of secrecy – of conspiring.

They'd set up their instruments too. As expected, the needles registered very high levels. There was electromagnetic energy here, electrostatic electricity in the walls and the cabinets. Their temperature gauges were reading low too – unusually low, despite the hot-water pipes that ran the length of the cellar from the boiler room.

This place was haunted. There was no doubt. Their instruments confirmed what the message in blood on the wall was telling them.

The question was, had it seen all the paranormal activity it was going to get? They decided to wait a little longer and then join the others at Westminster. They had a funny feeling that Bonati and his team would need their help. Something was being planned – they could sense it.

CHAPTER 53

THURSDAY 4 NOVEMBER: 7.40 P.M.

WINCHESTER STREET, PIMLICO, LONDON

The police officer on the doorstep was obliging enough. His guest didn't have to work too hard to get inside. And after all, he *was* telling the truth.

'There are documents in there that I must have access to, Officer. The minister was due to bring them to Parliament tomorrow. Sadly he will no longer be with us, as you know, but the papers he was working on *must* be collected.'

After checking the man's identity, the police officer said, 'All right, sir. I'm sorry to have to ask you for that – but rules are rules. You can go in now, but please leave the place as you found it. Detectives are coming back tomorrow, I think. I suggest you take your papers and leave the place undisturbed.'

'Thank you, Officer.'

The policeman led him up the stairs to the third-floor flat. He opened the door and remained in the hallway, watching him. There was a foul stench of congealed Chinese food and stale lager coming from the kitchen.

Dressed in his borrowed body, Fawkes knew what he was

looking for, of course. He needed to act swiftly before the officer changed his mind, but he couldn't help pausing to glance at the bed.

The little one's bed.

'Yeah, it's awful, isn't it,' said the officer, noticing that he was staring at it. 'Don't know what happened there. It's a mess, though. Forensics have already been over it.'

It *was* a mess. The white sheets were stained with what looked like blood. The little one's blood. Evidence of disobedience duly punished by the spirit.

But now, hidden deep within Black Rod's body, Fawkes felt a twinge of guilt as he stared at the scene. This whole flat was sad – unloved, as though the person living here hadn't cared for himself. A person's home – and especially his bed – holds a residue of its owner. Visit anyone's home when they're not there and you'll feel sympathy for them. Always. The slippers by the chair, the discarded clothes, the dirty plates stacked up in the kitchen, the towels on the floor. The things that surround us at home hold memories of us – they're a window into the private world we hide from others' eyes. Our space. Our things.

Fawkes could feel the guilt rising through his borrowed body. *What had he done?*

He'd known the little one for so long. He'd watched him grow. He'd been there every step of the way. And although the little one had now ruined everything, had let him down and betrayed all the martyrs for whom they'd resolved to find justice tomorrow, the master still felt the guilt. He'd silenced him. Left him for dead, his blood seeping across the floor of the train, as it had so often seeped into the dirty bed in front of him now.

Somewhere, buried deep within the anger and bitterness that had fuelled the master for so long, a deep sadness was growing.

What *had* he done?

And then he thought of the martyrs. The poor souls who'd suffered so badly. The ones he'd seen as a boy in York. The brave ones who'd lived their lives courageously. Who'd died for their faith.

The little one was nothing compared to them. Fawkes had spoiled him. He hadn't told him the true extent of the suffering his martyred friends had endured. Had Thacker known, he would never have risked everything for the sake of his own grievances against the CRYPT agents. Pulling a gun on that agent, in the church in Fawkes' own city, had been reckless and stupid. An act that had deserved to be punished.

How could he have been so stupid? All those nights they'd spent plotting. Everything was going to work, everything was set. They were just hours away from justice, or would have been if it hadn't been for Thacker's stupidity.

No, he'd deserved to die.

Fawkes would finish the job himself. And now, in his new skin – he'd managed to fool the officer well enough – he was resolved to see it through. Black Rod's fear had only served to strengthen Fawkes. He felt energised.

But he couldn't do it without the documents. He shook himself out of his pity and turned quickly from the bed to face the rest of Thacker's cluttered room.

It didn't take him long to find it. The bundle of papers was on Thacker's desk, bound together with a ribbon. He understood the coded title immediately: 'RC1701'.

He knew what that meant – the 1701 Act of Settlement, which barred the monarch from becoming, or marrying, a Roman Catholic. And beneath this antiquated legal document lay the first drafts of the new Bill. The Bill that would change the course of history – righting a wrong that had been allowed to run unchallenged for all these years.

Fawkes felt a renewed strength. He seized the bundle of papers and made straight for the door.

Parliament awaited.

CHAPTER 54

THURSDAY 4 NOVEMBER: 8.08 P.M.

BLACK ROD'S PRIVATE RESIDENCE, WESTMINSTER

'I've told you,' said Susie Farlington, rubbing her tear-stained eyes. 'I don't know where he is. He left here two hours ago. Said he was going back to Westminster.' She stared out of the living-room window, down at the evening traffic on Millbank and the dark, ominous trees beyond.

Lawrence Brooke-Jones, Yeoman of the Black Rod and Deputy Sergeant at Arms, really felt for Susie. Their families had known one another for years. They were close. To hear her so distressed was upsetting for him.

'So he left the building, Susie?' he said into the phone.

'Yes, Larry. I checked with the concierge. Apparently the lift got stuck, but only for a few minutes. They got it going again and he appeared eventually. The concierge said he thought he looked anxious and tired when he left, but that's because he was late for his meeting – and he's a little claustrophobic. Larry, you know what he's like.'

'I know, I know. But it's so strange that the security guards here said they've no record of his return. Honestly, Susie, I don't think he's back here yet.'

'Then *where* is he?' Susie cried.

There was the sound of a key in the door suddenly. It opened and Susie heard her husband's voice from the hallway.

'He's here, Larry!' she said, her voice croaking with emotion.

'Thank God for that!' said Larry. 'Tell him to call me if he needs to. Any time tonight. Otherwise I'll see him in the morning.'

Susie rang off. She placed the phone back on the table near the window and hurried out of the room.

'Geoffrey! Where've you been! We've been worried sick!'

'I'm sorry, darling,' said Black Rod, standing in the hallway. 'I've had so much to do.'

Susie stared at her husband. 'Are you all right? You look *awful.*'

'I'm tired,' he said. 'You know how busy it's been.'

'I know, darling,' she said, moving closer to him. She began stroking his brow. His face was pale and his eyes looked drained of emotion. His breath smelt stale and sickly.

'Don't *fuss*,' he snapped. 'I'm fine. I've got to work.'

'But you need to rest, Geoffrey. You don't seem yourself. You need—'

'*Peace,*' he said sternly. 'That's what I need. Peace and quiet. Tomorrow night I'll rest. It will all be over by then.' He pushed past her.

'But darling. I'm worried that you're overdoing it. That you're going to—'

'Please,' he interrupted. 'I've got a mound of work to do before tomorrow. Don't wait up. I'll see you in the morning.'

It was not the first time her husband had been so tetchy. Yet he seemed especially distant tonight. So . . . preoccupied.

But now was not the time to discuss his emotions, she knew

that. Years spent managing his moods had taught her when to give him affection and when to let him be. Tonight it was the latter.

'You eaten?' she said softly.

'Not hungry,' he snapped, walking to the open door that led into his study.

She backed off quickly and scurried back into the living room. The mood he was in, she didn't want an argument now. They'd make it up to each other tomorrow. They always did.

The study door was closed.

It remained shut for the rest of the evening. When Susie called from the hallway to say she was going to bed, 'Good night' was all she heard in reply.

It wasn't the first time she'd gone to bed leaving him to work late. But it would be the last.

It was another hour before he began calling them. He turned the room lights off, leaving just the lamp on his desk, then he spoke in a whisper.

'Catesby, Wintour, gentlemen. Rise.'

Nothing.

He called them again.

And again.

'Come, Catesby, Percy, rise up, Wintour, Wright. I am waiting!'

Slowly, in the dim light of the study, swirls of mist were forming. A glowing plasma was emerging from the shadowy corners of the room.

'Come, friends,' he said. 'Let us unite. Show yourselves. There is much to discuss.'

The clouds of plasma were thickening as the bulb in the desk lamp fizzed and crackled.

Soon the shapes were becoming figures. The ghosts were coming through from the afterlife. Appearing again. Stronger. Energised. The room was alive with electrical activity. A glowing red mist surrounded each figure, their faces becoming more defined by the second.

Within a few seconds, the gang leaders were together again.

Just like old times.

Chapter 55

THURSDAY 4 NOVEMBER: 11.58 P.M.

CRYPT EMERGENCY HQ, HOUSES OF PARLIAMENT, LONDON

The basement at Westminster resembled a suite of hi-tech labs – but a heavily guarded one.

Bonati had been battling with the House Authorities and members of the security forces for the last two hours, fighting for his agents to be granted access to all areas – above and below ground – and to be left alone to take their readings. Goode had said categorically that they were acting under the authority of the Prime Minister himself, with whom he'd met earlier that evening. No one could argue with that.

Dr Vorzek and her team had brought almost every conceivable piece of equipment at her disposal. Never had so many agents been sent to one place. But then never had there been such a colossal venue to investigate. Even with so many personnel in attendance, they were stretched.

While the police officers were concerned about security threats of a human nature, the agents worried about those of a supernatural kind. They organised themselves into teams of two, each one responsible for a room or stretch of corridor in the cellars. And above ground, Jud and Bex were in the two chambers with Jason Goode - the House of Commons and the House of Lords.

EMF meters, Geiger counters, electrostatic locators, motion detectors - they had it all. Thermal imagers were set up too. If there was paranormal activity anywhere in the building tonight, they'd catch it. And the very latest EM neutralisers were primed and ready in case things turned nasty.

The problem was, so far very few agents had found anything unusual. There had been the residual electromagnetic radiation in the location where the bodies of the officer and the engineer had been found. They'd expected that. And a dip in temperature too.

There was tragedy in the air at the site of any death. A lingering sadness - a residue that hung like an invisible mist. Grace and Luc had felt it the first time they'd entered the basement - Jud too. But there was little trace of such negative energy now.

It seemed like the spirits were playing games with them. Hide and seek.

Jud was getting exasperated.

Bex remained in the House of Lords with her instruments, while Goode and Jud moved across to the House of Commons.

They left the Lords chamber and walked down Peers' Corridor towards the Central Lobby. Giant oil paintings lined their walk, depicting scenes from the English Civil War. Silver rays of moonlight burst through stained-glass windows, striking the artists' work. Bearded gents in seventeenth-century costumes peered at them with intimidating expressions. But Jud passed unaffected - he'd become used to wrestling with ghosts in similar garb. He knew better than anyone how figures from history were not gone for ever. They lingered in the shadows, watching, waiting, biding their time. Only when you understood their grievances in life, the injustices that some had suffered, could you anticipate their return.

They walked on into the grand Central Lobby and onwards to the Common's Corridor. The long red leather window seats of the Corridor were now replaced by green ones, to match the green benches of the House of Commons chamber, which lay just beyond the Members' Lobby ahead.

Jud's extrasensory perception was in a state of high alert, but so far he'd detected nothing evil – just an overwhelming sense of power and authority. No wonder some politicians seemed full of their own self-importance, he thought. They must soak it up from the corridors of power by osmosis. Just being here every day would bolster anyone's confidence – make them feel special, and as removed as you could get from the daily grind of the commoners outside.

He followed his father into the Members' Lobby. The dim night lights and the moonshine from the sky outside gave the place an eerie quality. A giant statue of Winston Churchill stared straight at them. Behind, Baroness Thatcher was pointing accusingly at them.

Jud noticed that Churchill's right foot was shiny, unlike the rest of the dark sculpture.

'You've heard of the tradition?' said Goode, noticing Jud touching the shoe.

'No?'

'My politician friends tell me it brings good luck, that thing. It's shiny from all the polishing it gets. When MPs are about to deliver their maiden speech in the chamber, they rub it to bring them good luck. Don't know if it works, but it's a good story.'

They entered the chamber. Even in the dim light, the green leather benches were impressive – and the Speaker's chair with its ornate canopy.

Running down each side of the House was a thick red line. Two and a half sword lengths apart, the lines had been put in to keep MPs apart in the days when they could bring their swords into Parliament. If an MP crossed the line whilst speaking, the Speaker would order them to sit down and 'toe the line'.

'It's not as big as I'd expected,' said Jud.

'No, that's what most people say. I thought that when I first came for a tour of the place. Do you feel anything, J?' said Goode as he began setting up equipment on the large mahogany table near the dispatch boxes.

Jud remained still and breathed deeply.

'A sense of foreboding,' he said quickly. 'There's a real anticipation in this place – like the calm before the storm. I don't sense there's a presence here, but there's something on its way. I know it.'

Goode watched his son proudly as Jud slowly walked around the chamber, listening, sensing.

He'd never thought he'd be here with Jamie, leading agent in the nation's only paranormal investigation department.

It didn't seem real. And it would have been a proud moment, had the journey to reach it not been so tragic. It was at times like these, those rare moments when he was alone with Jamie, that he felt an acute longing for his wife. They were not complete without her. Maybe that was why he and Jamie saw each other so rarely. Jason always said it was work that got in the way, but was that the truth, *really*? Wasn't it just too painful?

'Do you miss Mum?' he said, before instantly regretting it.

'*What?*' said Jud, incredulous.

'I'm sorry, J,' said his father. 'I don't know why I said that. I shouldn't have. It's just, well . . . she'd have been proud of you, J.'

Jud stopped and stared at his father. He was wearing that empty, desolate expression again, the one he used to show in the first days and weeks after her death. When he used to visit him in prison. He had always tried to hide his sadness, for Jamie's sake, but his son could see through the facade. They felt the same pain, the same grief, and the same loneliness. They were just careful not to let it show when in each other's company.

'Yeah, whatever,' said Jud. 'Have you set the equipment up yet? I don't want to miss anything.'

'OK, OK,' said Jason. And then he stopped again. 'When all this is over, when the case is closed and you and I are back at the CRYPT, what say we go out for a night? Just you and I. We'll grab a meal. Have a chat . . . like old times?'

Jud looked nervous. Conversations like these had the potential to cut right through his armour and straight into his heart. He remained guarded.

'Yeah, OK. Whatever you want,' he said nonchalantly. 'Let's get set up then, shall we? It's going to be a long night in here, I think.'

CHAPTER 56

FRIDAY 5 NOVEMBER: 12.24 A.M.

PRIVATE RESIDENCE OF THE BLACK ROD, WESTMINSTER

'So you've killed him, Guido?' said Catesby incredulously. 'You mean you've actually destroyed our ticket to freedom. The man we've groomed all this time. Your own "little one". He who was to bring justice to—'

'Silence!' said Fawkes. 'I won't have dissension. Not now. You may have thought you could lead us back then, Catesby, but times have changed. I hold the reins of power now. I summoned you and you came. Now you listen to me. The man was weak. He was impatient. He *had* to die. He would have faltered. I knew it.'

'And now?' said Wintour, amused by Fawkes' self-appointment to gang leader. God knows, he'd seen he and Catesby fight enough times back then. Squabbling over how the plot would work and who would run things. That it was Fawkes who carried the can for the lot of them in the end was strange, but not undeserved. Guido was stupid enough to get himself caught in the cellars with the gunpowder. It was right he should be the one remembered for it. Though everyone knew at the time it was Robert Catesby who was the ringleader.

Centuries of symbolic burning of Guido's effigy on bonfires

across the land had left his spirit in tatters. Unlike the other gang members, left alone, their souls preserved in their anonymity, Guido was weak. Too weak to resume the shape of his living spirit. So to start the new uprising, and carry out his plan, he'd had to communicate through another. An innocent victim. Thacker had been chosen.

And now, although it seemed madness to have done away with the little one after all these years, for Fawkes to have inhabited the body of the Black Rod, well, he had to be given some credit for that. It was a master plan. The man's abject fear had been enough to give Fawkes the strength he needed. And now he sat before them, stronger and wiser.

But Catesby didn't share Wintour's new-found respect for Fawkes, and neither did Thomas Percy.

'I won't be silenced, not by you or by anyone!' shouted Catesby, rising. He went for Fawkes, seated at the other side of Black Rod's desk as if he owned the place.

He caught Fawkes by surprise and leapt at his throat.

'No!' cried Wintour. 'Don't be fools!'

'Leave him!' said Wright. 'You wreck his body and we stand no chance. Think of the martyrs! Think of their suffering. We owe it to them to see this plan through. Hear him!'

'It is just like before,' said Wintour. 'In the cellar on the Strand. There was no need for it then. Another victim dispatched. Another innocent woman lying dead. And for what, Catesby?'

'Oh spare us your piety,' shouted Thomas Percy. 'We are villains together.'

Wintour shot an evil glare at Percy. But he refused to rise to it. He would not sabotage Guido's plans now. 'Listen to Fawkes!' he pleaded to the ghosts in the room.

Catesby clung on, digging his fingers into Fawkes' neck. But he'd not allowed for the physical strength and presence of the body of Black Rod. Fawkes rose to his feet and swiped him away with one thickly set arm. The ghost fell feebly across the great desk and slumped to the floor on the other side. The red glow that engulfed him, engulfed them all, was dimming. He was losing energy.

Fawkes was worried the noise would wake Black Rod's wife, who was sleeping nearby. He spoke in a whisper.

'Catesby, you and I have many centuries more to settle this. We only have tonight to form our plans. When this is over, I shall accept your invitation to a duel. And I shall beat you. Until then, we work together, for the good of the gang, for the sake of our brothers and sisters who still suffer injustice. We *must* stay united. For them.'

Catesby slowly rose and stood in the corner of the room, brooding.

'Your neck, Guido!' said Wright. 'Your body is bleeding.'

The ghost was right. Black Rod's flesh had been punctured. This jeopardised everything. A bloodied and bruised Black Rod would certainly arouse serious suspicion at the State Opening.

'I shall dress the wounds,' said Guido, feeling no pain. 'Think not of it now, for we have much to discuss.'

'But first,' said Wintour, 'you talk of our friends who suffer in silence. What of them? Are they rising?'

Fawkes nodded, his facing forming a wry smile. 'And coming,' he said. 'I cannot stop them now. Mark my words. When the sun rises tomorrow, you shall see them.'

CHAPTER 57

FRIDAY 5 NOVEMBER: 8.31 A.M.

CRYPT EMERGENCY HQ, HOUSES OF PARLIAMENT, LONDON

It had been the longest night anyone at the CRYPT had experienced.

No one had faced danger, that was just the point. Whether buried in the basements or up in the stately corridors and chambers above, the agents had watched and waited, but sensed nothing.

Bonati had not known whether to feel relief or frustration. Though none of the agents had seen or connected with a spirit, all of them had experienced the same sense of foreboding that Jud had witnessed in the chamber of the House of Commons. Bonati had spent the night moving them around the building, briefing, redeploying, debriefing. Trying to keep their senses fresh and alert.

But here, gathered together in the main lobby of the basement for the morning's briefing, they had to face reality. They were no further forward than they were last night. No closer to offering any answers to the army of House Authorities and security chiefs who were now arriving at Parliament ready for the ceremony.

Khan had been there all night, of course. He shared Bonati's frustration. After all, he'd fought long and hard with his senior chiefs to give Bonati and his team the full access they needed throughout the night. But for what? So they could stare blankly at his superiors now and say they'd found nothing, just an innate sense that something might happen?

He remembered his initial scepticism about the agents' 'sixth sense' back on the Tyburn case. That was until he'd experienced first hand the power of the spirit world. Khan had nearly become a ghost himself. And that was enough to make him believe.

But now, in the full view of the security chiefs, neither he, nor Bonati, nor Jason Goode, were able to say conclusively whether the threats they all feared were real.

'All we can do,' said Jud to the assembled group of tired-looking agents, 'is stay alert. It's a waiting game. And we must *not* lose it. I believe – and I know you do too – that the events of the last few days are not the final chapter in this case, but only the beginning. We must be ready – neutralisers primed.'

The lift nearest to where they were assembled in the main basement lobby pinged. Who else was coming? wondered Bonati. Not another security boss or some meddling member of the House Authorities, here to give his judgement on the failings of the CRYPT?

The metal doors swung open and Black Rod stepped out.

He looked shattered – pale and gaunt. His eyes were framed by dark shadowy rings. But the civil servants and security forces in the room looked visibly relieved to see him. His deputy, Lawrence Brooke-Jones, had informed colleagues that the brigadier was safe and well, though he was just as anxious as they were to hear where he'd been last night and why he should have missed the six o'clock meeting.

'Everything OK, Geoffrey?' said Larry.

'Yes,' snapped Black Rod. 'Why?'

'Well, I mean, it's just that we missed you yesterday. At the meeting.'

'Yes, I'm so sorry. I was waylaid – you know how busy it gets in the run-up to today. But all's well, is it? No hiccups yet, what?'

Was that it? thought Larry. No more explanation than that? It was strange that the brigadier should miss a meeting at all, most unlike him. But he was here now, that was the main thing. He looked incredibly tired. Larry, like others in the vicinity, had assumed that there'd been trouble at home. But that wasn't his business. There was much to do.

Larry filled Black Rod in on the events since last night. How the crime scene investigators were there to assess the paranormal activity in the place since the bodies had been found in the basement. How he had negotiated on Black Rod's behalf to allow the CRYPT agents access to the building.

At this point Bonati spoke up.

'Good to see you again, Brigadier. My team have been holding a vigil all night – we've scoured the place for evidence of paranormal activity—'

'And?' interrupted Black Rod.

'What? Oh, er . . . well, I have to say we have recorded very little out of the ordinary.' Bonati felt as embarrassed as the agents around him. All this equipment, all this manpower and virtually nothing to show for it.

'Oh, right.' They noticed that Black Rod did not look disheartened. 'That's excellent news,' he said. 'We're clear for a good day.'

Neither Bonati nor Goode nor the agents shared his optimism.

'Well it's good news on one level – there's been no hostile activity recorded – but perhaps not so good given what our agents have all been detecting via their *senses*.'

'Which is?' Black Rod couldn't hide his cynicism.

'Well, a distinct sense of foreboding. They feel significant paranormal activity is imminent.'

'Well thank heavens we have you guys, then, I'd say!' said Black Rod, sarcastically. 'So, are we all set for the traditional search of the basement?'

'Search?' whispered Bex to Jud. 'What's he talking about?'

'It's a tradition,' said Jud. 'It happens on the morning of every State Opening – the Yeomen of the Guard do a sweep of the basement. You can guess when that tradition started.'

'No! The Gunpowder Plot? It wasn't!'

'Certainly was,' he whispered. 'After finding barrels of gunpowder hidden below the House of Lords, the very next year a search of the cellars was ordered – and it's happened every year ever since.'

'Wow! I'd say that's horribly prophetic!' said Bex. 'There may not be any gunpowder here, but I still think something's going to explode.'

'I have a horrible feeling you're right,' said Jud. 'What do you make of this guy, then?'

'Who? Black Rod?'

'Yes,' he said, keeping his voice down.

'Weird,' said Bex. 'No question. There's something about him. Do you feel it?'

'Yeah, there's a strange aura to him.'

'It could just be because of his position,' said Bex. 'I mean, he's in charge today, isn't he?'

'Yeah, and he knows it,' said Jud. 'Some leaders are like that. They give off a charisma – there's an aura to them you can feel.'

'Let's keep an eye on him all the same,' whispered Bex.

'We won't disturb your search, Brigadier,' said Bonati. 'Send your men down.'

'Thank you. I certainly shall,' said Black Rod. 'And during the ceremony? What will you be doing, might I ask?'

'What would you like us to do? We can be stationed anywhere you wish,' said Bonati.

'Well that's just it,' said Black Rod. 'I have a horrible feeling

Her Majesty and the noble persons here will not take kindly to a sea of agents, all measuring and recording and doing whatever it is you people do.'

'We can be a little more discreet than that,' said Jason Goode, who was getting exasperated by now.

'Oh, I've no doubt about that, but Her Majesty is most particular about the happiness and well-being of all those in attendance. She will *not* be pleased if there are those in the vicinity who have a disturbing influence over others. Seeing your agents with their black suits and their arms full of electrical equipment is likely to unsettle a great proportion of the parties present.'

'So what do you suggest?' said Jud impatiently.

'Well I'm glad you asked,' said Black Rod, fixing Jud with a stare like an overbearing teacher. 'I suggest you and your friends remain here in the basement, young man. We can provide you with as many monitors as you require. The whole place is riddled with cameras, so you won't be in the dark. You can watch the whole thing. You won't be bored.'

'*Bored?*' said Bex. 'I hardly think that is a concern. And in any case, if paranormal activity occurs, we will need to be there quickly.'

'Rebecca's right,' said Bonati. 'A rapid response will be essential should anything happen.'

'Fear not,' the brigadier said patronisingly. 'Should a nasty ghost appear, you will be the first to know.'

CHAPTER 58

FRIDAY 5 NOVEMBER: 9.16 A.M.

HOUSES OF PARLIAMENT, LONDON

The State Opening had begun. Her Majesty had arrived via the Sovereign's Entrance and had made her way to the Robing Room, her route lined with guards in ceremonial dress – shiny metal breastplates and long horse hair plumes, swords held at the ready.

When the Queen was finally in full regalia, the crown of state weighing her down – a metaphor for the heavy office she'd held for so many years – she proceeded towards the House of Lords. She was followed by a vast entourage of lords, senior judges and diplomats – many dressed in the traditional red robes, black stockings and long white wigs. It seemed almost unreal. Like something out of a fairy tale or a scene from Camelot.

And buried discreetly in the basement, the CRYPT watched the whole thing. None of them, not Bonati, Goode or any of the agents themselves, felt easy about being placed in the basement. Bonati had fought with Black Rod and other members of the House Authorities and the security forces to get closer access to proceedings, but they were having none of it. Fear was a strange thing. It started so very quickly and could spread like a forest fire. It didn't matter how real the threat was, they were not going to alter their plans and allow those in attendance to feel unsettled or worried by the presence of the agents. Like other security threats that had been ever-present at Parliament down the ages, and were still very real today, the dangers of the paranormal would have to take their place in the shadows – such threats would not force anyone to change anything they did. And besides, with so many dignitaries crammed into one place, there was no chance at all of any space to get closer to proceedings even if the CRYPT had been granted permission.

Especially as there were even more of them now – Grace and Luc had returned from the Strand in the early hours of the morning with nothing much to report. The anger they'd experienced the night before in that little cellar at the solicitor's office had slowly dissipated, and an overwhelming sense of foreboding had grown within them. They'd dashed back expecting to see Westminster on fire.

'Does anyone think it'll pass smoothly?' Jud said, as their eyes remained glued to the screens in the basement.

'Somehow I doubt it,' said Luc. 'I tell you, Grace and I felt sure something was being planned. We didn't see anyone, but we were *sure* something was happening here. I expected to see the place burnt down.'

'I have a horrible feeling about this, sir. It doesn't feel right,' said Grace.

'In what way?' said Bonati, a slight air of exasperation creeping into his voice. He'd been the most supportive of everyone when it came to preserving – and defending – the agents' special powers of extrasensory perception, but even he was beginning to tire of the same conclusion: 'It feels like something's about to happen.' *What?* he kept asking all night, but no one was able to give him any answers, only that there was this same old sense of foreboding about the place – and how much of that was imagination anyway? And then Grace and Luc pitched up and said exactly the same thing! It wasn't helping.

'Well, there is a heightened emotion about this place,' said Jud once again.

Bonati just stared at them. His face was lined and pale. A night in the depths of the cellars had put a strain on them all, including the professor. It wasn't just the monotony of waiting for something to happen. They'd been on enough vigils to cope with that. It was more the frustration of not knowing *why* the ghosts might be here. Why *now*?

It was a question they'd raised at the video conference the day before, but no one had truly been able to answer it. The connection to Guy Fawkes had been remarkable, but when Bex had regaled them all with her research at the York archives, it had seemed almost plausible. But no one, not even Bex herself, had been able to offer any theory as to why the ghosts should be stirring *now*.

Bonati hated it when a case was this elusive, so impregnable. They *had* to understand the ghosts' motives – it was what paranormal investigation was all about.

'If this is all true, and your theories and research prove correct,' he said, 'what have we done to upset the Catholic martyrs now? Why is Guy Fawkes returning at this time? Why was Simon Thacker enlisted now? Why not last year, or someone else a hundred years ago? Three hundred years ago? Why *this* year?'

'The State Opening of Parliament is about the Queen's speech, isn't it?' said Jason Goode, who'd joined them after yet another walk around the basement to try to relieve his impatience.

'Yes, that's right,' said Jud. He recollected his classes on British politics at school. 'It's when Her Majesty puts forwards the plans for the new Parliament.'

'Which means?' said Bex.

'Which means, well . . . I suppose it means she is listing the kinds of things the MPs will be debating in the coming year.

Setting the legislative agenda if you like – laying down what will be brought before the House in the next session.'

'And can we get access to that?' said Luc. 'To the content, I mean?'

'Doubtful,' said Bonati. 'Though I'm sure MPs are aware in advance, since they would have agreed the list in the first place.'

'A summary of it sometimes appears in the papers on the day of the Opening,' said Grace.

'Have we got one?' said Bonati hurriedly.

'No. We've been here all night, Giles!' said Goode.

Jud quickly approached one of the security officers who were still lurking around the place, watching the agents, bemused by their gadgets.

'Do you have a newspaper?' he said.

'What? Er, yeah. Wait a minute.' He went off towards the corner. Bonati could see a metal flask of coffee and a carrier bag on a chair. The security guard returned with a newspaper.

Jud quickly flicked through its pages.

And then he found it. He'd been scouring for references to the State Opening and quickly found an article. It gave a very brief outline of what was to be expected in the Queen's speech – the new Bills proposed.

'I've got it!' he said.

Bonati, Goode and his fellow agents came over to him.

'Listen to this,' said Jud.

'One controversial Bill proposed in the Queen's speech this year is the 1701 Act of Settlement (Revised). This newly extended Bill is likely to quash once and for all any hopes in the Catholic community for some equality. If there were those who opposed the original Act of Settlement, barring Catholics from succeeding to the British throne or even marrying a British monarch, then they will be sure to hate this new amended Bill, which not only keeps the same ruling, but extends it to include prime ministers too. The new extension to the 1701 Act will make it impossible for a Roman Catholic to become prime minister of Her Majesty's Government, since Her Majesty is head of state and as such is Supreme Governor of the Church of England. There are those MPs who feel it inconsistent to have a Catholic prime minister, answerable ultimately to the Pope in Rome, leading a government presided over by a Protestant head of state. This new Bill will go some way to redressing this.

'It is the same Bill once proposed by the then justice minister, Brian Maxwell, in 2005. Mr Maxwell tragically died just before he was able to persuade his fellow MPs to support it. But enough MPs have resurrected it, and if it is voted through in the new Parliament, it will become law within a year.'

'No wonder Fawkes has rallied the gang again,' said Bex. 'This *has* to be the reason. If you think about it, it's exactly why the plotters tried to take out the King and his government the first time – for the injustice. The way the Catholics were treated at the time. It's what Guy Fawkes witnessed when he was growing up in York.'

'And that's why Luc and I sensed something was being planned!' said Grace. 'That's where the plotters hatched out their scheme, wasn't it? In the Strand!'

'But surely no one is being sentenced and killed in this country today for being a Catholic!' said Goode. 'I mean, you can't be tried in court these days for harbouring Catholic priests!'

'Of course not,' said Bex. 'But this new Bill is the motivation for what they're doing. It has to be. It's why the ghosts are returning now. I'm sure of it. This *matters* to them, sir. And to all those who died for their cause. For their Catholic faith.'

'Bex is right,' said Jud. 'And it doesn't matter if we're talking about today or four hundred years ago – the spirits don't forget. We know some spirits cannot rest in peace if wrongs were committed against them that still haven't been righted. It doesn't matter when those wrongs were committed. This Act – the original one – has caused pain and anger all these years. And the fact that we're about to make it even *worse* for Catholics – and extend the rule to include the office of prime minister – would definitely be enough to stir the ghosts into action. No question.'

Bonati spoke. 'Jason, I think they may be right. Or at least we can't take the risk.'

'Meaning?'

'Meaning we've got to *stop this*.'

'OK, so you're saying we should go up there and tell them we think they're about to get a visit from the same plotters who tried to blow up Parliament four hundred years ago. Do you want to do that, Giles?'

'Yes, if I have to,' Bonati snapped back. 'You either trust our agents or you don't, Jason. You set up the CRYPT – you were as convinced as I was that they have a skill. Now *trust* in that skill!'

'It's not that I don't trust them,' said Goode. 'It's just that there's so much at stake. If we mess up here – we mess up big time.'

'*No!*' said Bonati firmly. 'There's no time for doubts. I share your worries, of course I do. We go up there now and nothing happens, we risk making fools of ourselves in front of every dignitary in the land – and it'll be the end of the CRYPT for sure. MI5 will distance themselves from us and it'll be over.' He glanced knowingly at Jud. 'And I know how *serious* that would be. But we've *got* to believe in these guys. Or else the CRYPT might as well die.'

Jud and Bex and the other agents close by couldn't fail to be impressed by this robust defence of them. *Go, Professor.*

'OK, OK,' said Goode. 'But how the hell are we going to stop this?'

'Look,' said Jud. 'No one says we have to stop it yet. But we've got to get up there at least. We've got to get closer in case something really does happen. There's enough of us – as long as we're discreet, we can fill every corner up there.'

'I agree,' said Luc. He glanced in the direction of the guards near the lift doors. 'Sir, why don't you and Mr Goode set up a diversion – take the guards off further into the basement or something, and we'll slip away. You could say you've found something, or heard a noise down there. They'll believe you.'

'Yeah, a ticking noise!' said Goode.

'It's a risk,' said Bonati.

'Any other ideas?' said Goode. 'Let's do it. And while we've got them, you guys jump into the lifts and get upstairs, OK?'

The agents nodded eagerly.

'And when we get up there,' said Jud to everyone, 'for goodness' sake be discreet. Keep out of the lights. If anyone asks you, we're part of the security forces – show them your card and they'll leave you alone.'

'OK,' said the professor. 'We'll join you up there as soon as we can.'

'But what happens when the guards see we've all disappeared?' said Bex. 'I mean, you can't distract them for ever, sir.'

'It'll be too late by then. You'll be upstairs hidden away,' said Bonati. 'Just stay safe. If your hunches are right, we'll need to act quickly, or I dread to think—'

'Yes, well we don't need to dwell on what *might* happen,' said Goode. 'These guys'll see us right. Let's go, Giles.'

'Oh, so you trust them now?' said the professor, but Goode had already begun striding down a pipe shaft, deeper into the basement.

A few minutes later, sure enough, the agents heard shouts from Goode and Bonati. 'Officers, come here, quick. I can hear something!'

The security guards and police officers in the vicinity ran in the direction of the shouts.

'Let's do it,' said Jud. 'Come on!'

They moved towards the two lifts. They filled both of them and within a few seconds they were at the floor that housed the chambers.

As the agents exited, police officers armed with rifles approached them.

Jud moved to the front, flashed his card and explained the situation.

'You can stay in the Central Lobby,' one said. 'You can't get into the House of Lords anyway, even if you could get clearance; there's too many in there. You can't move for peers.'

'In any case,' said another officer, 'they're about to come and get the MPs now. Black Rod's on his way down Peers Corridor.'

He was right. Black Rod and his staff were marching in their direction, heading for the chamber of the House of Commons at the opposite end of Central Lobby.

Bex was worried. 'What do we do, Jud? Are we seriously just going to wait here and watch?'

'There's nothing else we can do, Bex. But if something happens, at least we're here instead of down in the basement. We've all got neutralisers, and we can always call for an evacuation of the place.'

She could see in his eyes that he too was worried. But it was a waiting game and they both knew it. The truth was, no one quite knew what to expect. The CRYPT's motto – 'Expect the unexpected' – could never have been truer. But it didn't help now.

They saw Black Rod marching towards them.

'He's heading for the chamber,' whispered Jud. 'He knocks on the door and they slam it in his face.'

'They what?' said Luc, standing close to them. He'd always found the Brits' love of tradition and ceremony amusing. 'Why do they do that?'

'It's a symbol of the MPs' independence,' said Jud. 'They're answerable to the people, not to the monarchy. But don't worry, they open the doors again. Then Black Rod invites them to the House of Lords and they all file out to go and hear the Queen's speech.

'Does anyone feel anything?' said Grace.

'I can sense anger,' said Bex.

'Me too,' said Grace. 'It's just like in that office in the Strand. Do you feel it too, Luc?'

'Yeah. It's like before. It's like there's a storm brewing. There's real energy here.'

Agents were scanning the place, taking readings, watching. If something – anything – was about to happen, they'd certainly know it before anyone else did.

Black Rod now crossed the Central Lobby, in full regalia, staff in hand. As he walked past Jud and Bex, he turned to face them for a brief second.

And then Jud saw it.

Black Rod had blinked momentarily, and in the split second between blinks Jud had noticed something weird.

'My God,' he said. 'Did you *see* that?'

'What?' said Luc. 'See *what*?'

'It was his eyes. I saw him blink and I swear for a second he had no pupils.'

'What do you mean?' said Luc, looking puzzled.

'What I said. Just white eyes – plain, lifeless. And then he blinked again and they looked normal.'

'Are you *sure*?' said Grace.

'Yeah. Didn't anyone else see it?'

'He looked normal to me,' said Luc. 'Though I certainly felt something weird when he came near – like an anger again. What do you think, Bex?'

But she had gone quiet. Jud could see she was beginning to shake. There were tears in the corners of her eyes, and a startled look had surfaced across her face.

'Bex? What's wrong?'

'Oh God!' she whispered. 'It's Fawkes. I know it!'

'Who? Where?' said Grace. 'What're you talking about, Bex?'

'It's Black Rod. I went cold, freezing cold when he came past.

Then he looked at me. Jud's right. For a second he had white eyeballs. I tell you, it's him!'

'Well I didn't see his eyes,' said Grace. 'But I can't deny there's an aura to him.'

'We can't stop him unless we're certain,' said Luc. He was always the cautious one. That was why he was so good for Jud. Calm and considered, that was Luc. 'We need more proof,' he said slowly.

But it was too late. Jud had seen the fear in Bex's eyes, and that was proof enough for him. The last time he'd seen that expression was on the bridge in York. He knew she meant it. She'd seen something – and so had he. And they'd all felt something. Jud didn't need any more convincing. He'd broken loose and was now in the midst of the procession of dignitaries.

'Hey! Oi!' shouted one of the police officers. He and two colleagues went after Jud, guns primed.

'Jud, no!' shouted Luc. 'Don't be stupid! Get back!'

Black Rod had reached the door of the chamber. The Sergeant at Arms in the Commons duly slammed the great doors in his face.

'Don't open the doors!' shouted Jud from the back of the procession. 'Don't open them! *No!*'

Several of the dignitaries up ahead turned and scowled at Jud. Who was this kid?

'Officers?' someone shouted. 'Take him!'

Jud was swamped by men. Bex and the others pushed through the assembled dignitaries to try to reason with the officers, as Black Rod sounded three loud strikes on the door with his staff. The doors were opened.

It was too late.

Black Rod was inside the chamber.

CHAPTER 59

FRIDAY 5 NOVEMBER: 10.07 A.M.

HOUSES OF PARLIAMENT, LONDON

The MPs looked confused. Why had Black Rod entered the chamber? Protocol demanded that he remained at the open doors to give the invitation on behalf of Her Majesty to return to the House of Lords for the speech.

But he hadn't even spoken yet.

Instead, he made for the Prime Minister. He stopped within a few feet of him, closed his eyes and said, 'Come, spirits! Come to us. Show us the suffering you've endured. The pain, the injustice. Come!'

There was some laughter at first. Had the brigadier finally lost it? What was this? Some practical joke? MPs around him looked embarrassed.

The police officers holding Jud and Bex at the doorway released their grip and stood staring at the man in the middle of the chamber. Their hands twitched at the guns by their sides. But this was Black Rod. What the hell were they supposed to do?

Jud and the other agents now at his side grabbed their neutralisers from their pockets and stood braced.

The laughter trailed off when Black Rod opened his eyes again.

There were gasps in the front rows. His pupils had gone. Inflated white spheres now grew in their sockets.

He blinked again.

Red glowing spheres now shone from his face.

The room was alive with energy. There was some kind of mist gathering above Black Rod's head. And dividing. Smaller clouds of glowing plasma began spreading throughout the chamber.

'Get your neutralisers on, everyone!' shouted Jud as they ran deeper into the chamber. But the energy in the room just kept rising. Their hand-held neutralisers weren't enough.

Rooted to the spot, the MPs stared at the strange shapes and swirls that continued to form in front of them.

Figures started materialising through the smoky mist. Faint at first, hardly noticeable, but they were hardening now. The shapes were becoming opaque.

That was when pandemonium broke out.

MPs started fighting over one another, anxious to get through the packed hall to the exits.

But the spirits kept growing, and swelling in number. Six, ten, twenty, fifty. The great chamber was soon filled with ghosts. Haggard faces, skeletal limbs, even headless bodies were appearing, high in the air above them, swooping down. Though terrifying, none were causing injury. They wore tragic expressions – grief-stricken, as though they were enduring great pain. There were horrified screams from the awestruck politicians below them.

Officers rushed past the agents to the Prime Minster and began shielding him. They tried to bustle him towards the door, but it was too late.

Other spirits had materialised near Black Rod. Darker, more solid figures than the ghosts that swirled around the open space above the MPs' heads now flanked Black Rod.

It was the gang. They'd remained true to their word. The

plans they'd hatched out the night before were now happening for real. Catesby, Wintour, Wright, Percy. They'd not failed him.

Not this time.

The place was alive with fear, which flowed into the ghosts, strengthening them, hardening their bodies, turning the plasma solid and bringing a chilling glow to their eyes.

More armed officers entered the chamber, pushing past the MPs trying to exit. They made for Black Rod.

'No!' shouted Jud over the heads of the crowd. 'Don't!'

His words fell on deaf ears as the officers went for the ghosts standing together near the dispatch box.

It was carnage.

The gang of plotters lashed out, their limbs like razor-sharp swords, jagging into the officers' bodies. Blood was pouring.

One officer managed to fire off a round of bullets. They went straight through the ghosts' bodies, lodging themselves in the great solid beams above and behind them. The terrified MPs ducked under their seats, where they remained, shaking and shrieking like chickens in a battery shed.

One officer was thrown by Catesby towards the Speaker's chair. His body lay impaled on the ornate carvings on the canopy above.

Another had his eyes stabbed out by Percy and was then hurled over the great table that held the dispatch boxes. The blinded man slid across it and landed on the front row of the opposition, splattering the faces of shadow ministers with blood.

When a cabinet minister on the front bench stood up to move towards the door, Wintour grabbed him by his legs and swung him head first up towards the gallery. His head struck the solid wooden balcony and he dropped like a stone on to the MPs below, breaking his neck as he fell.

'For God's sake,' shouted the Deputy PM. 'Somebody do something!'

Jud climbed on to a bench and started shouting.

'Fawkes! Guido Fawkes!'

The politicians looked up open-mouthed from their hiding places beneath the benches.

Jud shouted again. 'Fawkes. We know why you're here.'

Black Rod slowly turned his face. The shock of his burning eyes chilled Jud to the bone, but he shouted again.

'It's for the martyrs, isn't it? The martyrs caritatis. For what happened to them. But we can make amends. We can give you the justice you seek!'

The Prime Minister stood up and brushed his bodyguards aside.

Black Rod motioned to his gang to stay still. To listen.

Gradually the screams in the chamber stopped. People were listening. The silent, tragic ghosts that swirled above their heads continued to move without a sound, centuries of grief etched on their stricken faces.

But the gang of plotters now stood still.

They were watching Jud.

'Careful,' Bex whispered, now at Jud's feet. 'Slowly, slowly.'

Goode and Bonati had arrived at the main doors. They stood watching with bated breath. 'What the hell have we missed?' Goode whispered to the professor.

They heard politicians close by saying, 'Who the hell is this kid?'

Goode resisted the temptation to shout, 'My son.'

'Speak,' said Fawkes as he stared at Jud.

'Politicians stood here centuries ago and were guilty of prejudice. Against the Roman Catholic community – and the martyrs who died for their faith. And their prejudice led to the Act. The Act of Settlement.'

The Prime Minister was listening now.

And so were the ghosts.

'The proposals to change the Act would see even more prejudice in this chamber. But it doesn't have to be this way.'

'Go on,' said Fawkes.

'No,' interrupted the Prime Minister, now approaching Jud.

Bex panicked. What was he doing? Was Jud about to be silenced, just when he was getting somewhere?

A chilling thought struck Jud like a blow to the stomach: was the PM in on it too?

'I am grateful to this man,' said the Prime Minister, his voice gaining strength each second. 'But I recognise what is my duty. I know to what this agent is referring and I know what needs to be done.'

He turned to Black Rod and the shadowy figures beside him.

'You have committed atrocities here today. You have maimed. You have shown a brutal disregard for human life.

'But our ancestors too carry a similar burden of guilt. For the atrocities committed against your people, the martyrs caritatis, we are truly sorry. Let there be no more pain.

'The Act of Settlement is a bad piece of legislation. It's discriminatory. It's anti-Catholic. The new Bill proposed would not only assure its future, it would worsen the prejudice within it. You cannot bar Catholics from high office. You *cannot* bar them from the office I hold as prime minister, or even from the throne of England.

'The crimes committed against your people were crimes against humanity itself. People were put to death for nothing but their love of God.

'But crimes can just as easily be committed with words. And that is what we are at risk of doing with this new Bill.

'Fawkes, if that is who you are, I believe you are here because you feel the martyrs' pain, just as you did four hundred years ago.

'So *let it end*. Right here. No more bloodshed.

'Ladies and gentlemen, let us repeal the very Act others are trying to extend. Let us abolish this piece of legislation *for ever*.'

MPs in the House were too shocked and drained and

frightened to express any response beyond a bewildered nodding of their heads.

Then Black Rod spoke.

There were tears in his eyes, which had softened in their intensity. The red glow was slowly diminishing.

'Prime Minister, your grace and mercy are received with heartfelt thanks. For your humanity, your understanding and your tolerance, you are truly worthy of the office you hold.'

He turned to face Jud. 'You are correct in your assumption. It is *justice* we seek.'

His hand was at the pocket inside his ceremonial jacket. Officers and agents stood ready.

What was he doing?

'No!' whispered Goode from the doorway. 'Please, no.'

But Black Rod removed a bundle of paper and held it above his head.

'This, ladies and gentlemen,' he cried, turning to take in his assembled audience, 'this is a new Bill. It repeals the evil Act of 1701. It preserves the right of Catholics to rise to the highest office in the land. It will end the prejudice. It will allow Protestants and Catholics to live together equally. And in so doing, it recognises the courage and calling of the very same martyrs you see above you now.'

The Prime Minister nodded his head slowly.

'It will be passed,' he said. 'It will be included in Her Majesty's speech.'

Fawkes looked up towards the high vaulted ceiling. The misty shapes were poised above him.

Jud and the other agents could detect that the energy in the great chamber had altered. Shifted. Emotions were slowly changing.

'Friends, martyrs, believers, listen to me,' said Fawkes. 'You have the word of the Prime Minister. You may trust in him. You may rest in peace knowing you did not die in vain. You died for a *cause* – a faith, a faith now recognised and welcomed in this land.

'Our plans are realised. You are released. It is over.'

He fell to the floor. Officers raced to him. Through the crowd, Jud could see that his eyes were becoming less and less intense. There was even a faint colour returning to his cheeks.

The spirit that had hijacked both the brigadier's body and his thoughts was finally leaving him. And somewhere, buried within the physical frame, hidden from view since last night, but still intact, lay the soul of the real Black Rod.

Jud turned to look up at the spirits in the room.

The shapes were shrinking. Ebbing away, just like the human fear they'd fed on. Glowing mists were fading. As anger and pain diminished, replaced by peace, so the energy and plasma slowly ebbed away, paling the spirits' bodies until they were but memories, left as residues in the great stones of the building.

Never to be forgotten.

CHAPTER 60

SATURDAY 6 NOVEMBER: 11.59 A.M.

PENTHOUSE, GOODE TOWER

Jud, Bex and their fellow agents piled into the room to watch the news bulletin.

'All right, all right,' said Goode, 'settle down everyone.' It was the first time many of the agents had been up to the penthouse.

He turned up the volume on the giant screen in front of them.

'Drink, Prof?' he said, turning to Bonati.

'Bit early, isn't it?'

The antique carriage clock on Goode's ultra-modern desk chimed the first of twelve rings.

'Nonsense. It's midday. Bourbon?'

'Why not.'

The lunchtime news had begun.

'After the unprecedented scenes at Parliament yesterday, we are told that everything is returning to relative normality. Our political editor Bill McIntyre is live at Westminster. Bill, extra-ordinary scenes, yes? But are things *really* back to normal?'

The picture changed to a balding, bespectacled man in a brown suit, standing in the Central Lobby at Westminster.

'Yes, well, Tina, it certainly was a day unlike any other. As you know, due to the heightened security this year, cameras were not allowed inside either of the two chambers during the State Opening, so there's plenty of speculation about what went on in there. We don't know – and due to the injunction order placed on the press so hurriedly last night, we may *never* know – the exact details of what happened in here yesterday, but it seems normal life has resumed. It's almost like nothing has happened.'

'And the Gentleman Usher of the Black Rod?' said Tina. 'Any news on him?'

'Yes,' said Bill. 'Good news. I'm told – and I have to say I can only go on the very limited press releases we're all being given from St Thomas's Hospital – that Brigadier Geoffrey Farlington is recovering. The official line is that someone spiked his drink with a very powerful hallucinogenic moments before he entered the chamber yesterday. Police suspect that some form of protester was responsible, but they're not saying any more than that. Doctors are trying to find out what the drug was. But I'm told he is recovering satisfactorily in hospital this morning.'

'And what of the MPs?' said Tina in the studio. 'The ones you've spoken to, Bill? They were there at the time. Have they confirmed any of these rumours we're hearing about *ghosts*? Was there *really* paranormal activity in the House of Commons yesterday, do you think?'

'Well, as I say, there is a very strict gagging order on what we can and can't discuss in the media. And it seems the MPs themselves are remaining tight-lipped too. Sources I've spoken to are unwilling – indeed they say they are prohibited, no less – to speak to me. Publicly, that is.'

'And privately?' said Tina, back in the newsroom.

'Privately?' said Bill, smiling. 'Well, I could write a book on what they tell me in private.'

Want a sneak preview of CRYPT'S next mission?
Head to **http://www.cryptagent.co.uk**
to read an exclusive extract of

CRYPT
COVERT RESPONSE YOUTH PARANORMAL TEAM

MASK OF DEATH

Out March 2013